Faking the Future

Never Give Up : Book Five

by

Suzie Peters

GWL
PUBLISHING

First Published in 2021
by GWL Publishing
an imprint of Great War Literature Publishing LLP

Produced in United Kingdom

ISBN 978-1-910603-97-0 Paperback Edition

GWL Publishing
2 Little Breach
Chichester
PO19 5TX

www.gwlpublishing.co.uk

Dedication

For S.

Chapter One

Isabel

"What's their problem? Don't they get it?"

My little sisters, Reagan and Ashley, walk into the kitchen of our parents' home, one after the other. As usual, it's Ashley who's leading the way, despite being the youngest. Like me, she has dark hair, although she wears hers much longer than I do, letting it fall to half-way down her back. Her eyes are paler than mine too, being amber colored and kind of exotic, instead of boring dark brown.

"What are you talking about?" I ask, as Reagan follows her, and they both sit down opposite me at the granite-topped breakfast bar. I've already put out cups for them, and they help themselves to coffee, gazing across at me.

"Men." Reagan shakes her head, trying to sound more knowledgeable than her twenty-one years. Her coloring is lighter than mine and Ash's. But then, she takes after our father, rather than our mother… neither of whom are here this weekend. Although that's not at all unusual. They're hardly ever here.

"And what is it that men don't get?" I watch as they sip their coffee, giving them both an indulgent smile. It is gone eleven o'clock in the morning, after all… and they're still wearing their pajamas. In fact, this is the first I've seen of them today. But that's my sisters for you. I've already cleared up the kitchen and been to the grocery store while they've both been sleeping.

"Anything," Ash replies, rolling her eyes.

"Can you be more specific?" It felt like they had a particular gripe when they were talking before and I want to make sure they're okay. I'm very protective of my little sisters. It's always been that way, for as long as I can remember. And even though they still live here at our family home in Vermont, while I now live in a small town in Massachusetts, I still like them to know I'm here for them if they need me.

Reagan sighs and puts down her cup, tipping her head to one side. "Do you know why men think they have to take the lead... all the time?" She gazes across at me, her blue eyes fixed on mine.

I swallow down my embarrassment together with a sip of coffee and take a breath. "Can you give me some context?"

"Sure..." She gets comfortable, making me wonder how long her story is going to take, and then says, "I spent yesterday evening at Damian's place."

"You mean, his parents' place." Both she and her boyfriend are still at college, and neither of them has a 'place' of their own. Unlike a lot of kids, both Reagan and Ash have chosen to go to college right here in Vermont. It takes less than an hour to get there, and they like not having to pay rent on an apartment. It probably helps that our parents are never home... so they also have the freedom of being able to do pretty much whatever they please. Especially as I'm not here most of the time, either. Of course, I went to the same college myself, but I don't think that influenced their decisions. I went there for very different reasons...

"Yeah, but they're away at the moment," she says, interrupting my train of thought and I notice the blush creeping up her cheeks.

"Oh." The word falls from my lips and I let out a sigh which seems to fill the space between us, wondering what she's about to tell me... and whether I want to hear it.

"We didn't *do* anything," she says, with a certain amount of emphasis, and that surprises me. Not because I think my sisters sleep around – either of them – but because of the way they were talking when they came in here. "Although he wanted to... obviously..."

Alarm bells ring in my head and before she can continue, I lean forward, reaching across the breakfast bar and putting my hand on her arm. "He didn't... he didn't force you, did he?"

"God, no." She shakes her head "But that's kinda the point."

I'm feeling very confused now, but I try not to let it show, as Ashley puts down her cup and says, "Exactly."

'Exactly' what? None of this makes sense and I wonder for a moment if this is an age-gap thing. I'm eight years older than Reagan and ten years older than Ashley... and maybe it's showing. Maybe teenagers and young twenty-somethings view the world differently to those of us who are in our thirties... which I'm not yet, but I will be next May.

"And what *exactly* did Damian do to you?" I ask, desperate to be put out of my misery.

"Nothing," Reagan says. "Well... nothing much."

"Then what's the problem?" I'm feeling truly exasperated now.

"That he – and just about every other man – seem to think they know everything about women. They're convinced they know what we want, and what makes us happy. I mean, we were there at his parents' place last night, kissing on the couch... and I sat up on his lap." She stares at me, shaking her head, and frowning. "He's always taking the lead, and I thought I'd see how he reacted if I switched things around."

"And?" I'm intrigued now.

"It didn't end well... because the next thing I knew, he'd flipped me over onto my back and had me pinned down on the couch. He made it very clear what he wanted, but I'd gone off the idea by then, so we just kissed for a while longer, and then he brought me home."

That sounds like a wasted opportunity to me, and I'm not sure I can understand Reagan's problem. I can't help picturing the scene, though, and I exchange Reagan for myself, as I imagine being held down by a man... not just any man, mind you. I conjure up the image of one man in particular pinning me to the bed, or the couch, or the floor... *oh, God.* It's a struggle not to sigh out loud as I feel a heated tingle rush through my body, and I picture him gazing down at me, his eyes filled with longing and desire.

"What's wrong with him?" Ashley says, getting in the way of my pleasant daydream.

"He doesn't realize it's the twenty-first century, that's what's wrong with him." Reagan rolls her eyes and takes another sip of coffee. "Men today don't seem to understand that we know what we want… and we're not afraid to ask for it." *We're not?* Personally, I'm terrified.

"Why do you think I've slowed things down with Jax?" Ashley nods her head as she speaks.

"Who the hell is Jax?" I ask. It's not a name I've heard before. The last time I was home, which was only two months ago, back in September, she was with someone called Eddie. I met him once. He was very good looking, but he struck me as dull.

"He's a guy from college," she explains.

"So you finished it with Eddie?"

"Yeah. I like to be with someone I can actually talk to… you know, have a conversation with about something other than football… and that wasn't Eddie." I'm surprised she didn't see that coming, but maybe she was blinded by his blue eyes and dimples.

"So you started seeing Jax?" I ask.

"Yes. We've been together for about a month now. And before you ask, I haven't slept with him… I'm not sure I will now."

"Why not?" I ask, slightly bothered by the way she said that.

"Because he's behaving like a caveman," she says with feeling. "I don't mind a guy taking the lead sometimes, but it gets really tired when they don't know how to do anything else. You know how it is?" She looks at me, a smile twitching at her lips. "Sometimes you just wanna grab a guy, put your hands on his shoulders… or his neck… or in his hair, so it gets all twisted around your fingers… and then kiss him. Really hard. And then you wanna step back and look at him and just say, 'More?' and have to wait for him to get his breath back, before he can answer you."

Reagan giggles while I contemplate Ashley's words and try to imagine putting them into practice, with that one particular man… the man of my dreams. Except all I can think about is him doing all of that to me, and how glorious it would be. If only…

"What do you think then, Isabel?" Reagan says, and I jolt back to my senses.

"About what?"

"About men. Are we wasting our time here, or do you think we'll ever find men who will let a woman take control in a relationship?"

"Yeah…" Ashley joins in before I get the chance to reply. "You've got more experience with men than both of us."

"Put together," Reagan says, and they both laugh.

"Thanks." I shake my head to hide my embarrassment.

"Sorry," she says. "I didn't mean that to sound like an insult… but the point is, you've had a lot more boyfriends than either of us. You can tell us… is there any hope out there?"

I'm pretty sure I'm blushing, and I do my best to cover it by taking a long sip of my coffee, finishing the dregs in the bottom of the cup, before I glance up at them again. They're looking at me expectantly, as though I'm the fount of all knowledge… when, in reality, nothing could be further from the truth.

"To be honest," I say at last, lying through my teeth, "I've been so busy with work, I've forgotten what it feels like to have a man in my life."

"How long has it been, then?" Ashley asks.

I think for a moment or two, wondering what would be an appropriate length of time… what would sound realistic. I only moved to Sturbridge in August and I suppose that would provide the perfect opportunity for claiming I'd broken off a relationship with some phantom man in Boston, where I used to live. Except three months is hardly long enough to have forgotten the concept of a male presence in my life. So what would sound better…?

"A year," I blurt out, because the silence has stretched for too long. And then I add, "Give or take," because it keeps everything nice and vague.

"Wow…" Reagan stares at me, a little dumbfounded.

"A year?" Ash says.

"Yeah." I nod my head, feeling guilty for lying to them.

"Did you fall in love with the last guy?" Reagan asks. "Is that why you're still on your own?"

"No. It's nothing like that. My training contract was a lot harder than I thought it would be." That's not a lie. The Elleston Clinic didn't really understand the concept of 'training' and threw me in at the deep end. "Once that had finished, I had to look for another position. I just haven't had the time for men…"

They both nod their heads, strangely in time with each other, and then Ashley smiles over at me and says, "You need to get out more. Stop working so damn hard and get a life."

She reaches over and gives my hand a squeeze, because she's being kind, not critical, and then they both get up, talking showers and lunch, and what they've got planned for the afternoon, as they head back upstairs.

I stay where I am, staring at the granite countertop, focusing on the gray and white sparkles in the dense black background as I contemplate how easy I find it to lie to the people I care about. I feel bad about that, but what can I do? It feels like I've been lying to them for years… or at least, they've been making assumptions for years, and I haven't been correcting them. That's more accurate. And as the reality of my situation hits home, the sparkles merge and tears fill my eyes. I'm so goddamn lonely, I could cry… and if I'm not careful, I'm going to.

I wipe my eyes on the backs of my hands and take a breath, refusing to give in to tears, and instead, I pull my phone from the back pocket of my jeans. It only takes a second or two for me to connect a call to Noah… although he takes until the fourth ring to answer.

"Hey," he says.

"Don't tell me you've only just woken up." I glance at my watch to see it's nearly noon. "Is small-town reporting keeping you up late at night?" Noah loves his job as a journalist, working for the local newspaper and has never been tempted to leave, even though he's had offers… some of them quite lucrative.

"Yeah, it is," he says. "I'm doing an in-depth feature on a local politician who has to remain anonymous for the moment, especially as he's behaving very badly."

"He is?"

"Yeah, and even though I love you dearly, I'm still not gonna tell you who he is, so don't ask."

"Okay. I won't. But can I guess that he's taking up all your spare time?"

"Not all of it, no. Why?"

"Because I feel like going out tonight."

"Are you here then?" He sounds surprised.

"Yeah. I got back last night, and I'm going back to Sturbridge tomorrow afternoon."

"You didn't tell me you were coming home."

"I know. It was a last-minute decision… based on the fact that I had nothing else to do." *When do I ever?*

He sighs. "Oh, I see how it is. I'm your oldest friend, and as far as I know, I'm still your best friend… and you're telling me you've only come to visit because you're bored?"

"Sorry." I can feel those tears gathering again.

"Hey," he says, sounding more serious now. "What's wrong?"

"Everything."

"Wow… it's that bad?"

"Yeah… it's that bad."

"In that case, I think we need to go to JC's tonight and get exceptionally drunk."

"That sounds p—perfect." I'm struggling to speak.

"I'll book a cab and pick you up at seven. I don't think either of us should be driving."

"Definitely not."

"Are you okay?" he asks.

"I'm fine." I'm not and he knows it.

"Don't start crying on me, will you?" he says. "I'm not dressed, and you know how I hate having to rush my morning routine."

"It's afternoon," I point out to him, almost managing a smile.

"It's the same routine, and I still hate having to rush it."

"You'd do it though, wouldn't you?" I need to know he cares… that someone cares.

"Of course I would. I'd do anything for you, Isabel. You know that."
A tear hits my cheek as he takes a pause, and then says, "Do you need me to come over?"

"No. I'll be okay. I'll see you later."

"Sure?" he asks, double checking.

"Absolutely. You can buy me a martini to cry into."

"I'll do no such thing. You'll cry on my shoulder, if you're gonna cry anywhere. You know they've always been reserved for you." They have too. I've cried on them a fair few times over the years... since we became friends in sixth grade, after his parents moved here.

"I'll see you at seven," I say, wiping away my tears.

"Okay. But call me if you need to."

We hang up and I put my phone down on the countertop, letting my chin fall onto my upturned hands and staring out the window at the last of the fall leaves, clinging to the trees, providing a bright contrast to the backdrop of leaden gray skies. I refuse to cry anymore, even though I'm desperately sad. Crying won't get me anywhere... but hopefully talking things through with Noah might. He's the only person I've ever been able to talk to. He knows all my secrets... every one of them.

Which is why it makes sense to tell him about Mason.

Mason

"Are we actually related to anyone here?" Oliver asks.

He's sitting beside me in an enormous marquee that's been set up at the back of Max Crawford's house. I think about my brother's question for a moment, studying the other guests around us, almost none of whom we know. I've never been to the wedding of a multi-millionaire before, but really it's no different to any other... except maybe the outfits cost a little more, and the cars are flashier.

"Apart from each other, and Dad… and Destiny, no."

We're certainly not related to anyone in the bridal party. We don't even know Max Crawford, and it's his wedding.

There is a connection between us, though… otherwise, we wouldn't be here. In fact, there are two. One is simple, and the other is more complicated.

The simple connection is that our father operated on Max Crawford when he was injured in the line of duty several years ago. Max was a soldier, serving in Afghanistan, and was shot in the leg. It was a serious wound and our father played an important role in his recovery… evidently.

The complicated connection is our sister, Destiny. She's just become engaged to a British archaeology professor, called Ronan Schofield… or Doctor Ronan Schofield, to be precise. It's him that provides the connection to the Crawford family, because his sister, Eva, is married to Chase Crawford… the groom's brother.

See? I said it was complicated.

We didn't know about the connection – actually, Oliver and I were barely aware of Max Crawford's existence – until Destiny brought her boyfriend home a few weeks ago to meet us all for the first time. Ronan explained about this sister living here in the States and who she's married to… and our dad joined the dots. That was soon forgotten, though, when Ronan asked our dad's permission to marry Destiny, and promptly proposed to her… in the living room… right in front of us all.

"Dad and Max Crawford seem to be getting along well." Oliver nods toward the front of the marquee, where our dad is standing talking to a tall man, who's obviously the groom. The tux is a huge give-away, as is the fact that he just exudes good cheer and happiness. He's dark haired, handsome and smiling down at our father, both of them talking animatedly, and occasionally laughing. I have to say, for a man who's about to get married, Mr. Crawford is showing no signs of nerves.

"Why wouldn't they?" I reply.

"No reason," he says and we both stand, behaving like gentlemen for once, as our sister comes over, accompanied by her new fiancé. Destiny is twelve years younger than me and has our mother's flaming red hair that I remember so well. She has Mom's gray-green eyes too, and she smiles as she sits down, leaving a space for our father between my seat and her own, while keeping hold of Ronan's hand, as he takes his own seat to her right, on the end of the row. I'm not sure exactly how old Ronan is, but I'm guessing around thirty, which makes him five or six years younger than me. He couldn't look less like an archaeology professor if he tried. I'm not sure if that's because of his beard, or his slightly tousled hair, or just his laid-back attitude, but if we didn't know his career, and have evidence of it, in the form of the fact that he's just been employed by Boston University, I'd say he was probably a musician, or a poet. Not that any of us really care what he does for a living, because he makes Destiny happy… and that's all that matters.

"It'll be your turn soon," Oliver says, talking around me, being as he's sitting to my left.

"I know." Destiny smiles, looking every inch the bride-to-be. They might have only become engaged a few weeks ago, but the plans for their wedding are already nearing completion, and that's just as well, because it's due to take place in two weeks' time, on the Saturday before Thanksgiving. When they announced that, a couple of days after Ronan proposed, I think we all wondered whether there might be a reason for their haste. They assured us there wasn't… not the obvious one, or even Ronan's immigration status. It seems they just wanted to be married… and that's the way it is when you find the person you want to spend the rest of your life with. You don't want to wait; you want to start spending your life with them right away.

I know I do…

"Who's the guy with the buzz-cut standing with Dad and Max Crawford?" Oliver directs his question to Ronan and I glance up at the giant of a man Oliver is clearly referring to. He might be paying attention to the conversation, and even joining in every so often, but he's also glancing around, all the time.

"That's Colt," Ronan replies, leaning forward and edging a little closer, so we can all hear him. "He's the best man. He's Max's oldest friend… and his bodyguard."

That explains his vigilance, I guess.

"You forgot the most important part," Destiny says, shaking her head.

"Oh, yeah… he's married to Max and Chase's sister, Bree," Ronan adds.

"Which one is Bree?" I ask, still trying to make sense of who everyone is and all their connections.

Ronan sits up and looks forward through the sea of heads. "She's sitting in the front row, next to Eva."

I know Ronan's sister Eva, because he introduced us earlier, along with his brother-in-law, Chase and their son Thomas, who's nearly eighteen months old. Eva's got long blonde hair, is absolutely beautiful, with sparkling light blue eyes, just like her brother's, and she's about six or seven months pregnant. And while I can only see the back of her head right now, I'm guessing Bree must be the woman beside her, with the curly dark mane flowing down her back.

The music, which has been playing in the background ever since we arrived, suddenly stops. That seems to be a signal for everyone to take their places, and Dad shakes hands with Max, before quickly making his way back to us, squeezing past Destiny and Ronan and sitting down beside me.

"Okay?" I ask him.

"Yes… fine, son." He smiles at me and then the music starts up again, playing a more processional piece this time, making it clear proceedings are now underway.

From the rear of the marquee, a little girl appears. She's wearing a peach colored dress, with flowers in her dark hair and is carrying a tiny posy of flowers. At first glance, I thought she might be a flower girl, but she actually seems to be a bridesmaid. She walks forward, looking directly ahead, her eyes fixed on Max Crawford, and I turn and glance at him, to see the most wondrous expression on his face. I don't think I've ever seen a man's face more filled with pride and love, and he watches the little girl, smiling and nodding his head, as she steps ever closer to him.

Once she's walked past us, Ronan turns, leaning forward again.

"That's Tia," he says in a low whisper, just loud enough for us all to hear. "She's Max's daughter from his first marriage."

We all know the story of Max's first wife, Eden, who was kidnapped and killed a few years ago. It was a tragedy... one from which many would never recover, especially as Max was there when his wife died. But I guess miracles can happen.

I look back up and see that, although the bridesmaid would normally stand to the left of the aisle, Max is holding out his hand and Tia takes it, going to stand beside him, as they both look back toward the rear of the marquee. Everyone else copies them, and there's a collective gasp, as we all let our eyes focus on the sight before us... the bride.

Cara looks stunning... except she doesn't, because that's not a powerful enough word to describe her. She's glowing. She's awe-inspiring... and, although I've never seen her before, it's obvious she's also terrified. Her dress is simple, but elegant, in an off-the-shoulder style, which hugs her slender figure. Her hair has been tied back from her face, but left long so it's hanging around her bare shoulders, and as she stands at the door to the marquee, she hesitates for a moment... long enough that I can see her swallowing and breathing deeply. I look around and notice Max giving her a nod of his head and then turn back to Cara as she smiles and walks toward him. I'm not sure whether anyone else noticed that moment – other than Max – or whether my psychology training gives me a better insight into people and their behavior, but I give a slight sigh of relief, because for a moment then, I wondered whether she was going to run. She wouldn't have been running from Max, though, not given the way she responded to his encouraging nod. I think she'd have been running from the rest of us.

Cara reaches the front of the marquee and, while he keeps Tia's hand in one of his, Max reaches out with the other and takes hold of Cara, pulling her close and whispering something to her. She nods her head, and he says something else, before they pull apart slightly and face the celebrant who's standing before them.

While she's speaking, beginning the ceremony, I allow myself a quick glance at Destiny and Ronan, to find my sister is leaning against her fiancé, her head on his shoulder... and I imagine she's thinking about their forthcoming nuptials. Considering they've only known each other for roughly five months, I suppose we should caution her to slow things down. But there really wouldn't be any point. Not only is Destiny clearly in love with the man beside her, but she's always been headstrong and willful, so we'd be wasting our breath.

Destiny was born with a certain wanderlust about her. So I guess it made sense that she'd leave Sturbridge at the first opportunity... which arose when she went to college. Oliver and I had done the same thing, but we'd come back home again to work. I think we knew, even as Destiny was waving us goodbye, that she'd never return. And she didn't. Oh, she visited, but that was all she ever did, and once she graduated, she got a job, working at her old college, for one of its top professors.

Dad was so proud of her when she came home and told us she was gonna be Professor McLean's assistant. And she was so proud that she'd landed the position without Dad's influence, or anyone else interfering. She'd done it all by herself.

Maybe it was that self-same pride that stopped her from coming to us when things went wrong – which it seems they did, almost from day one. That's what she implied, when she finally told us the truth of the matter... after she'd met Ronan, fallen in love with him, and he'd rescued her. If that sounds a little melodramatic, I don't care. It was melodramatic... because there's no other way to describe the feeling of having your sister, standing in front of you, in your childhood home, telling you that her boss has been sexually harassing her... and that she didn't feel she could come and tell you about it.

She could have done. She could've come to me, or Oliver... or our dad. We'd all have helped her. Dad would probably have used his influence at the college to have the professor removed from his position. Oliver would have driven into Boston, found the professor and performed some kind of painful surgery on him. He told me that afterwards. He even told me which parts of the professor's anatomy he'd have removed... and how. Not that he's a doctor, you understand... well, he is. He's a veterinary, but the principle is the same.

As for me? If she'd come to me? Well, I'd have talked to her. I'm a psychologist, after all. So, I'd have tried to persuade her to take action against the professor. I'd have convinced her none of it was her fault, and I'd have been a shoulder for her to cry on. And, when all of that was done, I'd have gone and found him myself. I wouldn't have wanted to talk to him though, and while I'm also a doctor, I'm no good with a scalpel... so I'd have used my fists to make my point. That would probably surprise Destiny... and the rest of my family. I'm renowned for being placid, a little shy, and quite calm in just about any situation... but when it comes down to it, no-one hurts my little sister.

I jolt back to the here and now as someone coughs and everyone stills, and I realize the bride and groom are about to make their vows. I wonder how Cara's gonna cope with this...

"Max," she says, in a quiet voice, taking a deep breath, and gazing up into his eyes. Her focus is on him alone, which is a good idea. She can pretend they're by themselves, and the rest of us aren't even here. "I've only known you for fifteen months, but sometimes it feels like we've already done enough to fill a lifetime. We've fallen in love, we've had a baby, we've got married." She stops talking and then says, "Well, we're *getting* married. You've rescued me... so many times. You've brought me back from dark places and you've shown me so much love, I sometimes find it breathtaking... even now." She falls silent and takes a step closer to him, reaching out and cupping his cheek with her hand. "I—I want you to know," she says, her voice a little stronger. "I want you to know – no matter how scared I am of standing up here and talking in front of all these people – that I love you. I love you with everything I have. And I will always love you... not just because you rescued me, or because you gave me Tia and Sapphire, but because you're a man who deserves to be loved." She lets her head rock forward, and he copies her, until their foreheads meet, and they stand for a moment, together. Then he whispers something and they move apart again, and Max smiles down at her.

"I wrote my vows weeks ago," he says, pulling a piece of paper from his jacket pocket, which he unfolds, glances down at and then throws over his shoulder, making everyone laugh. "I learned them too," he adds. "I just brought the written version for back-up."

"Really?" Cara says, tilting her head.

"Yeah. Really. I'm not gonna forget a single word I need to say to you, and if you ask me nicely, I'll tell you my original vows later on… but for now I'm gonna say something different."

"You are?" She's surprised, and I think everyone else is, too. Colt, the best man, seems to be. He raises his eyebrows and then looks down at his feet, shaking his head, like he expects this to end badly.

"Yeah," Max says, taking a deep breath. "To start off with, I'm gonna be annoyingly pedantic… because I'm gonna tell you that you haven't known me for fifteen months at all. You've known me for fourteen months, three weeks and five days. I'm counting, baby. I count every day with you, because they're all a blessing. That's what it feels like, having you beside me… like a blessing." He coughs, and then says, "That's why, every time I look at you, I give thanks you walked through my door and rescued *me*. Because that's exactly what you did. No-one here, apart from you, knows what my life was really like before, but you – and you alone – brought me back into the light, and gave me back my future. And while the last fourteen months, three weeks and five days have been kind of eventful, I'm gonna do whatever it takes to make sure that from here on in you're always safe, you're always happy, and that you always know you're loved… enough to last a lifetime."

There's a collective sigh around the guests as Max stops speaking and I notice a few of the women nearby wiping tears away from their cheeks as the celebrant completes the formalities, declaring the couple standing before us to be husband and wife.

Everyone stands and applauds as the bride and groom kiss, and then the atmosphere changes, as it always does on these occasions. Before and during the ceremony, there's always an element of tension, in case anything should go wrong, I suppose. Afterwards, it's as though the air is filled with happiness… and maybe relief, too. The noise level goes up, everyone chatters and moves around, leaving their seats and congregating in small groups here and there, while the bride and groom mix and mingle.

We're soon approached by Ronan's sister, Eva and her husband, Chase, together with their son. Eva is carrying a baby, who I know to be Cara and Max's daughter, Sapphire, but before they even reach us, Eva hands the infant to Chase, and stretches her back, clearly struggling. He places his hand behind her, rubbing her back, and then leans in and whispers something, which makes her smile. With them, they bring Chase's sister Bree. I hadn't been able to see before, but she's also carrying a baby girl, aged roughly six months old, I'd say, who's smiling up at her. And now I can see Bree properly, I can't fail to notice that – like Eva and Cara – she is also exquisite.

At that moment, Colt comes over and puts his arms around his wife, from behind.

"How are my favorite two girls?" he asks.

"We're both fine," Bree says, looking up into his eyes and smiling, and the love I see pass between them in that moment is breathtaking.

The people around us are all so happy, and so in love, that for a second or two, I feel like excusing myself… like taking myself off to a quiet corner, just to escape them.

It's not that I'm jealous. I'm not. It's that their open affection and joy merely brings into sharp relief the abject misery of my own life.

That's not because I haven't found love myself, though. It's because I have.

The problem is that the object of my desires, the woman who owns my heart, doesn't even know I exist. Well, she does… because we work together. So she knows I exist as a psychologist, a colleague, and a mentor. But as a man? I might as well be invisible.

I'll admit, I'm finding the whole situation quite stressful. Obviously, working with someone you love, who barely acknowledges your existence, isn't ever going to be easy. But it's made doubly difficult because I don't even understand my own reactions. It's not like I'm a teenager, stumbling over my first love… or even my first girlfriend. I'm thirty-six years old. I'm not entirely inexperienced with women… and yet, I'm behaving like a complete fool. At least I am when I'm around Izzy. It's ludicrous. Not that long ago, I accused Oliver of becoming tongue-tied and pathetic when he's around his receptionist, Jemima, who he's fallen for in a big way… and while that's perfectly true, I had no right to say that to him, when I'm no better myself.

When I have nothing else to do, I sit at home, in my house outside of Sturbridge, creating scenes in my head, in which I'm actually able to speak to Izzy, like a normal human being. I practice my lines; I rehearse what I'm going to say, and in these scenes, I'm lucid and coherent. Our conversations aren't about work, because the reality is that, when she comes to me – as she often does – to ask my advice about a client, or anything work related, I'm more than capable of talking to her, and even sounding quite sensible.

It's the rest of the time that I have a problem.

It's the times when I yearn to invite her to dinner, or to join me for a drink after work, in the hope it might lead to dinner. It's the times when she's in the kitchen at our offices, making herself a coffee, and I've walked in behind her and longed to take her in my arms – like Colt did with Bree just now – to tell her how much I love her… and how I can't stop thinking about her… every single minute of the day. And it's the times when I've wished I could just march into her office and tell her I need her more than I need to breathe…

Those are the scenes I create and rehearse… and in those scenes, she always says yes to dinner, or to the drinks that lead to dinner. When I tell her I love her, she says she loves me too… right before she kisses me. And when I march into her office, before I've even opened my mouth, she's on her feet, walking around her desk, undoing her blouse, her eyes on fire, her need matching my own.

Of course, that's only make believe… none of it's real. They're just scenes I invent… scenes where I let myself call her 'Izzy' out loud, instead of just in my head. She likes it, too, because that's the kind of relationship we have… in my dreams.

"Congratulations!" My dad's voice breaks into my thoughts, and I realize we've been joined by the bride and groom themselves, who are standing, arm in arm, beside my father. They've brought a group of people with them, who look like a family, comprising a mom and dad, and three kids, aged roughly between sixteen or seventeen, and about nine or ten. I wonder for a moment if they might be related to Cara, although I'm not sure how. The mom doesn't look quite old enough to be Cara's mother. I guess she could be an older sister... maybe. Cara is now holding Tia's hand, and she's looking around at all of us, a little in awe, which isn't surprising, being as all the men here – my father included – are over six feet tall.

We all offer our good wishes to the happy couple before Max turns Cara toward Dad.

"I've never had the chance to introduce you, baby," he says to his wife, "but this is Doctor John Gould. He's the man who saved my life, when I got back from Afghanistan."

"Didn't Uncle Colt save you?" Tia says and we all look down at her.

"Yes, he did," Max replies, smiling indulgently at his daughter before he raises his eyes to his best friend, best man, and bodyguard... oh, and brother-in-law, I guess. "Uncle Colt saved Daddy when he was shot, but I'm talking about when I got back here, into the hospital. That's when Doctor Gould saved my life."

Dad shakes his head. "I think you'll find I just saved your leg," he says, blushing. I'm not sure I've ever seen that happen before, and it surprises me to see my dad like that.

"You saved my life," Max insists, not letting this go. "Because of you and what you did, I'm able to live the life I have, to be the man I am, to be a father to my daughters... to stand up here today and marry the woman I love."

"That's as may be," Dad replies, taking a deep breath, clearly affected by Max's speech. "But it wasn't just me. There was an entire team of us who worked on you... and your leg."

"I know," Max says. "But it wasn't the team who came and sat with me during the night, after each of my surgeries, was it? It wasn't the team who stood on the sidelines while I was having my physio, telling me to push harder, and not give up. You're the one who gave me the determination to walk again... no-one else."

"I think you had more than enough determination of your own," Dad says.

"Maybe," Max replies, with a shrug of his shoulders. "But I couldn't have done any of it without you. They told me I might never walk properly again, and I don't even have a limp, thanks to you. Hell, Cara didn't even notice the scar until…" He stops talking and Cara looks up at him, blushing.

"Until when?" Chase says, grinning, and I'm reminded of the way Oliver and I rib each other, as only brothers can.

"I shouldn't have started that sentence," Max says. "And I'm sure as hell not gonna finish it… not with so many children present." Everyone laughs, and then Max releases Cara for a moment and offers his hand to our father, who takes it. As they shake, Max looks him in the eyes and says, "I owe you, Doctor. Remember that."

Dad shakes his head and is about to say something when Colt leans forward and says, "Don't dismiss the idea. You'd be amazed at how useful it can be to have a multi-millionaire in your pocket."

We all laugh again, and Max steps back slightly, turning to the mystery family and smiling. "I guess, while we're on the subject of saving people, we should probably introduce Cathy and her family," he says, and Cara smiles up at him before he looks at the rest of us. "Cathy owns a coffee shop," he explains, "and she gave Cara a job, and then persuaded her she could try her hand at being a nanny, which, as I think you all know, is how we met." They smile at each other again. "So, without her, I think it's safe to say, we wouldn't be where we are today."

Cathy blushes, and then Cara introduces her husband, who's called Martin, and her three kids, the oldest of whom is Michelle, and the two youngest, Declan and Lucy. She seems fascinated with baby Sapphire, who's just started to grizzle, and Cara steps forward to take her from Chase.

"I think she needs her diaper changing," Cara says. "I'll take her up to the nursery."

"Do you want me to do it?" Max offers.

"I'll be fine," Cara gives him a smile. "Although tackling the stairs in this dress, while holding her could be… entertaining."

"And dangerous," Max says, taking the baby from his bride. "I'll go."

"That's the secret," Eva says as he exits the marquee. "Wear long dresses if you want to get your husband to change nappies."

"Diapers," Chase says, and she looks up at him.

"They're nappies where I come from."

"Me too," Ronan adds, and the two of them smile at each other.

"Are you picking on me?" Chase says, even though his lips are forming into a cheeky grin.

"Picking on you?" Ronan replies. "How? There are two Brits here, and heaven knows how many Americans."

"In which case, the British contingent is outnumbered and nappies should be referred to as diapers," Destiny says. I know she and Ronan often joke about our supposedly shared language, and this looks like one of those occasions.

Ronan leans in to her and whispers something, after which she turns to him and says, "I think you mean panties," and he shakes his head, while everyone laughs, except Lucy and Tia, who just look confused.

"I used to scold your brother for lowering the tone of the conversation," Dad says, narrowing his eyes at Destiny with a smile on his face. "But it looks like I'll have to have a quiet word with you too."

"Great," Oliver says. "That'll give me a break."

I hold the wine bottle over Oliver's glass. "Do you want some more?"

He startles to attention, dragging his eyes away from the roaring fire we made up as soon as we got back to my place, about an hour ago. His chocolate labrador, Baxter, is curled up in front of the hearth, his head resting on his paws. He's spent the day by himself at Oliver's cabin, but as we had to drive past it to get to Dad's place and then come on here, Oliver stopped off and picked him up, because he hates leaving Baxter for longer than he has to.

"I'd better not."

He's stayed sober all day, having agreed to drive Dad and me to the wedding and not drink, but judging from the look on his face, I wonder if he's regretting that decision.

"You can stay, you know?"

It wouldn't be difficult. I've got four bedrooms in my house… not that I need them. I just liked the house. It's quiet, set in its own area of woodland, well away from the town center and my clients… and their problems.

He looks up at me, hesitates for a moment and then offers his glass.

"Do I have to make up my bed?" he asks.

"No. There's one still made up in the guest room from the last time you stayed."

It doesn't happen very often, being as Oliver only lives fifteen or twenty minutes away, on the other side of town, but occasionally we get together and one or other of us has too much to drink… so it pays to have a contingency plan.

I top up his glass, and then my own, and settle down again at the other end of the couch to him. We both stare at the flickering flames in the hearth for a few moments, sipping our rounded Merlot, until Oliver lets his head rock back and says, "I felt like such a loser today."

I glance over at him. He has reddish-brown hair. It's a slightly more interesting shade than my own, which is just a kind of lightish brown, or darkish blond – depending on the light. In Oliver's case, the red part comes from our mother, like Destiny's, although she's far more auburn than either of us. He's only two years younger than me, and I don't really remember a time when he wasn't there. It's the same for him – obviously – and while we might bicker, we also know when not to… and judging from his expression and the tone of his voice, this is one of those times.

"Why?" I ask.

"Because we were surrounded by people who were so in love, and yet we were there alone."

"So, you're saying I should've felt like a loser too. Is that right?"

He sits forward and turns to face me. "Well… didn't you?"

I put down my wineglass on the low table in front of us and remove my tie, folding it up and placing it next to me on the couch. We both took off our jackets when we got back here, and Oliver undid his tie, leaving it hanging loose around his neck. I'm buying time at the moment, though, and he knows it.

"Well?" he prompts, eventually.

"Yes, I felt like a loser… okay?"

"No, it's not okay. I'm sick of being alone."

I know how he feels. "Why didn't you ask Jemima to the wedding?" I say, to deflect his attention.

He narrows his eyes at me, because he hates talking about her, even though he's in love with her. "Why didn't you ask Isabel?" he replies, employing the same deflection technique and playing me at my own game.

"I asked first," I counter, and he lets out a long breath.

"I never seem to find the right moment with her," he says. "And anyway, I don't even know if she's free. She's always so secretive about her personal life."

"Have you actually asked her?"

"Not directly, no. I've never had the chance."

"You mean she's worked for you for nearly a year, and you don't even know whether she's married?"

"She doesn't wear a ring." He's clearly checked. "But that doesn't mean anything these days, does it? And even if she's not married, she could still be living with someone… or have a boyfriend."

"She's never mentioned one, though?" I ask.

"She never mentions anything," he says, shaking his head. "She just comes to work, does her job, and goes home again." He frowns, focusing on me. "Don't you think that's kinda weird?"

"A little. It wouldn't be so strange if you were working in a big office, with lots of other people, but when there are only two of you, it seems odd that she hasn't mentioned something… even if she was just telling you what she's done over the weekend, or her plans for the holidays, or something like that."

"I know… and every time I think about asking, she either goes home, goes to lunch, or comes up with something she desperately needs to do. It's like she knows when I'm going to ask her about her personal life and does everything she can to avoid it."

"She's not psychic, Oliver. She can't possibly know what you're going to ask."

"No… she's just avoiding me." He sounds really miserable, but then he takes a deep breath and says, "So, what's your excuse?"

"What for?"

"For not inviting Isabel to the wedding."

"Oh… I left it too late." I don't see the point in lying. "I took ages plucking up the courage, trying to work out how to ask her… and when I finally got there and went into her office, she was on the phone with someone. It was clearly a personal call, and she was getting near the end of it, so I waited, because I knew if I went away, I'd never get my courage up again… only when she came off the phone, she told me she'd been talking to her sister, and she was going home to Vermont for the weekend."

"What did you do?" Oliver asks.

"I made up an excuse about why I needed to see her, and didn't bother mentioning the wedding at all."

"You should've asked her sooner," he says. "We've known about Max and Cara's wedding for weeks."

"Yeah… but I'm not sure it would have made any difference."

"Why not? Isabel's plans were kinda last minute. I'm sure if she'd had nothing else to do…"

"Thanks for that." I shake my head at him.

"I didn't mean it like that."

"I know, but I doubt she'd have said 'yes' anyway, regardless of when I asked her."

"You don't know that," he says, shaking his head at me.

"She sees me as her colleague… occasionally her mentor, but certainly not as boyfriend material."

"At least she talks to you." He takes a long drink of wine, before reaching out and grabbing the bottle, filling his glass again.

"I'm not sure what's worse," I say, taking the bottle from him and copying his action. "Loving someone who doesn't see you at all, or loving someone who doesn't see you as a man."

"They both suck," Oliver replies, and we clink our glasses in mutual despair.

Chapter Two

Isabel

"Come on, let's find a table," Noah says, as we enter JC's.

"Okay." I nod my head and look around. It's busy in here tonight, but then it's Saturday, so that's hardly surprising. With Noah following in my wake, I make my way toward the rear of the bar, past crowded booths, filled with people who don't look old enough to be in here… which just goes to show how old I am.

JC's has been our favorite haunt for years. It's got a 'country' vibe, which is tolerable, because it's not over the top. The bar is in the middle of the room, in the form of a square, and while there are tables in neat rows, filling the floor space, I prefer a booth. Somehow it feels more private…

I find one against the side wall, even if it is a little too close to the jukebox for my liking, and take off my jacket, throwing it onto the seat before sitting down and looking across the table at Noah. It's been a while since I've seen him, but he hasn't changed in the slightest. He's easily the handsomest man here, and he dresses well, putting me to shame. While I'm wearing jeans and a chunky sweater, he's in smart pants, a button-down shirt and a casual jacket. I might have put my hair up in a ponytail because I couldn't be bothered to style it, but his short, dark hair is groomed to perfection. I decided against wearing makeup, but he's clean-shaven and smells divine… like he's clearly made an effort.

"What can I get you, honey?" A waitress, clad in a short black skirt and white blouse, comes over and stands between us at the end of the table, although she's focused entirely on Noah, her eyes twinkling and her breasts heaving a little too obviously.

This happens all the time and we're both used to it.

Noah looks at me. "Martinis?" he says and I nod my head, before he turns to the waitress and says, "Two please… very dry."

"Coming right up, hun." She flashes him a twenty-four carat smile and walks away, giving him a pronounced wiggle of her hips.

He's not even looking at her, though. He's focused entirely on me.

"Wanna tell me about it?" he says.

I know I asked to see him. I know I asked if we could come out tonight, but faced with the reality of telling him what's wrong, I find myself tongue-tied. It's not like I've ever said any of this out loud before. I've only admitted it all to myself… in my head.

"I—I…" I stammer, unable to find the words.

"Isabel…" He frowns, looking really concerned. "You know you can tell me anything, don't you?"

"Yes." I look into his deep blue eyes, and I'm reminded for a moment of Mason… which doesn't help in the slightest.

"Then talk," he says, like it's that simple.

"Well… I…"

At that moment, the waitress re-appears beside us, carrying a tray, from which she offloads two cocktail glasses, containing clear liquid, each with an olive on a stick. She glances at Noah again, giving him another smile. "If you need anything else, just holler… I'm Bonnie." She points to a black name tag, with white lettering, pinned just above her right breast… her very ample right breast, and then she tilts her head to one side, biting her lip, and looking very coquettish… or trying to.

"Thanks, Bonnie. We'll let you know if we need you," Noah says, being as politely dismissive as he can.

"Sure thing."

She leaves, thank God, and before Noah can press me into talking again, I raise my glass and wait for him to do the same. He does, after just a moment's pause, and then we clink them together, and I take a very long sip, swallowing down half of my drink in one go.

"Can I guess you needed that?" Noah says once I've put my glass back on the table again.

"Yes."

He reaches across the table, capturing my hands in his and gazing into my eyes. "Okay, you've prevaricated long enough. What's wrong?"

"If you must know, I've fallen for my boss. There... I've told you my latest dark and dirty secret."

He stares at me, totally unfazed by my announcement. "What's dirty about it?" he says, his lips twitching up just slightly at the corners.

"All the thoughts that go through my head whenever I'm with him... or whenever I'm thinking about him."

He laughs, throwing his head back. "There's nothing wrong with that," he says, and then he frowns again, looking confused.

"What's the matter?"

"Just that I didn't think you had a boss. I thought you were working *with* this guy in Sturbridge... not *for* him. I thought you'd set it up as a kind of partnership."

"We did. Mason was looking for an associate... someone he could grow his practice with. When he interviewed me, he told me – straight off the bat – that he'd never enjoyed doing relationship counseling, especially not with couples. He said he'd been getting lots of inquiries, though, and he wanted someone who could build that side of the practice, while he focused on the things he wanted to do."

"That's something you've always been good at, though, isn't it?" Noah asks, making it sound like I've been practicing psychology a lot longer than I have.

"I don't know if I'm any good at it, but it's a side of the business I enjoy. Since I've been there, I've been building up my own client base, and it's going pretty well. It's a bit like working for myself, but having the back-up of a partner at the same time. We both bill our hours, and then we take a percentage and leave the rest in the business."

"Did you have to buy your way in to get that kind of deal?"

"No." I shake my head and take another sip of my drink… a smaller one this time.

"That was generous of him, considering the practice was already established, and entirely his."

"He's a generous man." I think back to the interview I had with Mason in July, and how – when I wasn't staring into his blue eyes, and studying his handsome face – I raised exactly this same question, pointing out to Mason that I couldn't afford a buy-in. I'd only just completed my training, and to be honest, I was amazed he was even willing to consider me. "He explained he wanted someone who'd stick with him for the long-term; who'd have a vested interest in the practice. … not an employee who was just there to pick up their paycheck at the end of the month. So, we came to our agreement. At the moment, I have thirty percent of the practice, which is more than fair, considering my lack of experience, and the fact that he's been doing this for a lot longer than I have."

"And that you've fallen for him," Noah says, returning us to our original conversation.

"Yes… I have."

"Does he know?"

"No, of course not."

He frowns. "Why do you say it like that?"

"Because Mason only sees me as a fellow psychologist, someone he's helping… mentoring. And he's good at both those things. He's fantastic at what he does, and I'm learning a lot from him… but I wish – just once in a while – that he'd see me as a woman, and not someone he's in business with."

"You're sure he doesn't?" he asks.

"Absolutely positive. Outside of work, I might as well be invisible."

I finish my drink and Noah glances around, clearly spotting Bonnie and raising his hand, holding up two fingers and pointing back to the table again. Fortunately, she must have got the message, because she doesn't come over, and he leans in a little closer as he says, "I can empathize."

"About what?"

"Being invisible."

"I doubt that. Bonnie can't take her eyes off of you... and the same goes for every other woman in here."

It's true. Noah's the center of attention among most of the female clientele... but that's quite normal.

He smiles. "And why would I welcome their attention?" he says, shaking his head.

"Because it's better than nothing?" I suggest, before I reach over and take his hand in mine. "Have you met someone?" I ask. He nods his head.

"Yeah. And guess what? I'm in exactly the same predicament as you."

"You mean, you've fallen for your boss?" I frown at him. "Wait a second... I thought your editor was a woman."

"She is," he says. "And I think we just established that the guy you've fallen for isn't your boss, is he?"

"No..."

"He's a colleague," Noah says, sensing my confusion.

"Oh... so what you're saying is, you've fallen for someone at work? Someone who isn't your boss?"

Bonnie appears again, depositing two more martinis in front of us, simpering at Noah before she leaves again, and he rolls his eyes as I take a sip of my drink.

"Yes. He's the new photographer." He sighs, tilting his head and looking kinda dreamy, and I wonder for a moment if that's how I look when I talk about Mason.

"And?" I prompt.

"And nothing." His shoulders drop and he lifts his glass to his lips, drinking down a significant amount of his cocktail.

"Oh... you mean, he's not gay?" I lower my voice as I speak, leaning in close to him.

"No. I mean, he doesn't know I exist."

"So he is gay?"

"Yes."

"If it's not a stupid question, how do you know?"

"You just know," he says, as though the answer is obvious. "Not that it makes any difference."

"Why not?"

"Because, like I said before, I can empathize. Aaron never even looks at me, except to look through me."

"His name's Aaron?" I pick up on that.

"Yeah."

"What's he like?"

Noah hesitates for a second and then says, "Gorgeous." He smiles, although it doesn't touch his eyes. "What's Mason like?"

"The same."

"This sucks, doesn't it?" he says and I nod my head as I lean forward again.

"I really hate being the oldest virgin in town, you know?"

Noah smiles properly this time. "You're not."

"I'll bet I am."

"No," he says. "Flora and Lydia Massey… you remember them? They live with their brother out at Applewood Farm?"

"Oh, yeah? What about them?"

"Well, I'm fairly sure no-one's ever been anywhere near either of them in their entire lives… and Flora celebrated her eightieth birthday a couple of weeks ago."

I have to laugh. I can't help myself. "At least that gives me something to aim for," I mutter. "Try to get laid before I'm eighty."

"You'll do it," he says, with a lot more conviction than I feel. "And look on the bright side… at least you don't have to live here and pretend to be something you're not."

I can hear the sadness in his voice and see it in his eyes, and I reach across the table, taking his hand. "Hey, don't be sad."

"I'm not."

"Yeah, you are."

"Okay. I am. I'm not ashamed of being gay; I never have been. But I'm getting really sick of having to keep it a secret." He shakes his head, looking down at his half-empty glass. "If only my parents were more enlightened."

"If only my parents were here."

"You don't mean that" he says.

"No, I don't. It's probably the martini talking." We both stare at each other for a second and then laugh.

"Where are they these days?" he asks.

"I have no idea. Reagan and Ashley might know, but they haven't told me. Knowing Mom and Dad, they're probably on a cruise somewhere. That's where they usually are."

"When did you last see them?"

His question takes me by surprise, and I have to think for a moment. "It wasn't last Christmas… or the Christmas before that. So, probably nearly three years ago." I shake my head. "I'm not sure I'd recognize them, if they walked through the door tomorrow."

"We make such a happy couple, don't we?" he says, sighing. "Maybe we should get married."

I release his hand and take a sip of my drink, raising my glass to him. "I offered you marriage once, if you remember? Well… kind of."

He chuckles. "I don't think I'll ever forget the look on your face when I turned you down… and then told you I'm gay."

"Are you surprised?" I put my glass down again. "I didn't have a clue."

"I know. I'm good at hiding it."

"Which is probably why I suggested we could be each other's back-ups if we both got to thirty and were still single. I still can't believe you let me wax lyrical for twenty minutes about how I was sure it wouldn't happen, but if it did, I could think of a lot worse people to be married to than my best friend… and only then did you burst out laughing, and tell me I'm the wrong damn sex."

He shrugs his shoulders, staring into my eyes. "It would never have worked."

"Why not? Apart from the obvious… naturally."

"You're way too insecure." His lips twist upwards into a smile. "And you over-think absolutely everything."

"I know… and you're too sensitive for me."

"In that case, it's just as well I turned you down, isn't it?"

"Yeah, it is."

He reaches out and gently cups my face with his hand. "You love me anyway, though… don't you?" he says.

"Of course… and you love me too."

"Yeah, I do… always."

"Thank God someone does."

He gives me a sweet smile, his hand dropping back to the table as he searches around for Bonnie… because it seems we both need another drink.

Mason

Oliver spent the whole of yesterday with me in the end. It's not something we do that often, but I don't think either of us felt like being alone. We woke up late, after a fairly heavy Saturday night that involved opening a second bottle of wine and watching a truly awful movie. Then, after a brunch of bacon and scrambled eggs, he offered to help me chop some logs. I found him some jeans and a sweater to wear and we spent the afternoon behind the house, filling my log store, while Baxter ran around the forest, making up for having spent the previous day cooped up in Oliver's cabin. It was freezing cold out there, but the exercise was invigorating for all of us, and fortunately, neither Oliver nor I felt the need to talk… which was just fine. I made us some ribs for dinner and then he and Baxter left at about nine-thirty, being as we've both got work today.

He told me before he left last night that his appointment book is slammed for today, although mine isn't. In fact, I don't have anyone to see until eleven… and while, in the past, that might have meant I'd have stayed home and given myself a few extra hours in bed, I don't do that anymore. Now I make a point of being at the office from just before eight in the morning until the last client has left. I tell myself that's so I can be on-hand in case Izzy needs me. In reality, it's because I need her. She might not acknowledge my existence, but I still enjoy being around her. I'm not kidding myself… not really.

I park my car behind our brick-built office on Main Street, a few minutes before eight, as usual, and wander around to the front of the building, letting myself in, before I quickly switch off the alarm. The place is in semi-darkness, so I open the blinds that cover the small windows at the front. It's still too dark in here though, because it's overcast outside, so I turn on the lights, revealing our small reception area. We don't have a receptionist… because I never needed one when I worked here alone, and that doesn't seem to have changed since Izzy joined me back in August. *Can it really only be three months?* I guess so, although it's hard to remember a time when she wasn't here. In that first week, we discussed hiring someone to sit in the front office and greet our clients, make coffee, and take phone calls, but we decided against it. That's to say, Izzy asked what I'd done in the past and when I said I'd never used a receptionist, she suggested we should continue doing just that. We both make our own appointments, which works well for us, because like most people in our profession, we can ensure there's a gap between each client, allowing us time to make a coffee, or use the bathroom, or − most importantly − to gather our thoughts. That's necessary sometimes, because you can hear things you need to process, and it doesn't pay to go straight into another session without having had the chance to do so.

I wander down to my office, toward the rear of the building, by-passing Izzy's, which is on my right, and go inside, taking off my coat and hooking it up behind the door. The space I've created in here is, hopefully, calming and professional, with pale gray walls, a few landscape pictures, and a long couch against the far wall. There's a wing-backed chair off to one side, where I sit during most sessions, and between those two pieces of furniture is a low table, on top of which is a box of Kleenex. My desk is by the window, and I open the blind in here too, then switch on my table lamp, remove my jacket, placing it over the back of my black leather chair, and sit down to fire up my computer. As I do, I let out a sigh and gaze across at the chair on the other side of my desk, picturing Izzy sitting there, just like she did when she came for her interview, back in July. She was nervous, but she hid it well, behind a dark gray suit and white blouse… and a very shy but sexy smile.

I think I fell for her then, if I'm being honest. It wasn't difficult. She's the most beautiful woman in the world, so falling came naturally. It wasn't just her beauty I fell for, either. It was her enthusiasm, too. I loved the way she talked about our job. I loved her attitude to work, and to clients… to everything, really. She was inquisitive; she wanted to learn, she saw life as an education… and I liked that. It was refreshing.

I'd advertised for an associate… and in those circumstances, I'd been expecting to see people much older than Izzy, with years of experience and enough money to buy their way in to my practice. By the time she arrived, I'd already interviewed four or five of them, and hadn't been impressed, but we were only fifteen minutes into our interview when Izzy made it clear she couldn't afford a buy-in. I know there are many people who would say it was my libido talking when I said it didn't matter… and maybe it was… in part. But I wanted to work with her, and if she'd subsequently told me she'd lied on her resume and she wasn't single but was married with two kids and a dog, I'd still have offered her the same deal… and I wouldn't have been wrong. She's like a breath of fresh air, she's good for the practice, clients think she's great… and revenues are well up.

As it is, she didn't lie. She's single… and I'm in love with her.

Once I've checked my emails, I leave the room again and head further toward the back of the building, to where the bathroom and kitchen are. I call it a kitchen, but really it's a small alcove with a sink and countertop, where we can make coffee.

I'm just adding water to the machine when I hear the front door open and close, signaling Izzy's arrival, and I immediately spill the water over the countertop.

"Damn," I mutter under my breath. Why do I always have to behave like such an idiot around her… I mean, she's not even here, in the same room as me, and I'm being a clumsy fool.

I mop up the spillage and add the coffee grounds to the machine before switching it on, grateful I didn't get anything else wrong.

"Good morning."

I jump at the sound of Izzy's voice right behind me and turn to face her, my breath catching in my throat. *How can anyone be that beautiful?*

"I—I didn't hear you come in," I lie, stammering as usual. "Would you like a coffee?"

We usually get our own, but if we happen to both be out here, one of us will make a drink for the other… mainly because there's so little space.

"I'd love one," she says, giving me that shy, sexy smile and looking down at her feet. She's wearing high heels, like she always does. They make her legs look really shapely and long, and today, they're black, matching her stockings. I guess she could be wearing pantyhose, but I like to think not. Her suit's the same color, and the skirt – which ends just above her knees – clings to her hips, leading up to a pale gray blouse, which is open at the neck. She's my idea of a perfectly formed woman, with a narrow waist, flat stomach, slightly flared hips, rounded ass, and breasts which are neither too big, nor too small, but which I know would fit my hands just right.

The coffee machine beeps, halting my visual feast and I turn and grab a couple of cups from the cabinet, relieved that Izzy didn't look up in time to see the way my eyes were gorging over her, like a hormonal teenager… which means she also won't have noticed my raging hard-on. That's the effect she has on me, every time she's near me, and there's not a damned thing I can do about it.

I'm aware of the silence between us, and of the fact that I'm pouring the coffee, which means she'll go back to her own room soon… and I'll be alone again.

Except I don't want to be alone. I want to be with Izzy.

"H—How was your weekend?" I say the first thing that comes into my head, in my desperation to keep her here for a little longer.

I turn as I'm speaking, handing her one of the cups of coffee, being as we both take it black. She takes it from me and looks up through her long eyelashes, her dark eyes twinkling slightly. "It was fine," she says, and every nerve ending in my body sparks.

"How were your parents?" I turn back and grab my own coffee, hoping my hard-on isn't too noticeable… or at least that she's distracted by my movements and by the coffee. Not that she's probably looking in that direction, anyway.

"I didn't see my parents," she replies, and I can't help noticing the way her chestnut hair frames her face, or how she puckers her lips as she blows across the top of her cup to cool her coffee. I struggle not to groan out loud, as I think about pressing my lips to hers, and I almost step forward, just as she adds, "I never do."

"Excuse me?" That seems like a strange remark, and she's said it with such sadness, that even though I'm still staring at her, and even though I'm still in love with her, and I still want to kiss her more than anything, I have to say something. "Did you just say you never do?"

"Yes. My parents have hardly been home since I became old enough to care for my sisters… so for roughly the last thirteen years."

"Since you were sixteen?"

She smiles. "I hate the fact that you know I'm twenty-nine," she says and I have to smile back, because this is the most personal conversation we've ever had, and I like it… a lot.

"It was on your resume," I explain and she nods her head.

"Yeah… but there are times I wish I'd lied."

"Why?"

"Because twenty-nine sounds so old. It's so nearly thirty."

I lean back against the countertop behind me. "It's not old… not compared to thirty-six, anyway."

"Are you thirty-six?" she asks, tilting her head to one side.

"Yeah…" I wonder for a moment, if that bothers her… if she'd rather I were younger. But then I scold myself. Why would it matter to her how old I am? She's not interested in me… not like that. "You were saying… about your parents?" I prompt her, getting back to the conversation, so she won't leave.

"Oh, yeah. Just before my sixteenth birthday, they won a small fortune in the state lottery. They paid off their mortgage and Dad gave up work, and then a couple of weeks after I turned sixteen, they announced they were going on an extended trip around Europe for the entire summer, leaving me in charge of my little sisters."

"How little were they?"

"They were only eight and six, and while I'd looked forward to spending a long, hot summer with my friends, I found myself babysitting."

"It was a bit more than babysitting, wasn't it?"

"Yeah. It was full-time parenting."

"Your mom and dad came back though, didn't they?" I know she said her parents have hardly been home since she was sixteen, but that must have been an exaggeration. They must have been there while she went through college, surely. She's got a doctorate in psychology… I know how much work that takes.

"Reluctantly," she says, rolling her eyes and taking a sip of coffee. "They came home just before the end of the summer recess, and that became their pattern for the next few years. They'd stick around while we were at school, and then – leaving me with enough money to keep us fed and watered – they'd take off again the moment school ended."

"How did that feel?" I'm astounded by what I'm hearing.

"What?" she asks.

"When they left like that?"

She looks at me for a moment and then says, "It hurt," and I wonder how many times she'd admitted that to anyone… including herself.

"How did you cope, looking after your sisters by yourself, and getting through school?" I sense she might be uncomfortable discussing her feelings… so talking about practicalities seems a better way to go.

"I just did. It wasn't optional. I studied hard, and every time my parents left, I raised my sisters. I graduated from high school and went to college."

"In Vermont?" I say, recalling her resume again.

"Yeah. That wasn't my choice. I wanted to go to Boston, but I had to be somewhere within driving distance of home. By the time I completed my doctorate, last year, my sisters were both at college themselves. They're doing really well… and between them, they're driving all the boys crazy." She rolls her eyes again and I smile.

"So you finally moved to Boston?"

"Just to complete my training, yes."

"What made you choose the Elleston Clinic?" I ask, wondering why I didn't pose that question at her interview… other than that I was busy falling for her… obviously.

"I was sucked in by the brochures… just like their clients," she says.

"You didn't enjoy it there?" I drink down some more of my coffee.

"No. I hated it. Aside from the fact that they didn't really seem interested in the 'training' part of the contract, I didn't like their work ethic."

"Is that why you didn't stay on once you'd qualified?"

"Yes. They offered me a position, but there was no way I wanted to stay at a clinic that treated its clients like numbers, and was more concerned with their income than the patients' outcomes." This is the reason I took her on. She's not all about the bottom line… and she cares. "Are you familiar with the Elleston Clinic?" she asks.

"Yes, but only because I know someone who used to work there. He went there to complete his training too and stayed on for a while."

"Oh? Will I know him?"

"No. He left and started his own practice about five years ago."

"He must have liked it there, if he stayed on for so long?" she says.

"Yeah… but Calvin always was an idiot, so we won't set too much store by his opinion."

She giggles and my body shudders, which I only disguise by pushing myself off of the countertop and turning around to deposit my cup in the sink.

"How was your weekend?" she asks, surprising me by keeping the conversation going herself this time, and I turn back to face her. She's looking up at me, her cheeks slightly flushed, and I gaze down into her eyes.

"M—My weekend?" I'm stuttering again.

"Yeah… how was it?"

"I went to a wedding," I reply, remembering how to speak properly at last.

"Family, or friends?"

"Friends... I think."

"You mean you don't know?" She smiles at me.

"The groom was one of my dad's former patients," I explain. "But his sister-in-law is also the sister of my soon-to-be brother-in-law... so I really don't know if that qualifies as family."

"It qualifies as complicated," she says, and we both laugh.

"Yeah, it does."

"Was it a nice wedding?" she asks.

"It was okay." *It would have been so much nicer if you'd been there with me.*

"Don't you like weddings, then?" She sounds intrigued.

"I guess. But we didn't really know anyone. It wasn't like one of those weddings where you're catching up with people you haven't seen for years. It was one where you're constantly trying to remember who everyone is."

"We?" she says, picking up on that, rather than anything else.

That's an interesting response, especially when it's coupled with the blush that's creeping up her cheeks, and I actually take a half step forward before I reply, "By 'we', I mean my family and me... and by 'family', I mean my brother and my dad. My sister and her fiancé were there too, but they knew a lot of the other guests, because of Ronan's connection with the groom's family."

"The connection being... his sister?" Izzy says, hesitating slightly and tilting her head to one side.

"Yes... well done. You've picked it up a lot quicker than I did."

She giggles again, and because I'm more prepared for the effect that has on me, I'm able to control the shudder this time.

"Did you say the groom was a former patient of your dad's?" she asks.

"Yes."

"So you dad's a doctor?"

"He's a retired surgeon."

"There are two doctors in your family?"

"No… there are three. My brother Oliver is a doctor of veterinary medicine… and I guess you could say there will be four of us when Ronan and Destiny get married, because Ronan's a doctor of archaeology."

She gazes up at me for a moment and then her lips twitch up into that glorious, sexy smile. "Do you know anyone who just does a 'normal' job, like… I don't know… working in a hotel, or a bookstore, or something?"

I laugh, throwing my head back and Izzy stares at me until I stop and shake my head. "You won't believe this, but the groom was Max Crawford, the…"

"As in Crawford Hotels?" she says, interrupting my explanation.

"Yes."

She laughs herself now. "You move in exalted circles."

"Not really. I told you, the connection was very loose."

"And complicated," she says.

"Yes… it was good though."

"What was?"

"At the wedding… seeing Dad get the recognition he deserved."

"For what?" she asks.

"For saving Max Crawford's life. Dad always says he just operated on Max's leg after he was shot on active duty in Afghanistan. But Max made it very clear yesterday there was a lot more to it than that." I stare down at the space between us, which is about a foot wide, or just over, and then I look back at her again. "I know my dad is a great guy, but it was fantastic to hear someone else tell him that… in public."

She smiles up at me. "I hope you take the time to tell him that yourself, from time to time… in private."

"Probably not as often as I should." I can't remember the last time I said something like that to my dad, but Izzy's right; I should make the effort.

"Did your mom enjoy the wedding too?" she asks, and I feel like I've just been drop-kicked in the chest.

"My… my mom's dead," I reply in a whisper.

Izzy's face pales and her eyes widen, and before I can react, she reaches around behind me, putting her cup down on the countertop, and then places her hand on my arm, just above the elbow. I'm still feeling numbed by her question, but I can feel the heat of her touch too... and those two things, put together, are kinda confusing.

"I'm so sorry, Mason, I should've realized, when you didn't mention her," she says, with heartbreaking sincerity, and my confusion melts in an instant. I don't want her to feel like this... all sad and sympathetic.

"It's okay." She takes her hand away and I want to ask her to put it back, because despite the confusion, it felt good to have her touch me.

"When did it happen... if you don't mind me asking?"

"I don't mind at all. It was a long time ago... twenty-four years, to be precise."

"You were only a child?" She's shocked.

"Yeah, I was twelve." I don't know why I said that. She could easily have worked out the math herself, being as I've already told her my age. "Oliver was ten," I add, to cover my stupidity.

"Was it an accident?" she asks, still staring up at me.

"No. She was giving birth to our sister."

"To Destiny?" She's remembered my sister's name... I like that.

"No... not Destiny. She'd already been born a few minutes beforehand. It was Destiny's twin."

"You've got two sisters?" She looks confused, which isn't surprising, being as I haven't mentioned another one.

I shake my head. "No. Something went wrong. Mom had a massive hemorrhage, and the other twin was starved of oxygen. That's how Dad explained it, a few years later, when Oliver asked for more information and Dad felt we were old enough to understand. I've never asked for more detail than that."

"God... that must've been hard," she says, shaking her head.

"It was. Obviously, it was hardest of all for Dad. He'd lost his wife, and his child."

She puts her hand back on my arm again and takes a step closer, looking up into my eyes. "You'd lost your mom, Mason. Never underestimate that."

"I don't. I never did." Any more than I'm underestimating this conversation. "I think the hardest part for Oliver and me was trying not to resent Destiny when Dad brought her home from the hospital. We'd expected him to come back with two babies and our mom, and he just brought her. I—I remember running up to my room and wishing he'd just take her away again and bring Mom back instead." My voice cracks slightly, but then, this is the first time I've spoken about any of this in years.

"That's understandable." Her voice is soft, kind, deeply concerned.

"Is it?" I've never been sure.

"Of course it is. You were twelve. It was a lot to handle."

I nod my head, because I know what she's saying is right. My training tells me that, if nothing else, and I know it's what I'd say to a client in the same position. "It was Dad who got us through it," I tell her. "He sat us down and made us see it wasn't Destiny's fault. She hadn't asked for any of it… and she wasn't responsible for what had happened. No-one was. He never forced us to spend time with her, and she had a nanny to look after her when Dad was working… but he showed us how to love her. He let us talk about mom, whenever we wanted… and he reminded us all the time, how lucky we were that we had our memories of her, which I guess also reminded us that Destiny had none."

"Your dad sounds like a very special man," she says.

"He is. He's the one who made me realize I wanted to help people… like he helped Oliver and me."

"You do," she whispers. "I've seen what you do, and you help people all the time, Mason. You're great at what you do. You're a brilliant psychologist… you're…"

Oh, God… please don't start talking about work… don't make this like it normally is when you come to me for advice. It's been so…

The doorbell rings, interrupting my train of thought, and she startles back, letting her hand drop from my arm, down to her side.

"Shit… that's my nine-thirty." She glances around, looking flustered.

"It's okay." I place my hands gently on her shoulders and suck in a breath, because she feels so good to touch. She stops her unaccountable panic and stares up at me. "You go to your office and get straightened out, and I'll show your clients in."

"Oh… thank you," she says, and I release her, watching as she walks away, and then I follow a few steps behind, going through to the front door.

I open it and smile a greeting at the couple who are standing on the doorstep, waiting. I'd say they're in their early forties. He's graying at the temples, but is handsome enough, and she's very attractive, with blonde hair and a lovely smile.

"Good morning," I say, standing aside to let them in out of the cold.

"Hello," the man says. "We're Mr. and Mrs. Jackson. We've got a nine-thirty appointment with Miss Banks."

I nod my head. "Come this way."

I lead them to Izzy's office and knock on her door, waiting until she says, "Come in," before I push it open.

"Mr. and Mrs. Jackson to see you," I say, with a smile, which she returns, and I notice she's removed her jacket now. Like me, while she always looks professional, she prefers to dress fairly informally to see clients. It puts them at their ease.

Stepping forward, she widens her smile and then says, "Lynda… Barry… come in. Take a seat. How was your weekend with your friends from Vancouver? Oh, and how did they get along with your new puppy?"

Mrs. Jackson starts talking as I quietly close the door and lean back against the wall beside it.

That was impressive.

Very impressive.

As I wander back to my office, I'm blown away that she knew her clients well enough to greet them like that, or that at least she'd bothered to make notes on their personal lives, because it's not always about people's problems. You have to focus on what's wrong, obviously, but sometimes you just need to let them talk. That way, you can often learn a lot more than you might expect... and knowledge is always useful, even when you don't think it will be.

I sit at my desk, forgetting about Izzy's clients for a moment, still reeling from that conversation we had in the kitchen. I hope I'm not reading too much into it... I hope she wasn't just being as polite with me as she seems with everyone... because I'd really like this to be the start of something.

Something special.

Chapter Three

∽∞∽

Isabel

I kick off my shoes, letting my jacket drop onto the couch, before flopping down myself, feeling like my body has deflated.

It's only six in the evening, but it's been one of those days, and I allow myself a few minutes before I have to summon the energy to cook dinner... or maybe shower. I can't decide which. I feel like I need a rest, and I twist around and put my feet up, nestling back into the soft cushions of my pale blue couch. Like everything else in my apartment, it's small... but it's comfortable enough, and I smile to myself as I think back over a busy Monday.

I think I lulled myself into a false sense of security, because my first appointment wasn't until nine-thirty... but why I thought it was a good idea to spend so long talking with Mason in the kitchen is anyone's guess. The talk itself was fabulous... it was the timing of it that was the problem, because it threw me into a panic when Lynda and Barry Jackson arrived for their appointment. Mason stepped in, though, all calm and efficient, and saved the day, giving me time to go to my office, take off my jacket and check my notes from their last session, while he went to the door to greet them.

I made a point of skimming through the brief hints they'd dropped when I'd last seen them... about their friends who were coming to stay from Vancouver, and how their new puppy was getting along. So, when Mason showed them in, I could greet them with some personal questions, which always makes a client feel more relaxed. I know they've come to see me because they're having issues, but if we only focus on the negatives – on the reasons for them being in my office in the first place – it can make them forget that there's more to life than problems.

Once Lynda had sat down at one end of the couch, she told me that the weekend had gone really well... even if their puppy had chewed his way through one of their guest's slippers. Fortunately, he'd seen the funny side, pointing out that his mother-in-law had bought him the slippers for Christmas, and that he hated them anyway... before giving the puppy the other one to play with.

I noted Barry hesitated before sitting, and then took his place at the opposite end of the couch to his wife, and I wondered whether things had maybe taken a downturn for them, despite their good weekend.

"So, how are things?" I said as I sat down in the chair facing them, signaling the beginning of the session.

They looked at me, and then Lynda glanced at Barry and shrugged, before he said, "They'd be going a lot better if Lynda would stop obsessing about her weight all the time. She wouldn't even let us go out for dinner when Colin and Susan were staying... and I wanted to take them to the new steak house."

"Yes... where I've heard they serve the most incredible fries... and onion rings to die for," Lynda replied, shooting him a glare. "Do you want me to put on even more weight?"

"I've already told you, I don't care what you weigh," he replied, raising his voice slightly, and I held up my hands to get their attention. I wished he'd added, 'I love you, regardless,' or words to that effect, but he just looked away, doubtless making Lynda feel like he didn't care at all... about her, or her weight.

Lynda isn't that overweight. In fact, the problem lies more in her perception of herself than anything... and in the fact that, after nearly twenty years of marriage, I think she's feeling a little under-appreciated.

Today was our third session though, and I wanted to do a little more than skirt around the edges of their problems. So, I turned the tables on

Barry at that point and asked him what he did care about. He stared at me for a very long moment, and I wondered if he was going to refuse to answer. He's been a difficult client since the beginning, regarding my services as a waste of money, I think. But eventually, he sighed and murmured, "I care about us not doing anything together anymore."

Lynda turned and looked at him, surprise written all over her face. I didn't let her talk though, for fear they'd argue. Instead, I said, "What would you like to do together?"

He thought for a few seconds and then said, "I'd like us to go out for a drink every so often... or for dinner... like we used to."

"Yes, but we can't all eat a ten-ounce steak and not gain four pounds," Lynda huffed, folding her arms across her chest and looking out the window.

I knew she was exaggerating, and so did she, but she also wasn't budging.

"That's because I do some exercise," he said, and she turned back to him.

"You have time to exercise." She sat forward slightly, getting up a head of steam. "Between work, the house, the garden, and my writing classes, when do I have time for exercise?" They glared at each other and I wondered for a moment if I was about to lose control of the session... if they were going to descend into a full scale row.

"What exercise do you do?" I asked Barry, and he turned to face me.

"I play golf twice a week." I struggled not to yawn at the prospect, but nodded my head and shifted my gaze to Lynda.

"Is there any reason you can't do likewise?" I asked.

"You're suggesting I take up golf?" she said, frowning at me.

"Not necessarily, but surely you could cut down on the gardening and maybe take up tennis, or something?"

"I wouldn't mind if you came to play golf with me," Barry said, and we both looked at him in surprise. "Don brings his wife on a Saturday afternoon, and they have dinner afterwards in the clubhouse."

"Why does everything always have to revolve around food?" Lynda wailed, bursting into tears.

Barry sighed and although I willed him to comfort his wife, he didn't. He just sat and looked down at his hands until eventually I felt duty bound to hand Lynda a Kleenex from the box. She took a few moments, drying her tears, and then apologized.

"You don't need to say sorry," I told her. "But I think Barry has a point." He sat up slightly and Lynda opened her mouth to speak, but I held up my hands, wanting to say my piece. "Why can't you try playing golf with him on a Saturday afternoon... but maybe not going to the clubhouse afterwards? That way you wouldn't have to worry about food, but at least you'd be doing something together *and* getting some exercise."

She looked at me while he studied her until eventually she shrugged her shoulders and then nodded her head. "I guess we could try it," she murmured.

Barry smiled then, and I saw a younger version of the man appear in his eyes as he shifted along the couch, getting closer to his wife. "I— I could maybe help you in the garden on Sundays... if you'd like me to?"

"You wouldn't mind?" She smiled up at him.

He shook his head and moved even closer still.

I coughed, breaking into their moment, before they got carried away.

"That's great," I said. "But we mustn't lose sight of why you came to see me."

"Because of our relationship problems, you mean?" Lynda said, looking confused.

I wasn't sure that was how I'd have phrased it. They had a communication problem, which was easily resolved, but that didn't get to the heart of the issue... Lynda's lack of self-confidence. "When you came to your first session, you told me you felt as though Barry didn't love you anymore... is that right?"

"Yes," she mumbled.

I turned to Barry. "Was that ever true?" I asked.

"No," he said, surprising me, being as he'd been unwilling to comfort his weeping wife just a few minutes earlier. "I've always loved her."

"Then tell her."

He stared at me, his eyes widening.

"N—Now?" he stuttered.

"Yes. Pretend I'm not here."

The look on his face told me he thought such a concept was impossible, but then he let out a long breath and turned to face Lynda, moving along the couch enough that their knees were touching. He reached out, taking her hands in his, and after blinking a few times, he said, "I've loved you since the day you walked into my dad's store, over twenty years ago. There isn't a day that's gone by when I haven't thanked the Lord that your dad sent you to buy his nails, rather than coming himself. I know I'm not great at telling you how I feel, but nothing's changed from that day to this. To me, you're still the prettiest girl in town... and I don't care what size you are, I still wanna take you out and show you off. I just wish you'd let me... because I'm so damn proud you're mine."

I hadn't been expecting that, and neither had Lynda, because she promptly dissolved in tears. This time, rather than ignoring her and looking uncomfortable, Barry took her in his arms and held on to her... and she let him.

I gave them a few minutes, getting up and wandering over to my desk, where I pretended to study my computer screen, while they whispered to each other, and Barry dried Lynda's tears. Then, once it seemed safe and polite to do so, I wandered back.

"I think I'd like to see you by yourself from now on, Lynda," I said, looking at her, as she nestled against her husband, while he put his arm around her.

"I'm sorry?" She looked up at me, her eyes a little puffy from crying. "You want to see me? Why?"

"Because I think the relationship we really need to examine here is the one you have with food... not the one you have with Barry. This isn't about Barry loving you or not loving you. This is about how you feel about yourself."

"C—Can you help with things like that?" she asked, biting her bottom lip.

"Of course. If you want me to."

She looked up at Barry. "Do you think we can afford it?"

He smiled. "If it's what you want, then yes."

She turned to me and nodded her head, saying, "Okay," in a quiet voice.

We arranged our next appointment before they left, which will be next week, with Lynda… by herself. And then, once they'd gone, I took ten minutes to myself, to muse over what had happened, and to prepare for my next clients.

It's been like that all day really, flitting from one client to the next, with varying degrees of success. Sometimes their problems feel quite trivial, like the couple I saw immediately before lunch, who couldn't stop arguing – even during the session – about their youngest son. He was refusing to behave, and the situation was becoming intolerable… according to both his mother and his school. His father thought the solution lay with the mother, and that she wasn't firm enough. She believed it would all be resolved if her husband spent a little more time at home. I tried pointing out that they needed to focus on their son – and their other two children – rather than fighting between themselves all the time, but I'm not sure they even heard me… they were fighting so much.

I was glad it was time for lunch after that. I needed a break, and my only disappointment was that Mason's lunch break didn't coincide with mine. We have copies of each other's diaries, just so we know what we're doing, and his 'morning' sessions weren't due to finish until one-thirty, while that was the time for the first of my afternoon ones.

That was unfortunate, because I would have quite liked to continue our conversation from this morning… or maybe start another one. It was good to talk, even if the timing was difficult in the end. And it was good to let him talk, too. It was the first time either of us has really done that… opened up to the other about our personal lives, and I liked the fact that he listened. He didn't just pretend to be interested. He really was.

I also liked the fact that he'd remembered little details from my resume, although I'm doing my best not to read too much into that.

Apart from Noah, he's the only person I've ever spoken to about my parents and what they did. None of my other high school friends knew they'd taken off and left me in charge of my sisters. I didn't want to admit to the rejection… because that was what it felt like, and while I didn't explain that fully to Mason, I admitted it had hurt.

I've come to terms with it now… with the fact that having fun themselves was more important to my mom and dad than their responsibility toward their children. I don't even know where they are most of the time. They rarely bother to tell us, and I gave up asking them to stay in touch years ago. I keep them at arm's length, as do Reagan and Ashley… and we're all better off.

Except I have to admit, when I think about what they did… it still hurts.

Not long after I'd surprised myself by telling Mason that this morning, we reached a kind of lull in our conversation. It happened quite naturally, and he turned to put his cup down on the countertop. I felt a powerful urge then to ask him to hold me. I wanted to feel safe… like there was someone who'd look out for me, for once. Of course, I couldn't say that out loud, so instead, I inquired how his weekend had gone, just so he wouldn't leave. We'd gotten into the swing of talking by then, and although I was fairly sure he'd only asked about my weekend to be polite, I hoped he'd be willing to stay a little longer… and he was.

I never expected him to tell me about his mom. I had no idea she'd died… or in such tragic circumstances, and I wanted to hold him then, to take him in my arms and comfort him. That would have been impossible, but I reached out to him instead, and touched his arm. I wondered if he'd make an excuse to end the conversation. I'd have let him, if he'd wanted to… but he didn't. He told me about his resentment toward his sister, how he'd blamed her for their mother's death, with all the irrationality of a child in the depths of grief… and how their dad had helped him and his brother come to terms with their loss, if such a thing is possible.

I don't know how many people have heard him tell that story in the last twenty-four years… and I don't care either. The point is, he was sharing it with me, and that felt special.

Talking with Mason was about the most special thing I've ever done… although that's not saying very much, and I'm aware I need to stop over-thinking, as Noah would say. Mason probably only started the conversation because he had some spare time before his first appointment of the day, so I need to stop acting like it mattered… even though it did.

I stand, stretching my arms above my head, and glance over at the tiny kitchen area in my apartment. The whole apartment is tiny, so the kitchen is in perfect proportion to the rest of the place, and for a moment, I contemplate making something to eat before I decide on taking a shower first. Then I can cook and settle down in front of a movie… a fairly typical evening for me.

I wander through to the bathroom, undoing my blouse and letting it fall to the floor, before removing my bra, and then unzipping my skirt. It hits the floor beside my blouse and I bend to pick them up, dumping them into the laundry basket, unfastening my stockings and rolling them down my legs, and then removing my garter belt. I smile as I add them to my other clothes, reflecting on the fact that I've grown accustomed to not wearing panties. I stopped wearing them – unless I absolutely have to – not long after I moved here and started working with Mason. It was a bit of an experiment because I found that every time I was within touching distance of him, I got so wet, my panties were literally soaked… and I wondered one morning if it might be easier not to bother with them.

It was not only easier, and more comfortable, but I get even more turned on, knowing I'm naked beneath my skirt… knowing that if he brushed past me, he might feel my bare skin beneath my clothing. Not that he ever gets that close, of course. He maintains a very respectable distance between us… unfortunately.

Still, a girl can dream.

She can also touch herself whenever she gets the chance. Speaking of which…

I climb into the shower and turn on the water, adjusting the temperature slightly before I lean back against the cool tiles and let my hands wander over my body, closing my eyes as a gentle sigh escapes my lips…

Mason

Henry Bayliss sits on the couch, his hands clasped in his lap, looking across at me with a glint in his eye. I know it's not a reflection from his dark-framed glasses. There's definitely a glint there… and that has me worried.

"I've had an idea," he says, and my worry deepens.

Henry's been coming to see me, every Tuesday at eleven-thirty for nearly six months now, and it's been slow progress, getting him to come to terms with the fact that his wife left him at end of last year, and that she's not coming back.

"Oh, yes?" I try to sound enthusiastic, even though I'm not.

"I worked out, you see," he says, sitting forward and resting his elbows on his knees, "that I need to change."

"You do?"

"Yes. It's obvious when you think about it. That was why Madeleine left me. She was bored. She told me that when she walked out. But I've realized that, if I do something about my appearance… maybe lose the beard, and switch to contact lenses… and spend a little less time reading, and more time going out and doing things, then she'll come back to me."

I sigh, not bothering to disguise it, and put my notepad down on the table between us, leaning forward slightly myself. I'd thought I was getting somewhere with Henry… but evidently not.

"That's not gonna work." I do my best to sound reasonable.

"B—But…" he says with a stammer, looking up at me.

"Madeleine's gone." I don't worry so much about being reasonable now. He needs to understand this. "She moved in with Carl Simpson on the same day she left you." That shouldn't be a surprise to him. He was the one who told me when he came knocking on my door after his wife walked out on their twelve-year marriage, and the sense of loss got too much for him.

"But don't you think…?"

"I think if you want to make those changes for yourself, then that's absolutely fine, Henry," I say, interrupting him. "But you must do them for you, and not with any hope of regaining Madeleine's affections."

I know I'm being harsh, but there's a part of me that wants to take Henry by the shoulders, give him a shake, and just tell him to be himself. And if being himself means having a slightly untidy beard, and wearing dark-rimmed glasses and beige cardigans, then so be it. He can't go through life pretending to be something he isn't. No-one can. Because faking it never works…

"You really think she's gone for good?" God, he sounds despondent.

"Henry," I say, with a sigh. "You're the one who told me she'd left you. You're the one who told me she'd emptied her closet and your bank account, and taken everything she possessed with her, before she moved to Carl's place. She'd been having an affair with Carl for nearly two years before she did any of that. She wants a divorce. Her lawyer's already sent you the papers to sign. I think it's time to face up to the realities of the situation, don't you?"

"How?" He removes his glasses and looks at me, as though he's about to cry. It wouldn't be the first time… and I'm fairly sure it won't be the last.

"By looking forward, instead of back."

"How am I supposed to do that?" he asks, his voice cracking.

"It's something we'll work on… together," I say, and he tilts his head to one side. "Don't expect a quick fix." I add a word of caution. "You didn't ask to be put in this situation, and it's going to take time to come to terms with it and move on… but you will do it."

He doesn't reply, but just continues to stare at me for a while, before he replaces his glasses and blinks a few times.

"You think I should sign the divorce papers, don't you?"

"That's not for me to say, Henry. I'm not your lawyer. But I can't see any benefit in not signing them. You're just delaying the inevitable."

"Am I?" I don't answer, because his question seems rhetorical, and he turns and gazes at the seascape picture on the wall beside him for a minute or two, before he says, "I loved her so much."

"You still do. You don't stop loving someone, just because they're not with you anymore."

"Then how am I supposed to move on?" he says, sounding desperate.

"We'll work on it." I reassure him again. "But first you have to grieve."

He frowns. "Why? She didn't die."

"No. But your relationship did. You have to come to terms with that. It's a process. And when we've worked it through, you won't look back on the death, you'll look back on the life… on the happier times you had together. It will get better."

He takes a breath and slowly nods his head… and I feel like maybe we've made a breakthrough.

We agree to meet next week, and I ask him in the meantime if he can write down some happy memories of his time with Madeleine. I don't need to read them, I just want him to recall them… to remember that he's capable of happiness.

Once he's gone, I put my notebook back on my desk and shrug on my jacket and coat before heading straight out of my office. I'm having lunch with Oliver today and I'm running a few minutes late, although I ignore that fact and pause for a moment or two outside Izzy's office. She's got a client with her, unfortunately, or I would have canceled on Oliver and invited her to join me instead. After that conversation we had yesterday morning in the kitchen, I've decided I really want to try and spend some more time with her.

Still… I suppose there's always tomorrow, or the next day…

It's not like I'm going to fall out of love with her.

Fortunately, my next appointment isn't until two-thirty, so running a little late doesn't matter. I've got two hours to kill, and I make my way out of the building, turning left and walking along Main Street to the café where I arranged to meet Oliver.

He's already here, sitting at a table near the window, Baxter lying obediently by his feet. Oliver's wearing his green scrubs, with his jacket over the back of his chair, as he studies the menu, but he looks up as I take off my coat and sit down.

"Difficult client?" he asks, raising his eyebrows.

"Not difficult… just emotional."

He nods his head, but doesn't inquire further. He knows I won't tell him. I won't betray a client's confidence.

I pick up my menu and open it. "I think I'm going to have to employ the art of active forgetfulness on this one."

"Is that a complicated way of saying you wanna forget the client came in?" he says.

"No." I roll my eyes. "It means I want him to learn to forget."

"Is that even possible?"

"According to Nietzsche, yes."

"Oh, God… are you gonna go all philosophical on me?" He shudders, over-dramatically.

"No." I say, and study the menu, trying to decide what to eat.

After a few minutes, Oliver says, "Okay… explain."

"Explain what?" I look up at him.

"This active forgetting thing."

"I thought you didn't want me to go all philosophical on you."

"I don't… but I'm intrigued."

I smile and lean forward slightly. "It's a theory that Friedrich Nietzsche had, that you can actively forget your past."

"How?"

"By selectively remembering."

"That's just another way of saying the same thing."

I chuckle. "Yeah, it is. You've gotta love philosophers, haven't you?"

"Not especially."

I put down my menu and let out a breath. "Essentially, Nietzsche's idea is that memories aren't always good for us. Our past experiences may not be beneficial to our future life, so sometimes it's better to forget them."

"Just like that?"

"No… not 'just like that'. It's not as easy as saying, 'Today, I'm going to forget all the bad things that have happened in my life,' because if it was that simple, I'd be out of a job." He smiles and I add, "We can all suppress memories, or unpleasant experiences, and replace them with good ones, if we choose to. People do it all the time. We have… both of us."

"I haven't," he says, defensively.

"Yes, you have. With Mom." I pause for a second. "Tell me, what's the first thing that comes into your head when you think about her?"

"Pancakes," he says, without hesitating. "And the way she always hummed to herself when she was cooking, and how she used to tie her hair up in that crazy loose bun thing behind her head… and the color of her eyes." He stops talking and I smile across the table at him.

"I remember chicken pot pie and how the smell of it used to fill the house, and Sunday afternoon walks, and that scent she had… like jasmine and roses, or something… and sitting beside her on the couch, you on one side and me on the other, leaning against her, while she read us stories."

Oliver stares at me and nods his head, our memories aligning.

"You see?" I say. "Neither of us instinctively remembers the day she didn't come home from the hospital. The memory is there… and it always will be, somewhere in the back of our consciousness, but it's not our first thought, because we don't want it to be. We've chosen to put that to one side, because we want to think of the good times… before she died."

"I get it," he whispers, and gives me a slight smile, just as the waiter comes over to take our order.

Oliver's already decided on the Portuguese Omelet, so I have the same, and he orders a sparkling water, while I ask for iced tea, and once the waiter's gone again, taking the menus with him, Oliver sits back and stares at me for a moment.

"What's wrong?" I ask him.

"Nothing," he says. "It's just that we rarely talk about Mom, do we?"

"No… although I did yesterday."

"Oh?" He tilts his head, clearly intrigued.

"Yeah… I had a long conversation with Isabel."

He sits forward again. "You did?"

"Yeah."

"And you talked about Mom?"

"Yeah. I told her everything."

"Everything?"

I nod my head. "Everything. I told her how Mom died, what it felt like when Dad came home without her, how he helped us come to terms with losing her, and accepting Destiny…" I fall silent and he stares at me for a moment.

"Wow," he says eventually. "You really did tell her everything, didn't you?" He pauses for a moment, frowning. "Was this a professional conversation? Did you… did you need her help?"

"No. We just got talking over coffee."

"And it got that deep and meaningful?"

"Yeah. She was telling me about her weekend up in Vermont, and how her parents basically abandoned her and her little sisters."

"At the weekend?" he says, his brow furrowing in confusion.

"No. When she was sixteen."

"Oh… that had to be hard."

"I think it was. She said it hurt." I got the feeling it still does.

"And you told her about Mom?"

"Yeah… she asked about my weekend too, and I told her about the wedding, and about you, and Destiny and Dad. She asked about Mom, and I ended up telling her the whole story."

"How did that feel?"

"It felt good. It felt… like the beginning of something."

"You're not reading too much into it?" he says, sounding a note of caution.

"I hope not. But I was gonna invite her to lunch… maybe later in the week, so I'll let you know."

He smiles and then sits back again. "I think I'd sell my soul for a conversation like that with Jemima," he says wistfully. "Actually, I'd sell my soul for any kind of conversation with her."

"She's still not saying anything, then?"

"She says 'hello', and 'goodbye', and she talks to me about work and clients, and ordering supplies and which accounts to pay, or not pay. But that's it. There's never anything personal… ever."

"Have you tried just asking her about her weekend or something? That's how I got talking to Isabel."

"I've tried everything I can damn well think of," he says. "Nothing works."

I don't reply, because the waiter chooses that moment to bring our drinks, but as Oliver takes a sip of his water, I think about how unlike him this is. He's been like this ever since Jemima arrived in his office, but before that, he was about the most confident person I knew… at least where women were concerned, anyway. I've always envied him that… until now.

"That wedding at the weekend got me thinking," he says, putting his glass down.

"About what?"

"About how useless we both are with women these days."

"I suppose it's the past catching up with us." I stare down at my hands, which are clasped on the table.

"Your past or mine?" he says and I look up at him to see a smile on his face.

"Well… both, I suppose. We both had our fair share of women at college."

"Hmm… and in our twenties." His smile widens.

"So what happened when we turned thirty?"

He shrugs his shoulders, just as the waiter returns, bringing our food this time, and we sit in silence for a few moments while he asks if there's anything else we need. We both decline and he moves away again, and as we start to eat, Oliver leans in and says, "When did you last have sex?"

I think about my answer for a moment and wonder whether to lie… except I can't. "Eighteen months ago."

His eyebrows shoot up. "Wow… that's a dry patch."

"Dry?" I say, shaking my head. "That's the understatement of the century." I pick up my fork and then put it down again. "I wouldn't have minded so much if I'd been in a relationship… if I'd been spending those eighteen months getting over a broken heart, or something, but my last time was with a woman I met at a conference I went to in New York."

"I remember," he says. "You weren't sure whether to go."

"Yeah. In the end, I went, and spent the entire three days in bed with one of the other delegates. She was from Wyoming and neither of us was looking for anything more than a few days of fun,… which is exactly what we got. Of course, I never expected that to be my last time…"

"It won't be your last time ever," Oliver says with a smile.

"It might be, if I can't work things out with Isabel."

He nods his head like he understands. "Yeah… it's weird, when you meet *the one*, isn't it? You don't want anyone else."

"No, you don't." We both take a few mouthfuls of omelet. "What about you?"

"What about me?" he says.

"When did you last have sex?" I feel entitled to ask, being as I've told him.

"It was last December." He lets out a sigh. "I dated Mandy Tucker for a while… just a few weeks. We had sex a couple of times, but to be honest, it wasn't that great… and then Jemima pitched up at my office, looking for work, so I ended it with Mandy, and I haven't been able to look at another woman since."

"Even though a lot of your clients only come in to flirt with you?" I can't stop myself from smiling.

He narrows his eyes while eating. "Yes, even then."

"And you don't think having all those women playing up to you might be what's putting Jemima off?"

He stills, with his fork halfway to his mouth. "I—I hadn't thought of that," he says. "Do you—?" His voice is cut off by the ringing of his phone, and he puts down his fork and reaches behind him, into his jacket pocket, pulling it out and studying the screen for a second, before he smiles. "It's work," he says, connecting the call. I smile to myself as he says, "Jemima… hi," in the softest of voices. He listens for a moment and then says, "It's okay. I'm only having lunch with my brother." He glances up at me and I mouth, 'Thanks' at him, although he ignores me, a frown settling on his face. "When was this?" he says, before pausing, and then adding, "Okay, I'll be back in two minutes."

He hangs up, getting to his feet at the same time. Baxter raises his head and then stands in an instant, clearly realizing they're leaving.

"An emergency?" I say, looking up at him.

"Yeah. A dog's been brought in. All Jemima said was that there's blood everywhere and the owner's panicking."

"Go. I'll pick up the check for lunch… you can pay next time."

He's already turning away, pulling on his jacket as he walks toward the door, with Baxter at his heels. "I'll call you," he says over his shoulder… and then he's gone.

I finished my omelet, but didn't really feel like sitting in the café all by myself, so although I had two hours to kill, I've come back to the office to catch up on some paperwork. I let myself in, shuddering against the chilly breeze that's blowing down Main Street now, and close the door quietly behind me, wondering if it might snow before I get home tonight. The office is in silence, although I notice Izzy's door is ajar. She's probably gone out to get something to eat, and I make my way toward the back of the office, wondering about suggesting we could have lunch together tomorrow, when I hear a sound coming from her room. I stop in my tracks… surely not.

The sound I just heard is one I'm very familiar with, even if it has been eighteen months…

I stand, waiting, and then I hear it again… a definite sigh. It's the kind of sigh a woman makes when she's close to coming, and I'm torn. Whatever is going on in Izzy's office is none of my business. I know I should ignore what I've just heard and go to my room, regardless of my aching hard-on… but how do I know who's in there with her? It could be anyone, and although that thought is killing me, I know that if she's having sex with a client, I need to put a stop to it… because that's wrong on so many levels.

I take a step toward her office, but then I stop myself. She wouldn't do that. I know she wouldn't, and I should just leave her in peace… with whoever the lucky guy is. Then I hear a moaning sound, and without even thinking about it, I take the final steps, and peer through the gap in the open door… just as she lets out a more urgent, throaty groan. That's quite fortunate, because the noise she's making is enough to disguise my gasp, as I take in the sight before me, realizing immediately that Izzy isn't with anyone. She's completely alone. But that doesn't mean I was wrong in my assumptions about the noises and their meanings, because she's sitting right on the edge of her chair, her skirt pulled up around her hips, with one high-heeled shoe balanced on her desk, while the other leg is thrown over the arm of her chair. From where I'm standing, that leaves her completely exposed. I can see her black lace-topped stockings, and garter belt, although where her panties are is anybody's guess, because she's not wearing any… and I can see her perfectly shaved pussy, her fingers caressing over her clit in slow, circular movements. She shifts slightly and lets her head rock back on the chair, my eyes drawn upwards, to where she's undone her blouse and pulled down the cups of her bra, revealing firm, rounded breasts. I was right about them… they would fit my hands perfectly, and while she continues to stroke her pussy, she uses the fingers and thumb of the other hand to tweak at one of her nipples. The other is hardened and elongated and I long to walk in and lick it… no, bite it. As she groans a little louder, my eyes are drawn back to her pussy again, where she's now rubbing herself much harder. She's grinding her hips, rocking back and forth and I'm fairly sure she's about to come, as she moans again, sucking in a breath and sighing, and I reach down and stroke my hand along the length of my straining cock, unable to help myself. I'm about to unfasten my pants, when suddenly Izzy stops what she's doing and sits up, and fearful that she's seen me, or heard me, I step back, holding my breath, until I hear a zipper, and I peek back into the room.

Izzy is delving inside her purse, which she's balanced on her desk – fortunately to one side of her, not obscuring my view – and after a moment or two, she surprises the hell out of me by pulling out a dildo. It's flesh-colored with pronounced veins, and it's not very big, being only around six or seven inches in length. Still, it's a dildo, and I struggle for control, leaning against the doorframe and watching her avidly as she shifts back in her seat again, raising her legs into position once more and taking a breath. She studies the dildo for a moment, eyeing it hungrily, before she raises it to her lips, and I hold my breath as she sucks it into her mouth. God, I wish that could be me... I wish I could stand in front of her, and feed her my dick right now. But before I even have time to imagine what that might feel like, she removes the dildo and shifts her ass forward slightly, so she's right on the edge of the chair, and then she slowly inserts it into her vagina. She takes her time, sucking in a breath, biting her bottom lip, as she sinks the dildo inside her, inch by inch. She seems to enjoy the sensation of being penetrated, her eyes fluttering closed and her body shuddering as she sits still for a moment, impaled. Then she pulls the dildo almost all the way out, before the starts to pump it, in and out... hard and fast, while her fingers go to work on her clit again. Watching her fuck herself is almost too much for me, and while I'm longing to touch myself, I don't want to move. I don't want to risk being seen or heard. So I stay absolutely still, staring at her, listening to the sounds the dildo makes as she pounds her drenched pussy. I bite my lip, to stop myself from groaning out loud, when I see her juices flowing over her leather chair, and dripping down onto the wooden floor below, and it's all I can do not to crawl in there on my hands and knees and lick them up. She brings me back to reality though as she parts her legs wider still, and suddenly arches her back, letting out a plaintive cry as she comes apart, her body curling in on itself, pleasure rocking through her. I study every movement, every twitch and shudder, every whimper and sigh, until eventually she stills, and lies back... spent.

I should go. I daren't risk being caught...

I'm about to step away, when she pulls the dildo from her soaking pussy, and raises it to her lips again, and I have to bite on my knuckle this time to stop myself from making a noise as she sucks on it and licks it clean.

God... that's hot.

Finally, when she's satisfied, she sits up a little and grabs a Kleenex from the box on her desk, wiping the dildo, before putting it back into her purse. Then she stands, pulling her bra back into place, fastening her blouse and straightening her skirt. There's still no sign of her panties… but regardless of how much that thought turns me on, I shouldn't be here.

I turn away, as she's pulling more Kleenex from the box to wipe down her chair, and I tiptoe back to the front door, which I open, and then slam closed again, making a show of returning from lunch.

I don't call out to her, because I'm not sure my voice will work. Instead, I go to my office, my head full of the images I've just seen… and with thoughts of turning back around again, going straight to Izzy's office, bending her over her desk and fucking her. She'd be wet enough, I know that. She clearly needs fucking, too… and with something a lot bigger than that dildo.

Chapter Four

Isabel

I throw the Kleenex into the wastepaper basket, letting out a gentle sigh.

God… I think that was the best orgasm I've ever had.

Mind you, I needed it. I fell asleep in front of a boring movie last night and was too tired to do anything but go straight back to sleep when I finally got into bed. But all I've been able to think about since that conversation with Mason yesterday morning is how much I wanted him to take me over the kitchen countertop. So today, when I finished my last appointment of the morning and realized he'd gone to lunch, I thought, why not? I mean, he wasn't about to take me, because he doesn't think of me like that, but that didn't mean I couldn't do something for myself, did it?

I knew it was a bit of a risk, but it wasn't like I was going to be interrupted. No-one can get in here, other than Mason and myself, and I knew he'd be out for ages…

So, I got myself comfortable.

I didn't undress… not completely. I just pulled up my skirt and pulled down my bra, because I like having my breasts exposed. It didn't take me long to get really aroused, either. Within about ten minutes, I was close… really close, and then I remembered the dildo. I'd taken it up to Vermont with me at the weekend, and used it in the shower before coming home on Sunday, as a result of which I nearly forgot to pack it, and just bundled it into my purse at the last minute. I'm not in the habit of carrying dildos around with me, but it certainly came in handy just now, adding a touch of realism to my fantasy about Mason coming into my office and bending me over my desk…

Still… based on what just happened, I guess I could leave it here for future use…

At least I could, once I've washed it. I check the time on my watch. It's one-forty-five, so I've got a few minutes before my next clients arrive… enough time to visit the bathroom, anyway.

At that moment, the door slams and I jump out of my skin, rushing to my half-open door and peering through, just in time to see Mason striding to the rear of the building, toward his office. My heart pounds in my chest, and I close my eyes, leaning back against the wall. Thank God he didn't come back five minutes ago. That would have been really embarrassing. I let out a long sigh, calming myself and a smile slowly forms on my lips as I contemplate what might have happened if he had returned sooner than expected… if he had seen me. My skin tingles at the thought of being watched by him… or better still, at the prospect that he might have liked what he saw enough to join in.

If only…

I shake myself back to reality, remembering that standing here daydreaming isn't getting me anywhere, and I grab my purse before I open the door, heading toward the back of the building… and the bathrooms.

Mason has left his door open and I pause outside, because it seems churlish to ignore him, even if my head is full of inappropriate images of him.

"You're back early, aren't you?" I say, for the sake of conversation.

He looks up, staring at me a little strangely, seeming to focus on my hair before he nods his head and says, "Yeah. Oliver had an emergency call, and I thought I'd come back and do some paperwork."

I glance down at his desk, noting that there's nothing on it, apart from his computer and keyboard, and I wonder why he's not doing said paperwork… although I don't really have time to inquire.

"I'd better go," I say. "I've got my next appointment at two."

He nods his head, before looking at his computer screen again, and I move away, wishing I could have gone in to his office and found some way of lengthening that conversation.

Instead, I head for the bathroom, where I spend a few minutes tidying my disheveled hair, noting the flush on my cheeks and the sparkle in my eyes. I know why, of course… because I've just had a fabulous, mind-blowing orgasm. But that's my secret.

I smile to myself, and then pull the dildo from my purse, giving it a thorough wash. And then I dry it off, stash it back in my purse, and wash my hands, making my way back to my office.

Once there, I retrieve the dildo again, holding it in front of me, studying the deeply veined surface and swollen head, for just a second or two, before opening my top drawer and shoving it right to the back. It'll be safe there, and I can always get another one to use at home.

I can't stop smiling at the thought of repeating this lunchtime's performance, but I straighten my desk and put my purse away, just in time for my two o'clock appointment… which is with a couple called Vanessa and Ian Stevens.

This is their second session with me… their first having been a fact finding mission, during which it became clear that Ian is reluctant to be here. That much is obvious from his expression, as he sits looking out the window. Still, I don't blame him. Based on what I discovered last week, it seems to me that Vanessa is looking to create drama in their marriage, where it doesn't need to exist.

"How are you feeling this week, Vanessa?" I ask, as she's the only one who's paying attention to me.

"Frustrated," she says. I study them for a moment, finding them an interesting couple, who on the surface seem to be well suited. Ian is thirty-five and told me last week that he owns a construction company, which he started seven years ago. He has a muscular physique – probably because of the manual work he's always done – and is handsome, with a deep tan, and dark hair. Vanessa is a couple of years younger than her husband, and although I know they have three children, her figure is incredible… and certainly something to be proud of. She dresses conservatively though, today wearing gray pants and a cream-colored sweater. She's got strawberry blonde hair, and pale blue eyes, set in a beautiful face. They look good together. They just don't seem to want to look at each other.

"Would you care to elaborate?"

She glances at her husband before she looks back at me. "It's like he's forgotten who I am."

Ian turns to her. "No, I haven't," he says.

This is going well…

Vanessa twists in her seat, so she's facing him. "Okay… when did you last notice what I'm wearing, or tell me my hair looks nice? When was it last worth actually getting dressed up for you?"

He shrugs. "I don't know. But when was the last time you said any of those things to me? I didn't realize compliments were a one-way-street."

I struggle not to smile, because I think Ian has a point. But I keep a straight face and lean forward, getting in the middle of their brewing argument.

"Where do you think the problem lies, Vanessa?" She's the one who wanted to come here… so she must be the one who perceives there to be an issue.

She sighs. "It's just not like it used to be. Ian was always so… romantic… so attentive. And now…"

"You're being unrealistic." He interrupts her. "It was easy to be romantic in the beginning. It was just the two of us back then, and we were having fun, getting to know each other. We've got fifteen years of history now. We've got three kids and my business to think about. It can't be the same as it was… it's just not possible."

"I don't see why not… not if you wanted me, which you clearly don't."

"Oh, for Christ's sake." Ian rubs his hands down in face in despair. "How many times do I have to tell you… I still want you. You didn't have to drag me to a shrink to get me to say it. I tell you that all the time."

"Then why don't you actually *do* something?" she says, with a whining tone to her voice.

"When?" He raises his voice in response. "When am I supposed to find the goddamn time? Between me running the business and working all the hours God sends, and you volunteering at the hospital and taking the kids to their soccer and swimming practice, we're hardly ever in the house at the same time these days." He pauses and takes a breath to calm himself, and then says, "When we first met, the only thing we had to worry about was studying, not getting caught out by our parents, and not getting you pregnant. It was a very different time, Vanessa… with very different responsibilities."

She stares at him for a long moment, without saying a word, and then she looks back at me, and although this is only the second time I've met her, I can tell she's not happy. Ian's speech may have seemed perfectly reasonable to me – if a little harsh, perhaps – but it wasn't what she wanted to hear.

"I've been thinking about this since we last came here," she says, tilting her head to one side. "And I've been wondering whether the problem might be me, rather than Ian."

I'm intrigued, in that case, about why she's been hurling accusations of neglect at him since they walked through the door, but I nod my head. "In what way?"

"I've never been with anyone else." She looks down, studying her clasped hands, and then twists her wedding ring on her third finger. "I lost my virginity to Ian when I was eighteen. He's two years older, and he'd been with… well, let's just say he'd been around the block a few times before we met. But I've only ever been with him."

Ian sits forward, moving a little closer to her.

"Are you saying you wanna sleep with someone else?" he asks in a hushed whisper. "Are you saying you wanna have an affair?"

Vanessa doesn't answer. She doesn't even look at him, but Ian's expression gives away his fear and worry, and I put down my notepad on the table.

"Vanessa," I say, getting her attention, and she looks up at me. "You need to be honest here. You need to tell Ian what you're looking for."

She turns to her husband, but before she can say anything, he leans in a little and says, "Do you wanna have sex with another man? Is that what this is all about?"

I wish he'd be quiet for a minute and let Vanessa speak, because while I know he has to be confused and scared, I'm not sure he's helping.

"I don't know," Vanessa says eventually and Ian flops back in his seat, shaking his head.

"I may have slept around before we met, but I'd never cheat on you now… and I can't believe you're thinking about cheating on me. I— I thought this was just some kind of bored housewife thing…"

I want to tell him not to underestimate a bored housewife, but he doesn't need to hear that right now.

"Vanessa said she didn't know." I try to calm him.

"Yeah, which means she's thinking about it." He turns to look at me. "I've never looked at another woman since I met her. I've never wanted to."

"Have you told her that?"

"Yes," he replies.

"Not lately," she says at the same time.

"Is this how you wanna play things?" He turns back to Vanessa, narrowing his eyes. "Every time you feel like I'm not paying you enough attention, you wanna threaten to sleep with another man?"

"No!" she yells, getting to her feet. "That's not what I want at all."

I'm aware I'm losing control of the situation, and the session, and I stand myself, moving a little closer to Vanessa.

"Please sit down." I keep my voice calm, even though my stomach's churning. "We need to work things out."

"How?" She turns on me. "How the hell are we supposed to work things out, when he won't even listen?"

She's being unreasonable. It's not like she's actually said much for him to listen to.

"I'm not sure I wanna carry on with this," Ian says, getting to his feet as well and Vanessa startles, turning to face him.

"Carry on with what?"

"This session. I don't feel like we're getting anywhere."

I'm inclined to agree with him.

"Would you both be able to come back on Friday?" I ask. "I know we agreed to weekly meetings, but I'm not sure I want to leave it that long… and I think if you could both take a couple of days to think through what's been said today, and then come back and discuss exactly what it is you want from your marriage, we might be able to move forward."

They both stare at me for a moment, and then Vanessa nods her head, while Ian shrugs and says, "I guess…"

I go over to my desk, bringing up my calendar. "I can fit you in at twelve-thirty." That means I won't get lunch, but their needs seem greater than mine at the moment.

"I can work around that," Ian says and Vanessa just nods again.

Considering she's the one who wanted these sessions in the first place, I wish she'd show a little more enthusiasm for working out their problems, rather than just running through them, over and over.

I show them out and make my way back to my office, sitting down in my chair, and thinking back over that minor disaster. I'm not sure I've done the right thing in letting them go like that, but what else could I do? They didn't seem to want to stay, we weren't getting very far, and I've got more clients coming soon. Even so, I can't help thinking I should have done more… or at least tried to. Should I have tried harder to reason with Vanessa? She was being quite difficult, after all. Or should I have tried to get Ian to take Vanessa more seriously? He was quite dismissive… at least until she hinted at having sex with another man. I don't think she'd go through with it… but you never know, and thinking about that makes me wonder whether I should have tried to keep them here…

I scratch my head, and then let it fall into my hands. What if I've screwed up their marriage? What if she goes out and sleeps with another man, and it's all my fault because I'm just not experienced enough to handle situations like this?

I hear Mason outside, greeting his client, who's running late and being very apologetic about it, and I decide I'll find the time to talk to him about Ian and Vanessa. I'm not sure when, being as both our schedules are slammed at the moment… but sometime before Friday, I'll make the time.

Mason

What is it with work at the moment?

It's Thursday already, and not only have I not had the chance to ask Izzy to have lunch with me, but I've been so busy, I've barely had time to think about what I saw the other day, in her office. I know the sight of her masturbating has kept me awake at night… although having an aching hard-on all the time hasn't helped. And while I know I could do something about that, I don't want to… because now I've seen her, I want her more than ever. The last thing I want is to jerk off fantasizing about her; I know I'll only end up feeling disappointed afterwards. Besides, I've jerked off while fantasizing about her enough already… ever since she first walked through my door, in fact. In my fantasies I invented yet more scenes – very erotic scenes – of breathless, heated intimacy. I even created dialogues, during which I can tell her how I feel, and what I want… in graphic detail.

It's weird… I've watched women masturbate before. I've actively encouraged it. As far as I'm concerned, it's a huge turn-on, and there's nothing I enjoy more than watching a woman who knows how to pleasure herself. Well… there are one or two things I enjoy more… like joining in, for example. But there was something different about Izzy. There was something different about watching her, too. Maybe it was because she didn't know I was there. I felt like a voyeur. Hell… I was a voyeur, let's not kid ourselves here… and yet, I don't feel guilty. I ought to. At the very least, I should feel ashamed. After all, I intruded into a very private moment. I should have backed off and left her to enjoy herself in peace. Except I didn't want to. I felt like I belonged there... like I was part of it. Maybe that's because I'm in love with her... so I naturally feel like I'm a part of everything she does. I don't know...

What I do know is that I've never seen a woman masturbate quite like that before. There was a kind of sexual abandonment about her... an obvious need, and a deep-seated satisfaction in everything she was doing. She's clearly a woman who enjoys sex... and I like that. I think it's joyous, actually. I know a lot of men don't want to be with women who've had a lot of sexual partners in the past, but I've never worried about things like that. As long as they're exclusive at the time I'm with them, I'm okay with whatever has gone before. In Izzy's case, I'm very okay with it, because her experiences have obviously brought her to where she is... namely, right to my door. And I'd like her to stay here. Although that's not strictly true, because what I'd really like her to do is come right on in through that door and make a home with me... forever.

That's assuming I can ever find the time to have another conversation with her, of course.

I sit back in my chair, checking the time. It's okay... I've got fifteen minutes until my next appointment. Unfortunately, Izzy's with someone, so I can't take the chance to speak to her. But glancing over at the door, I can't help remembering the last time she stood there... on Tuesday lunchtime, when she came out of her office, on the way to the bathroom, after she'd climaxed so hard. It was so hot, watching her lick that dildo clean, but then, watching her stand in my doorway, with her hair a little out of place, that beautiful blush on her cheeks, and her eyes sparkling right at me, was almost as thrilling. If I hadn't known what she'd just been doing, I probably wouldn't have thought her appearance was anything unusual. But knowing that she'd just made herself come, the sight of her had me buzzing with need... and the thought that the last time I'd seen her, she hadn't been wearing any panties, was almost too much for me. It took every ounce of willpower not to get up from my desk, stride over to her, and discover for myself whether she still wasn't. I know she would have been, of course. Just because I couldn't see her panties anywhere in her office, didn't mean they weren't there. Even so, the fantasy was a good one... it still is.

It's almost as good as the thought that I'd really like for it to be me who'd got her looking like that… who'd put that 'just fucked' look in her eyes.

I groan, shifting in my seat, as my erection presses hard against my zipper, and I pull forward my keypad, clicking on the folder for my next appointment, and opening up my notes. This involves doing the almost impossible… forgetting about Izzy for a few minutes while I focus on Diane Shaw. She's my twelve-thirty, and I need to concentrate on her for the time being, no matter how hard it is not to think about Izzy.

I quickly skim through my notes from our last session, recalling the progress we made. It was promising, considering how bad things were when Diane first came to me nearly a year ago. She was in a bad place then, barely able to function, having lost both of her parents in quick succession. She's an only child and had been very close to both her mother and father, and her predominant feeling at the time was one of abandonment. Her husband, Rob, was very supportive, and he came to those early sessions with her. She still needed time, though, and some help, to work through the grieving process and to come to terms with such a massive and sudden loss. We've made a lot of progress since then, and for the last couple of months, she's been coming to see me by herself. Last time, before she left, she said she wanted to try seeing me less often. She assured me it wasn't a financial decision. She and Rob both work, they don't have kids, and to be honest, if money had been the problem, I'd have found a way around it… if I thought she still needed to see me on a weekly basis. Except I don't think she does… and clearly, neither does she. So, we agreed to meet up this week, and then skip next week, and see how she goes. Today's session will give me a chance to check she's really strong enough to do this, to make sure she's got her coping mechanisms firmly set… and to reiterate, that if she feels the need to come back sooner, then that's not a problem. It's also not a failure; it's not even a setback. It just means she wasn't quite ready yet… and that's perfectly okay.

I close the notes folder and take a sip of water from the glass on my desk, just as my computer pings, letting me know I've got a new email. It could wait until after I've seen Diane, but I've still got a few minutes, so I click on my mail app, and let out an audible groan when I see it's from my old college. The subject headline doesn't surprise me, but I read it anyway… 'Reunion reminder'. Did I need reminding? Probably… being as I've spent the last three months doing my level best to forget I agreed to attend this damn thing.

I click on the message, noticing that there's an attachment, and scroll down, seeing that some idiot has made the date flash up in red letters… Thursday, November 18th. One week from today.

Fabulous.

The attachment is right at the bottom and is named 'List of Attendees'.

Okay… this could be interesting. I open it up, drumming my fingers impatiently on my desk, and hoping Diane won't be early now, as the document appears on my screen.

"Marcus Collins," I muse out loud as I scroll through the alphabetical list. I'd forgotten he even existed. "Good Lord… Lance Fisher, too." It might be good to catch up with both of them. We always got along okay at college, although I've got no idea what they're doing now. They're both bringing someone with them, though. Next to Marcus's name it says 'Tanya Collins', and beside Lance is the name, 'Laura Fisher'. 'Lance and Laura'? How kitsch.

My name appears, with simply 'plus one' beside it, and I shake my head, trying to remember if I was drunk when I accepted the invitation to attend this function. I don't think I was, but if not, what on earth possessed me to say I'd bring someone with me when I don't have anyone to bring? Come to think of it, why did I say 'yes' in the first place?

"Oh… shit…" I shake my head. Someone, somewhere, must hate me. Because not only do I appear to be the only person on this page who doesn't have a named guest, but immediately below my name is one that makes my skin crawl… Calvin Hart.

I must have been drunk. Otherwise, it would have dawned on me that Calvin would be bound to attend the reunion… if only so he could show off to everyone else. He's got plenty to show off about, after all. Not only did Calvin walk into a senior role at the Elleston Clinic, right after he'd completed his mandatory training period there, simply because his father knew someone on the board, but as I told Izzy, he also left there and set up his own clinic. I know I have my own clinic too, but mine isn't in the center of Boston, and I don't have several associates working under me… unlike Calvin Hart. To make matters worse, he married a model. Her name is listed beside his, so I know she's called Naomi, and I know she's a model because she's just about famous enough for their wedding to have made the newspapers, even out here in Sturbridge. Ordinarily, I wouldn't care about things like that, but when we were at college together, Calvin always made a point of being super competitive… mainly with me. I don't know why, but he always felt he had to out-score me, and out-do me… at everything. I'm not just talking grades, but *everything*…

He even insisted on comparing notes over the one or two girls we both dated – at separate times – while we were at college. I refused to join in, because I'm not that kind of guy, but he took my refusal as an admission of inferiority, and promptly spread rumors to that effect… which was just typical of Calvin.

My eyes settle again on the 'plus one' beside my name and I realize how much of a loser I'm going to feel, not only going to the function without a beautiful wife or girlfriend… but going without the 'plus one' at all.

I wonder for a second about responding to the message and saying I can't attend… and I move the cursor over the 'reply' icon, letting it hover there, when I hear Izzy's voice, as she comes out of her office, bidding farewell to her latest client.

Could I…?

Could I ask her to come with me?

I notice a third voice outside and realize Diane must have arrived. So, quickly closing my mail app, I put all thoughts of reunions to one side for the moment and head outside, catching a quick glimpse of Izzy as she heads into her office, before I greet Diane, wondering whether I might have hit on the answer… or whether I'm maybe about to make the biggest mistake of my life.

Chapter Five

Isabel

I glance at the time on my computer screen… heavens, how can it be five o'clock already?

I promised myself I'd talk to Mason before tomorrow's appointment with Vanessa and Ian, and I'm nearly out of time. I don't know how I've got to Thursday afternoon without managing to speak with him, but I'm going to put it down to my period starting on Tuesday. It might happen every month – or every twenty-four days in my case – but it always seems to throw me.

At least my last appointment of the day has just gone, but I know Mason's got someone booked in for five-fifteen, and although fifteen minutes isn't really long enough to discuss the situation with my clients, I feel I still need to run things by him, just to make sure I'm not screwing up completely.

I get up, straightening my skirt and go out into the reception area, before making my way to the rear of the building, where he's left his office door slightly ajar, a light streaming out into the hallway. I knock, just once, and he calls out, "Come in," knowing it must be me, I guess, and I push the door open, although I don't go inside. Instead, I stand on the threshold and look at him.

God… he's gorgeous.

"Is this a bad time?" I ask, given that he hasn't looked up from his computer screen yet.

He glances over at me. "I'm sorry," he says, smiling. "I've had a message from my next client to say they're not gonna make their appointment, and I'm just seeing if I can reschedule." He clicks on his keyboard a few times and then rolls his eyes. "Honestly… I could've been getting ready to go home if I'd known they were gonna be a no-show."

"Oh… are you in a hurry to leave then?"

He shakes his head. "Not particularly. I'm having dinner at my brother's place, but that's not for another couple of hours yet. Why? Do you have a problem?"

"Not a problem, per se, but…"

"You could do with some advice?" he says and I smile.

"Is it that obvious?"

"No… but you only usually come and see me when you need advice, or help."

I realize how true that is, and it makes me feel kinda sad that, apart from our conversation the other morning over coffee, we've never just talked.

"Hmm… I suppose," I murmur.

"Do you wanna sit down and tell me about it?" He nods toward the chairs in front of his desk.

I move forward, taking a seat, and look over at him, trying not to be too mesmerized by his blue eyes, as he shifts his keyboard aside and leans forward, resting his elbows on the desk, and gazing right at me.

"It's this couple I'm seeing," I say. "They're called Vanessa and Ian."

"Okay." His voice is encouraging, as usual. "How long have you been seeing them?"

"We had our second session on Monday."

"And?"

"It didn't go very well."

"In what way?"

I shake my head. "In just about every way. It was Vanessa's idea to come here. She made the original inquiry and booked their first appointment, and she and Ian made it very clear at both sessions that he didn't want to come. She's obviously feeling neglected by him…"

77

"How long have they been married?" he asks, interrupting me.

"Fifteen years."

He nods and says, "Okay," with a smile that tells me I should keep talking.

"On Monday, she was saying how nothing's the same as it used to be, how Ian's different to the man he was when he was younger… and he was saying – not unreasonably, I thought – that their whole lives are different. They have three kids now, not to mention a mortgage and a business. She also volunteers at the hospital, so they barely have time to say hello, let alone…" I stop talking because I realize I was about to say, 'have sex', and I don't want to talk about sex with Mason… not when he's the man who makes my orgasms so incredible these days.

"I get the picture," he says, tilting his head to one side. "She's frustrated."

"Yeah. That's exactly what she said… right before she hinted at having an affair."

"She did?"

"Yeah. That worried me. It worried Ian too."

"Why?" Mason says. "I mean, I get why it would worry her husband, but why did it worry you?"

"Because I'm not sure I handled the situation very well. I had another client due right after them, so I had to let them go, rather than continue talking to them. I've arranged to see them again tomorrow, instead of waiting until next week, but I wondered afterwards if I should have done something more… or at least something different."

"Like what?" he says.

"Like maybe kept them talking longer?"

He shakes his head. "You can't do that. You know perfectly well how this works. The next client might have something even more pressing to talk about. You have to stick to schedules for that very reason."

He's right. I know he is. But that doesn't stop me from worrying. "What if…?"

"What's really bothering you?" he asks, leaning a little further forward.

"I think it's the fact that I don't really understand what their problem is… or, to be more precise, what Vanessa's problem is."

He smiles. "She sounds like a bored housewife to me."

I smile back. "That's exactly what Ian said. Bored housewives shouldn't be underestimated though, should they?"

"No."

"Especially not when they're threatening to sleep with someone else."

He tilts his head again. "Would she do it, though? Or was she just trying to get a reaction from her husband?"

"I don't know. She made a point of saying Ian is the only man she's ever slept with, and that she'd lost her virginity to him when she was eighteen years old. She said he'd slept around before they met, but she'd never had sex with anyone else, except him." What's wrong with me? I just told myself I wasn't going to talk to him about sex, and here I am doing just that. I cough, and hope I'm not blushing. "I—It seemed important to her… and I got the feeling she might want to find out what she's been missing."

"Who says she's been missing anything?" Mason frowns, clasping his hands together in front of him. "It sounds to me like she's jealous of the fact that he slept around and she didn't."

"You think?"

"Yes. Otherwise, why bother even raising the subject, or telling you she'd lost her virginity to him. It's not relevant to their problems, is it?"

"I don't know." That's the whole point of this conversation.

"It doesn't sound very relevant to me," he says, shaking his head, like he's thinking. "Why is it that women place so much importance on the past… and in particular on their virginity, and losing it?"

That feels a little random, and I stare at him for a moment, wondering where it came from. "Sorry… have I hit a raw nerve?" I ask, because it feels like I have.

"No," he says, his frown instantly turning into a smile. "My comment wasn't personal. It was a general observation."

"Based on?" I say, without thinking, and his eyes bore into mine.

"Personal experience," he replies.

"So it's not just a general observation, is it?"

"No… I guess not. But what I'm trying to say is, the experiences weren't painful for me, so my comment was based on my observation of my experiences, rather than my feelings about them. If that makes sense."

"It does. Although just because the experiences weren't painful for you, doesn't mean they weren't painful for the women involved."

"No… although, in both cases, I think everyone concerned agreed that breaking up was for the best."

"You broke up?"

"Yes."

"Over your girlfriends' virginity?" I can't hide my surprise.

He chuckles. "No. I broke up with a couple of exes who had issues with the past."

"Oh, I see. Yours or theirs?" I probably shouldn't ask that. It's none of my business. And yet, I want to know.

"Theirs," he says. "I don't really have that much of a past, and certainly nothing that would cause anyone any anxiety. But someone I dated in my late twenties couldn't get over an ex-boyfriend of hers… the guy she'd lost her virginity to, as it turned out. It got so bad, she kept saying his name at the most inappropriate moments." He smiles again and I have to smile too, even though I'm not sure why, because that sounds kinda hurtful.

"What about the other one?"

He pauses and stares at me, and then says, "She had problems going way back to an abusive relationship she'd been in during her late teens and early twenties, and to be honest, she needed a therapist, not a lover. I couldn't be both."

"So you broke up with her and became her therapist?"

"No. I broke up with her, because she wasn't in the right place to be in a relationship at the time… and I recommended someone else to be her therapist. It wouldn't have been appropriate for me to counsel her… not when I'd been sleeping with her for the previous three months."

"No. Of course not."

"She did okay, though. She's married now, with twins."

"You stayed in touch?"

"For a while, until I knew she was okay."

"That was kind."

He shrugs. "It was the right thing to do." He sits back slightly. "Now… back to your client and her virginity."

I smile. "That's not her only problem."

"No, but it seems to be something she's fixated on… the fact that she's only been with her husband, and she's intrigued."

"Yeah, it does."

He sits right back in his seat, taking a breath. "What were you taught about virginity? When you were at college, I mean?"

For a moment I feel completely thrown by his question, but then I remember my lectures… my training. "Is this the myth theory?"

He nods his head. "Yeah. What do you think about it?"

"It's a matter of perspective, really. Naturally, there's the medical side of things…" I stop talking, wondering why I started that sentence.

"You mean the fact the tradition tells us a woman can only lose her virginity when her hymen is broken through penetrative sex?"

How did he just say that without blushing?

"Y—Yes. But I'm not sure that's what we're talking about here. We're talking about whether the concept of virginity itself is a myth, aren't we?"

"Yes, because we're doctors of psychology, not medicine." He smiles, and I have to smile back. "So, what do you think?"

"I—I think it's up to each person – each woman, I suppose – to decide what her virginity means to her."

"So, are you saying you believe in virginity?" He gazes straight at me.

"Do you?" Deflection seems like the best way to go, because there's no way I can tell him I believe in it very firmly. I still feel like a virgin, even though I use a dildo… for the simple reason that I've never had sex with a man. I want to – obviously – with the man who's sitting right in front of me… the man who's making my body hum with need, right now.

"I guess it's not something I think about too often," he replies with a slight shrug of his shoulders. "Like most men of my age, I'm beyond having to worry about such things."

He smiles, and I smile back, although my body's just stopped humming and my heart feels heavy on hearing his words. He thinks he's past the age of sleeping with virgins... which I guess rules me out. The disappointment is overwhelming, and out of sheer confusion, I ask, "Have you ever taken a woman's virginity?"

I hear my words floating in the air between us, and I immediately want to apologize and take the question back. It's out there now, though, and he tilts his head and says, "Do you regard it as being 'taken'? Or that you 'give' it to a man? Is that how it feels?"

How the hell would I know?

"Well, it's not something a woman can ever get back, is it?" I avoid a direct answer to his question.

"No... I guess not. Does that matter, though?" I don't feel like we're discussing the myth anymore, but that he wants my opinion, based on my own experiences... and I don't have any.

"Probably... to some people." I'm being evasive again. "But you didn't answer my question."

"Which question was that?" he asks, and I wonder if he's stonewalling too.

I think about saying it doesn't matter, but somehow I don't think that'll work with him, and besides, I want to know... so I decide to be direct. "Have you ever slept with a virgin?"

"No," he says, without hesitation.

"In that case, do you have the right to judge?"

He pauses and sits forward again, and then says, "I have the right to an opinion. I also have the right to point out that your view is very biased toward women."

"Of course it is."

"Why? Why did you say that each *woman* has the right to decide what her virginity means to her? What made you say that virginity isn't something a *woman* can ever get back?"

"Because both statements are correct." I'm not sure what his point is.

"I know. But what about men in all this?"

"What about them?" He can't mean what I think he means… surely not. "I'm sorry… are you saying you think men should have the right to decide what a woman's virginity means?"

"No," he says, smiling and shaking his head. "I'm saying that men lose their virginity, too. Only society doesn't place the same significance on that as it does for women."

My half-formed anger dissipates, and I stare even more closely at him, taking in the slight stubble on his square jaw, and the way his thick, dark blond hair is slightly messed up, like he may have been running his fingers through it, before I came in here.

"Why is that?" I think about his comment, and the injustice of it.

"Oh, I imagine it's because men are supposed to sow their wild oats, and women are traditionally meant to remain chaste… at least until marriage, anyway."

I giggle because I can't help myself. "That's not even possible. If all the women are being chaste, who are the men sowing their wild oats with?"

He laughs. "That would be telling," he says, and we both relax a little.

"Okay," I say, feeling a little braver. "What did it feel like for you? Did you feel as though you were giving up something when you lost your virginity?"

He shakes his head again, still smiling. "It was so long ago, I'm not sure I can remember how I felt… other than relieved that I didn't screw up too much. She was more experienced than I was, and I didn't wanna get a reputation as the guy with no staying power… or the guy who couldn't get it up." He stops talking, and I'm almost certain I can see a slight blush on his cheeks. It's kinda cute, and very unexpected… and it also makes me feel a little uncomfortable, because I'm not sure I wanted to hear that.

"I'm assuming you didn't?" I say, my lips working on auto-pilot.

"Didn't what?"

"Get a reputation for either of those things?"

"No. It went okay."

I frown. "Only okay?"

"It was nearly twenty years ago... it was my first time... give me a break." He smiles.

Nearly twenty years ago? He's been having sex for twenty years, and I'm still a virgin. The contrast between us couldn't be more obvious if it was lit up in neon lights. I sit right forward in my seat. I've heard enough now. "Well... thanks for your help." I make it clear I'm bringing our conversation to a close, before he can question me any further about my virginity, or tell me anything else about his past...

"I'm not sure I have helped, have I?" he says, frowning. "Your clients sound to me like an unhappy housewife and a busy and maybe slightly complacent husband, who just need to spend some time together, instead of living separate lives. Unless they want to live separate lives, of course?"

"I don't think they do," I tell him, relieved to be back on topic. "I know Ian doesn't... at least based on his reaction to the idea of Vanessa having an affair, anyway."

"And Vanessa?" he asks.

"If she wanted that, why did she book the sessions? Why did she insist on Ian coming to see me? And why warn him in advance that she's thinking of having an affair? Why not just do it? It makes little sense."

"Hmm... I agree. In which case, my advice – if you're still asking for it – would be to see them separately. Get each of them to talk to you on their own tomorrow, while the other one waits in the reception. They might open up more that way and tell you how they really feel, instead of either saying what they think the other person wants to hear, or playing games."

That sounds like a good idea, and I could kick myself for not thinking of it first. That way I wouldn't have had to sit through that embarrassing conversation... a conversation I'm wishing I'd never started now.

"Thanks," I say, getting up, surprised by the tears that are forming in my eyes. *Dammit.*

He stands, a little too quickly, almost knocking his chair over. "A—Are you okay?" he says.

"Yes. I'm fine." That's not true. I'm a long way from being fine. "I should let you go. You need to get to dinner with your brother... and I've kept you far too long."

He goes to move around the desk, but I make it to the door first. "Isabel?" he says and I turn back to him.

"I'm fine, really, Mason. I'm just tired. It's been a busy week. Thanks again for your help... I'll see you tomorrow." Before he can reply, I bolt through the doorway, running to my room and grabbing my jacket and purse, before I flee from the office.

It's a ten-minute walk to my apartment, but I make it in less than that and slam the door closed behind me, leaning back against it, before I let my tears flow... rolling down my cheeks as I slide to the floor.

What on earth possessed me to get into that conversation? I know I needed help with Vanessa and Ian's case, but why did I let it get so personal? It was me who did that, not Mason. I was the one who changed the emphasis. I did it, because I wanted to know more. And he answered every question. Only now I'm wishing I'd stayed quiet. Not because I didn't like his answers, but because the way he gave them made it clear, I mean nothing to him... not in the way I want to. That conversation was just like my lectures with Professor Green at college. It was open, and yet professional. It was personal, and yet philosophical. We were talking about sex, like it was just another topic of conversation. There was nothing romantic or sexual about it. He had opportunities to make it romantic and sexual, but he didn't take them... and I guess that's because there's nothing romantic or sexual between us. If there was, he'd have answered my questions differently. At least, I think he would. I think he'd have shown more consideration for my feelings... for how I might react to hearing about his past. He'd probably have kissed me, reassured me that the past meant nothing to him... but that I do. Except I don't. Because he doesn't think about me like that...

No matter how much I wish he would.

Mason

I'm gripping the steering wheel so tight, I'm in danger of losing control, and it's been this way ever since I left the office. In fact, I've been in danger of losing control ever since I saw the tears in Izzy's eyes, and she bolted from my room. The need to hold her then was almost overwhelming, and I could kick myself for not going straight after her. Except her tears confused me. I couldn't understand why she'd be so upset. Yeah… I got that she's worried about her clients, but not to the extent of crying, surely? I couldn't think of anything I'd said that would get to her that much either, but after about thirty seconds of thinking things through, and getting nowhere, I came to my senses and realized that wasn't the issue. She was… or at least comforting her was. So, I ran after her, only to find she was already on her way out the door, making it very clear she wasn't interested in talking anymore… even though I'd have happily talked to her all night. I'd talk to her forever, if she'd let me.

I contemplated following her, but what would have been the point? She'd already dismissed me twice… and even I can take a hint when it's that obvious.

I try to relax my grip, although it doesn't help. I'm still so damn tense I can't concentrate. All I can think about – apart from Izzy's tears – is the conversation we had immediately before she got upset. Like I say, I'm fairly sure I didn't say anything that would have made her cry, but I wish I'd thought through my answers before opening my mouth. If I had, I'd never have discussed my sex life with her… or at least, not like that.

First, I'd have taken her over to the couch, sat her down and held her, while I explained that the past means nothing to me… and that she means everything. I'd have told her that, yeah… losing my virginity to Dawn Reynolds in the back of my car three weeks before my eighteenth birthday, was pretty damn momentous at the time, but now, compared to the idea of just sitting in the same room as Izzy, it's irrelevant. I'd have tried to draw a firmer line between the philosophical elements of our conversation, and the personal ones… because it all got kinda muddled.

I'd also have made it very clear to her that I don't care how she lost her virginity, as long as the guy didn't hurt her. I don't care who he was, or when it happened. All I want is for us to be together… forever.

Except… now I come to think about it, she never answered my question. When I asked her how it felt to lose her virginity, she deflected. She wouldn't say whether being unable to get it back mattered, either. I lift my foot off the gas a little, wondering whether that means something, or whether I'm over-thinking. That's perfectly feasible. I've been doing it a lot lately… but I guess it's possible she declined to answer because she lost her virginity to someone who mattered. And if the relationship didn't last, I guess that would make losing her virginity – or having it taken – more significant than my teenage fumble in the back of my car with Dawn Reynolds. After all, she and I only dated for another two months after that 'momentous' event, before we both moved on to pastures new.

I slow right down, barely focusing on the road now, the darkness shrouding in around me, as I wonder whether Izzy might be like Debbie… the girl I mentioned to her earlier. I wonder whether she might still be so hung up on the guy who was her first, that she'll be incapable of not saying his name at inappropriate times, just like Debbie did… every single time I made her come.

God, I hope not.

She certainly didn't say anyone's name when she came in her office. She didn't say mine, that's for sure… but then, I'm not that man for her. I'm not the one who fills her head when she's pleasuring herself. I'm not the one who sets her body on fire with need… no matter how much I want to be.

I arrive at Oliver's cabin by the lake and park my Mercedes alongside his Jeep, climbing out and walking up the steps to his door.

I don't knock. He's expecting me, and he rarely locks the door… unless he's got company, which, as we both know, is a rarity these days.

"Hi," he calls out from the kitchen, which is on the other side of the vast living space. "You're late… as usual."

"I know."

He frowns, as I take off my coat and jacket, hooking them up beside the door, before making my way over to him, by-passing his over-stuffed, deep red couches, and the oak dining table with benches on either side. "What's wrong?" he asks.

I contemplate telling him everything… about my conversation with Izzy, about how I think I must have screwed up somehow, because she left my office in tears… that my love for her is consuming me, and seeing her every day and not being with her is killing me… slowly and painfully. But that I'm going crazy trying to work it all out.

Except I'm not really in the mood for talking… not about Izzy, anyway.

Oliver's never been great at letting things lie, though, so I tell him about the other thing that's still bothering me, even if it has been overshadowed by my conversation with Izzy.

"I got an email today," I say, leaning against the countertop by the sink and studying the ingredients he's already spread out next to him by the stove. From the looks of things, I'd say we're having steak and salad, which is just fine with me.

"And?" he prompts.

"And it reminded me that the college reunion I said I'd go to is next week."

He looks across at me, a slight smile forming on his lips. "I told you not to accept," he says.

"Yeah, and no-one likes a smart ass. I guess I thought it might be a chance to catch up with a few people… but they sent me through a list of attendees, and Calvin Hart's gonna be there."

He pulls a face. "Oh. That's a shame." He knows about my history with Calvin. After my first two years, Oliver joined me at college, and we shared an apartment until I'd finished my doctorate, so he got to see some of the wreckage first-hand. It wasn't pretty. Calvin did a lot of damage with his rumors and innuendos, and my self-confidence took a battering. I think it's one of the reasons I can be shy around women now… because I was shot down in flames too many times.

"Yeah… especially as he married a catwalk model, and he's bringing her with him."

"That'll be nice," he says, with just the right amount of sarcasm. He reaches across the stove for some oil, and then says, "Is everyone taking someone with them?"

"Yeah… it looks that way."

I didn't actually look through the complete list, because Diane arrived, but I saw enough to make me dread next Thursday.

"And, let me guess… you're not?"

"I said I would," I reply, feeling stupid now.

"Why?" He frowns at me.

"Because I had the option of adding a 'plus one' and I ticked the box."

"Yes. I get that… but why?"

"I don't know. I wasn't thinking straight."

"Was there a reason for that?" he asks, his frown clearing and his lips twisting upward.

"Yeah. Isabel had just started working with me. I wasn't capable of thinking clearly… about anything."

He nods his head, his smile filling out a little. "Were you thinking you might take her with you? Is that why you ticked the box?"

"No. That didn't even occur to me. Not then…"

"But it has now?" he says, picking up on my comment.

"It did earlier today… just briefly."

"Why only briefly?"

"Because she wouldn't want to come." I already knew that before the conversation I had with her this evening. Now, I'm absolutely positive. But I'm not about to tell Oliver that.

"How do you know that?" he says, shaking his head. "This could be the perfect ice-breaker for you. After all, it's kinda work-related, isn't it? Or you could make it sound that way."

I stare at him as he seasons the steaks, my mind spinning. "I guess," I murmur, contemplating what he's just said. "Everyone there is in our line of work…"

"Exactly. And you said you were gonna look up a few people, so… there you go. It's perfect."

I nod my head, even though I'm not sure it's anything close to 'perfect'. "If I kept it professional and told her we'd be going there to meet some business contacts, that wouldn't be asking her on a date, would it?"

"Not any date I've ever been on." He sounds kinda doubtful about the whole thing now, which is surprising. "But if she says yes to that enticing offer, what are you gonna do with her all evening… glad-hand your old college friends and talk about work?"

"No, of course not."

"Oh… so you're gonna wait until you get to wherever this reunion's being held and then tell her you got her there under false pretenses?"

"No." Does he think I'm insane?

Oliver puts down the knife he's holding. "Good," he says, his brow furrowing. "Because I wasn't suggesting you treat the whole thing like a business meeting… with benefits."

"You weren't?" It sounded that way to me.

"No," he says. "I was suggesting you could use the work element as an ice-breaker… as a way of introducing the reunion into the conversation. Then, you could maybe tell her what you've just told me."

"You're suggesting I tell her about my arch nemesis from college and how he's made more of a success of his life than I have… and married a supermodel into the bargain?"

"No, I'm not. Because that would be really stupid… even by your standards. It also wouldn't be true. His wife isn't a supermodel… she's just a model. And, while he may be a financial success, that doesn't mean he's happy. You know the two things don't always go hand-in-hand. So stop making comparisons."

"I'm not. I'm just saying I'm not sure that's the best way to go with Isabel."

"Good… because that wasn't what I was saying, either. I was saying I think you could use the business to introduce the reunion, tell her you're going and that you're gonna look up some old friends from your college days… and then ask if she'd like to come with you… as your date."

I shake my head, because the thought of saying anything like that to Izzy – especially after our earlier conversation – seems alien to me. "Or I could just tell her it's gonna be good for the business," I say.

"So you wanna lie to her?" He steps away, leaning back on the countertop and folding his arms across his chest. "Lying isn't a great way to start a relationship, Mason."

"I know. But I think it might be the only way to start this one."

He sighs. "It might be a great way to end it, too. I think you'll be making a huge mistake if you do this. By all means, use work as the way into the conversation, but be honest with her. Tell her you wanna take her to the reunion and don't mess with her feelings. It's not fair."

"I know that." I'm not an idiot.

"Then why are you thinking about faking it? You know it never pays off… especially when you're talking about something as important as your future… and hers."

"I'm not thinking about faking it," I say, justifying myself. "I want to be with her… how is that faking it?"

"Because you're not planning on telling her that, are you?"

I shake my head at him. "So now you're saying, not only should I ask her to the reunion as my date, but I should tell her I wanna be with her?"

"Not in so many words…"

"Good. Because I don't think I could say that… not to Isabel."

"Why not? You're in love with her, aren't you?"

"Yes… but…" I fall silent, my admission ringing out between us. "Could you say it to Jemima?" I ask.

Oliver thinks for a moment and says, "Considering she barely acknowledges my existence… probably not. I'm too scared I'll get shot down in flames." He shakes his head. "It's not that easy, is it?"

"No, it's not. It's damn hard."

He lets out a long breath, staring across at me. "Don't fake it," he says. "You'll only regret it. Just keep things simple. Be honest with her… ask her to the damn reunion. Who knows? She might surprise you and say 'yes'. And then you can bring her to Destiny's wedding next weekend, and introduce her to the rest of us."

"Trust me, if she says 'yes' to coming to the reunion with me, I'm gonna be lucky to make it to Destiny's wedding. I'm gonna be too damn busy."

He chuckles. "You can hope… and anyway, you know damn well, if you don't make it, Dad will come after you."

I roll my eyes, although I'm already thinking about how it would feel to have Izzy with me at Destiny's wedding, to introduce her to my family, to hold her hand, to look into her eyes, to kiss her… and then, later on, take her back to my place…

God, that sounds so perfect.

All I need to do is persuade her I'm not a complete loser, and talk her into coming with me to the reunion, without giving away how much I love her, and want her… and need her.

So, no pressure then.

Chapter Six

Isabel

It's been a horrible week.

I've had a few tough sessions with clients, which didn't help, but to be fair, it hasn't all been bad. The conversation with Mason on Monday morning was lovely. The thing is, that was Monday. It was days ago… a distant memory. So distant that the conversation has been obliterated in my head by the talk we had last night, which I'm still doing my best to forget.

I'm failing dismally, because whenever I think about him – which is almost all the time – I can't help but remember the way he made me feel like he's my mentor and I'm his student. Like everything between us is professional. And while I know that's true… that's not how I want it to be.

I want to be so much more to him than that.

At the moment, though, I'm just grateful that at least I haven't seen him since last night, which means I haven't had the chance to embarrass myself any further… or to be reminded that I'm nothing to him. And at least I've survived another week, and have a restful weekend to look forward to. It's not much, but it's the best I can do right now.

I power down my computer, clear my desk, and grab my coffee cup, taking it through to the kitchen to wash, thinking about spending a couple of days in my apartment, reading, catching up with laundry, and maybe watching old movies. I allow myself a smile, because my new dildo arrived this morning. It's identical to the one I've left here in my desk drawer, but at least now I've got one at home too, so as well as reading and watching old movies, I can keep myself satisfied… and I think I might need quite a lot of that this weekend.

"Do you want me to take that?"

I look up, startled by the sound of Mason's voice, glancing down at his outstretched hand.

"I—I was just gonna wash it." I don't know why I said that. It's fairly obvious why I've brought my cup out here.

"I've already done mine," he says. "I'm happy to do yours."

"Oh… thanks."

I hand over my cup, wondering if this is his way of dismissing me, and am about to turn away when he says, "How did it go today?"

"Um… okay. It was busy, but that seems to be quite normal at the moment."

He turns, looking at me over his shoulder, while he washes my cup in the sink. "That wasn't what I meant." He surprises me with a smile. "Weren't you seeing those clients of yours today? The ones we were discussing last night?"

Did he have to remind me? I can feel myself blush and look down at the floor between us. "Yes."

"So? How did it go?"

Can he have forgotten that I ran out of his office – and out of the building – in tears?

Of course he can. He probably didn't even notice, and rather than bring that up, or anything else about last night, I stick to answering his question. "It went well. I saw them at lunchtime… and I followed your advice, and talked to Vanessa first, because I felt she was the one with the problem, not Ian."

"I think that was sensible," he says, drying his hands on a towel, before folding it, and leaning back against the sink. We're standing in the same places we were in on Monday morning, when we had that really lovely talk, and I suck in a breath, hoping that might be a good sign, and that I'm not reading too much into simple things... like geography. "What did she say?" he asks, reminding me to talk.

"That she's bored." I recall the conversation I had with Vanessa, and wonder how much of it I want to reveal to Mason... not because of client confidentiality, but because of the subject matter. Based on our talk last night, I'm not sure it'll end well.

"Bored with what?" he asks, and I'm faced with the choice of telling him the truth and risking the consequences, or lying... and I've never been great at lying.

"With Ian," I say.

"Generally, or specifically?"

"Specifically... in bed." There, I've said it. I've raised the specter of sex... again. Even though I know I'll probably regret it.

"Is this a recent thing?" he asks.

"Fairly, I think." I lean back on the wall behind me. "She didn't go into details, but she said it had gotten kinda mundane, which implied it hadn't always been that way."

"By 'it', do you mean sex?"

Is he trying to embarrass me? It's hard to tell. The look on his face isn't giving anything away. He's just staring at me, all gorgeous and intense and sexy. "Yes." I refuse to be intimidated... or at least I refuse to show it.

"Well, I guess that can happen, after time..." he says.

I'm tempted to ask if he's speaking from experience, but I got burned the last time I went down that road. "So, you're saying you think that's normal?" That feels like a safer way to go... I think.

"Not normal, no. I'm just saying it can happen, if you let it." He stares at me, and I stare right back, until he says, "Was that all she said?"

"Oh... no." I remember that we're talking about Vanessa, and recall our conversation. "She told me she'd joined a book club."

"A what?" He frowns.

"A book club... you know... where you get together and..."

"I know what a book club is," he says, shaking his head. "I'm just amazed that, when she really needs to be spending more time with her husband, and working on the marriage she claims is in so much trouble, she's doing something that takes her out of their home."

I push myself off of the wall again and take a half step toward him. "I can see what you mean, but I think I'd underestimated how many hours Ian works. He leaves the house before six in the morning and he's rarely home before eight at night, and he works most weekends, too. I think she's lonely, as much as anything. She said she joined the group to meet new people."

"New men?" he asks.

"I wondered that, but she told me all the other members are women, so I guess not."

"Fair enough," he says. "But how is the book club relevant?"

I smile, just slightly. "Because it's a double-edge sword."

"In what way?"

"Like I said, all the other members are women… just like Vanessa. From what she said, they're all roughly the same age, all bored, and all looking for something to spice up their lives."

"That sounds terrifying," Mason says, and I laugh, feeling myself relax slightly.

"It does, doesn't it? And it gets worse, because from what I could gather, their reading matter seems to be almost exclusively erotic fiction."

"Oh, dear." Mason lets his head fall into his upturned hand. "Don't tell me… this fueled the fires of Vanessa's imagination, did it?"

"Well, it certainly seems to have been the catalyst for making her think she's missing out on something."

"Doesn't she realize…?"

I hold up my hands, and he stops speaking. "You don't have to tell me… I know she's comparing fiction with reality. I told her that… repeatedly. I explained that she's confusing real men with the creations of a novelist's imagination, but she wasn't listening. She'd got it into her head that her husband ought to be more like one of the alpha studs in her books."

"Excuse me… did you just say 'alpha studs'?" he says, smiling.

"Yes. I did." I wish I hadn't, but I did.

"I think I'm gonna have to look up exactly what that is," he says, his smile widening.

"Oh… I don't think so." I let my eyes wander over his muscular body, wondering for a moment whether Mason qualifies as an alpha. He has the physique – the masculinity – which is normally associated with that type, but I'm not sure about his personality. Alphas are notoriously arrogant and egotistical, and often sexist too… and I don't think Mason displays any of those qualities. He's probably more like a…

He coughs, interrupting my train of thought, and I blush, realizing I'm staring at him… directly at his chest.

"What happened next?" he says, perhaps sensing my embarrassment, and saving me from it – thankfully – by getting us back to the point of the conversation.

"I talked to Ian," I reply.

"What books had he been reading?" he asks, and I smile, feeling even more grateful that he's injected some humor into the situation.

"None that he told me about… thank God. He just sat in my office, like a broken man, and told me he's terrified Vanessa's gonna leave him. Evidently, he'd built the whole thing up in his head, imagining her with someone else, not just having an affair, but actually walking out on him and their kids… because she'd found someone 'better' than him. He said he hadn't slept since they were last here… and I have to say he looked completely washed out."

"He loves her," Mason says.

"Yeah. He does."

"So, what did you do?"

"It was my last appointment of the morning, and I didn't mind skipping lunch, so I got Vanessa to come back into the room, rather than sending them home with no resolution… and I sat them both down and told her to tell him exactly what she wanted. No holds barred. I told her Ian's not a mind reader. She can't expect him to understand what she wants if she doesn't tell him. She said she wasn't sure she could, so I told her to pretend she was reading from one of those books."

Mason raises his eyebrows at me, but I just shrug my shoulders. "I figured I had nothing to lose… and neither did they."

"Did she do it?" he asks.

"She was kinda reticent, which was understandable, I guess. But then she got a lot closer to him, and he held her… and I think it was the physical contact that did it, because then the floodgates opened, and she told him in no uncertain terms, exactly what she wanted him to do to her."

"Wow," he says, tilting his head to one side. "How was that?"

"Embarrassing."

"And did it work?"

"Yeah, it worked. Although I had a scary moment when Vanessa first stopped talking."

"Why?"

"Because Ian just sat there and stared into space for about a minute and a half."

"Yeah, well, some men are easily shocked," Mason says with a smirk.

"It wasn't that… although some of what Vanessa said had been quite full-on. I think he was just trying to work out where to start." He laughs. "And then he stood up, grabbed her hand and pulled her to her feet, and told her they were going home… and that he was gonna call her mom to get her to collect their kids from school, and see if she could have them overnight."

Mason laughs again, throwing his head back this time, which is a glorious sight. "I guess that was one way to resolve the problem." He lets his eyes fix on mine. "You should charge double for being so inventive."

I shake my head. "I think I should probably pay commission to whoever wrote that damn book she was quoting from."

"You're sure she was quoting?"

"Yeah… I doubt even the best of alpha males could do some of the things she was describing. In fact, I think some of them were physically impossible."

"You never know," he replies, his voice dropping slightly. "Not until you try."

I don't know why he's staring at me like that, or why his mouth is slightly open, but I can't think about that at the moment, because my pussy is tingling and clenching and although I'm wearing panties, for obvious reasons, it's all very distracting… especially as I recall some of Vanessa's words, and imagine Mason holding me upside down and 'eating me out', while he 'fucks my mouth', and then flips me around 'suspended in his arms' and 'fucks me till I'm screaming'. That sounded like one of the more physically possible things Vanessa was describing. I've got no idea what any of that would feel like, of course, but I know that I'd love for Mason to do it all to me… whatever it is… repeatedly.

Mason

I'm so turned on right now, I'm struggling to breathe. If Izzy would just lower her eyes from mine by about three feet, she'd see the effect she's having on me, because there's no way I can hide it… and I'm not sure I want to.

Somehow, we've ended up talking about sex… again. Only this time, the atmosphere between us is better. It's more electric… more intense. Maybe that's because we're not talking about ourselves, but about Izzy's clients. Although there seems to be something profoundly intimate lying just beneath the surface of our words.

I'm not sure which one of us brought the conversation around to sex this time. It was me who asked how her appointment had gone… partly because I wanted to know, and partly because I wanted to keep her here, with me, for just a little longer. So I think it must have been Izzy who first raised the subject of sex, although she didn't do it deliberately. She did it by way of explaining about her clients' problems. And, I have to say, her method of dealing with those problems was certainly different... and effective, based on what she told me of the result. I don't know how she sat through that session, with Vanessa explaining to Ian in graphic detail exactly what she wanted him to do to her. I struggled to keep a straight face when Izzy said the words 'alpha stud'. So I don't think I'd have been much help to them... and I guess that's why I don't do couples counseling.

It was interesting, when Izzy said that, though, because she blushed, and although I took pity on her and made a joke out of it, I couldn't help noticing the way her eyes roamed over my chest. I've got no idea what she was thinking. Maybe she was wondering whether I consider myself to be an alpha. I don't. I don't feel as though I fit into any personality type. But I can't help wondering to myself whether Izzy might prefer her men to be more 'alpha'... more arrogant and ruthless... more dominant. Or whether she goes for beta types... men who are quieter, calmer, more domesticated... a little more boring. Men who'll probably never rock your world, but who'll also never break your heart. Then I remember the sight of her at her desk, the way she came so hard, and licked her juices from that dildo with such gusto, and I realize a beta guy would never work for Izzy. She needs a man who'll not only rock her world, but who'll make her body pulse... repeatedly.

We're staring at each other, and neither of us has said a word, or moved a muscle, for far too long. She's not upset, which is good, after what happened the last time we spoke, and she doesn't seem to be in any rush to leave... which is especially good, because I enjoy having her here.

"You feel it was a successful outcome?" I say, since one of us needs to break the silence.

She startles, like she's coming out of a trance, and smiles. "I guess I'll find out when I next see them. Although I'm gonna have to send Vanessa a text message about our next appointment."

"Oh? Why's that?"

"Because they ran out of my office so fast, we didn't get the opportunity to make any arrangements."

I laugh. "I guess there's a chance they might decide they don't need to come and see you anymore," I tell her and she shrugs.

"I guess. But I'm gonna encourage them to come back, if I can."

"Why?" I ask. I agree she needs to see them again, but I want to know her reasoning. I'm here to help her, after all.

"Because I think they're papering over the cracks. I get that sex is the manifestation of the problem, but there's more to it than that. It's about Vanessa feeling neglected… taken for granted."

"Do you think she is?" I ask.

"Not necessarily, but that's how she feels… and that's what's important. I want to sit them down and get them to see that, no matter how much great sex they have, they still need to appreciate each other, preferably outside of the bedroom."

She looks up at me, biting her bottom lip and I want to kiss her… so damn hard. I want to bite that bottom lip myself, and push her back against the wall, so she can feel how turned on I am.

"Am I right?" she says, blinking twice.

My carnal thoughts evaporate as I see the doubt in her eyes and hear it in her voice. She's really not sure about this.

"Of course you are." I step closer… but not too close, because no matter how much I want her, she needs reassurance. Professional reassurance. "A successful, long-lasting relationship can't be based on sex… great, or otherwise. There's gotta be more to it than that. It's not just about physical appreciation, either. It's not just about a man telling a woman she's beautiful all the time, or complimenting her on how great she looks…"

"Oddly enough, Vanessa brought that up," she says, interrupting me.

"And?"

"And Ian pointed out that compliments are a two-way street, and that Vanessa hadn't been paying him that much attention either."

"What did you say?" I ask. "When that came up?"

"I don't think I got the chance to say anything. It was during our earlier session… and it degenerated into an argument between the two of them quite quickly after that." She pauses and then says, "But I agreed with Ian's perspective."

"Why?" I ask. I'm not quizzing her, and she knows it. We both know that getting our thoughts out is beneficial. It helps us understand our clients better.

"Because I feel that if a woman finds a man attractive, she should tell him."

"She shouldn't wait until he says it first?" I challenge her... not because I believe what I'm saying, but because I want her to justify her own ideas... to herself, not me.

"No. Why should she?" She challenges me right back, which makes me smile.

"Maybe because it's more conventional?"

"To hell with convention," she says with feeling and we stare at each other briefly, before she steps to one side, breaking the moment. "I— I've taken up a lot of your time."

"N—Not at all." She's going to leave, I can sense it, and I don't want her to. I haven't even had the chance to invite her to the reunion yet... and it's less than a week away now. "I—I've been meaning to ask you," I stammer, and she looks up at me again, "w—would you like to come to my college reunion with me next Thursday?"

I've actually said it. Okay, so the words came out in a rush, and I did kind of fumble the beginning, but I didn't make it about work. I made it sound like a date... I think.

Izzy stares at me, blushing slightly, and then she bites her bottom lip again, and lowers her eyes, clearly embarrassed. Oh, God... this is going so wrong. I might have been viewing our conversation through romantic eyes, but she obviously hasn't. It's been entirely professional for her... and I've just blown it by asking her out.

"Everyone who's going to be there studied the same course as me," I say, before she can answer. "They'll all be in the same profession as us, on one level or another, and it'll be an excellent opportunity for us to network. It should be good for business..."

I've done the very thing Oliver warned me against. But what choice did I have?

Izzy's face clears, proving me right. She's not interested... not in me, anyway.

"So, it's about the business, is it? That's why you want me to go?"

"Yes... of course." It's amazing how easy it is to lie when you have to.

She nods her head. "Email me the details," she says. "I'll meet you there."

Just like that? I don't think so. "It's in Boston. We might as well go together... I'll drive us."

"Okay." She smiles, and then tilts her head to one side. "I guess I'd better head home."

"Fine. Have a good weekend."

"You too." She moves away, walking down the corridor, and heading toward her office.

I want to call her back. I'm aching to hold her in my arms and tell her I lied... that I want her to accompany me because I love her, and I want to spend every waking moment with her. But I don't. Instead, I switch off the kitchen light and make my way back to my room, where I sit down at my desk, letting my head rock back, and staring at the ceiling.

Could that have gone any worse?

I don't think so.

Except, I guess she could have said 'no' to coming with me at all, because she was definitely going to say 'no' to coming with me before I made it about the business.

I pick up my phone and connect a call to Oliver, feeling the need to talk to someone. He answers on the second ring.

"Please don't tell me you wanna meet up tonight, I'm too tired to stand."

"I wasn't going to."

"What's wrong?" I guess he can hear the dejection in my voice, so there's no point in trying to pretend everything's fine.

"It's Isabel," I say.

"What happened?" he asks, his tiredness forgotten.

"I just asked her to come to the reunion with me... as my date."

"And?"

"She looked like I'd suggested we should elope. She was blushing and flustered... and so embarrassed, I had to turn it into a work thing, just to save face."

"Shit..." he whispers. "How did she react when you made it about the business?"

"Oh, she was fine with it. She was quite happy to accompany me and said she'd meet me there. Obviously, I said 'no' to that, because the reunion's being held in Boston, and it doesn't make sense for both of us to drive, but..." I let my voice fade, because I can't think what to say next.

It seems Oliver can't either, and he falls silent for a moment before he says, "I'm sorry, man."

"She's so clearly not interested." I state the obvious, pushing my fingers back through my hair. "I wish I'd never asked her now."

"Why?"

"Because I've gotta get through Thursday evening, pretending she's just a colleague, and not the woman I wanna spend the rest of my life with."

"You don't think...?" he says, and then stops talking.

"I don't think what?"

"You... you don't think you might be able to turn it into something romantic once you get there?"

"No. Like I say, she's not interested."

I shake my head, and close my eyes for a second, imagining the scene... arriving at the hotel on Thursday night with Izzy, not being able to touch her, or even look at her... not closely, anyway. I picture us surrounded by couples. Marcus and Tanya... Lance and Laura. Calvin and Naomi. Oh, God... why couldn't Izzy have said 'yes'? Why couldn't she have pretended an interest, even out of pity?

"Are you gonna back out?" Oliver asks.

"How can I? It'd look really weird."

"Yeah... I guess."

The thought of all those couples is still filtering through my mind, just as another idea forms... "But..." I muse out loud.

"But what?"

"I guess there might be a way to make it slightly less painful… if I can work out how to make things *look* romantic."

"What are you talking about? I just asked you that and you said you didn't think you could turn it into something romantic. You said she wasn't interested." He sounds confused, which isn't surprising, being as I'm fairly confused myself… and thinking on my feet here.

"She isn't, and nothing's gonna happen between me and Isabel – that much is obvious – but at least I could try to save face with Calvin Hart."

"How?"

"If I can get him to believe Isabel's there with me romantically."

"And how are you gonna do that?"

"By doing exactly what I just said… making it *look* romantic."

He sighs. "This sounds like a recipe for disaster, if you ask me."

"I wasn't asking you. And anyway, what does it matter? Isabel doesn't think of me like that… so she's not gonna care what I do, and if I can pull this off, and pull the wool over Calvin's eyes for a few hours, at least I won't have to feel like such a loser."

"No… you can just be one," he says. "You do realize you're talking about using the woman you claim to love, to score points over someone who really doesn't matter, don't you?"

"I'm not using anyone. I'm just a colleague to Isabel. Nothing more, nothing less. She'll never even know what's going on."

In fact, she's so blind to me, she probably won't even notice…

Chapter Seven

Isabel

I make it back to my office, my mind in a whirl, and I collapse into my chair, staring into space.

Did that really just happen?

Did Mason really just ask me to go with him to his college reunion? He must have done.

I can remember him making the arrangements to drive me there.

But it's not a date, is it? I mean, it sounded like one when he first blurted out his invitation, and I could kick myself for not just accepting him, there and then. Except he'd caught me unawares. I was feeling distracted by our conversation. I'd been thinking about all the things I wanted him to do with me, and then, like he could read my mind, he stared at me for ages, his eyes on fire. At least they looked that way to me... and for a few moments, I allowed myself to dream... until he started talking about Vanessa and Ian again. I didn't want our conversation to end, so I went along with it, and asked his opinion about how I'd handled things... and he was typically kind and helpful. He raised the subject of compliments, and I told him what Ian had said – about it being a two-way street. He challenged me, because he likes doing that, and we both know I find it helpful. But then, as we were talking, I realized I wanted to tell him how attracted I am to him. I wanted to tell him I think he's the handsomest man I've ever seen, that I can't stop thinking about him... that he fills my darkest fantasies...

I didn't say any of that, of course.

I just got embarrassed and was about to leave when he invited me to his reunion… and I guess, because my brain was still full of all my darkest fantasies, I reacted the way I did… like a stupid little schoolgirl. Which gave him the chance to explain that it wasn't a date… it was business.

I suppose I should be grateful I didn't answer him before he'd had the opportunity to tell me that. Just imagine how much more embarrassing it might have been, if I'd acted like there could be something romantic between us, when all he was thinking about was the business…

I sigh deeply and pick up my phone, finding Noah's number and connecting a call to him. He takes a while to answer and is out of breath when he does.

"Is everything okay?" I ask.

"Yes. I've just walked in the door and had to put the groceries down, and then I couldn't get my phone out of my pocket," he says.

"Oh… that's a relief. I wondered if I might have interrupted something."

"If only." He sighs and then adds, "Just give me a minute to pour myself a glass of wine."

"Why? Do you need one?"

"I think I'm going to. You never usually call this early, so I'm guessing something's up."

"You've guessed right. I'm just wishing now that I'd waited until I got home to call you. Then I could have had a glass of wine too."

"Are you still at work?" he asks. I can hear a clinking sound in the background, which I know will be him getting a wineglass from the cabinet beside his refrigerator, and then I hear a cork pop.

"Yes."

"You're that busy?"

"I'm busy. But I'm not *that* busy. I just happen to still be here."

"Because…?" he says and I hear wine being poured, which makes me even more jealous.

"Because Mason just asked me to go with him to his college reunion."

"Oh, my God. He asked you out? But that's fantastic. I'm so thrilled for you. When is it? What are you gonna wear... I..."

"Noah, will you slow down?" I interrupt him before he starts planning my wedding... a wedding I know will never take place. "It's not a date."

"It's not?"

"No. It's about work."

"How?" He sounds almost offended.

"Because the people who'll be there are all psychologists, too. We'll be able to network... at least, that's what Mason said."

"Nice." I can hear the disdain in his voice.

"Don't blame him and don't criticize him. It's not his fault if I read too much into the situation, is it? How was he to know I'm in love with him? He was just thinking about what's best for the business."

"Hey," Noah says, getting in the way of my outburst. "Calm down. I wasn't being critical."

"Yes, you were."

"Okay, I was. Because I love you and I don't like to think of you being hurt." He pauses for a second and then says, "You are hurt, aren't you?"

A lump rises in my throat, and I say, "Yes," around it, my voice cracking.

"Don't cry, Isabel."

"I can't help it." A tear falls onto my cheek.

"Do you want me to drive down there?" he asks. "I've only had a few sips of wine... and I can be there in a couple of hours."

I know it's not a hollow offer, because Noah doesn't make those, any more than I do. And while I'm tempted to say I'll be fine, I don't think I will be.

"Could you stay the weekend?" I ask.

"I can stay until Sunday lunchtime," he says. "How does that sound?"

"It sounds perfect."

"Shall I bring my groceries? They're only gonna go to waste otherwise."

"Okay."

"And I'll bring the bottle of wine I've just opened too."

"I think we're gonna need more than one bottle," I say.

"We'll work it out. Give me twenty minutes to pack a bag and I'll be on my way."

I let out a sigh, struggling not to cry again. "Thanks, Noah."

"Anytime," he says, and we end our call.

I still feel downhearted, but I know I'm going to have someone to share it with… at least until Noah goes home again on Sunday lunchtime. After that, I guess I'll just have to keep myself busy until Thursday… and hope to survive the evening with Mason.

Once that's over with, I'll have to find a way to get over him… because I can't keep on like this.

I sigh and stand up, switching off my desk lamp, grabbing my jacket and purse, and making my way to my door.

I open it, and glance to my right, seeing that Mason's door is closed, although there's a light visible underneath it, so I know he's still here. I stand still for a moment and listen. Our rooms are fairly well sound-proofed, but I can hear his voice, which I guess must mean he's on the phone.

I don't want to think about who he's talking to… so instead, I walk over to the front door and let myself out, closing it softly behind me.

"Hey, you," Noah says, once he's come into my apartment, dropped his bag, put down the groceries and turned around again. "Give me a hug."

I close the gap between us and fall into him, and without warning, I burst into tears. He tightens his grip and lets me sob into his chest, soaking his shirt.

"Have you been holding that in since our phone call?" he asks, pulling back and looking down at me. He's a blur, but I nod my head, and he takes my hand and pulls me over to the couch, sitting us both down, and letting me rest against him.

I can't seem to stop crying, not properly, but he's undaunted, and just sits beside me, handing me Kleenex from the box on the coffee table, and waiting… and waiting… until eventually I regain enough control that I can speak.

"Why does this have to hurt so much?" I ask, looking up at his handsome face.

"I don't know," he replies and I shake my head.

"Why did I have to fall for him? Why did I have to over-interpret everything?"

"Like what? What have you been over-thinking now?"

"Everything."

"Care to elaborate?"

"Okay… take earlier on… before he asked me to his reunion, we were talking about…"

"About what?"

"About a client. Which means I can't tell you what we were talking about… not in any detail. But it was to do with relationships, and sex."

He shifts slightly in his seat and looks down at me. "You talk to him about sex?"

"Yes. Sometimes."

"Isn't that kinda awkward?"

"It can be."

"Why? Because you're in love with him?"

"Partly," I say.

"Or because you've never had sex?" he asks, with his usual perception.

"Thanks for the reminder."

"You need reminding?"

"No, but thanks anyway."

He frowns, tilting his head, and then says, "I get you might need to talk about your clients, but how do you have a conversation about sex with the man you love… and not make it sexual? Even allowing for the fact that you've never had sex."

"If you say that one more time, I'm gonna send you straight back home again," I say through gritted teeth.

He holds up his hands. "Okay. I'll do my best not to mention it again. But how do you discuss sex with Mason, knowing you wanna jump his bones?"

"You have such a way with words, Noah."

"I know. It's a gift… now answer the damn question, will you?"

"It's not easy," I say. "In fact, sometimes it's almost impossible to be in the same room as him, talking about really intimate things, and not tell him how I feel. I—I was tempted to tell him earlier on this evening."

"You were?"

"Yeah. Thank God I didn't – obviously – but there was this moment, when we were talking, and he was looking at me… and I just wanted to tell him all of it." I pause for a second, remembering the moment. "There was a look in Mason's eyes, you see."

"What kind of look?" Noah asks.

"I don't know… like they were on fire. That's how it seemed to me."

"And what was he looking at, at the time?"

"Me."

Noah leans back a little and frowns. "He was looking at you, and his eyes seemed to be on fire?" he says.

"Yes. Clearly they weren't. I know that now. I misinterpreted that. Just like I always do."

"You're sure about that?"

"Yes. I'm positive, because just a few minutes later, he asked me to the reunion. So I know he's not interested."

"Oh… well, of course. That clinches it then. It makes perfect sense, now you've explained it. A man you work closely with, and with whom who you often share intimate carnal discussions, looks at you, with a burning desire in his eyes, and then asks you out. Naturally, that means he's not interested in you. Why didn't I work that out for myself?"

"Because I didn't say he had 'burning desire' in his eyes. I said he had fire in his eyes."

"And they're so different, aren't they?"

"How the hell would I know?"

He sighs. "Well, unless he was about to get really mad at you over something, and the fire was anger, I'd say they were pretty much the same thing," he says, shaking his head.

"What are you trying to say?"

"That I think Mason is just as hot for you as you are for him."

"That's ridiculous."

"Why?" he asks.

"Because he doesn't want me."

"Really? And how do you know that?"

"He ignores me most of the time."

"Maybe he's shy."

"Even if he is, he made the invitation to his reunion all about work."

Noah pauses for a moment and then says, "Okay... I don't have an answer for that. But I also don't think you should give up."

"Are you serious? This really hurts, Noah. I'm not sure how much more of it I can take."

"And what if I'm right? What if this guy likes you... or even loves you? What if he wants to be with you, just as much as you want to be with him, but he just doesn't know how to put that into words? Are you willing to throw away your chance with him, just because you think you've misread the situation?"

"No... but I don't think you understand how this feels."

"Yes, I do. I spend every working day with Aaron, and he doesn't even acknowledge my existence... so I know exactly how this feels."

I swallow down my pride and lean into him. "Oh, Noah... I'm sorry," I whisper. "I'm being selfish."

"No, you're not. And even if you were, you're allowed to be a little selfish when you're feeling bruised." He kisses my forehead. "The point is, you shouldn't give up hope."

"Even though Mason's made it very clear he only thinks of me as a business colleague?"

"Has he?" Noah narrows his eyes.

"Yes."

"I don't have any business colleagues who look at me in the way you say Mason looked at you. Trust me, I wish I did. I wish Aaron would.

But I live in hopes, and you should do the same. You should certainly try to turn this reunion into something, if you can."

"What does that mean?" I sit forward and look back at him.

"Well… why don't you wear that little black dress of yours?"

"You mean the one I can't wear a bra with, because it's so low cut at the back?"

"Yes… that's the one. And wear the highest heels you've got… because they'll make your legs look longer."

"Any other suggestions to make me look more like a hooker?"

"You won't look like a hooker. That's not even possible. You'll just look… sexy. Alluring."

"Yes… and I can spend the evening going unnoticed."

"Or you can spend the evening either being watched by 'Mr. Fire In My Eyes', or being admired by every other heterosexual guy in the room, which might just light the fire in Mason's eyes… if you get my meaning."

"You think I should try to make him jealous?"

He smiles. "If you wear that dress, you won't need to. You'll have him eating out of your hand… or anywhere else you feel like being eaten."

I giggle. "Noah… that's very rude."

"Maybe. But I also know it's one of your darkest fantasies."

Not any more, it isn't… I've moved on since then.

Mason

I've spent the whole time since last Friday night beating myself up about the way I asked Izzy to tonight's reunion.

My weekend was terrible.

In the end, despite his tiredness, Oliver invited me over to his place on Friday evening, and I ended up drinking too much and staying there. Once I got home on Saturday morning, nursing a fairly dreadful hangover, I decided against drinking anything else for the rest of the weekend, and just spent my time wandering in the woods that surround my house, trying to think up ways in which I might make things up to Izzy.

I didn't reach any conclusions, although I decided I wouldn't go through with that awful plan I'd suggested to Oliver… the one where I'd said deceive Calvin into believing Izzy was my girlfriend. Oliver was right; that would have been using her, and I can't do that. I feel bad enough not telling her I want her at the reunion with me because I'm in love with her, and not so we can 'network' while we're there; I'm sure as hell not going to lie about anything else.

The rest of my week, until today, hasn't been much better than my weekend. Izzy and I have both been really busy, with back-to-back clients taking up every minute of the day. I'll admit that's great for business, but it's not ideal when you want to sit down with someone and explain that you've asked them to attend an event under false pretenses. I really feel now that I should come clean before we go, and I'm not sure I can go through with the evening, with the shadow of my own dishonesty hanging over us.

Except I won't get the chance, because although I noticed Izzy had no appointments on her schedule after four this afternoon, what I didn't realize was that she'd freed up the time so she could go to the beauty salon. She informed me of that as she was running out the door, and I called out to her that I'd pick her up at six-thirty… and then she was gone.

So now, I'm standing outside her apartment, wearing my tux, and feeling like the biggest loser in the world, because the woman I love doesn't know I'm too much of a coward to be honest with her.

I might have walked up two flights of stairs, but I'm wondering whether to forget about knocking on her door, and to walk away and call her instead. I could lie again and say the reunion's been canceled, and I'm about to step back when she opens the door, peering around it and surprising me.

"I thought I saw your car across the street," she says. "I wasn't sure if you were waiting for me to come down."

I struggle to speak for a moment, struck dumb by how beautiful she looks. She's wearing a black cocktail dress that hugs her gorgeous figure, and high heels that make her legs look long and sexy. Her hair's curled – which it isn't normally – and she's worn it up, in a loose arrangement, with a few stray strands framing her perfectly made-up face… and a part of me wonders about abandoning the reunion and suggesting dinner instead. Just the two of us… at my place.

"Shall I get my coat?" she says, when my silence has stretched beyond belief.

"Y—Yes."

She turns and I groan out load, as I see the way her dress dips down at the back, to maybe six inches above her ass, displaying her beautifully soft skin, and making it clear she's not wearing a bra.

Oh, dear God. Maybe we could skip dinner, too…

She's disappeared from sight for a moment, and I stand on the threshold of her apartment, pulling down my jacket to hide my hard-on and quickly reaching the decision that dinner and skipping dinner aren't options. I've invited her to a college reunion, and that's where we're going. There's no way I'm going to tell her I lied about the purpose of tonight's event. I'm not taking the risk. What I am going to do is take this God-given chance of spending the evening with her, to show her I'm not all about business, and that I want to be with her for her, for reasons that have nothing to do with work. This isn't about scoring points over Calvin, either. It's about Izzy, and me… and the 'us' I'd like us to become.

"Okay," she says, coming back into my sight, wearing a dark gray coat, which covers up that beautiful dress, but will at least keep her warm on such a chilly night. She grabs her purse and joins me outside, pulling the door closed behind her. "Sorry." She looks up into my eyes. "I should've invited you in."

"It's fine. Don't worry about it." I needed the opportunity to calm down and think things through. I place my hand in the small of her back and lead her down the stairs and out onto the sidewalk, and then across the street to my car, where I open the passenger door and help her inside.

"I—I meant to say, you look stunning," I say as she settles in her seat, and she startles, looking up at me.

"Th—Thank you." Even in the dim street lights I can see she's blushing. It's really cute, and I have to smile. "You look very impressive, too."

"Impressive?" My smile fades a little and I lean down, gazing at her.

"Yes." She lets her eyes roam over me. "Very."

Her lips twitch upward into a sexy smile, but before my cock actually explodes, or I overreact by reading too much into that, I smile back again, and close the door, floating around to the driver's side and getting in beside her.

I start the engine, wondering to myself how we're going to get through the hour's journey to Boston. I don't want to make it in silence, or with an awkward atmosphere between us, so I need to think of something to talk about… something safe, preferably.

"I saw Vanessa and Ian today," Izzy says, as I check my mirrors and pull away from the curb.

I'm not sure if that's a 'safe' topic, being as it always seems to end with us talking about sex, but at least we're talking… and it was Izzy who started the conversation. I glance at her and smile.

"You convinced them to come back again, then?"

"It didn't take much convincing. I sent Vanessa a message, and she came back straight away and said they wanted to see me. They seemed very keen."

"Both of them?"

"Yes."

"How did it go?" I ask, pulling up at a set of lights and looking over at her.

"Not as well as I might have liked."

"Oh?"

She sounds a little forlorn and turns in her seat, which makes her coat gape open and her dress ride up a little, revealing her toned thighs. That's kinda distracting, but I keep at least one eye on the lights while watching her.

"They said they'd talked everything through over the weekend, but I'm not sure they had."

"Why not?"

"Because the conversation we had kept going back to sex all the time…" *Oh hell… we're back on sex again. And so soon.* "I tried to explain that there's more to it than that, but I'm not sure they were listening. I think they're finding all their answers in bed at the moment, so they're not looking anywhere else."

I roll my eyes while shaking my head, just as the lights turn green and I accelerate across the junction. "My advice, if you're still looking for it, would be to keep seeing them. You don't have to make their sessions so regular, but I'd put serious money on them hitting a wall at some point, probably when exhaustion gets the better of them, or when Ian loses his inner alpha again. When that happens, they're gonna need some help to get through it and out the other side."

"Inner alpha?" she says, and although I can't look over at her, because the traffic's kinda heavy, I can hear her smiling.

"Yeah. Isn't that what Vanessa was looking for?"

"It was. But surely Ian's a classic beta, isn't he? They've got three kids and a mortgage, so he's the settling down type… a homemaker."

"Have you been studying up on your personality types?" I say, teasing, although God knows why I think that's a good idea, considering my cock is still pressing uncomfortably hard against my zipper… a situation which isn't helped by Izzy twisting even further in her seat and revealing yet more of her gorgeous thighs.

"I didn't need to study up," she says, and I wonder if I've offended her.

"Sorry. I didn't mean to imply anything. I—I was teasing."

"You were?"

"Yeah. I'm not very good at it, though. I'm out of practice." She giggles, which has a painful effect on me, and I glance over to find she's staring at me. I have to look back at the road, because we're just joining the interstate and I'm able to put my foot down a little, but I want to keep the conversation going, so I say, "If you're so knowledgeable on personality types, which one am I?"

What's wrong with me? I'm flirting now… and that's even dumber than teasing.

"Hmm," she says, like she's thinking about my question. "I don't know… you're certainly not an omega."

I take another glance in her direction. She's smiling, her eyes shining, and I have to smile back.

"No, I'm not an omega. I'm not a geek. Never have been. Never will be."

"And I really hope you're not a zeta."

Where did that come from? Why choose zeta next? Is she trying to tell me something? "A lone wolf? Really?"

"I said I hope you're not… but then you worked alone for a long time, so…" She lets her voice fade.

"Yeah, but that was work. In my personal life, I don't choose to be alone. I am… obviously. But that's not out of choice, and zetas are renowned for being celibate… which is just plain dumb, if you ask me."

I half expect her to laugh, but she doesn't and when I look over at her again, she's gazing back at me, although it's too dark to read her expression.

"So you like sex, then?" she says, quietly… so quietly I have to strain to hear her.

"Doesn't everyone?" I'm deflecting again, in the hope she might open up a little, just for a change. She doesn't reply though, and I take my foot off the gas just slightly. "Sorry… I didn't mean to get so personal."

"You didn't. It was me who asked the question."

"I know it was, and I haven't given you an answer, have I?"

"No. And you don't have to. I shouldn't have…"

"I like sex," I say, interrupting her as I speed up again. "I like sex a lot. But I guess, as I'm getting older, I'm also getting more choosy about who I have sex with. It seems to matter more now."

"I see," she murmurs, but she adds nothing more to the conversation. She's clearly not going to give me her perspective – not voluntarily – and I wonder if I've given her more of an answer than she was expecting… whether, in my attempt to be completely honest and open with her, I've gone too far. I'm just trying to decide whether I should apologize, or elaborate further… or risk it all and ask her directly how she feels about sex, when she says, "Tell me you're not a delta," getting back to our original topic. I don't mind that. At least she's still talking to me.

"I'm not a delta, no. I'm not that dark… and I don't think I've suffered enough to wear the tag."

"You don't? Not even after losing your mom?" she asks.

"No." I clench my fingers around the steering wheel, although hopefully it's dark enough that she won't notice. "I'm not gonna say I'm over that. I don't think you ever get over something like losing your mom, especially not when you're only twelve at the time… but I don't live my life around it. Besides, I like to think I'm a lot more fun than most deltas."

"Hmm… I think you probably are," she says, and I release the steering wheel completely, in shock, quickly grabbing it again, and reminding myself that she's just stating a fact, not paying a compliment. After all, it's quite easy to be more fun than a delta. They live their lives with a 'couldn't care less' attitude, and that's definitely not me.

"You don't think I could be an alpha, then?" I get us back on course, suggesting the most obvious personality type… the one that started this whole conversation.

"God, no," she says, with a chuckle.

"Well, thanks." I'm not sure if I should be offended by her reaction, but the words spill out of my mouth, regardless.

"I didn't mean to offend you," she replies, leaning a little closer and reaching out, placing her hand on my arm, which does all kinds of things to my body, and makes my cock so painfully uncomfortable, it's hard to focus on the road.

"You didn't." *Much.* "I'm just intrigued now. Why don't you think I'm an alpha?" Given her response, I feel like I'm entitled to know her reasoning. "Don't you think I'm man enough to qualify?"

"Of course I do," she says. "I just don't think you're the love 'em and leave 'em type. I don't think you have the ego to be a true alpha."

I think that was a compliment… and even if it wasn't, I decide to take it as one. "Thanks… I think."

"You're welcome." She sighs deeply, like she's troubled by something.

"What's wrong?" I ask. "Are you feeling okay?"

"Yes, I'm fine. I'm just trying to work you out… and I'm stuck between gamma and sigma."

"Why can't I be a beta?"

"You mean you want to get stuck in the friend-zone?" she says.

"No." *Of course I don't. Not with you, anyway.*

For a moment, I wonder whether her comment might mean she doesn't want me stuck there either, but that's probably just me overthinking things. To be honest, I'm a little disappointed that she's ruled me out as a beta so easily. I thought women went for betas more than any other type… so does that mean she's dismissing me?

"This is harder than I thought," she says.

"Why?"

"Because it's difficult to narrow it down to one type."

"Do I have to be just one type?" I ask. "Can't I be a crossbreed?"

"A crossbreed?" she says, and I can hear her smiling.

"Yeah. Why can't I be a fairly laid back, reasonably nice, empathetic guy, who likes the beautiful things in life… who's looking to settle down, but only with the right woman… who knows what he wants and won't make do with second-best?"

"You think you can be all those things? At the same time?" she says.

"I know I can."

"Really? That sounds like a mass of contradictions."

"Welcome to the human race, Izzy." *Oh shit*… did I really just say that out loud? Did I really just use my fantasy name for her? How could I do that?

"Did you just call me 'Izzy'?" she says.

"Yes. I'm sorry." I feel like such a fool, and I know I'm blushing. I'm just grateful she can't see me in the darkness.

"Why are you saying sorry?"

Because it's the name I've called you in my head for months now… especially when I'm fantasizing about making love to you. "I don't know," I say out loud, fumbling for a suitable excuse for my apology, because I sure as hell can't tell her the truth. "My brother hates people shortening his name to Ollie, so I guess I just assumed you'd hate it, too. I shouldn't have…"

"I don't hate it," she says, interrupting me.

"Oh. Does everyone call you that then?"

"No."

"Really?" It seems like the natural thing to me.

"Yes. Really. You're the first person who's ever shortened my name."

"In that case, I apologize again."

"Why? I liked it."

I really want to pull over and kiss her. I even want to tell her the reason I just called her Izzy. But I can't. I'm scared I'm reading too much into this conversation. Just because I want it to be personal and meaningful doesn't mean she does… and I've got to remember that before I make an even bigger fool of myself.

"You… you know that these personality types don't just apply to men, don't you?" I say, getting us back onto our main topic of conversation, for my sake, as much as anything. It feels slightly safer… just.

"Yes, I know."

"So… what type of woman are you?"

"Confused," she says, and I laugh. "I think you should try to work me out, don't you? I've just spent the last thirty minutes analyzing your personality…"

"And you want me to analyze yours?"

"Why not?"

I can't decide whether she's teasing, being serious, or has decided she doesn't care anymore… and that being the case, I'm not sure I'm the best person to judge her personality, being as I can't seem to read her at all. Still, she has thrown down the challenge.

"You're not an alpha," I say straight away.

"No, I'm not." Her voice is firm, so I guess I got that right and I fall silent for a moment, thinking. "Is that all you've worked out?" she says. "That I'm not an alpha?"

"No, but…"

"But what?"

"I think you're like me… I don't think you fall into any one category."

"You don't?"

"No. Why? Do you?"

"I guess if I had to pick one, I'd say I'm more beta than anything," she says. "I'm friendly, and I enjoy helping people."

"Yeah, but you have a lot of gamma qualities, too. You're organized, and you're independent."

"I am? What on earth makes you think that?"

"Your parents left you to raise your sisters. You had to be organized and independent. You weren't given a choice."

"Oh… I suppose so," she says.

"But then, I can see some omega in you as well."

"The over-sensitive part, you mean?"

"No. I was gonna say that you're intelligent… and I think you're probably quite romantic."

"Do you?"

"Yes, I do. But when someone says something like that, you go kinda delta on them."

"Are we talking about my shyness now?"

"Yeah, and the fact that you're self-conscious, when you don't need to be."

She pauses for a moment or two, and then says, "So, the only thing I'm not is a sigma."

"I didn't say that."

"Please tell me you don't find me intimidating."

I chuckle, even though she's intimidating the hell out of me right now. "No," I lie, being as I can't tell her the truth. "But I think you're fiercely loyal, and that when you fall, you fall hard." I stop talking, because I know how that feels myself, but I don't want to think about Izzy falling hard for anyone… unless it should happen to be me.

She doesn't say a word, and I glance over at her, to see she's staring through the windshield, like she's in shock.

"Have I offended you?" I ask.

"No, not at all." She sounds kinda dreamy and I look back at the road, just as we pass a sign.

"Shit… did we just miss the turning?"

We arrive at the venue, roughly twenty minutes late, even though we didn't actually miss the turning. The traffic in Boston was heavy, though, and it took a little longer to negotiate the city roads than I'd expected. Not that I care. I'd have happily carried on driving all night.

I hand my keys over to the parking valet, who's already helped Izzy from the car. She walks around to me and, although I'm tempted to take her hand, being as I feel we know each other so much better than we did an hour ago, I don't. Instead, I nod in the direction of the glass doors and put my hand in the small of her back. That feels less intimate… although I'm not sure it is, not when I remember how low-cut the back of her dress is.

She looks up at me through her long eyelashes and walks ahead, through the doors. I follow, just a step behind, and when we get inside, she looks around, her eyes wide open.

"Wow," she says, turning back to me. "This is…"

"Over the top?" I take in the glass chandeliers, thickly piled carpets, and gilded furniture, and I lean in a little closer. "This is enough to give you a headache, isn't it?"

She chuckles and nods her head as she removes her coat and I stand behind her, taking it from her, and sucking in a breath as her naked back is revealed again.

"I—I'll just take this to the cloakroom for you," I say, with a stutter.

"Oh… thanks."

"Stay right here. I won't be long."

She nods her head, and I make my way to the side of the lobby, where there's a cloakroom, handing Izzy's coat over to the attendant, and being given a ticket in return.

I return to her, noticing that every other man in the room – even those who are accompanied by women – stares at Izzy as he walks past. Some even have their mouths open, and I wonder if she's aware of the effect she's having… especially on me.

"Shall we?" I say, as I get to her, nodding toward the reception room at the rear of the lobby, which has a sign outside announcing that the reunion is being held inside.

"Okay." She smiles up at me and I place my hand in the small of her back again, forgetting that she's no longer wearing a coat, and startling as my fingers settle on her bare skin. I think about pulling away, apologizing even, but then I notice a guy in a tux, heading for the reception hall too, passing us by, and almost tripping over his own feet as his eyes linger on Izzy's body… and I actually put my arm around her, pulling her a little closer to me, claiming her in the only way I can. She's mine… even if she doesn't know it.

She doesn't pull away, or say a word. She doesn't slap me either. So I lead us into the reception hall, which is – thankfully – slightly less garish than the lobby, in terms of its decor. The carpets and drapes are both red, but at least there's no gilding in here, and we walk forward to the bar.

"What would you like?" I ask Izzy, looking down at her.

"Red wine?" she says and I nod my head, ordering the same for myself from the barman, who also seems to admire Izzy, as he hands over two large glasses.

I pay him and then turn around, to be faced with the vaguely familiar form of Brett Stewart, bearing down on us. He's put on some weight in the last few years, and has lost some hair too, although what he's got is still dark brown, matching his smallish eyes, which are gazing at Izzy.

"Mason Gould," he says, like I've forgotten my own name.

"Yes," I reply, because I haven't.

"You remember me, don't you?" He drags his eyes away from Izzy and turns to me at last, frowning slightly.

"Of course I do... Brett." I leave a slight gap before saying his name, just to unnerve him, because I don't like him staring at Izzy like that.

He looks back at her again, and I realize I'm going to have to introduce them. "This is Isabel Banks," I say, without telling him who she is exactly. I can hardly call her my girlfriend, or anything of that nature, but to call her my business partner feels like a truly inadequate description for the woman I'm in love with... at least it does to me.

Izzy holds out her hand and Brett takes it, raising it to his lips and kissing her fingers, which makes me want to do something very uncharacteristic... namely, punch him. Except I don't need to because Izzy pulls her hand away, which makes me smile.

Brett turns to me again. "You're a lucky son-of-a-bitch," he says, shaking his head. "I remember you always did screw the hottest girls around when we were at college... and it seems nothing's changed."

Before I can tell him how offensive he's being and to get lost, Izzy turns to him and says, "I assume you didn't have the same luck yourself?" tilting her head to one side. "But with that attitude, I'm not surprised." She takes my hand in hers and pulls me away from the bar, and I follow, gladly. Once we're far enough away, she stops walking, takes a large sip of her wine, and looks up at me. "I'm sorry," she says.

"What for? I was gonna say something very similar... only with a few expletives thrown in, just for good measure. What he said was offensive, and I'm the one who should be apologizing."

"Why?"

"Well, he was a vague acquaintance of mine."

"I'm glad he wasn't a friend." She shakes her head.

"No, he was never that."

She looks down at my tie for a moment and then says, "I—I didn't mean... with my outburst... I didn't mean to imply that you and I... that I think you see me in that way, or..."

"Izzy..." I interrupt her rambling speech and she looks up, startled... presumably because I've called her by that name again. "Stop apologizing. You didn't imply anything. You just put an obnoxious asshole in his place, like the true alpha woman that you are."

125

She frowns, and I smile, and then she realizes I'm kidding – or at least trying to lighten the moment – and she smiles too.

"I'm not an alpha woman."

"You were doing a damn fine impression of one just then." I'm still smiling, and she shakes her head slowly from side to side, taking another sip of her wine. I copy her, only now noticing that we're still holding hands... and being as she doesn't seem to mind, I grip on to her a little tighter.

We've made it to nine-thirty and I haven't punched anyone... yet. I've come close a few times, with guys who've literally just stood and stared at Izzy, like she's a piece of meat, but I've controlled myself... just. I think the wine's helping. We've both finished our fourth glass, and Izzy's gone to the restroom while I wait by the bar. As she walked across the room, I noticed most of the men around her followed her every move, and it made me angry at my fellow man I'll admit I've been admiring Izzy all night, but I admire her every other day, too. And there's nothing superficial in my admiration. I love her brain, and her smile and the sparkle in her eyes, just as much as I love her body, and I know I always will.

"Mason? Is that you?"

The familiar voice makes my skin tingle... but not in a good way, and I turn to see Calvin Hart standing a few feet away. He hasn't changed a bit. He's still tall, dark and handsome, his arrogance still hidden behind a thin veneer of smoothness. Hanging off of his arm is an exquisite woman. She's easily five foot ten, with a slender figure and short blonde hair.

"Calvin." I plaster on a smile and hold out my hand for him to shake.

"It's good to see you," he says, once we've both released each other from a bruising grip. "Are you here alone?"

"No. My... my date's just gone to the ladies' room."

"Oh." He nods his head like he doesn't believe me, and for a moment, I don't blame him. Because despite everything that's happened... the holding hands, the touch of her skin, the smiles, the laughter, the flirting… despite my love and admiration, Izzy isn't my date. I asked her here on a lie, and she deserves better than that.

She deserves better than me.

Chapter Eight

Isabel

I open the door to the ladies' room, stepping out into the reception hall, to be greeted by a wall of noise and warmth, which makes my head spin. Okay, so the four glasses of red wine might also have something to do with that, but there's no getting away from the fact that there are a lot of people in here.

I hook my purse over my shoulder and straighten my dress over my hips as I step away from the door, smiling to myself. I really wasn't sure about wearing this dress, even though Noah advised me to. He made a point of reiterating his suggestion several times before he went home on Sunday lunchtime, and in the end, I did. It had nothing to do with making Mason jealous. I'm not into playing those kinds of games. It was just that, by the time I sat down with Noah on Sunday morning, I'd had the chance to think about what he'd said on Friday night. I still wasn't willing to admit he could be right – because I never am – but I was willing to admit that giving up was futile. Apart from anything else, I don't even know how to give up on loving Mason, so I decided to wear this dress and see what happened.

There's no denying he noticed me. Right from the moment I opened my door when he called for me, he got that look in his eyes again… the one I called 'fire' and Noah called 'burning desire'. I still think 'fire' is a more accurate description, but just seeing that look was enough to make me forget my manners… or at least forget to ask him inside. He didn't mind that I left him standing out in the hallway, though, and when he helped me into his car, he said I looked 'stunning', which took me by surprise. Of course, compliments are a two-way street; we've established that. So I told him he looked impressive. I'm still not sure why I chose that adjective. I could've just said 'lovely', but I didn't… I said impressive. That seemed to confuse Mason too, but luckily he didn't ask for an explanation… he just smiled and closed the door.

I wasn't sure what to say then. I certainly didn't want to drive all the way to Boston in silence… especially not when I'd decided not to give up on loving him, so I started a conversation, and to be on the safe side, I made it about work, and updated him on my session with Vanessa and Ian. I'm not sure how wise that was, being as it led us into talking about sex… yet again. But then Mason turned the conversation around to personality types… at least I think it was him who did that. I don't think it was me.

Either way, analyzing him was fun… even if I did stupidly ask him whether he likes sex. I don't know what came over me then, but he answered me, much to my surprise, and with an alarmingly honest response. He said he'd become more choosy as he's gotten older, and I wanted to ask him to stop the car then… so he could look at me properly and I could ask him to choose me. I couldn't do that… not in real life. I'm too shy… and I was too scared he might reject me. So instead I turned the conversation back to personality types, and he surprised me again by being so willing to laugh at himself.

What threw me completely was when he called me 'Izzy'. No-one's ever done that before, and it sounded strange on his lips… strange, but special. I wished the setting could have been more romantic, because he started analyzing me then, and he wasn't wrong. I can be a romantic at heart… sometimes.

He wasn't wrong about most of his assessments of me, actually. They were very insightful, although they were also too generous and very kind. I'm not the paragon he painted me to be, but it felt like he'd taken all my personality traits and turned them into positives.

When he said that I'm a person who falls hard, I wanted to tell him he was right. I wanted to explain that I've fallen for him, but it was at that moment he got confused about the turnings and had to concentrate on getting us into Boston… and I didn't feel like I could turn the conversation back there again. It would have been contrived, and I worried it might have looked like I was trying too hard.

Of course, there haven't been any opportunities to say anything to him since… not about falling for him, anyway. Although he brought up personality types again, just briefly, after I put his friend – or rather acquaintance – in his place. I guess that was kind of alpha of me, but the man was being obnoxious at the time… and Mason agreed with me.

Fortunately, everyone else we've met since has been much more pleasant. There was a man called Marcus, who was married to a woman whose name I can't remember. They were nice enough. He works for a large clinic in New York and they'd come here just for the reunion. She made a point of saying they'd left their kids with her mom, and were making the most of having a long weekend. She kept looking up at Marcus while she was talking, and was clinging onto his arm, and I couldn't help but be reminded of Vanessa and Ian…

We also met a couple called Lance and Laura, which I thought was very alliterative. Lance works exclusively with children, which was fascinating. It was a field I considered entering while I was studying at college, although I decided against it, fearing I might find it too traumatic. We talked for quite a while, over our second glass of wine, and I enjoyed the conversation. It's the kind of thing I imagined us doing when Mason told me we were coming here specifically for work… gleaning information from people who are experts in their own field. It was useful, but whether we are here specifically for work, I'm not so sure… because this has felt like the polar opposite of a business function. Not only have we drunk four glasses of wine each – the last one of which is definitely going to my head – but we've laughed, we've flirted – or at least, I have – we've talked incessantly, about all kinds of things, mostly not work-related at all… and Mason's been so attentive too. He's been by my side the whole time, making sure I'm okay, introducing me to his friends, like I'm his date, even though he's never referred to me as such… or in any way that wasn't professional. Above and beyond all of that, though, he's been touching me. There's been nothing inappropriate – nothing untoward – but there's barely been a minute during the evening when he hasn't had his hands on me, most often in the small of my back, his fingers touching my bare skin. I'm not complaining. I've enjoyed every second.

I just wish I knew what it meant… or if it means anything at all.

My head's still spinning, but I glance over toward the bar, where Mason said he'd wait for me, and sure enough, he's still there. He's talking to someone, but he looks in my direction, and our eyes meet, a smile crossing his lips at the same time as mine twitch upwards. My heart flips over in my chest, but I mentally slap myself. I've got to stop reading too much into this. He's just being a gentleman… right?

Right.

He raises his hand, waving me over and I walk across the thickly piled carpet, wishing I'd ignored Noah's advice about the shoes. I'm not convinced they do anything to my legs at all, but they're killing my feet.

As I approach, Mason takes a step away from his friend, who I notice is accompanied by a very beautiful woman, and he reaches out to me, taking my hand in his and pulling me close to him… closer than before, so I'm standing right beside him, with his arm around my waist. This feels different, but in a nice way.

"Calvin," he says to his friend, "let me introduce Isabel Banks."

I vaguely recall Mason mentioning someone called Calvin during our conversation the other day, when he was asking me why I'd chosen to complete my training at the Elleston Clinic. The man in front of me is not as tall as Mason, and he's more athletic than muscular, but there's no denying he's handsome, and he smiles down at me, with a slight twinkle in his dark eyes.

"It's a pleasure to meet you," he says, holding out his hand, which I shake, rather than getting into that whole finger-kissing thing the other man did earlier. I glance in the direction of the woman standing beside him, who's looking around the room, and he adds, "This is my wife, Naomi."

She turns, on hearing her name, and I say, "It's nice to meet you."

Her smile is a little half-hearted, and although she's looking at me, it's clear she's struggling to focus, and I wonder if she's even more drunk than I am. She doesn't say a word though, and just turns away again as I look up at Mason, who raises his eyebrows.

"I believe you used to work at the Elleston Clinic?" I say to Calvin, before the silence becomes too awkward.

"Yes, I did. That was years ago though."

"Hmm… Mason said it was before my time." I hope he won't think I'm suggesting he's old.

"Oh? Do you work there?" he says.

"I completed my training there, before I moved to Sturbridge in the summer."

"You moved out of Boston to sleepy Sturbridge?" There's more than a hint of disdain in his voice, and I take an instant disliking to him, even before he says, "You weren't interested in having a career then?"

"It can't be about the money for all of us." Mason comes to my defense… not that I need him to, although it's nice to have him on my side, especially against a man with an ego the size of Calvin's.

"I was interested in helping people," I say for myself. "I wasn't getting that from the Elleston Clinic, so I didn't see the point of staying on there."

He shrugs his shoulders. "I will admit, their policies are a little cut-throat."

"And yours aren't?" Mason says.

"I run a tight ship." Calvin narrows his eyes at Mason before he looks back at me, smiling. "I have my own clinic now… it's quite a lot bigger than Mason's place. I started it about five years ago and I've already got nine associates working under me, with another two starting in the New Year. You might have heard of it… it's called CHC."

"I can't say I have." I shake my head. "And it's not Mason's place. It's our place."

Mason's grip around my waist tightens slightly and I wonder if I've said the wrong thing, even though I've told the truth.

Calvin tilts his head to one side, frowning slightly. "Oh, I see. You two work together, do you?"

"Yes. We're partners."

"In every sense of the word... evidently," he mutters under his breath, just loud enough for me to hear. Before I can ask what he means, he says, "What's he like to work with?" nodding in Mason's direction.

I sigh and bite my bottom lip, as though I'm pretending to think... and I notice Calvin's eyes drop to my mouth, settling there for a moment. The last thing I want to do is to attract the attentions of this egotistical, arrogant man, and I release my bottom lip straight away and say, "Professionally, he's a brilliant teacher. I've learned more working with Mason for the last couple of months than I did during the whole of my time at college, and at the Elleston Clinic, put together. He's got a gift for this field... and I think anyone who works with him, or is treated by him, should consider themselves very fortunate indeed."

There's a moment of hushed silence, and then Calvin glances to his right, and says, "That's Carolyn Walsh, isn't it? I need to catch up with her. I've been trying to head-hunt her for ages. Do excuse us, won't you? It's been lovely meeting you."

I'm not sure which of us he's talking to, but it doesn't matter, because before we have the chance to reply, he drags his bored-looking wife away.

"Wow," Mason says, his mouth quite close to my ear, and I look up to see he's smiling down at me... with that fiery look in his eyes again, which is very distracting. "Was that you being an eager to help beta, or a loyal to a fault sigma?"

"Both? Neither?" I say, feeling confused still by the look in his eyes.

"Well, whichever it was, thank you for the glowing reference. Even if it's not true, it got rid of Calvin."

"Who said it's not true?"

He frowns slightly. "You mean... all that was for real?"

"Yes."

"In that case, thank you." His smile returns. "Calvin was quite competitive at college," he says, turning me toward him so we're facing each other and then bringing up his free hand and resting it on my waist. I can hardly breathe, being held like this, and I lick my lips, staring up at him for a moment or two, until he says, "Well, I guess he still is."

"Really? I didn't notice."

He chuckles. "It used to really get to me... especially when he made it personal."

"Does it still get to you?" I ask.

"No... not when I've got you here, singing my praises." His smile becomes the most perfect grin. "And anyway, I'm not competitive... not anymore."

"Hmm..." I muse, leaning into him slightly, feeling the warmth of his body seep into mine. "No... you're not."

"Oh, are you saying it doesn't fit with my beta/gamma/sigma personality, then?" he says, his eyes twinkling.

"I have absolutely no idea. I've had far too much to drink to work it out."

His smile fades, and he takes a deep breath, his chest expanding into me. "I know how you feel," he says, tilting his head. "I—I've just realized... there's no way I can drive."

The reality of his words hits me like a blast of fresh air, and although I'm still feeling light-headed, I register the seriousness of our situation.

"How are we going to get home?" I ask, looking up at him.

"Good point," he says. "But on the bright side, we are in a hotel, so I'm guessing they have rooms."

"You think? With all these people here?"

He shrugs his shoulders and pulls away from me, letting me go, which I'm not sure I like. I was enjoying being held by him.

"I can go ask," he says. "You stay here, and I'll find out whether they've got a couple of rooms for the night."

"Okay."

He takes a step or two away and then turns back. "Don't go anywhere, will you?"

"No." I shake my head and he smiles, and then walks off into the crowd.

Left standing by myself, I feel a little unsteady on my feet, and I move closer to the bar, leaning against it, and wondering whether Mason did this on purpose. He must have known he couldn't drink if he was going to drive us home... and he could easily have stayed sober, if he'd wanted to. Although he did just say 'rooms', not 'room', which I guess means he doesn't want to spend the night with me. So, regardless of the fact that he's just been holding me in his arms, and looking at me with fire in his eyes, it looks like I'm overthinking things... yet again.

Mason

I make my way through the crowded room, wishing I could have been honest with Izzy, right from the start. Not only does she deserve it, but if I'd told her the truth – that I love her and want to be with her – then we'd have been here on a date. I could have tried to find a way to suggest we get a room together... and make use of it. Instead of which, I'm going to have to get us two rooms, and probably lie awake all night, ruing yet another missed opportunity... probably the best one I'm ever gonna get.

There are a couple of people already waiting at the reception desk, so I stand in line, waiting... and thinking. Because while this isn't a date, and I'm fully aware of that, I'm also aware of the fact that I've had my hands on Izzy for most of the evening, and she hasn't once objected, even just now, when I was holding her and looking down into her eyes. That all came about, of course, because Calvin had doubted Izzy's existence. So, when she came back from the ladies' room, I went all alpha male on her and put my arm around her, pulling her close to me and claiming her in the only way I could. Even once I'd proved she was a real person, and not a figment of my imagination, I still wasn't sure Calvin believed she was here with me, which of course she isn't... not in the way I'd led him to believe. But what could he say? He couldn't call me a liar in front of her. Not that I needed to worry... as usual with Calvin, he was more interested in talking about himself, presumably intending to impress Izzy. It didn't work, I don't think. In fact, I got the feeling she didn't like him very much, especially after he made that comment about her leaving Boston and moving out to Sturbridge because she didn't care about her career. It was meant as a jibe at me, of course, but Izzy wasn't to know that, and I loved the way she responded to him. She showed nothing but contempt for his clinic, of which he was being so boastful, and then embarrassed him by pointing out that my clinic is actually hers too. I got a little worried then that he might pick up on the fact that we're business partners... and nothing else. But I heard his whispered comment about us being partners 'in every sense of the word', so I guess he didn't work out that this is all fake, thank God... because I also noticed the slight change in the way he looked at Izzy after that... like he wanted to consume her. I couldn't believe he could do that, while his wife was standing right beside him... but he did. *Asshole.*

Izzy didn't seem fazed by his attentions, though. It was then that he asked her what it was like to work with me... and I'll admit I was intrigued by how she was going to answer that. She took her time, mulling it over, and I wondered if she was trying to work out how not to offend me in front of Calvin. But then she blew me away. She paid me the biggest compliment of my professional career... of my life, actually. Sure, I've had clients thank me in the past for helping them, but I've never had someone who matters – someone who actually gets this business – say anything like that about me. Calvin hated it, of course, and made a lame excuse to get away, claiming to have seen someone we used to know. I know he invented that, because not only does the thought of him 'head-hunting' anyone sound ridiculous, but I've never met anyone called Carolyn Walsh in my life. There was a Caroline Fletcher on our course, and I think there might have been someone called Monica Walsh, who wasn't actually studying psychology at all, but who used to hang out with a couple of people who were. So where he got the name Carolyn Walsh from, I don't know.

Either way, I was glad to be rid of him. It gave me a chance to be alone with Izzy, even if we were still in a room full of people. And it gave me a chance to thank her for her compliment, which she reassured me was genuine… and that's when I turned her toward me and put my hand on her waist. My other arm was still around her, so that meant I was effectively holding her. It was like a dream come true for me… I was holding Izzy in my arms and as far as I was concerned, if the world had ended there and then, I'd have been a happy man. She looked up into my eyes at that moment, and while I expected to see confusion, and to be told to back off, or at least to be asked what the hell I thought I was doing, what actually happened was that we just stared at each other. I think she licked her lips, but I can't remember anything else, other than the look in her dark brown eyes… which was a little baffling. It was as though there was some kind of expectation there… but expectation of what? I have no idea…

"Can I help you, sir?"

I startle back to my senses and notice that the line in front of me has disappeared.

"Oh… yes. Sorry." I step forward and the blonde receptionist gives me her best smile, which does nothing for me whatsoever. "Do you have two rooms, please?"

"For tonight?" she says.

No, for the second Thursday in February. "Yes, for tonight." I'm the one who's drunk, so why is she asking such stupid questions?

"I think we're fully booked." She bites on her bottom lip. "I'll just check…"

She taps on the keyboard in front of her, studying the screen, before tapping again, and I wonder what I'll do if there's no availability. I guess I'll just have to find another hotel, get a cab to take us there, and come back for my car tomorrow. It's not like I have any choice. I can't drive anywhere…

"You're in luck," she says, looking up at me again with that simpering smile. "We've got a suite available."

"A suite?"

"Yes."

"How many bedrooms does it have?" I ask.

"Only one, but there's a living area with a large couch, if that helps?" She's clearly worked out – quite correctly – that I'm looking for separate sleeping arrangements, and I feel grateful that at least I didn't have to explain myself to her.

"Can I have my key please... room five-twenty." I'm not surprised that it's Calvin who's interrupted my conversation with the receptionist. It's just typical of him... too impatient to wait his turn.

"I'm just seeing to this gentleman," the receptionist says, turning to him with less of a smile, which almost makes me laugh. "Do you want to take the suite, sir?" She looks back at me again.

Before I can reply, Calvin gets there first, leaning on the reception desk and facing me. "Oh, Mason doesn't mind me interrupting, do you?" he says, while holding out his hand for his key. "If you'd been better organized and pre-booked like the rest of us, you wouldn't be standing here trying to get a room, would you?"

"No... I'd be standing here, picking up the key to my room. But either way I'd still be standing here... in front of you." I turn to the receptionist. "I'll take the suite, thanks."

Calvin lets out a whistle, and I glance back at him. He raises his eyebrows. "You must be doing well for yourself," he says.

I don't respond and turn back to the receptionist, who looks up from her screen and says, "That'll be twenty-five hundred dollars... I'll need to take a credit card now, if that's okay."

Twenty-five hundred dollars? "Of course." I try to sound as though I pay that much for a hotel room all the time, as I reach into my back pocket and pull out my wallet, handing over my credit card. It's not the expense I mind... I just wish I was spending twenty-five hundred dollars on a room I was going to be sharing with Izzy, rather than on a suite in which she's going to be sleeping in the bedroom, while I lie awake on the couch... dreaming about what might have been.

"Thank you, Doctor Gould," the receptionist says, having read my name on my credit card, which she hands back to me, together with the room key. "I hope you enjoy your stay."

"Thanks."

I turn and make my way back into the reception hall, ignoring Calvin, my only thoughts being how on earth I'm going to explain to Izzy that we don't have separate rooms. I just hope she doesn't think I've done this on purpose…

"Hey… Mason." I turn at the sound of Calvin's voice as he comes up behind me.

"What?" I know I sound impatient, but that's because I am. I'm fed up with him.

"I was just gonna say… if you need any help keeping Isabel satisfied, you know where I am. Room five-twenty."

"I don't need any help with anything, Calvin. And I'm fairly sure your wife will have something to say if you sneak out of bed in the middle of the night."

He smiles, rolling his eyes at the same time. "Naomi's so high most of the time, she doesn't notice anything."

"Excuse me?" I can't believe I heard that right.

"Naomi takes prescription meds… Valium, to be precise…"

"Enough to make her high?" I say.

He steps closer, lowering his voice. "She had a big problem with anxiety attacks a few years ago, when her career really took off, and she came to the Elleston Clinic…"

"Is that how you met?"

"Yes. She wasn't my patient, you understand. She was being seen by someone else."

"Someone who prescribed Valium?"

"Yeah."

"And now she's addicted?" I guess.

"She's not addicted," he says, stepping away again and going all defensive.

"You're sure about that?"

He pauses for a very telling second and then says, "I'm positive."

I shrug my shoulders. "Okay… well, if you change your mind about that, and you decide she needs to talk to someone, you know where I am."

He stares at me, blinks a few times, pushes his fingers back through his hair, and then turns and walks away.

I think I surprised him with my offer, but I meant every word. Not that Calvin's surprise, or his wife's addiction, are uppermost in my thoughts right now…

I find Izzy exactly where I left her, although she's leaning up against the bar now, rather than standing beside it, which makes me smile.

"Are you okay?" I ask as I approach her.

"I'm fine. I'm just struggling to stay upright."

The thought of her not being upright, but lying down… beneath me… is very distracting. But I have to stop thinking about that, especially as I've yet to break the news to her that we're going to be sharing a room… or at least, a suite.

"How did you get on?" she asks.

"They didn't have any rooms," I reply and her face falls. "But they had a suite."

"A suite?" She frowns.

"Yeah. There's a bedroom and a living area, with a large couch, evidently. So I'll sleep on that."

"Oh… okay."

It's hard to read her. I can't tell whether she's pleased, or disappointed, and even if I could work that out, I'm not sure what it would mean. If she's pleased, is that because she doesn't have to share a room with me, or because – in a way – she does? And if she's disappointed, is that because she'd hoped to have a room entirely to herself, or because she wishes we could spend the night together? I'm so confused by her right now. But then, I'm also quite drunk, which isn't helping.

"Do you want to go up to the suite now? Or would you rather stay down here for a while longer?"

"I certainly don't want anything else to drink," she replies. "And my feet are killing me."

"Shall we go up then?"

"Okay," she says, pushing herself off of the bar and stepping forward a little unsteadily. I take her arm, guiding her through the crowd, and although I'm struck by her lack of enthusiasm, I can't say I'm sorry that – for us at least – the party's over.

Chapter Nine

Isabel

Why didn't I have the courage of my own convictions?

I had the perfect opportunity then to tell Mason that he doesn't need to sleep on the couch, no matter how large it is… because I want him to sleep with me.

Why didn't I say that, instead of losing my nerve and just saying 'okay'?

I'm probably never gonna get another chance like this again… and even if he has clearly gone out of his way to ensure that we don't have to sleep together, I could have tried… just one last time.

We ride up in the elevator, along with another couple, who are staring at each other, and look like they can't wait to rip each other's clothes off. That only heightens my sense of disappointment in myself. If I'd taken my chances back at the bar, and explained to Mason how much I want him, he might be looking at me like that right now too… assuming he didn't turn me down, of course.

Because that would have been awful…

So, maybe, on second thoughts, it was better to have said nothing.

I glance up at him, letting out a slow sigh, in the hope he won't hear it. No… I should've said something, because I think even being rejected would have been better than not knowing.

The doors swish open and the other couple exit first, turning to the left, holding hands and rushing along the corridor, clearly in a hurry to get to their room.

"We're in the Mayflower Suite," Mason says, and I follow the signs to the right, with him a few paces behind. There's no question of us holding hands, or hurrying, although my shoes and the wine aren't helping with that.

The door is right at the end of the hallway, and Mason opens it, waiting for me to pass through ahead of him. He flicks on the lights, and I suck in a breath.

"I—It's beautiful," I say on a whispered breath.

In contrast to the gaudy rooms downstairs, this is a sea of tranquility.

We've walked into the living area, which does indeed have a huge couch, in soft cream leather, along with a dining table and two chairs, a wall-mounted television, and a small desk. The walls are pale blue, and there's a view over the Charles River, and beyond it, the city… its lights twinkling in the darkness. To the right is a door, which is slightly ajar, but through which I can see a bed…

"Do you want a coffee before you go to bed?" Mason asks, putting the room key down on the desk, and adding his wallet and car keys from his pockets.

I don't think I actually want to drink anything else at all, but if I say 'no', it appears the alternative will be going to bed… alone.

"I—I don't think so," I say.

"Okay." He looks around the room. "I guess we'd better turn in then."

God, he really doesn't want me at all.

"I guess. Can I assume the bathroom is in the bedroom?"

He glances around again, clearly noticing – as I have – that there are no other doors in here.

"It must be," he says. "Shall I go in there first? Then you can have the bedroom to yourself afterwards."

"Okay."

He nods, still not looking at me, and heads for the bedroom, pushing the door open and flicking on the lights as he enters.

Part of me wants to follow him, but that would be intrusive... and anyway, he's had more than enough chances to suggest we spend the night together, and he hasn't taken any of them. So clearly it's only me who wants this.

I wander over to the window, looking out on the view of the city, the lights blinking back at me, and I struggle not to cry. I know Noah was right about not giving up, but being here now, so close to Mason, and not being able to do anything about it, is harder than I ever imagined.

I just wish he'd kept it about business tonight, rather than touching me and looking at me like he did... and getting my hopes up...

"We'll have to work out something for the morning." I startle at the sound of Mason's voice and turn around to see he's come back out of the bedroom. He's got his jacket over his arm, and has undone his tie, so it's hanging loose around his neck... and he looks so gorgeous... kinda relaxed and getting ready for bed. Or, to be more precise, getting ready to sleep on the couch, so he doesn't have to sleep with me.

"The morning?"

"Yeah. I'll need to take a shower, but I don't wanna come in there and disturb you. So... maybe you could give me a shout when you're dressed, or something?"

He doesn't even want to come into my room? Could he be any more dismissive?

"Okay," I say and walk over to the bedroom, stepping across the threshold, just as my curiosity gets the better of me, and anger overcomes embarrassment... not for the first time. "What has this evening been about, Mason?" I blurt out, turning around to face him.

"Excuse me?"

"I don't understand." I ignore the catch in my voice and hope he won't notice it, either. "You've been touching me all evening, and while none of it has been inappropriate, I don't understand why you'd do that, if you're not interested in me... which you're clearly not. Was it to humiliate me?"

"Of course not," he says, sounding offended.

"Then why? Why would you bring me here for a business gathering and then treat me like..."

"Treat you like what?"

"Like you care. I know you don't, but it's so unfair to lead me on, to make me think there could be something, when… please, Mason… can't you see how much I want you?"

He stares at me, his eyes widening and I'm just contemplating running into the bedroom to hide my humiliation, when he drops his jacket to the floor and strides over, capturing my cheeks between his hands, and gazing down into my eyes, his own blazing with need. Running is clearly not an option anymore, but before I can apologize for my outburst – or for saying something so stupid and needy – he raises my face slightly and leans down, brushing his lips against mine in a burning kiss. His lips are soft, yet demanding, and I sigh as his tongue darts into my mouth. He groans in reply, and then walks me backwards into the bedroom. Without breaking the kiss, he releases my face and undoes the zipper at the side of my dress, pulling it from my shoulders while we're walking, so it drops to my feet before we've even reached the bed.

Finally, he pulls back, looking down at me and while I want to tell him he doesn't have to do this if he doesn't want to… I don't want him to stop. Not now. Not ever.

"Y—You're not wearing any underwear," he says, stepping away, and gazing down at my body, with a hunger in his eyes that takes my breath away.

"No."

I'm standing in my garter belt and stockings, still wearing my high heels… and absolutely nothing else, and he groans before closing the gap between us and pulling me into his arms.

"Is there a reason for that?" he asks, kissing me again.

"This dress is too low cut to wear a bra." I'm so breathless, I can barely speak.

"I get that," he says, between heated kisses. "But what about panties?"

As he speaks, he reaches down between us, and then between my legs, his fingers instantly finding that sweet spot and I shudder, almost losing my mind at being touched for the first time by someone other than me. The words 'I never wear them around you' are poised on my tongue, but I can't say that, and even in my befuddled state, as he makes slow circling movements with the tips of his fingers, I say, "I just don't like wearing them."

"Never?" he says, leaning back and looking down at me, his fingers stilling, although he doesn't move his hand away.

"Not unless I have to."

He tilts his head to one side. "Does that mean you've been coming into work with no panties on?"

"Yes. Is that a problem?"

He doesn't reply. He just shakes his head and swallows hard… and then he drops to his knees. I miss him instantly. I miss the feeling of his strong arms around me, and his hard, muscular chest, tempered by the soft cotton of his shirt against my skin. I'm tempted to ask him to stand up again, to hold on to me, but then I feel his fingers touching me, parting my smooth lips, before he leans in and runs his tongue over my clitoris.

"Oh…" I struggle to catch my breath. This feels different to his fingers… so much more intimate, but with an intensity that's indescribable.

He shimmies a little closer and on some basic instinct, I raise my right leg and let it hang over his shoulder. I'm exposed to him, and I love it. He flicks his tongue over me and I tremble, reaching down and holding the back of his head, partly for support, but also because I want him to stay just where he is… forever. His tongue swirls across and around me and I slowly circle my hips, grinding against him as he feasts on me. I'm starting to understand the phrase 'being eaten' now, where I never really have before, because I feel like I'm being consumed… gorged upon by a starving man. I feel a familiar tingling in my core, too, and know I'm about to come… and I instantly regret the fact that I'm standing on one leg, in stupidly high heels.

"I—I'm gonna…" I try to warn Mason, but it's too late. My legs quiver, my body shatters, and although I'm aware of his arm coming up around my waist and supporting me, I'm overcome with heat and fire, pleasure pulsing through every vein and sinew, as I scream his name.

Eventually the throbbing sensation fades and I calm slightly, opening my eyes to find I'm still standing, and I look down to see Mason gazing up at me. He lowers my leg to the floor before he says, "That was amazing, Izzy. You taste incredible."

I smile, because he called me 'Izzy', but I can't reply. I seem to have lost the power of speech. Instead, I just watch while he gets to his feet and removes his shoes and socks, before pulling off his tie and unbuttoning his shirt, revealing his toned, muscled chest, covered with a fine layer of dark hair. I reach out and run my fingers through it, while he undoes his pants, lowering them and his underwear and I let my eyes roam downward…

Holy shit.

I don't think I'll ever speak again… and I'll certainly never be able to walk properly after tonight.

He's enormous compared to my dildo, and I raise my eyes to his, wondering if he'll notice my fear.

"Are you okay?" he asks, proving that he has.

How do I ask him if it's normal for a real man to be that size, and whether the dildo I've been using for the last few months is just a cheap imitation? I can't, can I?

"I—I'm fine," I say.

"Are you sure? You look a little scared."

"That's because I've never seen a man who looks quite like that." I lower my eyes again. Yep… he's huge. And I guess, being as I've never seen a naked man at all, that wasn't a lie, was it?

He smiles. "Quite like what?" he says, teasing, I think.

"Quite so big." There's no point in pretending.

His smile widens. "Thank you… but there's nothing to be scared about. I won't hurt you."

Somehow I think he's being optimistic, but I can't say that either, and instead I let him take my hand and pull me over to the bed. He sits me down and although I expect him to remove my shoes, he doesn't. Instead, he pushes me backwards, so I'm lying across the mattress, and then he kneels up. I go to part my legs, but he grabs one, pulling it up and over his shoulder, twisting my body, so I'm on my side, his arm around my raised thigh, while he straddles my lower leg. Then he looks down into my eyes, and I feel the head of his arousal against my entrance, before he pushes inside, flexing his hips, and pulling me onto him at the same time.

"Oh... Oh, God..." I grind out the words between gritted teeth as he stretches me.

"Okay?" he says, stilling, and I nod my head, trying to relax as he sinks in a little deeper. There's no pain, but then there wouldn't be... I broke that barrier a while ago. Instead, all I can feel is the deeply satisfying, exhilarating sensation of being penetrated... taken. He inches further inward, until I'm fully impaled and he stares down at me, the fire in his eyes igniting something deep within me. It's not a physical feeling at all. It's more than that. I've found the part of me that's been missing all my life. I've been lost without it... and now, I feel whole, at last. Mason shudders slightly and then he lowers his gaze, his eyes grazing over my body, pausing at my breasts, before moving lower still... to where we're now joined. Then he pulls back and I open my mouth to tell him not to break the connection, just as he thrusts right back inside again and I let out a scream of satisfaction as he really starts to move, his arm clamping around my thigh as he pounds into me.

"Fuck... yes..." he growls, grunting with every stroke, and I worry he might reach his climax before I do... because I need to feel this too. I need to know what it's like. The thing is, as much as I'm loving every second of what he's doing, I don't think I can come like this. I don't think I can get there. "Touch yourself," he whispers, like he's read my mind. "Make yourself come... for me."

"Y—You want to watch?" I gaze up at him.

Please say yes. Please say yes.

"More than anything." He pauses for just a moment and then says, "Rub your clit, Izzy."

Oh, God... that's so exciting, hearing him say that.

I don't hesitate. I reach down between my parted legs, recalling my fantasy of having him watch me masturbate, and rub my exposed clit, just like he said. He watches me, and then sucks in a sharp breath as I raise my other hand and tweak my nipples, one at a time, between my thumb and forefinger, rolling them, pulling them, creating incredible sensations in my body as he hammers into me, harder and harder.

"Come for me, Izzy," he yells, and that's all it takes to push me over the edge. I fall through misted clouds and hazy dreams, hearing my voice screaming out for more, begging him to take me. How can it be this good? How can it be this different?

Eventually, the clouds clear and the haze fades and I stare up him, aware that he's let my leg fall back to the bed, that I'm lying on my back and he's leaning over me, his face just an inch from mine.

"Are you okay?" he asks.

"Oh… yes. Did you…?" I feel guilty for missing his climax, but my own was too much for me to take… too much for me to notice anything else.

"Did I what?"

"Did you… finish?" I'm not sure how else to phrase that.

"You mean, did I come?" he says and I nod my head. "No… I'm not done with you yet."

He's not? Does that mean I'm going to get the 'more' I was just screaming for? I hope so.

I smile up at him. "What are you gonna do with me next, then?" I say.

"I'm gonna give you a taste…"

"Of what?"

"Yourself… and me… combined."

With that, he pulls out of me, making me wince, not with pain, but because I don't feel complete without him inside me. He doesn't give me time to think about that, though, and he crawls up my body… upwards and upwards, until I'm face-to-face with his hard, long, shining erection. I can't resist, and I raise my head slightly, kissing the tip, tasting myself on him. I taste good, and I lick around the bulbous head, and then take him into my mouth. He groans and then straightens his body along the length of mine, and flexes his hips, taking my mouth this time.

I moan and sigh, tilting my head back so I can take him deeper. He moves faster and then, with an urgency to his voice, I hear him say, "Fuck… that's good, Izzy. Suck my dick."

I love it when he says things like that… it's so different from the way he normally is with me. But this is just how I want him to be, and I suck him further down my throat.

He stills, seeming to catch his breath, and then moves again, a little harder. "Finger your clit," he says, and I obey, reaching down, spreading my legs wide and rubbing myself. It only takes a matter of minutes before I shatter once more, squealing and screaming beneath him as I buck and writhe through my third orgasm.

He pulls out of my mouth as I calm, and moves back down my body before he flips me over onto my front.

"You're still not finished then?" I say, looking at him over my shoulder.

"Did you notice me coming in your mouth?" he says with a smile.

"No." I think I'd have felt that.

I feel him lift my left foot off of the bed, and undo my shoe, hearing it fall to the floor, before he does the same with the right, and then he places his hands on my hips and lifts my ass off the bed, parting my legs with his own and entering me, giving me his whole length in one go this time.

"Put your hands behind your back," he says, and I turn my head to one side, letting my shoulders take my weight, and raise my hands up, moving them around behind my back. Mason takes hold of them, just above the wrist and pulls me backward, impaling me deeply… so deeply it almost hurts.

"God…" The word escapes through my clenched teeth and I feel him relax, feel his grip loosen on my arms.

"Is this too much?" he says.

"No… no. Don't stop. Please." I know I'm begging, and I don't care.

He doesn't say a word. He just pulls out… about half way, and then slams back into me again, harder and deeper than before, as he grips my arms again and takes me. This is so good… he's so good. He's like everything I've ever wanted… everything I've ever dreamed of.

There's a gentle brutality to him, which I know makes little sense. Although it does… to me. He's attentive and caring, considerate and kind, and yet he takes me so damn hard… like his life depends on it. Mine too. And that's exactly what I need.

"More… please… give me more…" I'm desperate for him, and as I part my legs a little, he stills, and then thrusts really hard and deep inside me, letting out a loud howl.

"Izzy… yes…" he yells and then he swells inside me and shudders, and I feel his release.

I remain completely still, until he flops forward on to me, his chest against my back, and then I feel his arm come around me as he pulls us both over onto our sides… spooning. At least I think that's what this is called.

"I'm sorry," he says in my ear.

I twist slightly so I can look up into his face. He seems genuinely contrite, and I frown. "What on earth for?"

"I wanted you to come again."

I shake my head. "You don't think three orgasms are enough, then?"

"Hell, no." He studies my face for a moment, like he's looking for the answer to a question. "Was that a bit alpha for you?"

"It was certainly very alpha… but I'm not complaining."

He raises my top leg, supporting it and moving inside me, making me aware that he's still hard.

"In which case, you won't mind if I fuck you until you come again… will you?"

I giggle as he takes my hand and moves it between my legs, holding my fingers against my clit as I grind back into him… loving every moment.

Almost as much as I love him.

Mason

I knew Izzy would be good.

I'd watched her in her office, so 'good' was a foregone conclusion. Even 'great' was predicable. But 'the best'? Could I have seen that coming?

I don't know.

But either way, she's the best.

She's like the Izzy of my dreams… and more.

When she stood across the room and told me she wanted me, I couldn't believe my ears. That declaration came on the back of her suggestion that I'd spent the evening humiliating her. I hadn't. I'd spent the evening feeling guilty for the way I'd arranged everything, and I suppose I should have taken that chance to straighten things out with her. Except she was looking up at me, her eyes wide, her body calling out to mine… the words 'please, Mason' echoing between us, and I needed her so much, words failed me.

So I didn't say anything. I just peeled her out of that dress, struggling for breath, because I couldn't believe how good she looked… even though I'd seen it all before.

Her breasts were the first thing to be revealed, and they were just as firm as I remembered them, her nipples hard and dark pink… and perfect. As I lowered her dress, taking in her garter belt, I found it more and more difficult to breathe… and then I thought my heart had stopped when I realized she wasn't wearing any panties. In the office, when I watched her, I hadn't been able to see any, so I had to ask if this was a normal state of affairs for her. She told me it was… and the idea that she's been wandering around at work, with no underwear, was almost too much for me. I had to taste her… so I did. On my knees, where I belong… worshipping her.

She tasted divine. So sweet… like honey. And when she came, she came hard, screaming my name, which sounded so damn good. I remembered how her juices had overflowed onto the office floor beneath her chair, and I lapped her up, swallowing down every drop of her, before I took her over to the bed…

I undressed then, my cock almost unbearably painful by that stage, and I couldn't fail to notice the way Izzy's eyes roamed over my body, until she let them roam south… and then she looked back up at me again, and I saw what looked like fear in her eyes.

That didn't make sense to me, but I had to make sure she was okay… I had to know. So I asked.

She said she was, but I didn't believe her, and eventually, she admitted she'd never seen a man who looked like me before… clarifying that by saying she'd never seen anyone 'quite so big'. I had to smile at her compliment, recalling the size of her dildo, which I guess she'd probably bought because it was nearer the size she's used to, but I reassured her I wouldn't hurt her… because that's something I'll never do. Then I pushed her down gently on the bed, and once I'd gotten into a comfortable position – for both of us – I entered her. She seemed a bit shocked, but then I guess she had made the point that she wasn't used to taking anything too big… so I gave her a minute to get used to the sensations…

It was a difficult minute. All I wanted to do was take her… hard. But I had to give her time, so I inched inside her really slowly, until she'd taken my entire length. Then I gazed down at her, feeling the connection between us… it was more than just physical. I felt as though, until that moment, my life had been like a puzzle with a missing piece. In joining us together, I'd found that piece and made myself complete. I didn't dare hope she felt the same, but the feeling made me shudder, as I looked down at her body beneath my own, taking in the beauty of her rounded, firm breasts, her flat stomach and slightly flared hips… and that miraculous place where we became one.

She was tight, clenching around me, and I knew I'd have to move, even though I didn't want to break that moment, so I pulled out and then plowed straight back into her again, with a force I've never used on any woman before. She screamed then, but I knew it wasn't pain… it was pleasure. And I knew she wanted more… which is why I suggested she should touch herself. I wanted to watch her, just like I said. I wanted it more than anything. Seeing her come apart was miraculous, and even though I'd seen it before, this was different. She really let go… she screamed my name, and she begged me to take her… the word 'please' echoing around the room.

I wanted to tell her she never needs to beg. Hell, she never even needs to ask. I'm hers. She can take me whenever she wants.

She confused me then, though, by asking whether I'd come. She didn't exactly phrase it that way, but that was what she meant. It seemed strange that she didn't know, but I didn't make a big deal out of that. I just told her I hadn't… because I wasn't finished with her yet. I don't think I'll ever be finished with her…

At that moment, I remembered her licking her dildo in the office, and I knew what I wanted. I wanted her to lick me clean, too.

I never expected her to do so with such enthusiasm, but she did, and it was all I could do not to come in her mouth, especially after I'd suggested she should rub her clit again. She came really fast… and hard. But that seems to be the norm for Izzy.

I wanted her to come again after that… so I flipped her over onto her front, and I took her so damn hard. I've never fucked like that in my life, holding her arms behind her back, and thrusting into her like my life depended on it. It did, I think. I know I couldn't have stopped… and when she begged me for more, I couldn't take it. I had to come. When I did, I felt like my spine was going to break… like my lungs were going to burst.

And yet… I haven't made her come again. Yet.

I catch my breath and fall forward, letting go of her arms as I rest my chest against her back, before I put my arm around her and pull us both over onto our sides. I'm still hard inside her… but I think I'm going to be hard for a while yet.

"I'm sorry," I say in her ear.

She pulls away slightly and twists around, so I can look down at her, which is nice, because she's kinda mussed up… just fucked, and utterly beautiful.

"What on earth for?" she says with a frown.

"I wanted you to come again."

She shakes her head, her frown fading. "You don't think three orgasms are enough, then?"

"Hell, no," I say instinctively. A lifetime of orgasms isn't enough…

I take a moment to really look at her… I study her deep brown eyes, noting the flecks of amber in the irises. I smile at the way her lips twitch upward, and the soft smoothness of her porcelain pure skin, and even though her hair's a mess now, it still looks incredible… because I'm the one who made it like that.

"Was that a bit alpha for you?" I ask, wondering if she's serious, if I've gone too far.

She puts my mind at rest immediately, smiling as she says, "It was certainly very alpha, but I'm not complaining."

Thank God for that… because I need to feel her come again.

I move downwards just a fraction, and then raise her top leg, holding onto it, as I flex my hips.

"In which case, you won't mind if I fuck you until you come again… will you?" I say, and she giggles. That sound makes my cock twitch inside her, and I take her hand with my free one, moving it down between her legs and pressing her fingers against her swollen clit.

She grinds her hips back into me, letting out a sigh, and I release her hand, leaving her to her own devices as I take her.

We've been making love for nearly four hours.

It's been non-stop, from that first taste of her, to our last gentle fuck, which I took a lot slower, lying between her parted legs and grinding into her, while she rubbed her clit, until we both came.

We've been curled up together for the last twenty minutes, facing each other, our limbs entwined, unwilling to be parted even for a second… and although it's gone two in the morning, and I know we should go to sleep, I don't want to. Not yet.

Still, I guess I have to give her the option.

"What time is your first appointment tomorrow?" I ask, running my fingers down her spine, which makes her shudder.

"Ten-thirty," she says, raising her top leg and bringing it across mine.

"Mine's ten. So, we're gonna have to leave here by eight. We'll both need to go home and change."

"Yes, I suppose we will."

"In which case, do you think we ought to get some sleep?"

She looks up at me. "Must we?"

I turn her onto her back and straddle her, raising myself above her. "Not if you don't want to… no."

She giggles and I roll us over the other way again, so I'm on my back and she's between my legs, my cock pressing into her. She's about to move, to straddle me, like she did about an hour and a half ago, when she came spectacularly on my cock, while I played with her breasts, pulling at her nipples and making her squeal with pleasure… but I stop her, placing my hands on her hips.

"What's wrong?" she asks.

"Nothing."

I smile, and then lift her up, turning her around, so she's facing the other way.

"Um…" She sounds doubtful.

"Sit on my cock," I say and she twists around, looking back at me. "Like this?"

"Yes. Kneel over me and sit back on my cock."

She does as I say, putting her knees on either side of my thighs, and then she shifts backward, giving me the perfect view of her beautiful ass, while I guide the head of my cock to her soaking entrance. She settles back, sighing as she takes my length, clearly more used to it now.

"Now… kneel up," I tell her.

She turns around again, looking down at me. "You want me to kneel up?"

"Yes."

"You mean, you don't want me to… to do it like I did earlier?"

I smile, recalling the spectacular way she rode my cock before… and while I'm not averse to a repeat performance, I've got something else in mind this time.

"No," I say. "Now… kneel up." I repeat myself and she faces away from me, doing as I say, kneeling right up, so my cock is halfway out of her.

"What do I do now?" she asks.

"Give me your hands."

She moves them around, and I take them in mine, holding them firmly behind her back.

"You realize I won't be able to touch myself," she says.

"Yes. But you won't need to."

Before she can ask me any more questions, I raise my hips, impaling her. She yelps and then shudders.

"W—What was that?" she says, stuttering in a breath.

"That was me."

"I know… but what did you do? It felt different."

"I hit your g-spot."

How can she not know this? Not that I care… she feels too good. "C —Could you do that again?" she says.

"Of course."

I flex my hips a second time… and then a third, building a rhythm, clenching her hands behind her as she strains against me. Her juices trickle downward, forming pools at the base of my cock and before long her legs shudder and her body twitches.

"This can't be… I'm… oh God… I'm…" Her words are incoherent, and then she lets out a scream as she comes, gushing over me, in a spectacular orgasm, every muscle in her body tightening, as she grips me… and I thrust upward one last time, filling her deeply.

I release her arms, and she flops backward onto my chest, nestling into me as I fold her up in a warm embrace. She twists and looks up at me, a smile etched on her lips.

"I didn't think that was possible…"

"What? Coming without clitoral stimulation? G-spot orgasms? Or female ejaculation? Because believe me, it's all possible. At least it is with you."

"I think you'll find it was you who made all of that happen."

"I just released the inner alpha in you," I say, and she smiles.

"Maybe…"

"But before we take this any further, I need the bathroom." Aside from anything else, she just came over me… and I need to clean up.

"Okay," she says, and kneels again, rocking forward until my cock pops out of her, before she flops over onto her side.

I slide off of the bed, unable to stop the smile that forms on my lips, because she looks so totally fucked right now… and it's a sight to behold. She's still wearing her stockings and garter belt, although they're a little twisted, and her pussy is pink and swollen… and very used… by me. She lets out a sigh and rolls over onto her front, crawling up the bed and resting her head on the pillow, and although I'm tempted to get back into bed with her, I need the bathroom.

"I won't be a minute," I tell her, and head over to the corner of the room, and into the white-tiled bathroom.

This feels so different to when I came in here earlier, before she told me she wanted me… before she practically begged me to take her… thank God. I recall standing here a few hours ago, staring at my reflection in the mirror and deciding that tonight was going to be a blow-out, and there was nothing I could do about it. As it turned out, I didn't need to worry. Tonight's been the best night of my life. It's been different, that's for sure. I've certainly been different. I've taken the lead and been more dominant than I usually am, and while I've got no idea whether that's the alpha coming out in me… it seems I can't help myself with Izzy. She does something to me. She makes me want more.

I turn out the light and walk back out into the bedroom, a smile settling on my lips, because while I might want more, Izzy's eyes are closed, her breathing is even and steady and I know before I climb into bed beside her, that she's fast asleep. And that's just fine with me, because there's always tomorrow, and the next day… and forever.

I settle beside her, pulling her close in my arms and she lets out a snuffled moan before she nestles against me.

This feels good… like another piece of that puzzle just slotted into place.

Something wakes me.

A noise, I guess. Or maybe the fact that I'm not in my own bed, but in a hotel. It's light outside, but not very light, and I gaze across the room, noting the leaden sky and droplets of rain on the window. Even the appalling weather can't dampen my mood. Nor can it stop me from smiling, because the memory of last night, of Izzy and how wonderful it was to finally be with her, is all I can think about. I turn over, my cock already hard, and put my hand out to touch her.

"Good mor—" My voice fades as I realize the bed is empty.

I'm alone.

I sit up, pushing down the covers slightly, and look around the room, letting out a sigh of relief, when I see Izzy's dress and shoes are still lying on the floor.

She hasn't left then.

"Izzy?" I call out.

"I'm in the bathroom." Her reply is muffled, and I smile, twisting around in the bed and sitting up on the edge, letting my feet rest on the thickly piled carpet. I stand and take the first couple of steps toward the closed door in the corner of the room, when I realize I probably shouldn't. She clearly wants some privacy, and no matter what we did last night, I don't have the right to just barge in on her.

So, I settle down on the bed again, lying back on the pillows, and pulling up the covers, before I turn on the TV to check the time on the breakfast news program. I ignore the headlines flashing across the bottom of the screen about a slump in the dollar, and a scandal involving a minor presidential aide, because I don't care about any of that. All I care about right now is that it's only six-thirty. We've got an hour and a half until we have to leave. We can easily spend forty-five minutes in bed, and both be showered and dressed in plenty of time. That's if we skip breakfast, of course, and hopefully, breakfast won't be uppermost is Izzy's mind this morning. I know it's the last thing I'm thinking about, because it's just occurred to me that, if we shower together, we could spend an hour in bed first…

The door to the bathroom opens, and on a waft of steam, Izzy comes out into the bedroom. She's wearing a white bathrobe, wrapped tightly around her, and has clearly showered already. It's a struggle to hide my disappointment that she didn't wait for me, because the thought of taking her in the shower, of hearing her scream my name, while she clutches onto me and I come deep inside her…

Oh, shit.

I stare at her. How could I have been such an inconsiderate idiot?

"The President has been placed in a very difficult position," the voice says on the TV, and I reach for the remote, turning it off and focusing on Izzy again. God, what have I done to her? She won't even look at me. Which I guess means she's probably worked out what a loser I am too. I came inside her three – no, four – times last night, and I didn't use a condom. Not once.

I kneel up on the bed and move toward her.

"Izzy…"

She startles, and her eyes lock on my erection before she blushes and looks up at my face. There's no hunger in her eyes this morning. In fact, she looks more embarrassed than anything… no, I'll go further than that; she looks mortified, like she'd rather be anywhere but here.

"I—I…" I say, but she holds up her hand and I stop speaking. Whatever she needs to say, I deserve it. I've been irresponsible and even though I can't regret what we did, she's entitled to be angry with me.

"Please," she says in a soft whisper. "Can you just let me… I—I need to say sorry."

What the fuck?

"What the hell for?"

"Because I tricked you."

She tricked *me*? I think she's got that the wrong way around. I'm the one who tricked her into coming to this reunion in the first place, so I've got no idea what she thinks she's guilty of.

"You tricked me?" I say.

"Well, 'tricked' might be the wrong way of phrasing it. But you'd made it very clear that last night was about work, and rather than just accepting that, I practically begged you to sleep with me. We were both drunk, and I should've just let you sleep on the couch, like you wanted, rather than forcing you to… well, you know."

"You didn't force me." How can she possibly think that? I was the forceful one. I've never been like that before. Not with anyone.

"It's nice of you to take it like that, but I still shouldn't have done it, and I'm sorry. I—I hope this won't cause a problem between us at work. I hope it's not gonna change anything…"

She wants us to go back to how we were before? Is she serious? How the hell are we supposed to act like last night didn't happen? And why would we want to?

Unless… was I *that* bad?

I kneel back and grab the covers, pulling them over myself, to hide my erection, which doesn't seem to be listening to her rejection and is still as hard as nails.

"Things won't be difficult between us, will they?" she asks, making it clear she expects me to answer, even though I'm not sure how.

I push my fingers back through my hair and, because I can't think what else to say, I just reply with, "Of course not."

She smiles, biting her bottom lip just briefly and then bends and grabs her dress from the floor, before she darts back into the bathroom, without another word.

I stare at the blank surface of the door, imagining myself – or at least the alpha version of myself – striding over there and barging through the door. I'd rip off that bathrobe, push her naked body back up against the wall and lift her into my arms before impaling her on my cock, and then I'd take her so damn hard. As I was fucking her, I'd tell her never to say sorry to me ever again. As I pounded into her, I'd tell her I never want to hear anything about regrets either. Because I don't regret a single thing about last night. I don't even regret not using a condom.

And then I'd come inside her, deep and hard, just to prove the goddamn point.

The sound of a tap running inside the bathroom brings me to my senses, and I realize she'll probably be coming out again soon. I can't just sit here naked. That'll only embarrass her more. So I get up and walk around to the other side of the bed, where I find my pants, shirt and underwear lying on the floor. I pick up all my clothes and dump them on the bed, pulling on my underwear and pants, because my underwear alone isn't doing a great job of concealing my erection, and then I sit on the edge of the bed, wondering how it all went so wrong.

I thought last night was perfect, but she clearly regrets it all.

I don't. But I can't turn back the clock. I can't turn Isabel into Izzy again.

Chapter Ten

∽

Isabel

I fasten the zipper on my dress and straighten the skirt, wishing now that I'd worn something else. Something less revealing. Because at seven o'clock in the morning, this dress feels very inappropriate.

I glance up at my reflection for a moment, trying to ignore the look in my eyes, which only speaks of guilty regrets… and I study my hair instead, hoping there's a hairdryer in the bedroom, because I look a mess.

I feel a mess too.

I was telling the truth to Mason just now, when I said I was drunk last night, and I shouldn't have begged him to have sex with me.

That wasn't the whole story, though, because while I meant to apologize for throwing myself at him, in my drunken state, what I meant to say was that I wished we'd talked first. I'm not denying that I wanted him, or that everything he did to me last night was incredible. It was perfect. It was everything I've ever imagined it would be… and more. I'm sure he knows that, though, given the amount of noise I made. It's just that I wish we'd been able to talk before he'd taken my dress off and shown me what a real man can do. That way, I might have a clue what's going to happen next.

As it is, I'm feeling kinda lost.

Like I said to him, I don't want things to change between us professionally, but I hope he won't expect everything to be like it was before. That's the last thing I want. In an ideal world, I'd like us to carry on from last night, and somehow find a way of working together, while also having that conversation we should have had before we got carried away last night... *and* hopefully building our relationship from there. Assuming he wants a relationship with me, of course.

The problem is, if he doesn't want the same thing, and is just thinking we can go back to how we were, then what am I supposed to do? How am I ever going to look him in the eye at work, knowing what he can do to me?

"Why?" I whisper, unfolding the tiny toothbrush the hotel has provided, and squeezing out some toothpaste before running it under the tap.

Why didn't we talk first? Why didn't I make it clear to him that, for me, this is serious... so he had the chance to back out?

God... I wish I could turn the clock back and maybe do things a little differently.

Rinsing out my mouth, I sigh, knowing it's too late now, and that I have to face him again, even though I don't know what to say to him, or how to behave. I open the door, going back out into the bedroom.

He's sitting up on the edge of the bed and stands the moment he notices me. He's wearing his pants, although it's impossible not to notice the bulge in the front, and I let my eyes settle there for a moment before focusing on his face again.

He looks tired, but then so do I. We didn't get much sleep last night, and I smile up at him, just as he says, "I'll take a quick shower and then we'll head back to Sturbridge."

His voice is impersonal, which I guess means my worst fears have come true. He's not looking for the same thing as me at all. "Oh... okay," I say, feeling more lost than ever.

He grabs his shirt from the bed and steps around me, going toward the bathroom, and then stops.

"Did you wanna stay for breakfast?" he asks.

"No, thanks." I don't think I want to stay here any longer than we absolutely have to.

He nods and, without another word, he goes into the bathroom, closing the door behind him, and I slump down on the bed, trying not to cry.

I glance at the rumpled sheets and swallow down the lump in my throat as I picture us here, clasped together in ecstasy, for hours on end. I remember the feeling of him deep inside me, of how I cried his name every time I came. And I remember waking up this morning, still wearing my stockings and garter belt, feeling a little cheapened by that, and looking over at his glorious body, lying on the bed, wondering what it had all been about… what it all meant.

I hear the shower starting up and startle back to my senses. He said he'd be quick, and I still need to dry my hair, so I get up again, and search the drawers beside the bed, finding a hairdryer on the third attempt. I have a small hairbrush in my purse and make a reasonable job of styling my hair, although it doesn't look anywhere near as good as it did when the lady at the beauty salon had finished with it yesterday. That was for a special occasion… at least, I thought it was…

I finish up, and put on some lipstick and mascara, which I also have in my purse, before tidying up the room a little and putting on my shoes.

I'm just fastening the left-hand one when Mason comes out of the bathroom. God, he looks good. He's wearing his pants and shirt, undone at the neck, and his hair is damp from the shower, and I wish more than anything that he'd come over and sit beside me, and tell me what he's thinking… what he wants from me.

He doesn't.

He goes and sits on the other side of the bed, pulling on his socks and shoes, before standing again and turning to face me.

"A—Are you okay?" he says, speaking at last.

No. I need to know if last night meant anything to you. I need to know if I mean anything to you.

"Yes, I'm fine," I lie, and he nods his head.

"We should go," he says, and I get to my feet, picking up my purse and following him out into the living area. We don't hang around, and he grabs his jacket from the floor where he dropped it last night. He shrugs it on and puts his tie into the pocket before heading straight for the door, which he holds open for me, as I pass through into the hallway.

I want to thank him for the best night of my life, but I can't talk, so instead we walk down the corridor to the elevators. We keep at least a foot of space between us, and he presses the 'down' button while I wait, staring at the wall, and wishing we could just get this over with.

Once the doors swish open, he hesitates, and then says, "After you," and I enter the elevator ahead of him, watching as he presses the button for the lobby, and then standing in total silence as we ride down. I wish there could be someone else in here with us, like there was last night. At least it would ease this awful tension there is between us. He said there wouldn't be any difficulties between us at work, but we can't even ride in an elevator together without it feeling like I can't breathe.

I actually heave out a sigh of relief when the doors open again, and Mason glances down at me, frowning, and then waits as I exit the elevator ahead of him.

"I just need to check us out," he says, looking over my shoulder toward the reception desk.

"Oh… okay."

He doesn't wait for me to say anything else and walks over, waiting for a woman to finish talking to the receptionist, and then goes through the procedure of checking out.

The receptionist is a beautiful blonde who smiles at Mason, fluttering her eyelashes at the same time. He leans over the desk slightly and they talk, and although I can't see him, because he has his back to me, I wonder if he's smiling at her too. I want to march over there and tell her he's mine. I want to tell him he's mine, too. Except he's not – no matter how much I want him to be – so I turn away and look at the painting on the wall beside me. It's a landscape, with the some flowers in the foreground, I think. I don't really care.

"Okay?"

His voice startles me, and I turn to look at him.

"Yes, thanks." He frowns, but that's not surprising. Even I can hear the harshness in my voice.

"I'll just get your coat."

"Oh. I'd forgotten about that." God knows how. "I could have been collecting it while you were… were with the receptionist."

His frown deepens, and he shakes his head. "It's not a problem," he says as he walks away toward the cloakroom, and I wonder how we've come to this. How can this be the same man who played my body like a musical instrument for hours on end last night? Who watched me touch myself and urged me to come, just for him, like it meant something?

He's back within moments, and stands beside me, holding out my coat so I can put it on. He doesn't say anything though, and just waits while I get comfortable, and then moves toward the main entrance. I follow, and we make our way to the parking lot. There aren't as many cars here as there were last night, and his black Mercedes is by itself now, over to the left. We walk toward it, with a suitably wide gap between us, and as we approach, he uses the key to open it, and then holds the door for me, while I sit down in the passenger seat. He doesn't make eye contact at all, and just gazes across the top of the car before he shuts the door. Tears prick behind my eyes and I struggle to blink them away as he walks around the front of the car and climbs in beside me.

He made love to me so hard last night, and now he won't even look at me.

We've been on the road for nearly forty-five minutes, and I've spent the whole of that time staring out the window, trying not to cry. I don't want to think about where it all went wrong, and why everything feels so different now than when we made our journey in the opposite direction last night. We had fun then, discussing personality types. We flirted. I'm sure we did. It felt like flirting to me.

The difference between yesterday and today is too marked not to notice.

Mason clears his throat in a rather obvious attempt to get my attention, and I look over. His eyes are fixed on the road though, and

I'm about to turn away again when he says, "I'll take you back to your place, so you can change and get ready for work."

"Thank you." I'm struggling to speak and I notice how his hands tighten on the steering wheel.

"Don't," he says, his voice cracking slightly, although I don't know why. "Don't, Isabel... please."

Don't what? I've got no idea what he means by that, and I can't ask him. I can't speak at all. There's a lump in my throat that I can't speak around, because it seems I'm Isabel once more... and I'm not sure I'll ever be Izzy again.

I close the door of my apartment, finally letting the tears fall. I've held them in for such a long time, I can't help myself.

And besides, I feel entitled to cry.

I've wanted Mason since the moment I first met him and the disappointment of it ending like this is almost overwhelming. It's not his fault. He wasn't to know it was my first time, or how much it meant to me, and it's not like he believes in things like that, anyway. Knowing it meant nothing to him, though... that's hard to take.

I check the time on the microwave. It's just before nine, so I've got plenty of time before I have to be at work, and I fix myself a coffee, bringing it back into the living area and sitting down on the couch. I grab some Kleenex from the box on the table in front of me and dry my tears, because crying won't do me any good, will it?

The only thing that'll do me any good is to talk to Mason, and I'm going to do it, even if it ends up being the most embarrassing conversation of my life. It's my fault we didn't talk last night, before we went to bed together. I'm the one who begged him to sleep with me, and he obliged... spectacularly. It's clear now that we're looking for different things, and that while I might want forever, he doesn't. I don't know why... maybe he's just too polite to tell me I wasn't very good... or maybe he's more of an alpha than I thought he was. Either way, we have to talk, because the idea of working together in this awkward silence is too much for me. So, even if he ends up telling me I was terrible in bed, even if he breaks my heart and tells me there can never be anything between us, we need to find a way through this… for both our sakes.

∞

Mason

I let myself into my house, throwing the keys down onto the side table by the door, and kicking it closed behind me.

How the hell did that go so wrong?

I wander through to the kitchen and put on a pot of coffee, leaning back against the countertop.

I've never put so much of myself into sex before. In fact, I don't think I've ever really made love before. Not like that. I've fucked plenty of times, but I've never made love. I hadn't appreciated the difference until I made love with Izzy… Isabel. No… she'll always be Izzy to me, at least in my head.

I came close to saying, "I love you," so many times last night, and this morning, especially when I came out of the shower and saw her sitting on the edge of the bed, trying to fasten her shoe and looking kinda lost. I was going to say it, too, until I remembered her words. She made it very clear… she regretted what we'd done, and it certainly didn't mean the same to her as it did to me. She said she wants us to go back to how we were before, and for it not to affect us at work. And that meant putting my feelings out there wasn't going to help. It was only gonna make things worse.

So, I buried my emotions, and we rode down in the elevator together, neither of us saying a word. That's probably why I could hear her sigh of relief when the doors opened. She was clearly glad to be free of having to spend time in that confined space with me, and she couldn't have made that any more obvious.

I pour myself a coffee and carry it upstairs, so I can get dressed for work, although I can't stop thinking about Izzy's regrets. She might have been embarrassed about how we'd ended up in bed, but I wasn't. I sure as hell didn't feel like she was begging me for sex, either. It might have felt like she was taking the lead, but I was perfectly okay with that. I'd spent most of the evening touching her and dreaming about being with her, but that didn't give me the right to take advantage of the fact that we'd ended up sharing a room. Why she felt the need to 'blame' herself for what happened is beyond me. If anyone got us into bed, it was me, not her. The moment she made it clear she wanted me, I didn't hold back – not for a second – and from then on, every move came from me. I was the one calling the shots, for Christ's sake. Wasn't my need for her obvious enough?

I take off my jacket, throwing it on the end of the bed and then sit down, putting my coffee on the nightstand as I lie back, thinking about making her come on my tongue, and how sweet she is. How the hell am I supposed to live if I can't taste her again? I recall her riding my cock while I sat up on the edge of the bed. I've forgotten how many orgasms she'd had by then, but she came really hard that time, as I held her ass and she ground down onto me, whimpering my name and biting on my shoulder. What am I supposed to do if I can't feel her again… can't touch her again?

I feel a lump in my throat, like the one that appeared there on the ride back here, in the car. We hadn't said a word to each other since we'd left the hotel. Izzy didn't seem to want to talk and I couldn't think what to say that didn't involve the words 'I love you', which felt like the last thing she'd want to hear. The silence was killing me, though, and I was desperately trying to clear that lump in my throat, so I coughed and she looked over, and I knew I had to say something. I just said the first thing that came into my head, telling her I was taking her back to her place, so she could get ready for work. That was kinda obvious, really. I was hardly gonna be taking her straight into the office, dressed like we were. As for taking her back to my place… well, I didn't think that was an option. I didn't expect her to say 'Thank you' with so much feeling though, and I had to tell her not to. The very last thing I needed from her was thanks. I was responsible for where we were. I'm responsible for where we are. It was me who tricked her into going to that damned reunion in the first place.

So, however you look at it, this is all my fault.

I sit up, looking at the time on my alarm clock.

"Shit…"

It's nine-thirty already. My first appointment is in a half hour, and I need to get changed. I sit up and gulp down some coffee before I go through to my dressing room, and get undressed, putting my clothes into the laundry hamper. I'm tempted to take another shower… a cold one this time, because thinking about Izzy has got me hard again. But I don't have time, so instead I wander over to my closet and select a pair of dark blue jeans and a white shirt. The shirt is standard work attire for me, but the jeans aren't. I don't care though. It's Friday and I'm tired.

Despite my tiredness, I know I've just had the best night ever, with the woman I want to spend the rest of my life with. I can also remember that feeling I got when I joined us together, like I'd found the part of me that had always been missing. And no matter what she says, I can't just walk away from that. We're going to talk. I'm going to ask her about her regrets, and do everything I can to help her overcome them… and then I'm going to apologize. Because, even though she didn't comment on it, I haven't forgotten that I failed her. I failed to protect her… and once I've said sorry for that, we need to talk about the consequences of my actions, and about the fact that I'm not walking away from them, either.

Once I'm dressed, I finish my coffee, stack my cup in the dishwasher and leave the house.

My journey back into Sturbridge takes a little under ten minutes, and I use that time to think about Izzy. I know I've been thinking about her since the moment I woke up this morning, to find she wasn't in bed with me. This is different, though, because now I'm thinking clearly. Or I'm trying to. I've decided I'm going to ask her to have lunch with me. I can't wait until dinner… I'm too impatient. We've both got a gap in our schedules around noon, and I'm thinking about asking her back to my place. That's a risky strategy, I know, because she might misinterpret my intentions, but I've got things to say, and I'm not sure a restaurant is the best place to say them. I've decided I'm going to come clean… I'm going to explain that I lied to get her to accompany me to the reunion. I know she might get mad, but I have to be honest with her, because I'm also gonna tell her I'm in love with her… deeply, passionately, totally in love with her. And, all things considered, I think I'd rather do that in private.

I sigh, while smiling, as Sophia Brent leaves my office. The sigh is genuine; the smile is as fake as they come.

It's not that Sophia is difficult, although I was struggling not to fall asleep during her session. She's only my second client of the day and I'm already exhausted. The last thing I needed was someone droning on about how her children have left home, and she no longer feels she has a purpose, and how her husband prefers playing golf to being with her. I wanted to yell at her to stop being so dependent on other people, and find something to occupy her time that actually satisfies her… for herself; not for her kids or her husband. But I didn't yell. I sat quietly and encouraged her to try and get more involved in the community, to find other outlets for her time and abilities. She seemed less than enthusiastic to start with, but then she remembered a book club that one of her friends joined a while back, and said she might consider that. I thought about Izzy's client, and how badly that had gone, but what could I say? I just smiled and said it was probably worth looking into, but that she might want to find out what type of books they read first. It seemed only fair to warn her.

I'm not seeing anyone now until after lunch, and Izzy should be free, so I go along to her office. Her door's closed and I can hear her voice, but it sounds like she's on the phone, so I go back to the kitchen and make myself a coffee, bringing it back to my room.

It's only just gone twelve. Izzy isn't seeing anyone until one-thirty and my next appointment is at two, so providing I can catch her when she comes off the phone, we can still fit in lunch… hopefully at my place, or maybe here, in the office, if we have to. I leave my door ajar, so I'll hear her door opening and am just taking a sip of coffee and looking over my afternoon appointments when my phone rings. It's Oliver and I answer straight away.

"How did it go at the reunion?" he asks, after we've said 'hello' to each other.

"Okay," I reply, although I struggle to keep the sadness out of my voice.

"Just okay?" he says.

There's no point in trying to hide anything from him, so I may as well come clean. "Isabel and I both had too much to drink," I explain. "So we had to stay overnight at the hotel."

"And?"

"And we slept together."

"As in slept? Or as in occupied the same bed, but didn't bother sleeping very much?"

"The latter."

"In that case, why the hell do you sound so damn miserable?" he says.

"Because this morning, when I woke up, the bed was empty."

"You mean she'd left already?"

"No. I mean, she was in the bathroom. And when she came out, she said she regretted it."

There's a brief pause and then Oliver says, "I know it had been a while, but were you that bad?"

"I don't think so, although I forgot to use a condom, so…"

"You fucking idiot," he interrupts.

"Thanks. Make me feel better."

"I'm not here to make you feel better," he says. "Is that why she regretted it? Because you'd been a fucking idiot?"

"No. She didn't even comment about that. She just said 'I shouldn't have done it', or something like that, and then said she hoped things wouldn't be difficult between us at work."

"Ouch."

"Yeah."

"Have you talked since?" he asks.

"About what?"

"Any of it."

"No. I was going to talk to her when she came out of the shower, but she kinda threw me with her regrets."

"Yeah. I can see how that would happen."

"I'm gonna ask her to lunch though," I say. "I owe her an apology."

"For forgetting the condom?"

"Yeah. Although I don't regret that."

"You might regret the consequences of it… assuming she's not on birth control."

"I don't know whether she is, or she isn't, but either way, I don't regret it."

There's a pause and then he says. "Really?"

"Yeah. Obviously, getting her pregnant might be kinda complicated, if she decides she never wants to see me again."

"That's putting it mildly."

"I know. But I'm hoping that won't be the case."

"Even though she said she regretted what you'd done?"

"Yeah. I'm hoping to persuade her that, even if I did screw up in some way, we can still work it out."

"You can't make her love you," he says.

"I know that. Believe it or not, I may be a fucking idiot, but I'm not completely stupid." I can't tell him that Izzy didn't seem to have any regrets last night… only this morning. And the more time I spend thinking about that, the less sense it makes, which is another reason I need to talk to her.

"You'll have to come clean, you know that, don't you?" Oliver says.

"You mean I'll have to tell Isabel I tricked her into going to the reunion with me?"

"Yeah, and about your shitty plan to make it look like she was your girlfriend, in front of Calvin."

"Oh… I didn't go through with that. I couldn't. And anyway, I didn't need to. No-one seemed to guess she wasn't my girlfriend. Not even Calvin. And to be fair, Isabel couldn't have played the part any better if she'd known about my plan."

"Hmm… well, you still need to come clean to her about the rest of it."

"I know. I have to tell her I lied to her."

"Yeah… and just hope she can forgive you."

I'm already aware of that and I'm just about to reply when I hear the slam of Izzy's door. *Shit… I don't want to miss her.*

"I've gotta go," I say to Oliver.

"Okay, but we still need to talk."

"Yeah, fine… but later…"

I don't give him a chance to reply. Instead, I hang up and dash out of my office, making my way to Izzy's, which is still closed.

I knock just once, waiting until she calls out, "Come in," and I push the door open, smiling at her, even though she's staring straight past me, like I don't exist.

What the hell have I done now?

Chapter Eleven

Isabel

My first clients of the day – and thankfully my only clients this morning – are new ones, which means going through an assessment session. They're always a little more complicated and time-consuming. I have to get to know the people, and understand their problems; their reason for coming to see me. In this case, it's the fact that he – Lucas – had a one-night stand when he went away on a business trip about four months ago, and while she – Penny – initially threw him out, they're now trying to patch things up. 'Patch' is the optimum word here, because at the moment, I don't think Penny's heart is really in it. She only let him move back for the sake of their daughter, who's two years old, but they've already told me they're sleeping in separate bedrooms, that they haven't kissed, or held hands, or touched each other since it happened. Lucas wants a reconciliation, though. He's the one who booked the sessions with me and based on what he said within the first ten minutes of entering my office, I think what he'd like most is to turn the clock back, so that he could avoid getting drunk, being persuaded to go to the woman's hotel room, and – as he put it – making the biggest mistake of his life.

"I don't know how to trust you anymore," Penny says, struggling not to cry.

"I know," Lucas replies, his own eyes shining with emotion. "I understand that, and I'm not expecting you to trust me. That's why I arranged for us to come here. So we can get some help, and maybe try to find a way back."

"How are we supposed to find a way back?" Penny says, giving in to the struggle and letting her tears fall. "You slept with another woman."

"I'm sorry. You know I'm sorry. If I could change it, I would... but I can't. It didn't mean anything, Pen..."

"Don't say that!" Penny shouts. "It means everything. You broke us."

"I know, and I'm sorry. What I meant was, it didn't mean anything to me," he says patiently.

This conversation could go on forever, in perpetual circles.

I sit forward slightly. "We don't need to talk about this now. I think we all know what the problem is. What I need to know is that you're both committed to doing something about it."

"I am," Lucas says, almost immediately, and we both turn to face Penny, who stares at me and then turns her blonde head to Lucas.

"I want to try," she whispers. "For Louise's sake."

"Louise is your daughter?" I check.

"Yes," Lucas replies.

I nod, keeping my eyes on Penny. "You have to want this for you, Penny, not just for Louise... or it won't work."

"Do you still love me?" Lucas says, sounding scared.

"I don't know," she sobs. "I don't know anything anymore, except you betrayed me. You betrayed us."

Lucas sits back in his seat, deflating, tilting his dark head down and staring at his hands. I shift a little further forward, so I'm right on the edge of my chair.

"I can help you," I say and they both look across at me, Penny rather bewildered through her tears, and Lucas kinda hopeful. "But you both have to understand that it won't be me doing the work; it'll be you. And it won't be easy." I turn to Lucas. "Your actions have made Penny feel insecure, Lucas."

"I know. My only defense is that I was drunk."

So? I was drunk last night, and I still knew exactly what I was doing when I begged Mason to take me to bed. I still knew exactly what I was doing when I let him undress me and make love to me. I could have stopped him at any time… if I'd wanted to.

"You don't have to defend yourself," I tell him, and Penny moves forward now, tilting her head at me.

"He doesn't?"

"Not to me, no."

"But he does to me?" she asks.

"If you want him to. If you think it'll help. I'm not sure it will, though. You've already heard his defense several times over, haven't you? He's explained how sorry he is, and that he was drunk. You know he feels bad about what he did, and that he'd do anything to change it. You know he regrets it more than anything…"

"I do. That's all true," Lucas says, interrupting me.

"Exactly. And does that help, Penny?" I ask. "Does knowing all of that make it hurt less?"

"No," she says, shaking her head and looking down at her hands. "But in that case, what hope is there?"

"There's every hope," I say. "That's why we're here. To work on your future… together."

"So I'm just supposed to forget that he slept with another woman?"

"No. But we might be able to help you accept it – as a mistake." I pause and sit back just slightly, looking at both of them now. "I'm not saying this is going to be easy. You've strayed from the path you were expecting to take, and we'll spend some time working out why that was…"

"Are you saying it's my fault?" Penny says, biting her bottom lip and frowning, before she turns to Lucas. "Was there something I wasn't doing? I know things were tough after we had Louise. I know I went off sex for a while, but I thought we were okay again, I thought…"

He reaches over and puts his hand beside her leg, not on it. She stares down at it, and then looks back up at him as he says, "It was nothing to do with you, or with anything you were, or weren't doing. I got how difficult things were after Louise was born. I understood all of that, and you're not to blame." He turns back to me.

"No-one is to blame," I say and they both frown. "I know you'll both probably say that Lucas is, because he's the one who had the one-night stand, but my point is, you can't keep playing the blame game. It won't help. You won't be able to move forward. All you'll do is stay exactly where you are now, going around in circles, and I don't think either of you wants that."

They both shake their heads, although I notice Penny does so with less enthusiasm than her husband. "This is the last thing I want," Lucas says, although Penny doesn't comment, and he shifts a little closer to her on the couch. "Please believe me, I never wanted to hurt you. I love you. I've always loved you."

"Even when you were making love to her?" Penny says, surprising me.

Lucas closes his eyes for a second and then opens them again, letting out a sigh. "I didn't make love to her."

"What did you do then? You told me you…"

"I fucked her." He interrupts her, raising his voice. "There's a difference."

Really? There is?

I'm distracted by that thought, my mind drifting back to Mason and everything he did to me last night. I thought what we were doing was making love, but now I come to think about it, I remember him saying something about fucking me. That just goes to show we were on different wavelengths. I should have realized then…

"What was her name?" Penny asks in a quiet voice, interrupting my train of thought.

"Y—You told me you didn't wanna know her name," Lucas says. "Or anything about her, and what we did."

"I've changed my mind."

He takes a breath. "Her name was Kayla."

"How old was she?"

"I've got no idea."

"Take a guess," she says, not willing to let it go.

"She's the company's new sales director for the mid-west. I can't imagine she'd have been promoted to that position if she was under thirty. She didn't look under thirty."

Penny nods her head. I think she'd expected him to say Kayla was a lot younger than that. "Where did you meet her?" she asks.

"In the hotel bar," Lucas says, with a sigh. "Work was going really badly, and the stress was getting to me. I hadn't met my sales target for the last two quarters and, to be honest, as much as I wanted to come home to you and Louise, I was grateful to be out of the office. It meant I couldn't be fired." He pauses for a moment and pushes his fingers back through his hair. "There was a whole group of us from the different regional offices, all feeling the same way, but most of them drifted off as the evening progressed and then Kayla suggested we go to her room. I'd had far too much to drink, and I stupidly said 'yes'."

"Did you think about me at all?" Penny asks.

"I don't remember thinking anything."

"W—What did you do when you got to her room?" Penny's clearly struggling with this, and I wonder if I should call a halt to their conversation... except I'm not sure if that's the best idea, and I wish Mason could be here with me, to guide me. I'm feeling a little out of my depth... again.

"We got undressed," he says. "It was all kinda fumbled. She was just as drunk as I was..." He stops talking and turns to Penny. "We... we had sex."

She narrows her eyes. "You had sex," she repeats slowly. "What does that mean?"

"It means we had sex."

"Yes, but how? Did she go on top, or did you? Did she suck you? Did you lick..."

"Don't do this," Lucas says, interrupting her.

"Do what?" Penny raises her voice, sitting forward on the couch.

"Don't torture yourself. It's not gonna help."

"You don't think I'm already feeling tortured enough?" she yells. "You fucked another woman."

He doesn't reply, but I guess there's nothing he can say that hasn't already been said.

Penny sighs, seeming to calm slightly. "Have you seen her since?" she asks.

"No. We woke up the next morning and realized what we'd done. She's married too, and we both knew we'd made a mistake. It's not one either of us wanted to repeat, so we agreed to forget about it."

"I knew," Penny muses, almost to herself. "I knew the moment I saw you that something was wrong."

"I wasn't going to tell you," he admits, and she turns to him.

"Really?"

"Yes. If you hadn't guessed something had happened and started asking questions, I'd never have told you."

"Why?"

"Because I'd rather have let the guilt eat away at me than hurt you. I'd do anything to stop this from hurting you. That's why I contacted Isabel. That's why I've changed jobs, because even though Kayla and I agreed never to let anything happen again, we were bound to meet up at some point. I'd never have been tempted – not a second time – but I wanted you to feel safe. Besides, my new job means I can be at home more. I hated all the traveling I used to have to do. I hated being away from you. Please, Pen... I want this to work. I love you too much to lose you."

She doesn't reply, but stares at him for a moment, and then they both turn to me.

"You probably didn't want to hear most of that," Lucas says with a very slight smile.

"It's fine." I smile back more fully, trying to look and sound reassuring, and then I take a breath. "We're running out of time for this morning's session, but I'd like to see you both again before next Friday." I get up and go across to my desk, checking my calendar. "Would you be free to come and see me again on Monday morning, at nine?"

"So soon?" Penny says.

"Yes. I want you to take the weekend to decide whether you both want this." I keep my eyes fixed on her. "We can't proceed if it's not something you're both keen to make work, Penny." She lowers her head for a second and then looks up at me again, nodding.

"Okay. I'll give it some serious thought."

"Good. While you're doing that, I want you to do something else for me." I walk back across to them, resuming my seat.

"What's that?" she asks.

"I want you to count to ten every time you feel like throwing Lucas's mistake in his face. I understand the temptation to bring it up at every opportunity, and I get you want to blame him for hurting you, but all the while you're doing that, neither of you can hope to move forward. This will be a good test of how much you want to, and it'll help me find out whether you're ready. You might not be... and that's not a crime. If you can spend some time together this weekend, by yourselves, and make a conscious effort not to use his mistake against him, I think it will help."

"So, I just count to ten?" Penny says, like she doesn't really understand.

"Not necessarily. While you're counting to ten, I want you to try and think about happier times. There's such a thing as active forgetting. I think it's a process you might find useful, and I want you to use it to put yourself in a better place."

"Active forgetting?" Lucas says, tilting his head.

"Yes. Bad memories, or negative experiences, are best left in the past, where they belong. By actively forgetting them, you can move forward more positively. It's not as easy as just deciding to forget, so we'll work on it together, assuming you decide you want to go ahead with the therapy."

"And this starts with counting to ten, does it?" Penny says, sounding even more confused.

"It might take longer than ten seconds. You might find you need to walk away from the situation and be by yourself for a while, but the point is to use that time positively. Think of better times you've shared. It's obvious the two of you were very much in love before this happened, so I'm sure you've got plenty of positive memories to choose from. It won't happen overnight, and you don't need to get hung up on the details of it at the moment. As I say, it's something we'll work on together. For now, I just want you to try not to focus too much on the negatives… and Lucas, you need to give Penny time to work this through in her own way."

"Of course," he says, gazing over at her and smiling. "I'll do whatever it takes."

"Good." I look back at Penny again. "So, can you both come back on Monday at nine, and tell me how it went, and whether you want to continue with the sessions?"

"I'll take the time off work," Lucas says, without hesitation.

"I—I guess I can call Mom and see if she can look after Louise." Penny nods her head slowly, and I get to my feet, signaling the end of their session.

They both stand, and Lucas holds out his hand to me. "Thank you," he says with feeling.

I want to tell him he has nothing to thank me for. His wife hasn't even decided she's willing to go ahead with the therapy… yet.

I think she might, though, and I move toward the door, letting us out into the reception area.

"Be kind to each other," I say over my shoulder, as they follow. "Don't think too much about the future, or the past. Just think about the weekend. Take things one step at a time… so just be together and concentrate on each other, and I'll see you on Monday morning."

We're by the main door now, and they turn to me.

"Thank you, Isabel," Penny says, with a very slight smile.

"You're welcome."

Lucas guides his wife out through the door, being careful not to touch her, I notice, and then he thanks me again, and I shut the door behind them, letting out a sigh of relief.

It's not that I don't feel sorry for them. I do. I feel sorry for both of them, actually. But I'm also exhausted. I'm emotionally drained myself… and just like my clients, I feel like my love life is in tatters. If I even have a love life, that is.

I know Mason has a client with him at the moment, although they're scheduled to leave in about thirty minutes, and I'm desperate to ask him to have lunch with me, so we can work out what happened last night, and this morning… and hopefully move forward ourselves.

In the meantime, I can't just sit at my desk for half an hour worrying. I need to talk. In fact, I'm desperate to talk… and there's only one person – apart from Mason – that I want to talk to.

I head back into my office, closing the door behind me, and wander over to my desk, picking up my phone, and calling Noah.

He answers quickly, although the line is fairly noisy.

"Where are you?" I ask.

"In my car. I'm just on my way to interview an informant about that bad-boy politician I was telling you about."

"Oh. Can… Can we talk?"

"Sure. Is something wrong?"

"I slept with Mason." Saying it out loud for the first time sounds weird, but I don't have time to think about that before Noah starts in with his questions.

"Oh. My. God," he begins, then adds, "Was this at that reunion thing? That was last night, wasn't it? How was it? Was he everything you dreamed he'd be? What happened? Did you wear that black dress of yours?"

"Yes, I did. But slow down, will you?"

"Sorry. I'm just so excited." *Lucky you.* "So, tell me, what happened?"

"We both got drunk."

"Okay. And?"

"And, because he couldn't drive us home, and the hotel only had one suite left, we ended up sharing it."

"It was fate," he says, with a dreamy voice.

"I don't believe in fate."

"Well, I do, so tell me all about it."

"I—I begged him to have sex with me." I blurt out the words, feeling the shame wash over me… again.

"You… you begged him?"

"Yes. He made it very clear he was gonna sleep on the couch in the hotel room, and I—I begged him not to. I threw myself at him, Noah."

There's a brief pause before he says, "At least he didn't turn you down."

"No. He didn't."

"So, what did he do?"

"He kissed me, and then he undressed me, and made love to me for around four or five hours, I suppose."

"Wow. So, he did the polar opposite of turning you down, then?"

"Yes. I guess. But we were both very drunk."

"He can't have been that drunk, not if he made love to you for four or five hours. Believe me, when guys are really, really drunk, things tend not to work properly… if you get my meaning."

"Maybe." My body tingles as I let myself remember Mason's touch, the way he looked at me, and how he made me feel… so damn much. "None of that matters, though."

"Why?"

"Because it all went wrong this morning."

"How?" he asks.

"I woke up, and I felt so embarrassed, and so guilty."

"What the hell for?"

"For begging him. What else?" Isn't that obvious?

There's a moment's silence, then Noah sighs and says, "Okay. You felt guilty. What did you do next?"

"I got up and bolted into the shower before Mason woke up."

"And when you came out?"

"He was awake."

"You're making hard work of this, Isabel. Just tell me what happened?"

"I apologized. I told him we shouldn't have done it."

"You did what?" he says, raising his voice slightly. "I hope to hell you clarified that, because if someone I'd just spent the night with came out of the shower the next morning and said those words to me, I think I'd feel insulted. In fact, I know I would."

A chill grips at my spine, and I try to remember my exact words to Mason.

"Tell me you clarified it," he says.

"I—I'm not sure. I can't remember now."

"For fuck's sake, Isabel." He raises his voice properly now, and I jump. "You need to speak to the guy. You need to explain to him why you apologized, before you blow this completely."

"But…"

"There are no 'buts'. Most guys have really fragile egos, especially about sex, and when you said you shouldn't have done it, that's all he'll have heard. Just that you regretted sleeping with him."

"But I don't. I don't regret…"

"How's he supposed to know that? He's not a mind reader." Noah sighs, sounding exasperated.

"Well, I was gonna talk to him," I say, defending myself. "I was gonna ask him to have lunch with me, so I can explain it to him."

"Good," he says.

"Did I catch you at a bad moment?"

"No. Why?"

"Because you keep biting my head off."

He sighs again. "I'm sorry. I just know this guy matters to you, and I don't want you to screw it up."

"Neither do I."

"In which case, you need to make sure he understands what you meant, and you need to apologize for hurting his feelings. Guys have them, you know?"

"Of course I know that. I didn't realize I had hurt his feelings, but if I have, I'll apologize. Happy now?"

"I will be… when you give me some details."

"What about?"

"About Mr. 'Drag me to bed please' Mason. What was he like?"

"I'm not telling you that."

"You're a real spoilsport."

"Maybe I am."

"It was your first time, Isabel. It must have left some kind of impression."

"It did." I can't help smiling. "But it's not an impression I'm gonna share with you."

"I can hear you smiling," he says. "And I'm your best friend."

"I'm still not sharing."

"Fine," he says, with a fake grumpiness. "At least tell me it was good."

"It was more than good."

"Was he gentle, bearing in mind it was your first time?"

"Not especially, but then he didn't know it was my first time."

"Oh, of course. I'd forgotten about you and your dildo. Still, you won't be needing that anymore, will you?"

"I hope not."

"Have a little faith, will you?" he says.

"But… but what if I can't work things out with him? I—I didn't realize he might have misunderstood what I'd said. What if I've really hurt him? What if he can't forgive me, Noah? I love him so much."

"Stop beating yourself up, will you? The first time is always hard, even if it's just with someone new, let alone it being your actual first time. You're bound to make mistakes. There are so many things to think about, what with all your own personal hang-ups, and worrying about how you look, and getting it right. Plus, there are things you need to talk about, which you don't necessarily want to, because you just wanna get on with it."

"Don't I know it," I murmur. "That's half the problem. Mason and I didn't talk about anything. We just got on with it."

"Nothing wrong with that," Noah replies. "But let's face it, even having the condom conversation can get in the way…" His voice fades into the background for a moment.

"The… the condom conversation?" My skin chills.

"Yeah. I mean, obviously I don't know what it's like when you're straight, but…"

"We didn't have the condom conversation," I whisper.

"Well, that's okay. At least he was responsible."

"No. You don't understand. He... He didn't use one."

"Shit! I nearly hit that car. Are you kidding me, Isabel? You're telling me this guy made love to you for four or five hours and he didn't use a condom? Not once?"

"No. I may have been drunk, but I wasn't so drunk I wouldn't have noticed that."

"In that case, I take it back. He wasn't responsible at all."

"Well, neither was I," I reason.

"In straight relationships, isn't it the guy's responsibility?"

"How the hell would I know?"

"Fair point." He sighs, yet again.

"I—I've only just had my period," I say, unable to control my stammer. "That'll be okay, won't it?"

"You're asking me?"

"Yes. Who else am I gonna ask?"

"I don't know, but I'm not exactly an expert."

"I—I'm sure it'll be okay."

"Then why don't you sound sure?" he says.

"Because my cycle is really short, and I'm trying to do the math."

He sighs. "Okay. Let's work it out. Not that I know the first thing about any of this, but when exactly did your period start?"

"Tuesday of last week."

"So... ten days ago." He's clearly doing the math, too.

"Yes. And my cycle is always twenty-four days."

There's a moment's silence and then he says. "Okay, so it's ten days down and fourteen to go until your next period. Is that right?"

"Yes..." I fall silent.

"When are the most dangerous days of the month?" he asks. "In terms of falling pregnant when you don't want to?"

"Um... I—I think you work it out from when your next period is due, rather than when the last one was, because everyone has a different cycle... and I think it's around two weeks."

"From when your next period is due?" he says.

"Yes."

We both stop talking, and then Noah says, "You need to talk to him, Isabel. Tell him you're not on birth control, and that there's a strong possibility you could be pregnant."

"Noah…" I hear my voice shake. "What if I am, and he doesn't want to know?"

"Then I'll be here for you. I won't let you down. But before you over-react, or think the worst, you need to tell him everything. Explain how you feel, and about your apology this morning and then tell him you're not on birth control… and take it from there. Do it in that order, though, so he knows that what you did together meant something, before you drop the bombshell on him."

"O—Okay." I suddenly feel really nervous.

"Don't be scared," Noah says, picking up on my fear, just like he always picks up on everything. "If you need to talk, you know where I am."

We end our call, partly because I don't know what to say to him now, but mainly because he's arrived at his destination and needs to get on with his day. Before he goes, though, he reiterates that I can phone him whenever I need to, and he'll call me back if he's busy.

I put my phone back down and stare at my desk for a moment. How did I not realize until just now that Mason didn't use a condom? I honestly wasn't that drunk.

I pull my keyboard forward and quickly go online to check my facts. After all, there's no point in worrying Mason if I don't need to. Getting pregnant, or not getting pregnant isn't something I've needed to think about before, for obvious reasons, but I do a quick search, to verify what I've just said to Noah, and sit back in my chair, when I realize I was right… and so was he. There's a very real possibility I could be pregnant, and I've got a lot to discuss with Mason now. Not only do I need to explain that last night meant everything to me, but I also need to apologize and make sure he didn't misunderstand what I said to him this morning. Then I have to explain that I'm not on birth control, and that while he may not have wanted a future with me, he may not have a choice now. The thing is… do I want that? Do I want us to be forced together because of a mistake? Do I want him to feel obliged to stay with me? No, of course not. But I want him to abandon me even less.

He wouldn't do that, would he?

"Of course he wouldn't," I murmur out loud.

Mason's not that kind of man. He might have made love to me like an alpha, but regardless of my doubts this morning, I know he isn't one... not really.

I take a deep breath and get up from my desk, going over to the door and pulling it open before stepping out into the reception area. I can hear Mason's voice, even from here. That must mean he's on the telephone, because I know if his client was still with him, the door would be closed.

I could maybe make us both a coffee and take it into his office as a peace offering. *Do I need a peace offering?*

Probably.

Besides, it'll give me something to do while he finishes his phone call.

I make my way past his office, trying not to listen to his private conversation, but stopping in my tracks when I hear the words, "No-one seemed to guess she wasn't my girlfriend. Not even Calvin."

Calvin was the name of Mason's friend... the one he introduced me to last night at the reunion. I can't help myself. I step a little closer to his half-opened door.

"And to be fair," he continues, "Isabel couldn't have played the part any better if she'd known about my plan."

Plan? What plan? What's he talking about? It's clearly to do with me and last night, but I don't understand. I move closer still, holding my breath.

"I know," he says, sounding a little despondent now. "I have to tell her I lied to her."

He lied to me? And he had a plan? I don't understand. But I can't stand here. What if he sees me? And anyway, I'm scared I might hear something else... something worse. I run back to my office, slamming the door closed and bolting to my desk, sitting down, trying to control my heartbeat, and my shaking hands.

His words echo around my head: 'No-one seemed to guess she wasn't my girlfriend.' What does that even mean? Of course, I wasn't his girlfriend. He told me the evening was about work. So why would anyone think I was there as his girlfriend?

I think back to last night and how attentive he was... and he was. Even with my lack of experience, I know that much. I also know that when I stood in that suite and asked him what the evening had been about, he didn't answer me. He'd told me earlier on, though, that Calvin used to compete with him. So was last night just an extension of their competitions? Was Mason trying to prove something? And was I just a pawn in his game?

It's starting to feel like it.

I startle at the knock on my door, and instinctively call out, "Come in," feeling a lump rising in my throat as Mason steps into my room.

I can't bring myself to look at him, to remember all the things he did and said to me last night, knowing it was all a lie. He doesn't feel the same way I do... that much is obvious. But this? This level of deception? It's too much... so I stare past him and he stands for a moment before he says, "I—I was wondering if you'd come and have lunch with me?" Is he serious? "I thought we could drive over to my place. We've got time, and I think we need to talk, don't you?"

"I can't. Sorry." I'm not sure why I'm saying 'sorry' to him. Although I'm not about to offer an explanation. I don't owe him one. I don't owe him anything.

"Isabel? What—"

"I'm busy, Mason." God, my voice sounds harsh. "I need to get on."

He frowns, stepping back. "Okay. I get the message."

Do you? Do you get how much you've hurt me?

He leaves, closing the door behind him, and although part of me wants to call him back, or go after him, I don't. I'm scared I'll cry in front of him if I do, and I'm damned if I'm going to give him the satisfaction.

I lean back in my seat and stare up at the ceiling.

How did I get him so wrong? There were times last night when I thought he cared. I even said that to him, I think... right before I begged him to take me to bed. I was mistaken, though, in so many ways. He's a player. A player who took my virginity like it didn't mean a thing, and who presumably came in here just now, looking for more of the same.

Because if he'd really wanted to talk, he'd never have suggested going to his place. He'd have suggested a restaurant, like I was going to do... when I thought we had a chance.

I've avoided seeing Mason all day, thanks to our schedules, and by being careful. I can't keep doing this though, and by the time I make it home, feeling exhausted and bruised, I've made my decision. It's one I need to act on straight away, so before I take off my shoes, or even contemplate the bottle of wine that's chilling in the refrigerator, I sit down at my laptop and start typing an email. It takes several attempts, because the screen keeps blurring, but I get there eventually...

Dear Mason,

It seems clear to me after today that we can no longer work together. So, I'm writing to inform you I'll be taking the necessary steps to terminate our partnership.

I don't know exactly what's involved in that, but I'm going up to Vermont for the weekend and I'll seek legal advice as soon as I can on Monday, when I get back. Then perhaps you can set aside some time later in the week so we can discuss how we move forward in our separate ways.

I have one appointment on Monday at nine, which I can't alter. My remaining sessions are in the afternoon and I'll endeavor to rearrange them for later in the week, by which time I hope to have found alternate premises from which to carry out my work. I can't abandon my clients, and if I'm unable to find somewhere suitable, I hope we'll be able to work in the same building, in the very short term, without any unnecessary difficulties.

I pause for a moment, wondering whether to just sign off, but I can't. I have to say something.

I was wrong about you, Mason. You're an alpha, through and through.

I sign off, formally, and press 'send' before I'm tempted to add anything else, because I also want to tell him I don't think he's a very nice man... not anymore.

Except I'm aware how hurtful words can be, and I've got no wish to hurt him.

I still love him.

That's why I have an ache in my chest that I don't think will be going anywhere, anytime soon.

I kick off my shoes now, and glance over at the refrigerator, wondering about opening that bottle of wine, and drinking it… all of it. I know I said I was going to go up to Vermont. But I can always do that tomorrow…

Then I remember last night, and what happened when I drank too much… how badly that ended. Except it didn't, because the night itself was perfect. It only went wrong this morning… when reality hit.

Reality.

God. What an awful word.

Especially as my reality is the prospect of a life without Mason, the potential of being pregnant, and the thought of being truly alone.

I can't face it. I really can't… not by myself.

I need to be with people who actually care about me, who don't lie to me, and who aren't playing games… and I need to be with them now.

Struggling to my feet and fighting back tears, I make my way through to the bedroom and pack a small bag. I need to see Ash, and Reagan… and, more than anything, I need to see Noah.

I need him to hold me and tell me it'll all be okay… even if I don't believe that for a second.

Mason

I don't know how I've made it to the end of the day, but I have, and as I say goodbye to my last client, I lean back against the door, heaving out a sigh of relief.

Izzy's door is closed, and while I'm fairly sure her last session finished about fifteen minutes ago, I want to just shut down my computer and write myself a note about Diane Shaw. I wasn't expecting to see her this week, considering she'd said last week that she wanted to come here less often. But she phoned late on Tuesday afternoon and said she'd changed her mind. She sounded kinda tearful, so I squeezed her in today, and while the session hasn't been exactly easy, I think it's been useful. If for no other reason than that she's accepted she wasn't quite ready to take a break from seeing me yet.

I write up my notes, reminding myself that we need to focus on potential triggers next week, because I think that was the problem this week. She met up with a friend on Tuesday, whose parents were celebrating their ruby wedding anniversary, and it triggered a memory for Diane... one she wasn't ready for. We're going to need to think that through. Or rather, she is... with my help.

I close my notepad, and shut down my computer for the weekend and then sit back for a moment, thinking about my own life, and how much of a disaster it feels right now.

Okay, so 'disaster' might be putting it a little strong, but it still doesn't feel great to be rejected – twice – by the woman you've just spent the night with. It was bad enough that she said she regretted what we'd done at the hotel this morning, but then to turn me down for lunch...

Still, I've given that some thought in between sessions, and I've realized that Izzy might have been offended by me asking her to come to my place. She might have assumed I was thinking of making love with her again... and I wasn't. I was just thinking that my place would have been somewhere quiet and private, where we could sit and talk together; where I could tell her how I feel. I wanted to get across to her that, no matter what her reservations are, we can work them out. I know we can, because I love her more than life, and there's nothing we can't resolve together. Okay... so, I won't deny I may also have been thinking that I might have stolen a kiss, and that a kiss might have led to something more. So maybe I was thinking about making love with her. But I've thought of little else since last night. I can't help it. I love her... I want her. That's how it is. That's how it's always gonna be. Even if I got something wrong. Even if I disappointed her, I'd at least like the chance to put it right. Surely she can give me that, can't she?

I get up and skirt around my desk, going out through my door and into the main reception area, where I find Izzy's door still closed. I know she can't have a client with her, so I knock. There's no reply, so I knock again, and when I'm greeted with silence a second time, I tentatively open the door to find her office in darkness.

She's gone?

Seriously?

I turn and lean back against the wall beside her door, letting out a long breath.

How can she have gone home already? Without even saying goodbye...

She might have made it clear she didn't want to come to lunch with me, and I might have said I'd got the message loud and clear, but that didn't mean I was going to stop trying. She must have known that, even if she doesn't know how I feel about her. We made love for hours and hours last night. I can still taste her. I can still feel her. Does she honestly think I'm going to just pretend it didn't happen? Does she even think that's possible?

I guess so. And I guess this is what she wanted... to pretend like it never happened, and for everything to go back to how it was. That was what she said, wasn't it?

Except I can't do that. I need her. God, do I need her... and we need to talk, for Christ's sake. I was going to ask her to have dinner with me at a restaurant. It might not be the most ideal place in the world to say all the things that need saying, but it's better than nothing.

I can't ask her, though, can I? Because she's already gone...

I push myself off the wall, wondering if I should go around to her place. We can talk there if she feels more comfortable. To be honest, I don't really care where we talk now... just as long as we do.

I make my way back toward my office to grab my jacket, just as my phone rings, and I pull it from my back pocket to see Oliver's name on the screen. For a second, I think about ignoring his call, but I can't really do that. It's not who we are.

"Yes?" I say, a little abruptly.

"What the hell's wrong with you?"

"Nothing," I say, shrugging on my jacket while juggling my phone. "It's been a tough day, that's all. Did you need something important?"

"No. I was just gonna ask whether you want me to drive tonight?"

"Tonight?" What's he talking about?

"Yeah... tonight. You cut me off earlier, but I told you we needed to talk... about the arrangements for tonight?" I'm still in the dark, but he continues, "I've been slammed all afternoon, so I haven't been able to call until now."

"What are you talking about, Oliver?" I cannot hide my impatience. I've got somewhere important to be, after all.

"I'm talking about Ronan's bachelor party," he says, like I'm stupid. And, to be honest, I feel kinda stupid. What's wrong with me? Not only have I allowed Ronan's bachelor party to slip my mind, but I've also somehow forgotten that tomorrow is our sister's wedding. Dear God... I know everything's been organized at the last minute, but that's no excuse to forget about it. Hell, Oliver and I even helped choose the restaurant we're going to tonight, because Chase Crawford – who's Ronan's best man – isn't familiar with Sturbridge. Ronan made a big deal about not doing anything extravagant or wild for his bachelor party. I gather Chase Crawford had something of a reputation before he got married, and I think Ronan was concerned about what might happen. But Chase has been true to Ronan's wishes. He emailed, asking me to suggest where we could all go, and then he and I got together with Oliver on a video call and planned the whole thing... and yet somehow, despite all of that, it's slipped my mind.

"You'd forgotten, hadn't you?" Oliver says, breaking into my thoughts. I don't answer, because I feel like such a loser, and eventually he adds, "Is this to do with Isabel? Did lunch not go very well?"

"Lunch didn't even happen."

"Why not?"

"She turned me down."

There's a moment's silence and then he says, "I'm sorry, man. Are you okay?"

I can't lie to him. "No, I'm not. I was gonna ask her out to dinner, but she's already left for the day, so I thought I'd go around to her place and find out what the hell I did wrong. Only I can't now, can I?"

"Not really. We're due at the restaurant by seven, and it's six already."

I check my watch. He's right. "Where are you?" I ask him.

"I've just got home. I'll need to change, but I can come pick you up, if you want?"

"Would you mind? I'm still at work, so I'm gonna need to get home and change… and I think I'd rather you drove."

"Why?"

"Because I need a drink."

Oliver knocks on my door just over thirty minutes later, and I let him in. I'm nearly ready and just have to put on my shoes and jacket.

"Are you okay?" he says, grabbing my arm as I turn away from him.

"No. But I don't wanna talk about it, okay?"

"You are gonna see her again, aren't you?" he says, ignoring me.

"Of course." I've already decided I'm going to call round there on Sunday morning, but I'm not about to tell him that. "I'll have to see her on Monday morning anyway," I say to fob him off.

He shakes his head. "Don't make this about work, Mason… not again."

"I'm not." I raise my voice. "She's the one who won't talk to me."

"Stop behaving like a fucking child. You love her, don't you?"

"Yes."

"Then make the effort. Talk to her."

"Says the man who can't even say 'hello' to the woman he loves."

He narrows his eyes at me. "I can say 'hello' to Jemima. It's Jemima who won't say anything back."

"Who's behaving like a fucking child now?"

"Grow up, will you? We're not talking about me, we're talking about you, and the fact that something went wrong between you and Isabel. You need to work out what it was… and you need to talk to her about the minor detail that you forgot to use a fucking condom."

"I know that. I'm trying to talk to her."

He opens his mouth and then closes it again. "Don't leave it until Monday," he says in a much calmer voice.

"I wasn't going to. If you must know, I'm gonna call round to see her on Sunday. I'd already decided that, but if you remember, I said I didn't wanna talk about it… and I don't."

"Sorry," he murmurs and I turn away, sitting down on the bottom of the stairs to tie up my shoelaces.

"Are you surprised Destiny decided to get married here?" Oliver asks me once we're in the car and on our way back into town.

"No. Why? Did you expect her to get married in Boston?"

"Yeah, I think I did. It's where she's settled now, and I think she's made it clear she's not coming back here."

"Maybe. But I think she's getting married here for Dad's sake as much as anything, don't you?"

"Yeah. I guess."

"Does it bother you she's settled in Boston?" I ask him, because his tone seemed kinda weird just now.

"No, not really. I miss having her around, but I get her job is there, and so is Ronan's now. She has fewer memories of this place than either of us."

I smile, which is a Herculean effort at the moment. "Yeah… but that makes sense. She doesn't remember Mom. Dad did a great job of bringing her up, but being cared for by a nanny isn't the same as having a mother in your life."

"Do you think that's why we've stayed here?" he asks. "Because of our memories of Mom?"

"No. I think we've stayed here because we like the place. It suits us and what we wanna do. But if something came up that meant leaving, whether that was personal or professional, I don't think either of us is so sentimental that we'd stay, just for the sake of Mom's memory."

As I'm speaking, I wonder whether I'll want to stay here if I can't fix things with Izzy. Moving away is a fairly horrible thought. I really like my house. I love being close to my dad and to Oliver, and I've spent years building up my practice. But the thought of sharing an office with Izzy, of facing her every day and knowing she doesn't want me, is like a nightmare. I can't even imagine how we'd make that work.

"Are you okay?" Oliver says, and I realize I've been silent for a while.

"Yeah. I'm just thinking."

"About Isabel?"

"Yeah."

"And can I assume you still don't wanna talk about it?" he says.

"I won't be able to stay here if I can't work things out with her," I tell him and he slows the car, looking over at me.

"You mean, you'll leave town?"

I shrug my shoulders. "I don't know what I'll do. Can you imagine if you slept with Jemima and then she gave you the cold shoulder? Would you wanna hang around to face her every day?"

He pauses for a second and then says, "No, I wouldn't."

"Then you'll understand how I feel."

"I understand you need to work things out. You can't leave. You belong here."

"I belong with Isabel."

"Then go see her."

"I will. Like I said, I was thinking I'd go round there on Sunday. But now I'm wondering about calling her tomorrow morning instead. I should have time before the wedding."

He speeds up again and lets out a sigh. "Make time."

I'm trying so hard to get into the swing of this party. Ronan's sitting at the other end of the table to me, and between us are my dad, Oliver, Chase Crawford, his brother Max, and Colt Nelson. We've made it through most of the dinner, and although I intended having a few drinks, I've only had two glasses of wine. After the second one, I realized that drinking wasn't the answer. It was just confusing me even more. So I've stuck to mineral water since then.

I smile, or at least, I try to, looking at Ronan. He's not at all nervous about tomorrow. In fact, he's more excited than anything, which is nice to see. He and Destiny drove out here from Boston this afternoon, and while Destiny is staying at Dad's place, Ronan's booked into the local hotel. I said he could stay with me, but as Chase is the best man, and all the Crawfords are here too, they decided to stay at the hotel instead. Ronan laughs at something, throwing his head back, and I feel a slight pang of envy for his happiness. He is happy, there's no doubting that. Why wouldn't he be? He's marrying the woman he loves, and they've got their whole lives ahead of them.

I envy him that… because, as things stand, I'm not sure I've got a future at all.

"Are you okay?" I startle at the sound of the male voice beside me and look up to see Colt Nelson staring at me.

"Me? Yeah, I'm fine."

He frowns. "Do you wanna run that by me again? You look like you've got the worries of the world on your shoulders."

"Not the world, no. Just my associate."

He nods his head slowly. "Ahh, so it's a work problem?"

"No. My associate and I, we… um…"

"You turned work into something personal?"

"Yeah."

"And it didn't work out?"

"That's one way of putting it."

He sighs. "I'm sorry, man. Is there nothing you can do?"

I shrug my shoulders. "To be honest, I don't know. I was gonna talk to her. I tried to talk to her. But she doesn't seem so keen on the idea."

"Of talking?"

"Yeah. The thing is…" I lean a little closer to him. "The thing is, even though she said she wants us to go back to how we were before, I didn't have her down as someone who'd hook up for just one night, you know?"

I know I shouldn't be saying any of this. It's personal. It's between Izzy and me, and somewhere deep inside me, there's a small voice telling me to shut up. Except, it feels good to have said that out loud. Because despite what I saw in Izzy's office the other day, I don't believe she is the kind of woman who'd have casual sex.

Colt tilts his head to one side, like he's thinking, and then he says, "Maybe she isn't. Maybe you need to try a little harder."

"I'm gonna call her tomorrow."

"You can't go see her?"

"No. My sister's getting married."

He smiles. "Ahh, yes."

"But I'll call her," I say.

"Good… and this time, don't be so easily defeated."

Oliver brought me home about twenty minutes ago, and while it's midnight already and I should head for bed, I'm feeling restless. I know I won't sleep, that's for sure, but I'm also not in the mood for a movie. I don't want to stay up that late.

So, I make myself a coffee and sit down in front of my laptop, deciding to check my messages. At least it's something useful to do, and it won't take too long.

I go to my mail app, and while it's opening, I take a sip of coffee, and then glance at the screen to see I've got seven new messages. My eyes immediately alight on one from Izzy and I sit forward, feeling a spark of hope in my chest. It's timed at six-forty-five this evening, so just around the time that Chase arrived to collect me. Unfortunately, I wasn't in the mood for checking my messages at the time, and we were running late, thanks to my forgetfulness. I just hope I haven't missed a chance with her, and that she didn't send this message as an olive branch, hoping we might meet up. If she did, she'll probably think I'm really rude for not replying.

I click on the message and sit back, reading…

Dear Mason,

It seems clear to me after today that we can no longer work together. So, I'm writing to inform you I'll be taking the necessary steps to terminate our partnership.

What the fuck? She wants to end our partnership? She's not even gonna give me a chance?

I pull my screen forward and continue reading.

I don't know exactly what's involved in that, but I'm going up to Vermont for the weekend and I'll seek legal advice as soon as I can on Monday, when I get back. Then perhaps you can set aside some time later in the week so we can discuss how we move forward in our separate ways.

Oh… so she'll talk about work, but not about us. Great.

I have one appointment on Monday at nine, which I can't alter. My remaining sessions are in the afternoon and I'll endeavor to rearrange them for later in the week, by which time I hope to have found alternate premises from which to carry out my work. I can't abandon my clients, and if I'm unable to find somewhere suitable, I hope we'll be able to work in the same building, in the very short term, without any unnecessary difficulties.

She won't abandon her clients, but she has no problem with abandoning me… evidently. I run my hands down my face, struggling to take this in, before I read to the end…

I was wrong about you, Mason. You're an alpha, through and through.

Yours sincerely,

Isabel

I'm an alpha, am I?

I may have fucked her like one, but in alpha terms, that's as far as it goes for me. I thought she understood that. Hell, we talked about it on the way to Boston before the reunion. She was the one who argued with me that I couldn't possibly be an alpha, because I don't have the ego for it.

I glance back at the screen, the formality of her words searing into my heart. She really wants to break up our partnership. She's going to see a lawyer on Monday, and she's left town, so I can't even see her. I can't reason with her, or tell her how much I love her.

But then, what would be the point?

She clearly doesn't love me.

I'm not sure she even likes me.

Hell, this really is my worst nightmare coming true.

Chapter Twelve

Isabel

It's nearly ten by the time I get home, and as much as I wanted to see Ash and Reagan, I'm kinda relieved to find they're both out. The journey up here has been filled with thoughts, and I'm done now. I just want to fall into bed and sleep for ten straight hours. I can talk to them in the morning… assuming they've made it home by then.

That thought makes me shudder, and as I lug my bag out of the trunk, into the house and up the stairs, I wonder if they routinely sleep with their boyfriends. I was never really clear on that when I was last up here. Sure, they talked about guys taking the lead, but did that mean they lead them to bed? It's not something we've discussed. It's none of my business, although I told them the facts of life when their periods started, because on both occasions, our parents were away, so the responsibility of dealing with the situation and explaining what it all meant fell to me. I focused mainly on the changes the female body undergoes and touched only briefly on the reasons behind those changes. I went into very brief detail about how babies are made, concentrating on being safe, which makes a mockery of what I've done with Mason. Ash found my explanations funny and Reagan thought them impossible, and then when I explained that everything I'd said was perfectly feasible, she told me she thought it was 'disgusting', and I had to tell her it wasn't at all… it was beautiful. Of course, I didn't know then how beautiful it could be.

I feel tears prick behind my eyes as I sit down on my bed and think about the beautiful night I spent with Mason. I can't deny it was beautiful, even if it was also built on a lie… and even if it ended so badly. The beginning was his fault; the ending was mine. So, I guess we're equally to blame. Except it doesn't feel that way, because I didn't lie, and he did.

I blink away my tears and pull my phone from my purse. I'm only here until Sunday night, which means I need to check whether Noah's free to meet me tomorrow. It's late, though, so I text him, rather than calling.

— *Hi. I'm here for the weekend. Can we meet tomorrow at JC's? Need to talk. xx*

I sit for a moment, clutching my phone, but there's no response, and after a while, it becomes clear there won't be, so I leave the phone on my bed and head into the bathroom, stripping off my clothes and stepping into the shower.

It seems weird that the last time I showered was this morning, in the hotel room, after my beautiful night with Mason. It also seems odd that, while I stood under the water, I was trying to work out how to apologize to Mason for begging him to sleep with me. If I'd known then what I know now, I wouldn't have bothered, and I certainly wouldn't have wasted so much time during the rest of the day worrying about whether I'd hurt his feelings. I know I didn't, because he doesn't have any feelings… not for me. He doesn't care, and he certainly doesn't love me. My eyes sting with tears again, because no matter how angry I am, I still love him. I wanted a future with him, and I'm never gonna have that now, because you can't build a future on a quicksand of lies.

I climb out of the shower and wrap myself in a fluffy towel just as my phone rings.

"What the…?" I dash through to the bedroom, dripping on the carpet, and grab my phone from the bed, turning it over and seeing Noah's name on the screen.

"Hi," I say, connecting the call.

"Hello. What are you doing here? The last I heard, you were going to ask Mason to have lunch with you, so you could work things out with him."

"Yeah. Lunch didn't happen."

"Why on earth not?"

"Because I walked past Mason's office and overheard him telling someone…" I struggle to talk past the lump in my throat.

"Are you okay?" Noah says.

"No," I sob.

"Hey, Isabel. Don't cry."

"I can't help it."

"Tell me what happened? What did you overhear?"

"I—I heard him telling someone that nobody at the reunion had guessed I wasn't his girlfriend."

"And? You weren't. I mean, you didn't go as his girlfriend, did you?"

"No, but that's not the point."

"Then what is?"

"That he said I couldn't have played my part any better even if I'd known about his plan."

"What plan?"

"I've got no idea."

"Who was he talking to?"

"I couldn't tell. He didn't say the person's name. But the last thing I heard him say was that he was gonna have to tell me he'd lied to me."

"About the plan?" he says.

"I guess. I don't know. Not really."

"I take it you didn't confront him?"

"No. I ran back to my office, and then he came and knocked on my door a few minutes later, once he'd finished his call."

"To apologize for lying?"

"No. To ask me to have lunch with him at his place. I said 'no'… obviously. It was fairly clear what he was interested in."

"Was it?"

"Of course it was." I roll my eyes, even though he can't see me.

"You don't think he might have just wanted to take you somewhere quiet, so you could talk in private?"

"We could've talked in a restaurant."

"Not in private."

Mason said we needed to talk... I'm sure he did. "What does it matter now?" I say out loud. "I—I feel used."

"Even though you're the one who begged him for sex?" he says

"Yes. That meant something to me. It meant everything to me, but he... he just took me to that reunion as some kind of trophy..." I'm struggling with that lump in my throat again.

Noah sighs deeply. "I'm sorry. Please don't get upset." I don't reply, because I can't, and then he says, "What are you gonna do now? You still have to work with the guy."

I cough, to clear my throat, and take a breath. "No, I don't. I've already sent him an email, telling him I want to end our partnership. I'm gonna find a lawyer on Monday and see how we go about that."

"Wow... you really mean this, don't you?"

"Yes, I do. He lied to me."

"I know. But he might have had a good reason."

"For lying?" Is he serious?

"Yes. You've heard one side of a telephone conversation. Don't you think you owe it to him to let him explain? It would've been better to wait and hear his explanation before sending him that email, wouldn't it?"

"No... and I don't owe him anything." Why can't he see this?

"Okay, okay," he says, trying to placate me, I think. I hear a muffled voice in the background, before Noah says, "Hold on a second, Isabel." The line goes quiet for a moment or two, and then he comes back again. "Sorry about that."

"Are you with someone?" I ask.

"Yeah. I'm with Aaron."

"As in, the guy from your office? The photographer?"

"Yes."

"Are you still working? At this time of night?"

"No. We're not working." I can hear the smile in his voice.

"You mean, you asked him out?"

"No. He asked me, actually."

"Oh, my God. Tell me... give me details."

"I thought we were talking about you and Mason."

"There is no me and Mason…" I can't believe how much it hurts to say that. "And anyway, I need the distraction. So, come on… tell all…"

He chuckles. "Okay. Well… I got back from that interview I was doing earlier. It was late, and the office was fairly deserted. There was just Aaron and one secretary left, because everyone has a tendency to go home early on a Friday. Anyway, I had to type up my report, and the secretary left after about ten minutes, and then Aaron came over and started talking."

"Just like that?"

"Yeah, just like that. He sat there and watched me working while we talked and then, when I'd finished, he asked if I wanted to have a drink with him."

"And you said 'no', naturally."

"Of course I didn't."

"So, where are you now? Still at the bar?"

"No. We're back at my place."

I feel awful now for interrupting their evening. "Oh, I'm sorry," I mumble. "I'll go. I shouldn't have… I mean. You'll want to be with Aaron, and…"

"Isabel, will you stop fussing," Noah says, and I can almost see him shaking his head at me.

"But you shouldn't have called."

"Yes, I should. You sent me a message saying you'd come home for the weekend and you needed to talk. What did you think I was gonna do?"

"Message back with a time to meet me at JC's tomorrow, like I suggested? I didn't expect you to call, and I sure as hell didn't expect you to interrupt your date."

"Will you chill about my date, for crying out loud? You're my best friend. You just had sex for the first time last night, and the guy you were with didn't use a condom. Added to that, you also screwed up fairly spectacularly this morning and apologized for sleeping with him, *and* told him you regretted it, or words to that effect. After all of that, when you send me a text saying you need to talk, you think I'm just gonna ignore it?"

"No… but I kinda wish you hadn't said all of that in front of Aaron."

"I didn't. He's in the kitchen, making some more coffee."

"Leaving you in the bedroom?"

"No. I'm in the living room. It's our first date. We haven't made it to the bedroom yet."

"I'm sorry, Noah," I say, feeling guilty. "I shouldn't have said that. We're not all sluts."

He sighs. "You are not a slut. Hell, the last time I saw you, you were calling yourself the oldest virgin in town. Even you've got to realize you can't have it both ways."

"Except it seems I can."

"No, you can't. Look, it's late, and I think the thing you need most right now is some sleep. You didn't get much last night."

"Don't remind me…"

"Why not? You said it was good. Don't forget that. Don't lose sight of what you had with him."

"I haven't. But I also can't lose sight of the fact that it started on a lie."

"Maybe… maybe not. Like I said, you don't know the full story yet."

I think I do. But he's right, I'm too tired now.

"We don't have to meet up tomorrow," I tell him. "You'll wanna spend the evening with Aaron, and…"

"I'll come by and pick you up at seven," he says. "Aaron's going home to see his family tomorrow, but even if he wasn't, I'd still make the time for you. I'm not gonna drop you, just because I'm seeing someone, and I hope you won't drop me either, when you finally work things out with Mason."

"Yeah… 'cause that's gonna happen."

"It might. It's too soon to tell yet. So, for tonight, will you just dry your tears and get some sleep? I'll see you tomorrow night. Okay?"

"Okay. If you're sure."

"I'm positive."

"Thanks, Noah. I love you… even if you are crazy."

"I'm not crazy. And I love you too… which proves it."

Mason

Destiny looks so damn happy, and so damn beautiful, I'm almost able to forget that my own life is falling apart. She's wearing a long white dress, with a plunging neckline I'm sure Ronan appreciates, and the lace bodice shows off her stunning curves too. I don't think I've ever been more proud of my little sister than I am today, and judging from the way Oliver's beaming at her, I think he feels the same.

Ronan hasn't been able to take his eyes off of her since the moment she walked into the barn where they're holding the wedding. It's a couple of miles to the north of the town, and is a well-known wedding venue, where they were lucky to get a last-minute cancellation.

Sitting here, with my dad to my left and Oliver to my right, and Baxter sitting quietly by his feet, I can't help feeling kinda sad, though. There aren't that many people here, because that's how Ronan and Destiny wanted it, but everyone around us seems to be part of a couple… except for the three of us. Oliver and I are seemingly useless at love – especially if Izzy's message from last night is anything to go by – and as for our dad… well, he's still in love with our mom. She might have died nearly twenty-five years ago, but she's clearly the only woman for him, just like Izzy's the only woman for me. I know she's left me, and she's breaking up our business partnership and washing her hands of me completely, but I also know I'll never love anyone in the way I love her.

And that's a really depressing thought.

I let out a deep sigh at the prospect of never knowing love again. It's an empty, hollow feeling, but it hurts too, and the pain is bone-deep, like nothing I've ever felt before. I think back to my conversation last night, when I told Oliver I'd have to leave town if I couldn't work things out with Izzy, and even though she's said she'll find premises elsewhere, I'm thinking a change of scene might be my only hope. Oliver gives me a nudge, and I sit up and pay attention. It seems we've got to the part where the bride and groom make their vows.

Destiny goes first and looks up at Ronan, her eyes glistening and a smile touching at her lips as she says, "From the moment we met, you gave me your love; your unconditional, honest, faithful love. You are the best and truest man I've ever known, Ronan, and that's saying something when you know I've been surrounded by three of the most honorable men in the world, since the moment I was born. You believed in me when I was at my lowest. I didn't deserve or return your trust, and I will spend the rest of my life repaying you, from this day forward, by giving you the thing you keep saying you want the most. I give you myself... always and forever."

I steal a glance at Oliver and see that he's just as shocked as I am to have been included in Destiny's vows, and in such a complimentary way. Neither of us says a word, and instead, we focus on Ronan, who smiles down at our sister and leans in, giving her a gentle kiss on the tip of her nose, before he stands up straight again and lets out a sigh.

"This is weird," he says, and Destiny tilts her head to one side, looking a bit confused. "We don't generally go in for this kind of thing in the UK. We tend to stick with traditional vows that have been written down and used for centuries. It saves us having to work out what to say, which is especially useful for men who aren't great at public declarations of affection. However, it became clear fairly early in the wedding planning process, I was gonna have to write some vows of my own, and not knowing what to do, I turned to Chase, my best man, because he's been here before... and he's American." There's a general ripple of laughter before Ronan continues, "Chase told me to be myself, and to just say whatever comes into my head. So, I took him at his word and didn't bother to write anything down." Destiny's mouth drops open and her eyes widen before she blinks a few times, clearly expecting disaster. "I haven't rehearsed this, and allowing for that, and the fact that I'm British, I hope you and everyone here will be kind..." He pauses and then takes a slight step closer to her before he says, "The first time you texted me, you made me smile, and I wanted to hear your voice. The first time we spoke, you made me laugh, and I wanted to meet you. When I met you, at the very moment I saw you, I fell in love with you... and the moment I fell in love with you, I knew I wanted to spend the rest of my life with you. The rest of my life starts now, and it will end when the last breath leaves my body." He reaches out and cups her face in his hands. "Whatever else you might think, you are my fate, you are my world to come... and, more than anything, you are my Destiny."

Our sister is in tears, and Ronan wipes them away with his thumbs, while I notice out of the corner of my eye that Dad is reaching into his pocket for a handkerchief to dry his own eyes.

Everyone sits in a kind of stunned silence, until the celebrant coughs and Ronan and Destiny face her again, and she completes the ceremony, eventually declaring them husband and wife.

Now the wedding service itself is over, and the guests are milling about in the barn, drinking champagne and waiting for the food to be laid out, it's easier to recall my own problems, and I sit by myself, to one side, feeling kinda desperate.

I barely slept last night, because I couldn't get Izzy's words out of my head. I couldn't stop myself from wondering how on earth I'm going to face her, how my life will ever be the same again, without her. It all got into a tangled mess at around five this morning, when I eventually drifted into an uneasy sleep, only to wake up a lot later than I'd planned, which meant I had to hurry to get ready for the wedding, and I only just arrived in time.

Now, I still can't think straight, and although I'd like to blame lack of sleep, I know it's just because the idea of living without Izzy – whether that's here, or somewhere else – is too much for me right now.

"Why were you so late getting here?" Oliver says, walking up to me, with Colt Nelson beside him. Colt's carrying his baby daughter in his arms, although I've got no idea where Bree is. "I thought I was gonna have to come find you." He smiles, but I can't smile back and he sits beside me and frowns. "Did the call to Isabel not go well?"

"The call to Isabel didn't happen."

"Why not?"

Colt sits on the other side of me, adjusting his daughter's position so she's more comfortable and he leans in slightly. "Did something happen?" he asks.

Oliver leans forward, looking at Colt. "You know about this?" he says, talking around me.

"Yeah. A little."

Oliver nods, sitting back slightly and then says, "So, what happened?" talking to me now.

"When I got back from last night's dinner, I found an email waiting for me… from Isabel."

"Saying what?" Colt asks.

"Saying that she doesn't wanna work with me anymore. Actually, I'm not sure she wants to see me ever again either, other than to break up our partnership. She's gonna see a lawyer about that on Monday, evidently, as well as finding new premises where she can see her clients."

"Jesus, man," Oliver says, leaning in to me slightly. "I'm sorry. I didn't realize things were that bad."

"Neither did I. I thought I still had a chance."

"Don't you?" Colt says. Oliver and I both turn to face him.

"You heard what I just said, didn't you?" I can't help frowning. It feels like he's being deliberately insensitive.

"Yeah. But what I'm not hearing is what you're gonna do about it."

"What can I do? She's made it very clear she wants nothing more to do with me. As Oliver said to me yesterday, I can't make her love me… and, if I'm not careful, I'll be accused of stalking her, or harassing her."

"I think you'd have to communicate with her, for either of those accusations to stick," Colt says, shaking his head.

He has a point, I guess.

"Even so, I can't make her feel something she doesn't, and she clearly doesn't love me. I don't think she even likes me."

"How would you know?" Oliver says, and I turn to face him. "Unless I'm mistaken, you and Isabel haven't actually spoken since you spent the night with her at the reunion… have you?"

"No."

"In which case, how do you know how she feels?"

"Her email was fairly explicit."

"Emails, letters, texts… anything that's written, it's all easily misconstrued," Colt says. "For all you know, she might be hurting, just like you are, and could be desperate to talk to you."

"Then why send me that message?"

"Maybe because she's mad at you," Oliver says.

"What for?" I ask.

"Well, you said she didn't comment on it at the time, but she might have realized since that you didn't use a condom. I'd say that would be enough to make most women pretty damn mad."

I hear Colt sigh and turn back to him. He's nodding his head and says, "Yeah, I'd agree with that."

"Okay. I know I've been an idiot, and that's one of the many things I was gonna apologize for, if I'd had the chance. If she hadn't left town."

"She's left?" Oliver's shocked.

"Yeah. She's gone back to Vermont."

"Forever?" he says.

"No. For the weekend."

"And you're just gonna sit here and wait for her to come back, are you?" Colt says. "Because I'm telling you now, that's not how this works."

"Not how what works?" I ask, looking up at him.

"Love," he replies with a slight smile. "You're in love with her, and you screwed up… maybe in more ways than one. That means you need to say sorry, and you need to tell her how you feel about her. You can't wait for her to come back before you do that, because if you do, all you're saying to her is she's not even worth your time."

"She is worth my time." I raise my voice slightly.

"I know. But don't tell me, tell her. Or better still, *show* her. Go find her."

"I don't need to find her. I have her address. It was on her resume."

"In which case, why are you still sitting here?" he asks.

"It's my sister's wedding." I frown at him, waving my arm around the room.

He smiles, rolling his eyes. "Okay. But after the wedding? What are you gonna do then?"

"There you are," Bree's voice interrupts my answer before I've even formed it, and we all look up at her. She's smiling at Colt, her eyes sparkling, and we all three of us stand as she approaches, tucking her mane of curly dark hair behind her ears. "Do you think I'm gonna have to keep dashing to the ladies' room all day?" she says, looking up at her husband and brushing her hand across her daughter's dark head at the same time.

Colt gives her a slightly stern look, although his eyes are still filled with love, and Bree bites her bottom lip. There's something in that interchange that speaks volumes.

"Are you okay, Bree?" I ask, lowering my voice, wondering if there's something medically wrong with her. I'm not a doctor of medicine, but I know a little and Dad was a surgeon, so between us, I'm sure we can be of use, if necessary.

She smiles up at me. "Yeah, I'm fine. I—I wasn't supposed to say anything."

"About what?"

Colt steps closer, lowering his voice. "About the fact that we've just discovered Bree's pregnant again," he says.

"Congratulations." Oliver and I both speak at the same time.

"Thanks," Colt says, while Bree smiles. "We only found out yesterday morning, and we weren't gonna say anything yet, were we?" He looks down at Bree. "Except it seems my wife can't keep a secret."

"I can," she replies. "I just can't control my bladder, that's all."

We all chuckle, and Colt moves a little closer to Bree, putting his free arm around her. "I guess, now the cat's out of the bag, we'd better go tell your brothers."

She looks up at him. "Do we have to?"

He frowns. "Why wouldn't we?"

"Because they're gonna think we're crazy."

Colt laughs. "No, they're not. They both know I can't keep my hands off of you." Bree blushes and Colt shakes his head and says, "Stop looking embarrassed. You know it's true."

"Even so, Max and Chase know how much I struggled with Willow when she was born. They both know I was useless at coping with sleepless nights. They're gonna say we're mad for doing it all again so soon."

"No, they won't," he replies, with a soothing voice.

"That's easy for you to say." Bree leans in to him. "You handled it all so well."

"Yeah, baby. Because I'm used to going without sleep, and being under enemy fire at the same time. Listening to a baby cry all night is comparatively easy." He turns to face her, like Oliver and I aren't even here. "Stop putting yourself down, will you? You're an amazing mom. You handled most of it, while I went out to work all day... and I'll admit, Max and I sometimes turned off our phones in the afternoons and had a quick power nap."

Bree leans back slightly and looks up at him, her eyes widening. "You did?"

"Yeah. Sapphire and Willow were born around the same time, and we were both feeling our age. We're the wrong side of thirty-five for all this shit."

"In which case, should we be doing it again?" Bree bites her bottom lip, looking doubtful.

"It's kinda late to be asking that question, baby. But you know me well enough to realize, if I didn't want this, it wouldn't have happened... so will you stop worrying?"

Bree relaxes into his embrace, nodding her head, and Colt says, "Come on, let's go break the news." He's about to turn away, taking her with him, when he stops and looks at me. "You never said what your plans are for after the wedding."

"I'm thinking of driving up to Vermont," I reply, and he smiles, before I add, "I'm the wrong side of thirty-five too," and his smile becomes a grin.

"Don't give up, man," he says. "Trust me, it might be hard, and even painful, but it's worth it."

"What is?" Bree asks, looking up at him with a puzzled expression on her face.

"Love," Colt replies, and Bree pulls away from him again.

"Are you saying that loving me is hard and painful?"

Colt steps back, shaking his head. "Man... I love it when you're pregnant. You misunderstand every damn word I say."

"What's to misunderstand?" Bree sounds like she's going to cry now. "You just said loving me was hard and painful."

"No, I didn't," he says patiently, looking down into her eyes. "I was just telling Mason that the road to love can sometimes be hard and painful, but that it's worth it. Isn't it?"

Bree smiles now. "Yes, it is," she murmurs. "I'm sorry. I overreacted, didn't I?"

"Yes. But don't worry about it. We've got another eight months of this to come yet."

Bree chuckles. "Do you think you can take it?" she asks.

"For you, I can take anything."

They both give us a smile and then turn away, heading toward Bree's brothers, who are over in the other corner of the barn, talking to Dad.

"You're really gonna drive up there?" Oliver says once they've gone.

"Yeah, I am. I love her. I have to try, one last time."

"And if she doesn't wanna know?" he says, and a sharp pain stabs at my chest and takes my breath away.

"Then I guess it'll hurt like hell."

I'm not sure how it can hurt any more than this, but something tells me it might.

"If you need to talk... later, you know where I am," he says and I nod my head and smile my thanks, because I can't talk.

Chapter Thirteen

Isabel

"It is you then," Ash says, coming in through the kitchen door.

She's still wearing her pajamas, and her hair's a mess, telling me she just got up, even though it's nearly eleven in the morning, and I've been up for hours. But I guess some things never change.

"Of course it's her." Reagan follows, in a fairly similar state. "Aside from us not knowing anyone else who drives a Lexus, we sure as hell don't know anyone else who'd park their Lexus on our driveway."

Ash shoots Reagan a glare, and then comes over to where I'm sitting at the breakfast bar, taking a seat opposite me.

"Were we expecting you this weekend?" she asks.

"No. Why? Is me being here a problem?" I wonder for a moment if they've got company; if their boyfriends are upstairs, trying to work out how to sneak out of the house without me noticing.

"Of course not," Reagan replies, sitting down beside Ash. "It's just that, what with it being Thanksgiving next week, we assumed you'd be coming back then."

I'd forgotten about Thanksgiving. How the hell did that happen? I guess because my life has just crumbled into tiny pieces, and I've got no idea how to put it back together again. I focus on my sisters, who are staring at me, looking a little perplexed, and kinda embarrassed, I think.

"If you guys have company..." I say, returning to my earlier thought, and they both look at me, like I've made the most ridiculous suggestion ever.

"Company?" Ash says.

"Yeah. I mean, if you've got your boyfriends here, I don't mind. Not that it's my place to mind. You're both old enough to know what you're doing, and it's your house, just as much as it's mine."

"Boyfriends? Here? At this time of day?" Ash is clearly scandalized by the thought. "Before I've even fixed my hair, and put on some makeup?"

Reagan shakes her head, rolling her eyes. "I think Isabel's implying our boyfriends might have slept over."

Ash blushes. "Oh. I see."

"The answer's 'no'," Reagan says. "We weren't even out with Damian and Jax last night. We went to JC's by ourselves and then met up with Margot and Anna, and spent the evening with them."

"We're seeing Damian and Jax tonight, though," Ash says, and then blushes again.

"What's wrong with that?" I ask, noting her expression.

"Nothing," Reagan says. "It's just that we're not only planning on seeing Damian and Jax. We've invited about twenty or thirty other people over too."

"So, you're having a party?"

"Yeah. We weren't expecting you to be here, and..."

"It's okay," I interrupt. "You don't have to explain yourselves to me. Like I just said, it's your house, just as much as it's mine."

"It's certainly not Mom and Dad's," Reagan says, with feeling. "I was gonna call you tomorrow to let you know they've been in touch."

"They have?" I'm surprised. They normally call me, not Reagan or Ash.

"Yeah. They said they didn't want to bother you at work, and they thought they'd call us to let us know they're not coming home for Thanksgiving, or for Christmas."

"Again?" I say, shaking my head.

"Yeah. If you want me to be honest, I think the reason they called us is that they knew you'd be mad at them."

"And you're not?" I shake my head.

Reagan shrugs, and Ash just sits there, staring at the countertop. "I think we're beyond caring."

I can understand that. Our parents have ignored them for most of their lives.

"Are you gonna come up for Thanksgiving?" Ash asks, tilting her head. "Or is that why you've come up now? To tell us you're not gonna make it."

How can I explain that my life's such a mess, I'd forgotten Thanksgiving was even happening? "I—I don't know," I say, my voice faltering. "I don't know what I'm doing."

Without warning, I suddenly burst into tears, like the floodgates have opened, and I sit, sobbing, as my sisters rush around the breakfast bar, standing either side of me, putting their arms around me and hugging me tight.

"Isabel? What's happened?" Reagan says.

"Don't cry, Isabel." Ash sounds distraught, but then, I rarely cry in front of them.

"I—I'm okay," I stutter.

"No, you're not." Reagan steps back a little and they both stare down at me. "Tell us what's wrong."

I wonder about lying; about maybe telling them I'm just tired or overworked. Except I can't lie. That said, I can't tell them the truth either. So I fudge things…

"I've fallen out with Mason."

"Is this the guy you work with?" Ash says, leaning her hip against the breakfast bar and folding her arms across her chest.

"Yeah."

"What did you fall out over?" Ash asks.

"Was it a professional thing that you can't talk about?" Reagan says, shooting Ash a glance and a frown.

"Not entirely."

"You mean you can talk about it? Or it wasn't professional?" Reagan frowns at me now.

"I mean, it wasn't professional. It was personal. It was very personal."

"Were you and he... together?" Ash asks.

"Yeah. Briefly. Until it all went wrong. I—I'd rather not talk about it... not yet."

Reagan huffs out a sigh. "God, I hate men sometimes."

"So do I." I look up at her and smile.

"How are you gonna work with the guy?" Ash asks.

"I'm not." Sitting up a little straighter, I square my shoulders, trying to feel brave. "I'm gonna see a lawyer when I get back to Sturbridge on Monday, and I'm gonna do whatever's necessary to end my professional partnership with Mason."

"Oh, but that was such a perfect setup for you," Reagan says.

"I know." It was. It was completely perfect. I got to work with the man I love, and be guided by him too... until I found out he's a liar. I can't say that out loud, though. Ash and Reagan will want details, and I can't give them that. I certainly can't tell them about Mason not using a condom and me not being on birth control. I dread to think how they'll react to that, when I've always drilled into them how important it is to be careful.

"So, are you gonna move back here?" Ash asks.

"I don't know. I've got quite a few clients in Sturbridge, and I don't feel as though I can just walk away from them."

"Can you find somewhere else to work that's close by?" Reagan says.

"Maybe. I'll have to check things out when I get back." It's not something I'm looking forward to. I never expected to have to go it alone, but it seems I got that wrong... along with everything else.

"Noah's here!" Reagan calls and I run down the stairs to greet him.

My sisters are getting ready for their party. I've been helping them all afternoon, just for something to do, but based on how loud the music is already, I'm glad to be going out.

Noah is standing just inside the door, wearing jeans, a white t-shirt and a leather jacket, and he smiles up at me. He looks happy, and while I want to be jealous of him, I can't be. I'm pleased for him.

"Ready?" he says, as I grab my coat from the hook and shrug it on.

"Definitely."

"What's going on here?" he asks, holding the door open for me and letting me go through ahead of him.

"Ash and Reagan are having a party."

"You don't wanna stay and join in?"

"God, no. I'm far too old for their parties… and I'm not sure I could handle all the noise."

He smiles. "In that case, shall we go?"

"Definitely."

He takes my hand and leads me out to his car, helping me into the passenger seat before he comes around and gets in beside me.

It's only a short drive to JC's, and while I'm tempted to ask him about Aaron, and I'm sure he's tempted to ask me about Mason, I think I need a drink first, so instead, he tells me about his nameless politician, and how he's hoping to complete his piece by the end of the week.

"Can't you tell me what he's done?" I ask. "Just calling him a bad boy covers a multitude of sins."

"That's because he's guilty of a multitude of sins," Noah replies, giving me a smile.

"Does it involve a woman?" I ask.

"Several."

"Really?"

"Yeah. And that's all you're getting out of me."

He parks up outside JC's and helps me from the car, escorting me inside. It's not that busy tonight, but then I guess a lot of the younger people in the town are going to be at our house.

We find a booth and I remove my coat, putting it on the bench beside me, along with my purse. The waitress comes over and takes our order, and for once she doesn't seem to want to flirt with Noah, which is a relief.

"A large, dry white wine, please," I say, looking up at her. She smiles and turns to Noah, who asks for a mineral water.

"I'm driving," he says, once she's gone, looking over at me.

"Why didn't we get a cab?" I ask.

"Because I feel like one of us needs to stay sober and sensible tonight, and given what you've been through in the last couple of days, I assumed it was gonna have to be me."

I sigh and lean back in my seat. "You're not wrong there."

"Promise not to get mad at me if I speak my mind?"

"I promise."

He nods his head. "In that case, I have to say, I think you need to speak with Mason."

"I tried. That's how I found out he lied to me."

"You didn't try. You went to ask him to lunch, you overheard his conversation and you ran out of the office." He frowns across the table. "That's what you told me."

"I know. What was I supposed to do?"

"I don't know, and in your shoes, I'm not saying I wouldn't have done the same thing. But can't you see? You only heard one side of his conversation. You don't know the full extent of what was being said."

At that moment, the waitress brings our drinks and we stop talking while she puts them down, and then leaves again.

"I know he said he had to apologize for lying to me," I reason, once she's gone, picking up my glass and taking a very long gulp of wine, which almost makes me choke.

"Which shows he's sorry," Noah says.

"It shows he lied."

He sighs deeply, resting his elbows on the table and clasping his hands in front of him. "I know lying isn't the best thing in the world, and it's certainly not a great basis for starting a relationship, but it's also not the worst thing he could've done. There could be a perfectly reasonable explanation, you know?"

"For what he said on the phone, or for lying?"

"Both. But all the while you're refusing to even talk to him, you'll never know, will you?"

"Do you have any idea what it feels like to be treated like a… like a fake girlfriend?"

"Obviously not. But you do."

"Excuse me?" What's he talking about? I drink down some more wine, hoping to make some sense of what he's saying. It doesn't help, but the wine's going straight to my head anyway, probably because I haven't eaten.

"You've been my fake girlfriend more times than I can remember."

"That was different, Noah. We both knew the score. We both knew we were pretending. I didn't realize the whole thing was a fake with Mason."

"Was it though? Did he make you feel like a fake?" Noah asks. "Are you seriously telling me that's how it was at the time? You begged the guy to sleep with you, and now you're saying you did that off the back of him making you feel like a fraud?"

"Well, no." I look down at his hands. "At the time, it felt very different. But now I know…"

"You don't know anything, Isabel," he says, shaking his head. "Because you haven't let the guy explain any of it."

I finish my wine and hold up my hand for the waitress, pointing to my glass when I get her attention. She nods her head and smiles, going over to the bar, and I look back at Noah. He doesn't comment, or even raise an eyebrow at the speed with which I've put away my drink.

"Why are you taking his side?" I ask him.

"I'm not," he replies, sipping at his water. "I'm on your side, Isabel. Just the same as always."

"It doesn't feel like it."

The waitress brings me a second glass of wine, removing the empty one, and I take a drink before looking up at Noah, who says, "Only because I'm not telling you what you wanna hear. I love you, Isabel, and the very last thing I want is for you to blow this over a misunderstanding." He reaches out and takes my hand. "I'll always be on your side, and I'll always be here for you, no matter what. But please, talk to the guy before you walk away. For me?"

I shake my head. "I can't. Not right now. It hurts too much." I'm struggling not to cry, and he grips my hand a little tighter as I swallow down some more wine.

"Okay," he says softly. "But promise me you won't do anything drastic until you've spoken to him. Don't consult a lawyer. Don't move out of your office. Not yet. The guy's good for you, professionally as well as personally, and think how terrible you'd feel if you broke up with him and then found out you'd misinterpreted his words."

"I don't understand you." I shake my head at him. "You're meant to be my friend."

"I am being your friend."

I glare at him for a moment, but he just smiles back. "Tell me about Aaron," I say, letting out a sigh.

"Is that a not very subtle change of subject?"

"Yes. I don't wanna talk about Mason anymore."

"Okay. But first you have to promise me not to do anything drastic."

"I can't. Don't you see? I can't go back to the office on Monday and carry on like nothing's happened."

"No-one's asking you to. I'm saying you need to talk to this guy first... before you do something you might regret. Apart from anything else, you need to discuss the fact that you could be pregnant." He frowns, grabbing hold of my glass. "Speaking of which, should you even be drinking?"

I take my glass back, holding it close to me and cradling it. "Why shouldn't I? It's not like he cares, so..." I let my voice fade, tears filling my eyes.

"You don't know if he cares, Isabel. You haven't given him a chance to say anything, even when he wanted to."

"When did he want to?" I reply, drinking yet more wine, despite Noah's disapproving glance.

"You told me, he came to your office and asked you to lunch at his place."

"Not to talk."

"How do you know?"

I don't, I suppose, but I'm sick of this conversation. "Tell me about Aaron," I repeat.

Noah nods his head and sits forward. "What do you wanna know?" he says.

"You said he asked you for a drink?"

"Yeah." He smiles. "I'll admit, I wasn't sure whether he was asking me on a date, or just as an after work kind of thing, because it was Friday and were both still at the office."

"But it was a date?"

"Yeah, it was a date."

"How did you know?"

"Because once we got to the bar, he touched my hand under the table, in a way that couldn't be misunderstood."

I shake my head at him. "You really need to come out of the closet, Noah."

"I know. But I wasn't sure whether Aaron had come out himself, so I could hardly ask him outright whether he was hitting on me, could I?"

"I guess not." I sip some more wine. "Has he? Come out, I mean?"

"To his family, yes… so he's one up on me. But then they don't live here."

"Where's he from then?"

"Saratoga Springs."

"Oh… so not far away."

"No. He can get home in about an hour. He's gone there today and will be back tomorrow afternoon. We're meeting up at his place in the evening." He runs his finger down the side of his glass, leaving a trail in the condensation. "He's got an apartment here in town."

"Two dates in one weekend?" I say, teasing him a little.

"Yeah, I know."

"You think he might be a keeper?"

Noah smiles. "I think he could be."

I grin across the table at him, putting my wine glass down again. "I'm so happy for you."

"I know you are." He reaches over and takes my hand in his once more.

"And I can't wait to meet him."

"He can't wait to meet you either."

"He knows about me?" That's a surprise.

"Of course he does. I told him about you last night, after our phone call. I wanted to make sure he wasn't gonna go all crazy jealous over the fact that my best friend is a girl."

"I'm twenty-nine years old, Noah. I'm not a girl. And surely, me being female makes me safe, doesn't it?"

"Yes. Safe, but complicated."

I narrow my eyes at him. "Don't call me complicated."

"Why the hell not? You're a woman."

I giggle. "Based on that insult, you can buy me another drink…"

Mason

Ronan and Destiny are talking to Oliver. To be honest, it's six o'clock, and I'd half expected my sister and her husband to have left by now. They may not be going on their honeymoon for a few weeks yet, but they are booked into a hotel for the night, and I'd have thought they'd want to get there sooner rather than later. I know I would in their shoes.

They seem to be enjoying themselves too much, though, and I guess that's fair enough. They're not going to do this again, so they might as well make the most of it.

Even so, if I'm going to get up to Vermont at a reasonable hour, I need to leave… and I need to leave now.

I wander over and tap Destiny on the shoulder. She spins around and looks up at me.

"I've hardly seen you all day. Where have you been?"

"Around," I reply. I wouldn't say I've avoided the happy couple, but I know I'm not the best company today, and I didn't want to rain on their parade.

"Is everything okay?" she asks, tilting her head.

"No."

She reaches out and puts her hand on my arm, moving closer. Ronan and Oliver step nearer, too. "What's wrong?" Destiny asks.

"It's a long story, but basically I've screwed up in a fairly major way with Isabel, and I need to work things out with her before I lose her for good."

"Lose her?" Destiny raises her eyebrows. "I didn't even know you were with her."

"I was… just briefly. But like I say, I screwed up. I—I don't wanna walk out of your wedding, but if I don't go soon, I won't make it."

"Where are you going then?" Ronan asks, looking confused.

"Vermont. It's a couple of hours' drive."

"She's in Vermont?" Destiny says.

"Yeah. It's a long story."

Oliver puts his hand on my shoulder and I feel like I'm being enveloped by my family, which I guess I am. It's a good feeling and it's one I'd quite like to savor, but it's one I know I'm going to have to walk away from, if I'm going to stand a chance with Izzy.

"Go," he says. "I'll explain everything to Destiny and Ronan."

"If you could leave out some of my more idiotic moves, I'd be grateful," I say, lowering my voice and giving him a glare. He nods his head, which I think means he understands I don't particularly want my little sister to know I had unprotected sex with Izzy.

I turn and give Destiny a hug, then shake Ronan's hand, and finally I ask Oliver to let Dad know where I've gone too, because I can't explain it all to him either. If I do, I'll never get away. Then I leave, making my way quietly to the door, and out into the parking area out front. Luckily, because I was late getting here, my car is easily accessible, although Oliver's Jeep is completely blocked in, which makes me smile.

I get in and, before I even start the engine, I undo the top two buttons of my shirt, along with my tie, leaving it hanging loose around my neck. Part of me wishes I had time to go home and change, but that would waste the better part of thirty minutes or more… and I don't have thirty minutes, because now I've decided to talk to Izzy and to find out why she sent me that message, I need for that conversation to happen as soon as possible. If that means turning up to her house in a tux, then so be it.

Fortunately, the email with her resume attached is on my phone, and it's a simple thing to call it up and copy the address into my sat/nav. What's not so easy is accepting that the drive is going to take two hours and forty-five minutes, which means it's going to be nearly nine pm by the time I get there. I hope that won't be a problem. But if it is, I guess it's just another thing I'll have to apologize for… among many others.

It's actually just after eight-thirty when I park up outside Izzy's house.

At least I assume it's Izzy's house, because the sat/nav is telling me so, but there seems to be a party going on, which is making me wonder. The property itself is set on a slight incline, with a steep driveway that's currently slammed with cars, all blocking each other in. There are other cars parked on the road, but I've found a space between them, and I get out, stretching my back, and locking my car, before walking up the driveway, in between the parked vehicles.

The house is quite large – similar in size to my place – and has wood cladding, just like mine, although I can't judge in the darkness what color it is. It's pale, but that's all I can tell.

There's loud music blaring out, but I ring the doorbell, more in hope than expectation, and am surprised when the door opens and I'm greeted by a young woman, who's probably in her late teens. She's the image of Izzy, and I know now I'm at the right place, because this has to be one of her sisters.

"I'm looking for Isabel Banks?" I say, raising my voice above the cacophony in the background.

"She's not here," the woman says, tilting her head and staring at me. "She's gone—"

"Who is it, Ash?" Another woman appears behind her, and while her coloring is lighter than Izzy's or than the younger woman in front of me, I know this must be Izzy's other sister. Her features are too similar.

"I don't know," the one evidently called Ash replies. "This guy is looking for Isabel."

"Who are you?" The second woman asks.

"I'm Mason Gould. I'm a—"

"So you're the guy," Ash says.

"I'm what guy?"

"You're the guy who made her cry."

I step forward, noticing that the second woman nudges into Ash with her elbow, like she wasn't meant to say that. "Isabel was crying?" I say.

"Yes, she was," the second woman replies defensively.

I already felt bad, but now… "I—I know she's probably told you all kinds of things about me, but I need to talk to her. I need to explain. There's been a terrible misunderstanding, and I need to apologize to her. Can you tell me where she's gone?"

They both stare at me for a moment, and then turn and look at each other, before the one called Ash steps forward a little onto the threshold. "She's gone to JC's with an old schoolfriend."

"What's JC's?"

"It's a bar."

Izzy's other sister moves forward now. "You'll need to turn your car around and head into town. JC's is on the right, on the main road. You can't miss it."

I step backwards, nodding my head. "Thanks," I say, and then I turn, running back to my car.

Turning around is tricky, being as the street was already narrow before the party guests filled it with cars, but I manage it eventually, and follow Izzy's sister's instructions, heading into town. Sure enough, I see the sign for JC's, lit up against the night sky, and I pull in, parking my car not too far from the entrance and getting out.

I feel kinda nervous, because I don't know exactly how I'm going to start this conversation, and I have no idea what kind of reception I'm going to get. But the fact that she was crying has to be promising…

surely. I mean, as much as I hate the idea of her being upset, it feels kinda hopeful. It means she cares.

I open the door to be met with a wall of noise and heat, and I glance around. I can't see Izzy to start with, and I hope she hasn't moved on somewhere else with her friend, because if she has, I'll never find her.

It's not that busy in here, but I still have to scan the booths, taking in all the different heads and faces, none of which belong to Izzy. I'm about to give up when I turn and see her. She's sitting halfway down the left-hand side, facing away from me, but I'd know her anywhere, and I stand completely still, taking in not just the sight of her, but the fact that her 'schoolfriend' is a man. He's a very handsome man, too.

Now I don't know what to do. My feet are glued to the floor. I can't decide whether to go up to her, or to leave, because while she might have been crying, she's clearly fully recovered now. She's laughing, not crying. She's throwing her head back, she's laughing so much… and she's drinking white wine out of an enormous glass. I'd expected to find her here with a girlfriend, dishing the dirt on me, no doubt. I never expected this… and now, I have to wonder whether her sisters sent me down here so I could see the consequences of my foolishness… so I could realize what I've lost.

The pain in my chest is more than I'd expected. It hurts like hell, and I'm struggling to breathe. I can't be here. I can't watch her with another man. It's too much.

I turn to leave, but just as I do, Izzy gets up and I see her properly, at least from the rear. She's wearing skin-tight jeans that seem to be glued to her, and a dark-colored sweater. She's got on high-heeled boots that accentuate her long legs and although my heart is broken, I still want her. In fact, I want her more than ever. The man she's with says something and she replies before she heads toward the back of the bar.

Something makes my feet move… and it's not in the direction of the door. They follow in Izzy's footsteps, leading me past her table, where I see the man at closer quarters. He really is very good looking, with dark hair and what appears to be an excellent physique beneath his leather jacket. He glances at me, with a slight smile as I pass, but I can't return the gesture, and I follow Izzy down a narrow passageway to two doors; one on the right marked 'Men' and the other on the left marked 'Women'.

There's only one place Izzy will have gone, and as much as I don't belong in there, I don't have a choice. The conventional, shy part of my personality might be telling me I should wait for her out here, but I can't. I have to see her. I have to know if we're really through… and she's the only one who can tell me that. So, taking a deep breath, I push on the door to the left.

Chapter Fourteen

Isabel

Three glasses of wine is enough to make anyone need the bathroom, and I grab my purse and shimmy along the bench, making it to the edge, before I stand up.

"Back in a minute," I say to Noah.

"I'd offer to get you another drink, but I don't think that's a good idea, do you?" he says.

"No, I don't." I've had too much already. The room's spinning slightly and for all my bravado earlier, he's quite right; I could be pregnant, and I ought to be vaguely sensible about that. "I'll have some water though, if that's alright?"

He nods his head, and I move away, feeling surprisingly steady on my feet, as I make my way toward the bathrooms at the rear of the bar.

The ladies' room is on the left and I push the door open, to be greeted by a line of four or five women waiting their turn.

Well, I didn't need this.

I know there are only six stalls in here, but it's not that busy tonight, which I guess means I just timed this badly.

I move from one foot to the other, wishing I'd come in here ten minutes ago. The line might not have been so long then, and even if it had been, my need probably wouldn't have been so pressing.

I reach into my purse for my phone, in the hope it might distract me, just as the door opens behind me, and the woman standing at the sink washing her hands, looks up and frowns.

"Excuse me, can't you read?" she says, sounding cross, and I turn to see what the problem is, letting out a loud gasp as I come face-to-face with Mason. He's wearing a tux again, although God knows why, and seeing him like this, my mind drifts back to Thursday night... which is the last thing I need. I ought to be concentrating on other things, like what he's doing here, how he found me, and why he's in the ladies' room.

"Get out," I say instinctively as he steps further into the room, looking down at me.

"No." He shakes his head. "You keep putting me off, and we need to talk."

"You don't have the right to come barging in here, just because you've decided you've got things to say." I square my shoulders and narrow my eyes at him. "Whatever you might think, I'm not a trophy. I'm not your fake girlfriend, either."

"What are you talking about?" he says, frowning slightly.

"I'm talking about your little plan, at the reunion."

He blushes and closes his eyes for a second, before he opens them again, takes a half step nearer to me and looks down into my eyes. "How did you know about that?" he asks.

"So it's true, then?" Even though I knew it already, I can't help feeling even more disappointed at having him confirm it.

"Yes," he says. "But how did you know?"

"I overheard you telling someone on the phone that I hadn't been clever enough to work it out for myself, right before you admitted you'd lied to me."

I hear a tutting sound and turn around to find I'm surrounded by about eight or nine women now, some of the stalls presumably having emptied. The women are of various ages; some younger than me, and some significantly older, all staring at Mason disapprovingly. One lady has her arms folded across her chest, and is positively scowling, and as I turn back to him, she whispers, "Shame on you," at him.

Mason glances at the woman, blinks a couple of times, and then looks back at me again.

"I'm sorry, Isabel... truly sorry. I never thought of you as a trophy. If it felt like that, then I apologize, but that wasn't how I thought of you."

"You lied to me, though?" That's what matters most, and I'm not letting him get away with it. He's already admitted it, so he's not going to hide behind apologizing for something else.

"Yes. I lied about the purpose of the reunion."

"The purpose of it? But it was about work," I say, tilting my head at him. "You made that abundantly clear."

"It was *never* about work." He shakes his head, sighing. "It was a date. Or at least, I wanted it to be a date."

Oh, God... what's he saying?

"I—I don't understand. If you wanted to ask me as your date, why didn't you?"

"I did," he says. "But I was nervous, and I kinda screwed it up, and even when I finally got the words out, you looked at me as though you'd rather have your toenails removed than spend time with me outside of the office. So I made it about work."

"That was the lie?"

"Yes."

"And was there a plan?" I ask.

"There was... kind of. Except I couldn't see it through."

"What was it about?"

"It was about scoring points over Calvin," he says, shaking his head. "Our history is a lot deeper than I've ever told you, and I thought if I could convince him you were my girlfriend..." His voice fades and he swallows hard.

"Like a trophy, you mean?"

"Well, yes. I suppose. But, like I said, I couldn't go through with it, and I never thought of you like that."

"No, you just thought of me as your fake girlfriend."

"Not my fake girlfriend, no... my real one. I know I made a mess of asking you, but I wanted to take you as my date... until you made it clear that wasn't what you wanted. When we were there, though, as far as I was concerned, there was nothing fake about any of it, and work was the last thing on my mind. It was all about us… you and me, nothing else."

"I—I guess it would have helped if I hadn't over-reacted to your invitation." I let out a sigh, cutting him a little slack, even though I'm still angry with him, and I still feel used.

"You didn't over-react." He moves closer still. "None of this is your fault, Isabel. It's mine. I should've been honest with you from the start." He stops talking and I'm about to disagree with him, when he says, "Despite the way I got you there, we had a good time, didn't we? I enjoyed the reunion; at least the parts of it I spent with you."

"So did I," I admit. "That's why I asked you to sleep with me."

There's a collective gasp from behind me, but I don't turn around. I'm not sure I want to. I'm not sure I should've said that, either… but it's too late now.

"I've wanted to make love with you since the moment I met you, so don't feel bad about asking. I'm the one who should feel bad for not acting sooner, and I would've asked you myself, or I'd have made a move, if I hadn't been so scared you'd turn me down."

"You… you wanted me?" I whisper, although I'm struggling with the concept of Mason being scared of anything.

"Oh God, yes. Wasn't that obvious? I'd already told you, I'm really choosy about who I make love with. I said, it matters. You matter." He sucks in a breath. "We made love for half the night. Didn't you get it? Even after that?"

"I guess," I murmur, biting my bottom lip, and I notice his focus shifting and his eyes widening.

"In that case," he says, his voice a little strangled, "why did you say you regretted it? And why are you here in this bar, two days later, with another man? I know I got something really wrong with you, but I don't know what it was… and you haven't been willing to talk to me so I could find out. Whatever it was, however I disappointed you, please don't let it ruin what we had, because as far as I'm concerned, it was perfect. You might have a problem with begging, but I don't, and I'm begging you, please don't do this. Please don't leave me. I'm so in love with you,

Isabel." My heart flips over in my chest and I hear a sigh from just about every woman behind me, as Mason says, "I've been in love with you since the first time you walked into my office. I'm just too damn stupid and too damn shy to know how to say that properly." *You just did.* "I— I know I don't deserve your forgiveness for the lie, or the shitty plan, but please, give me another chance. I'll only need one, I promise... because I'll never do anything to hurt you again."

I stare up at him, unable to believe I'm hearing all of this. Yes, I can't forget the lie, or the 'shitty plan', but can he really be in love with me? And can he have been in love with me all this time? Just like I've been in love with him?

Someone behind me coughs, and Mason startles and looks over my shoulder, like he's only just remembered I'm surrounded by an audience of women, and that he's in the ladies' room. He blushes and gazes down at me, then pushes his fingers back through his hair.

"It's okay," he says, his voice a soft whisper. "You don't feel the same. I get that. Whatever I did wrong is obviously too much for you. If it's the lie, or the plan, then I'm really sorry. You'll never know how much I regret that, and I'd understand if you hated me for it. If... if I somehow disappointed you in bed, then I wish you'd tell me, so I could try to put it right. I wish you'd give me that chance..." His voice fades and I blink, trying to find the words to say what needs to be said, except I can't... I'm still in shock. "I'm sorry," he says, shaking his head. "I'll go."

Without another word, he turns and leaves.

I want to yell at him to come back, because I haven't had my say yet, but before I can move, the women behind me shift forward, gathering around, and the one who was scowling at Mason earlier, with her arms folded, steps up to me and tilts her head to one side. "I don't fully understand what he did wrong," she says. "And maybe he wasn't great in bed..."

"No, he was," I interrupt. "He was amazing. I don't know why he thinks he wasn't."

"Maybe because you said you regretted it?" Someone else says and I feel my shoulders drop, knowing a lot of the misunderstanding between Mason and me is my fault.

"Either way," the first woman says, putting her hand out and touching my arm, "I've gotta say, if I had a man in my life who looked that good, and was willing to do something like he's just done to apologize for being an idiot, then I wouldn't be standing in the ladies' room looking at the door he just walked out of. I'd be running right after him."

I step forward to do just that, right at the moment that my pressing need, which I've somehow forgotten for the last ten minutes, suddenly becomes of paramount importance again.

"I need to pee," I murmur, and the women around me giggle.

"Make way, ladies," the woman with the scowl says, and they all step aside, giving me space to get to the stalls, all of which are available now, thanks to Mason's more interesting floor show.

I go into the first one, my need being urgent, and once I'm done, I come out and wash up.

"Good luck," the lady with the scowl says, and a couple of the others repeat her greeting, with smiles and winks. I smile back, and head out the door, into the bar.

There's no sign of Mason, but I'm not surprised. He said he was leaving, and I hope I haven't left it too late to catch him.

Noah's still sitting in our booth, and I walk over to him.

"I have to go," I say, leaning over and grabbing my coat from the seat.

"Go where?" He looks up at me, surprised.

"Mason was here." Noah looks around. "He just came into the ladies' room and told me he's in love with me, in front of a dozen other women."

"And what did you say?" Noah asks, getting to his feet and pulling a couple of twenty-dollar bills from his wallet to cover our drinks.

"I didn't say anything. I was too shocked. But I have to go find him."

"Yes, you do… and I'm coming with you."

He dumps the money on the table, nodding at the waitress as we leave, and helps me with my coat as we walk outside.

"Where did he go?" Noah says, holding the door open for me.

"I don't know. I just hope…" The cool evening air hits me, as my eyes fix on Mason, leaning against his car, close to the entrance. He must be cold in just a tux, and although I don't button up my coat, I pull it around myself, keeping out the chilly breeze. "He's there," I whisper, nodding, and Noah looks over, smiling.

"You have fabulous taste," he says.

"Not only is he straight, but you're spoken for," I remind him.

"Unless I'm very much mistaken, so are you." His smile widens as he takes my hand and leads me down the steps.

Mason looks up as we approach, and pushes himself off of the car, standing upright. I can see his face in the lights from the bar, and he stares at me for a moment, before his eyes settle on Noah, a frown forming on his brow.

"Mason, this is Noah." I make the introductions, and then, because I think it needs to be clarified, I say, "We've known each other since high school, and there's nothing going on between us, I promise. He's just a friend."

Noah holds out his hand, and Mason takes it without hesitation. They shake and Noah smiles. "The bit she hasn't told you is that I'm with someone else, and as my boyfriend would be happy to confirm, Isabel's the wrong sex for me… always was, always will be."

Mason says, "I see. Okay," looking bewildered, like he didn't expect to get that much information. I don't blame him. I didn't expect Noah to offer it. He never tells anyone about his sexuality… ever.

Noah turns to me, releasing Mason's hand. "Are you gonna be okay now?" he asks. "Or do you want me to wait in my car?"

I hesitate for just a second, and Mason says, "She'll be safe with me. I promise."

Noah nods his head, but still looks down at me, like he needs to hear me say it, too. "I'll be fine, but thanks for offering."

"Anytime," he says, and then he moves a little closer. "Remember… you need to talk. And more importantly, you need to listen. Okay?"

"Anything else?" I shake my head, kinda wishing he'd leave now, especially as Mason will have heard everything he's just said.

"No. But if you want someone to talk to later, you know where I am."

I nod my head and he bends, kissing me on the cheek, before he gives Mason a smile and a nod of his head and turns away, walking over to his car. He gets in and drives away, and once we're alone again, I turn back to Mason. He's staring down at me, his face unreadable.

"You wanted to talk to me?" he says in a gentle whisper.

"Yes."

"Okay. What did you wanna say?"

"I wanted to tell you you're wrong."

He frowns. "What about?"

"Well, first, I didn't say I regretted what we'd done."

"Yeah, you did," Mason says, leaning back against his car again. "You came out of the bathroom yesterday morning and said you were sorry, and you shouldn't have done what we did. That sure as hell sounds like regret to me."

"That might have been what I said, but it wasn't what I meant. I meant I was sorry for asking you to sleep with me... not for what we'd done together."

"Why were you sorry for asking? Like I said just now, in the ladies' room, I wish I'd asked you first... or done something about the fact that I've wanted you for as long as I've known you. But why shouldn't you take the lead if you want to? Why do you have such a problem with that?"

"Because I was embarrassed."

"I think I got that much," he says, shaking his head and staring down at the space between us. "The look on your face when you came out of the shower was enough to tell me that."

He seems so downcast still, even though I'm trying to make it right between us.

"I'm sorry I hurt you," I murmur, and he looks up again. "It wasn't my intention."

"I know it wasn't," he says. "You're too kind to intentionally hurt anyone. I think that's how I knew I must've done something wrong..." His voice fades and I step closer to him, looking up into his eyes.

"You didn't, Mason. That's the second thing you got wrong in there tonight." I tilt my head back over my shoulder toward the bar. "You didn't disappoint me, when we were together on Thursday night... not at all."

He sucks in a breath and lets it out slowly. "Are you sure?" he murmurs.

"I'm positive. Wasn't it obvious?"

He smiles for the first time since I came out here and nods his head. "Yes, it was. But can't you see? The way you responded to me when we were in bed is what made your reaction the next morning so damn confusing."

"I can see that now, and I apologize."

He nods his head. "Apology accepted." He pauses for a second and then says, "Is there anything else I got wrong back there?"

"Yes, there is." I step closer to him, so we're almost touching. "Please don't for one moment think I've forgiven you for lying to me, or for your shitty plan, because I haven't. But after the way you just publicly humiliated yourself in there, which I know can't have been easy, I feel it's only fair that I should tell you, I'm in love with you too."

"Y—You're what?" he says, pushing himself off of the car again, his body colliding with mine, and sending sparks to every nerve ending.

"I'm in love with you. I have been since the moment I walked into your office."

He smiles and I smile back. "You too?" he says.

"Yes. Me too."

I hiccup, unable to help myself, and Mason grins. "Just out of interest, how drunk are you?"

"I'm light-headed, not drunk, and before you ask, I know exactly what I'm saying. I'm definitely in love with you."

He nods his head, then pulls open my coat, reaching inside, and tugs me against him, holding me against the length of his body. I can feel his arousal pressing into me and I sigh as he leans down and whispers, "Are you too drunk to be kissed?"

Mason

Izzy looks up into my eyes, and although I think she might be a little more drunk than she's willing to admit, the moment she nods her head, I pull her closer, bringing one hand up to cup her face as I crush my lips against hers. She tastes good. Kinda like coming home, and I'll admit, I feel a little drunk myself, even though I've barely touched a drop of alcohol all day, other than to toast the bride and groom. I think back to how miserable I was at Destiny and Ronan's wedding, how heartbroken I was when I stepped out here just now, and compare that with the euphoria I'm feeling right now, and the contrast is too marked to be believed. Except I can believe it, because I'm holding the evidence of it in my arms, and she's moaning softly into my mouth.

I know I'm not forgiven yet. She made that very clear… but this a start. It feels like more than a start, and eventually I break the kiss and pull back, looking down at her upturned face. Her eyes are a little glazed over and she smiles up at me.

"You really are kinda out of it, aren't you?" I murmur, shaking my head.

"I think it's the cold air, more than anything," she says.

"Really? That's what you think?"

"Okay. I've had a few glasses of wine… but I promise, I don't do this kind of thing all the time."

"What? Kissing men in parking lots, or getting drunk?"

"Both," she replies, biting her bottom lip.

"Good." I brush her cheek with the side of my thumb and she closes her eyes for a second, letting out a soft sigh. "Would you like me to take you home?"

She opens her eyes again. "Yes, please."

I help her around to the passenger side of the car, opening the door and lowering her into the seat, tucking in her coat and making sure she's comfortable before I close the door again. Then I walk around to the driver's side and get in next to her.

"Where do you wanna go?" I ask her.

"Home," she says, turning and frowning at me. "Didn't we already esht... establish that."

Oh, great. She's slurring now.

"We did. But we didn't establish whose home. I can take you back to your place, or I can drive you back to Sturbridge. I feel I ought to warn you though, before you make your decision, that your sisters are having a fairly loud party."

"I know about their party." She nods her head and then frowns, like she regrets the move. "Believe me, Sturbridge is sounding more and more attractive by the minute."

I smile at her, because I was hoping she'd say that. "Is there anything you need to pick up from your house?"

"No. Nothing I can't live without."

"Not even your car?"

She raises her eyebrows, looking a little sheepish. "Ahh... yes. My car. I'd forgotten about that."

"Well, it's not like you can drive it now anyway, not with the amount you've had to drink. We'll work out a way of getting it back, and in the meantime, I'll take you back to Sturbridge."

"Okay," she says, and points forward. "Drive on." I select reverse to back out of the parking space and she giggles and says, "Or you can go backwards, if you prefer."

I can't help chuckling. She's kinda cute when she's drunk... and very sexy.

We've only been on the road for about ten minutes when I notice a change in Izzy's breathing and I glance over to see she's fallen asleep. To be fair, it's probably for the best, and I concentrate on driving. Not that I'm in any hurry... not now I've got her back. She said she's in love with me, and even if I am going to have to do some work to earn her forgiveness, I don't care. I'll do whatever it takes. I'll do whatever she needs. The point is, I've got a chance... and I couldn't be happier.

"Why are you wearing a tux?" Izzy's voice startles me and I glance over at her again. I guess we're about an hour out of Sturbridge now, but I hadn't expected her to wake yet.

"You've woken up."

"Yeah. Why are you wearing a tux?" she says again.

"Because I was at my sister's wedding."

"Today?" She sits up in her seat and twists around slightly so she's facing me.

"Yes. To be honest, I'd planned to invite you, if things had gone better on Thursday night."

"Things went perfectly on Thursday night," she says, in a quiet voice. "In fact, Thursday night was heaven. I loved everything you did to me."

"*With* you." I correct her. "And it's good to know I didn't get anything wrong... not in terms of making love with you, anyway." I've been so worried about what I might have done wrong, and knowing it was all a misunderstanding is such a relief.

"Well, you didn't. I just wish things could have been different. I wish I'd been able to come to the wedding with you..." She lets her voice fade and I reach over and place my hand on her denim-clad thigh.

"So do I. I'd have enjoyed it more, and been a lot less miserable."

"You were miserable?"

"Of course I was. When I got your email last night, I was devastated."

"I'm sorry," she says, putting her hand over mine. "I shouldn't have sent that. Noah told me I'd only heard one side of your conversation and I'd jumped to conclusions. He said I'd been too hasty in sending my message."

"He did?"

"Yes. He might be my friend, but he took your side."

"Is it a question of sides?" I ask, glancing over at her.

"Not anymore, no."

"Good. I hate to think of us being on the opposite sides of anything... even a bed."

I hear her suck in a breath and then she says, "So do I." I turn my hand over and clasp hers properly, entwining our fingers. "Tell me about the wedding," she says.

"It was just what they wanted it to be. Destiny looked beautiful, and it was all very romantic, especially Ronan's vows."

"Isn't that how vows are supposed to be?"

"Yeah. But Ronan's British, and he said they're not used to making up their own vows over there. They have traditional ones they use."

"Oh, I see. That must have made it hard."

"He coped." I tell her. "He made Destiny cry... and my dad too."

"In that case, he did more than cope," she says and I chuckle.

"Yeah, he did."

Keeping a hold of my hand, she twists a little further in her seat. "I'm not complaining," she says, "but if today was your sister's wedding, shouldn't you still be with your family, rather than here, with me?"

"No. I left early."

"You did?" She raises her voice a little, giving away her surprise.

"Of course. You'd sent me a message which basically said you wanted nothing more to do with me, and while I knew I couldn't make you love me, I wanted to at least tell you I love you. I wanted to apologize, too... not just for lying to you, and for my shitty plan, but for whatever I'd done to make you come out of the bathroom yesterday morning, so full of regrets."

"You didn't do anything... not in the way you thought. And you've more than apologized." She hesitates for a second and then says, "I can't believe you left your sister's wedding early... for me."

"What else was I gonna do? I've been going insane without you."

She leans over, resting her head against my shoulder. "Do you know how much I love you?" she whispers into the darkness.

"Yes. I think so. If it's anywhere near as much as I love you."

"Thank you for coming to find me," she says, and while I want to tell her she doesn't need to thank me, I can't... because my voice won't work.

We're about ten minutes outside of Sturbridge now, and Izzy's still leaning against my arm. We're still holding hands too, and she gives me a gentle squeeze. "This is real, isn't it? I'm not dreaming."

"It's real," I say, brushing my thumb over her skin. "Feel that?"

"Yeah."

"That proves it's real. We're here. Both of us... together."

"God... that sounds good."

"Yeah, it does."

I take the turning into the center of the town, and Izzy sits up slightly, looking through the windshield, and then back at me. "Where are we going?"

"I'm taking you home."

"To my place?"

"Yes. Why? Did you wanna go to mine?"

There's a brief silence before she says, "Would you mind?"

"Of course not." I take one of the turnings off of Main Street, which will bring me out on the road that leads to the south of the town, toward my house. "I know you haven't forgiven me yet, and I didn't want to take anything for granted," I explain.

"I'm glad to hear it, but I'd still like to see where you live," she says, with what sounds like a smile, so I drive us out of town, eventually pulling up outside my house. It's dark here, being as I live in the middle of nowhere, but there's a fairly strong moon tonight and the house is quite visible.

Switching off the engine, I get out of the car and go around to help Izzy, closing the passenger door behind her. I keep a hold of her, partly because she might still be unsteady on her feet, but mainly because I want to, and I lead her up to the front door.

"It's beautiful," she murmurs softly, leaning against me as I put the key into the lock.

"Thank you."

"I didn't know you were such a recluse."

"I'm not. I just like my own space, so I can escape at the end of the day."

I push the door open, feeling the warmth from within envelop us, as I stand back and let Izzy cross the threshold ahead of me.

"What are you escaping from?" she asks as I follow her inside, close the door behind me, and flick on the lights.

"Not you, that's for sure."

She looks up at me, her eyes shining, and she steps closer, standing up on her tiptoes, so she can kiss me. I pull her close, deepening the kiss, and she sighs into me, her tongue finding mine, and while it would be easy to lift her into my arms and carry her upstairs, I'm not ready for that yet.

I pull back, gazing down at her, aware that she's breathless and biting her bottom lip, and that I'd like to bite it back.

"Before we get into anything, we need to talk," I tell her.

She releases her lip. "Really?"

"Hmm… and if you think I'm making love with you while you're drunk, you can think again. We've done that once already…"

"Yes," she interrupts. "It was spectacular."

"I know it was, but the next day, you said you regretted it."

"No, I didn't. We've covered this already, haven't we?"

"Yes, we have… but we still need to talk. I don't want there to be any more misunderstandings between us."

I take her hand, leading her into the living room, to the right of the front door, turning on a couple of table lamps.

"Do you wanna sit down, and I'll go make us some coffee?" I take her coat and lay it over the back of the chair by the window, adding my jacket, although I leave my tie hanging loose around my neck.

"Are you trying to sober me up?" she says, with a twinkle in her eyes.

"It would certainly be an unusual move, but yeah, I told you, I'm not making love with you while you're drunk."

"In that case, bring me coffee," she says, and I chuckle, going through the archway into the kitchen.

It doesn't take long to make a pot of coffee and I pour two large cups, bringing them back with me. Izzy's standing over by the bookcase in the alcove next to the fireplace, looking at the photographs on the shelves.

"Is this your mom?" she asks, holding up a picture of Mom, with my brother in her arms, at roughly six months of age.

"Yes."

"Is that you she's holding?"

"No. It's my brother, Oliver."

She puts down the photograph and turns to me. "She was very beautiful."

"Yes, she was."

I leave the coffees on one of the low end tables and go over to Izzy, putting my arms around her and holding her close to me.

"Do you wanna come sit with me?" I ask her. She nods her head and I take her hand, leading her back to my huge L-shaped couch and sitting us both down, studying her hand, before I turn to her. "Can you explain why you were so embarrassed?" That seems like a good place to start. Her reaction to what we did feels like the moment where the trouble began. "Surely you realized from the things I did with you that I wanted you, so why did it matter who asked who into bed?"

"It wasn't just about that," she says, sighing. "I woke up yesterday morning, wearing nothing but my stockings and garter belt, and I felt... well, guilty."

"Why? I don't get it. We'd just had the best sex ever. What was there to feel guilty about? And why did you want to forget it had happened?"

"Best sex ever?" she says, her eyes widening.

"Yes. And stop changing the subject."

"I'm not. And I didn't want to forget it had happened. I told you that already. I told you, I didn't regret it... that was a misunderstanding."

"I know. That's not what I'm talking about. I'm talking about the part where you said you hoped there wouldn't be any difficulties between us at work."

"And? Us sleeping together was bound to change things, and..."

I close my eyes, realization dawning. "I thought you meant you wanted us to go back to how things were before, like it had never happened."

"No. Of course I didn't. I may not have phrased it very well, but that wasn't what I meant at all." She leans into me a little, looking up into

247

my face. "You have to remember, Mason, I didn't know what I was doing or saying. I've never been in that kind of situation before."

"In what way?" I ask before I realize what she's saying. "Oh... you mean you've never slept with a co-worker before? Well, neither have I, in case you're wondering. That was definitely a first for me."

She shakes her head. "That's not what I meant." A blush creeps up her cheeks. "What I'm trying to say is that I've never woken up with a man before at all."

"Really? You've never spent the night with a guy?"

"I've never had sex before," she blurts out, raising her voice.

I sit forward and turn, staring back down at her in shock. "Excuse me?"

She shuffles away, then goes to get up, but I reach over and pull her back toward me again, holding onto her. "Don't," I say firmly, looking into her eyes. "Can we just get one thing straight here?"

"What?"

"You need to stop getting embarrassed around me."

"But I am embarrassed."

"Why?"

"Because of what I just said."

"You mean that you've never had sex before? About Thursday night being your first time?"

"Yes. I'm sure there are a few more ways of saying I was a virgin until Thursday night, but that's the gist of it."

"That's nothing to be embarrassed about, or ashamed of. And if that's why you felt guilty yesterday morning when you woke up in your garter belt and stockings, you didn't need to."

"Seriously?"

"Yes. I'm the one who should feel guilty."

"Why?" She tilts her head.

"Because I didn't notice. I mean... I know I was drunk, but I feel awful now."

"I don't know why," she says. "It's not like you believe in virginity, or the importance of losing it. That's what you said, isn't it?"

I recall our conversation and shake my head. "I don't remember actually saying that, no. If my memory is correct, we talked through the myth and I played devil's advocate for a while. But I don't remember saying whether I do, or I don't believe in virginity, or the importance of losing it."

"Well, do you?" she says, like she's angry with me.

"I do now."

"Why?"

"Because it's you we're talking about, not just a general concept." Her face softens, and she sighs into me. "I wish I'd known, Izzy. If I had, I'd have been more gentle." I shake my head. "I can't believe the things I said to you… the things I did with you. God… if I'd known, I'd have gone about it all so differently."

She pulls away and looks up at me again. "I wouldn't have wanted you to," she says, her voice much calmer now. "I wouldn't have wanted you to change anything about what you did to me."

"*With* you." I correct her again.

She smiles and says, "Please don't blame yourself for not noticing. It had nothing to do with you being drunk, it was because… I mean, I—" She stops talking suddenly, blushing and looking away.

I place my finger beneath her chin, turning her face toward me again. "Are you talking about the fact that you use a dildo?"

She pulls back, or tries to… except she can't because I'm holding her. "H—How did you know about that?"

"Because I saw you last week… at your desk. I came back early from my lunch with Oliver, and I heard a noise coming from your office."

"You mean, you watched me?" she says.

"Yes. I'm sorry. I know I shouldn't have done, but I couldn't help it. I felt guilty, but…"

"Did you feel anything else?" she asks. "Other than guilty?"

"Yeah. I felt really turned on. You looked incredible, especially when you came so hard… and when I saw you pull the dildo from your pussy and lick it clean, I honestly thought I was gonna explode. Either that, or I was gonna have to march into your office and fuck you over your desk."

She shudders in my arms. "I wish you had," she says. "That's what I was fantasizing about when I came."

I have to smile, remembering her coming, and knowing now she was thinking of me. "I guess that was what made me think you must be experienced; seeing you with your dildo."

She shakes her head. "No. But when I turned twenty-nine, back in the spring, I decided I didn't wanna get to my next birthday and be a thirty-year-old virgin, so I went online and bought the dildo."

I pull her closer and put my lips next to her ear, whispering, "You realize that technically you were still a virgin, even after using the dildo?"

"Yes," she says, and I pull back slightly so I can see her face. "But I wanted to know what it would feel like."

"And? What did it feel like?"

"Which time?" she asks. "With the dildo, or with you?"

"Both."

She tilts her head, first one way and then the other, and then says, "With the dildo, it was kinda awkward. The first time I used it was in the bath, but I ended up getting water all over the floor."

"I'm not surprised. I've seen you come."

She laughs. "I'm not gonna say it didn't hurt a little, but I enjoyed it."

"And with me?" I ask. "What was that like?"

She looks up into my eyes. "Well, you're a lot bigger than my dildo."

"Thanks."

She smiles, and then says, "You felt incredible, and everything we did was so... so special. I—I can't think of any other way to describe it, except to say, it felt like I'd found the missing puzzle piece I'd been looking for all my life."

Oh, my God. Her too? "It was the same for me," I tell her. "I hadn't even realized part of me was missing until I joined us together, and found it... in you. I think that's why I forgot to use a condom..." I let my voice fade and she nods her head calmly, like I haven't just dropped a bombshell on her. It takes a second or two for me to realize that's because she's already worked out my carelessness for herself. "You noticed I'd been an idiot then?"

"I wouldn't say you were an idiot, but yes, I realized you hadn't used a condom... although not straight away."

"I'm sorry," I murmur.

"Are you gonna apologize for everything?"

"Yes. I keep screwing up, so I think I need to keep saying sorry, don't you?"

"You don't keep screwing up," she says. "What we did was magical, and I'd do it all again."

"Don't worry... we will."

"Good." She smiles up at me.

"About the condom, though," I say, trying to stay on topic, because it's important. "Are you on birth control?"

"No."

"So there's a chance you could be pregnant?"

"Yes, there is."

"How much of a chance?"

She looks at me, tilting her head. "Thursday was day ten of my cycle... and it's usually only twenty-four days long, so..."

"Quite a serious chance." I finish her sentence and she nods her head. She seems incredibly calm about this, but then I surprise myself by feeling exactly the same. I'm not fazed at all. In fact, the thought of Izzy being pregnant fills my heart with wonder.

"Does that worry you?" she asks.

"No... not in the slightest."

She frowns. "Really?"

"Yes, really."

"Then why do you look so concerned?"

"Because I failed you... and, if I'm being honest, I guess I'm kinda uneasy about the amount of alcohol you've been drinking tonight."

"You sound just like Noah," she says, rolling her eyes.

"I do?"

"Yeah, he told me I shouldn't be drinking either."

"So he knows you might be pregnant?"

"Yes. I hope you don't mind. I needed someone to talk to."

"Of course I don't mind. I told Oliver too... at least that I'd forgotten the condom. Obviously, I didn't know you weren't on birth control at the time, or that there's a very real chance you could be pregnant. I needed someone to talk to as well, and my lack of caution was one of the reasons I was so upset you wouldn't speak to me. I wanted to apologize."

She nestles into me, putting her arms tight around me. "What did Oliver say?" she asks.

"He called me a fucking idiot."

She giggles. "I think I'm gonna like Oliver. He sounds like someone who speaks his mind."

"Yeah, he does... and he wasn't wrong. I didn't protect you."

"I didn't ask you to. But if you are worried..." Why does she keep offering me a way out, when I've already said I'm okay with this? Is this a pregnancy thing? I guess it might be... at least I hope it might. And if she needs reassurance, she's got it.

"I'm not worried... I promise. I like the idea of you being pregnant with my child."

"Y—You do?"

"Yes. I do."

She doesn't say anything for a moment, but then she leans in to me a little further. "It's strange, but even when I worked it out for myself, I was never scared. I guess I thought things might be difficult if we couldn't work out our differences, but I knew you wouldn't abandon me. That's not who you are."

"No, it's not."

"Even if we couldn't be together, I..."

"We've always been together," I say, interrupting her. "Ever since you walked through my door and claimed my heart. That's why making love with you was like finding the missing part of myself. It's why, when you left, that part of me was torn away with you."

"I know. We're two halves of the same person. I'm not complete when I'm not with you."

"No, neither am I."

She twists slightly and gazes up at me. "I love you so much, Mason."

"I love you too."

I lean down and kiss her, letting my tongue explore for a while and when I pull back, she's breathless, her eyes alight with a longing which I'm sure matches my own.

"I'm feeling fairly sober now," she says, even though neither of us has touched our coffees.

"Really?"

"No." She smiles. "But I want you. I can't help it."

"I want you too…. but I meant every word I said. I'm not making love with you while you're drunk. I want you to remember every second of what we do together."

"I will," she says.

"I know. Because you'll be sober."

I stand and lift her into my arms, carrying her from the living room and switching off the lights as I go, before taking her up the stairs.

"Where are we going?" she says with a hint of a tease to her voice.

"You know perfectly well where we're going, Izzy."

"To bed?" she says.

"Yes, but that doesn't mean we're going to make love."

I open the door to my bedroom, turn on the lights, and set her down on the floor.

"I like that you're calling me Izzy again," she says, letting her hands rest on my chest as she looks up at me.

"I'll confess that in my head, you're always Izzy. You have been ever since I first met you. That has nothing to do with my brother not liking his name being shortened, either. It's because, when I'm dreaming about you, when I'm thinking about you – when I'm fantasizing about you – I always call you Izzy."

"Oh," she says. "And what are these fantasies about?"

I pull her close, letting her feel my arousal. "They're about us, making love."

"That sounds exciting."

"It is. But it's nowhere near as exciting as the reality."

"Wanna prove it?" she says, tilting her head.

"I will. When you're sober."

She shakes her head, narrowing her eyes at me. "You're a spoilsport."

"Yeah, I know."

I keep hold of her, walking her further into the room, toward the bed, and once we're beside it, I take a step back and place my hands on the hem of her sweater, pulling it up over her head. She's wearing a black lace bra, and I suck in a breath at the sight of her. She gazes at me as I reach around behind her and unfasten it, struggling not to lick and suck on her pert nipples. I've said I won't make love with her, though, so I can hardly tease.

I drop her bra, and turn my attention to her jeans, undoing the button and the zipper and pushing them down, stopping when I notice she's wearing black lace panties that match her bra. I look down into her eyes and frown.

"You're wearing panties?" I say.

"Of course I am."

"But I thought you said you didn't like them." My face falls. I can't help it. "Is this one of those times when you have to wear them?"

She takes my hand and pulls me to the bed, sitting us both down. "No," she says calmly, with a kind of mock patience in her voice. "If it was, I'd know I wasn't pregnant, wouldn't I?"

"Oh, yeah. Sorry. I was being dense then, wasn't I? Put it down to lack of sleep."

"Lack of sleep?" she says.

"Yeah. We didn't sleep much on Thursday night, and I barely slept last night either. I was thinking about you… missing you… feeling scared I'd never get to see you like this again, never get to hold you, or kiss you, or make love with you again."

She smiles and says, "I'm not stopping you."

I smile back. "But your drunkenness is."

She shakes her head, although her smile doesn't fade as she says, "I've got a confession of my own," looking up into my eyes.

"Oh?"

"Yes. I didn't tell you the truth when you asked me why I don't wear panties. I didn't lie exactly, because I honestly prefer not to wear them. But that's not the entire story."

"Then what is?" I'm intrigued now.

"It's just that, when I'm around you, I can't wear them."

I can't help smiling, as I ask, "Why?"

"Because when I started working with you, I found that being so close to you, I—I got really turned on, and because of that, I got really, really wet… so wet that my panties got soaked through. It was uncomfortable, so I tried not wearing them, and I found I liked it. Not only was it more comfortable, but I liked how it made me feel."

My smile turns into a grin and my dick presses hard against my zipper. "Well, I've gotta say, that turns me on, too. You told me you didn't wear panties, and knowing you'd been coming into the office without any on was already very stimulating. Now, knowing I'm the cause… let's just say it's gonna make it really hard to concentrate at work."

"Good," she says and I shake my head at her, even though I'm grinning still.

She chuckles and I push her back on the bed, making light work of pulling off her boots, jeans and panties, so she's lying naked before me. I'll freely admit, I'm really tempted to forget everything I've been saying to her since we got back here, and I know I won't regret making love now, even if she is drunk… and neither will she. But I want this next time to be when we're both completely sober and aware of everything we're doing. It feels important to me.

So, I pull back the covers and lift Izzy up the bed, lying her head on the pillow, before I cover her over again.

"You're really serious about this, aren't you?" she says.

"Yeah."

I switch off the lights and undress in the dark, so she can't get any ideas, and then climb into bed beside her. I know she's going to be more than aware of my erection, especially when I pull her into my arms, and she proves that by squirming into me, grinding her hips a little.

"I'm not gonna be persuaded," I say, kissing her forehead.

"In that case, will you answer me a question?"

I settle on my back, bringing her with me, and she nestles beside me, her head on my chest.

"Of course."

"You... You keep saying you won't make love to me while I'm drunk."

"No. I keep saying I won't make love *with* you while you're drunk."

"Okay, but that's not the point."

"What is?"

"It's just that tonight you're talking about us making love, but on Thursday night, you... you said you wanted to fuck me."

"I know. Because I wanted to fuck you."

"And now you wanna make love to me? Sorry... *with* me. You don't wanna fuck me anymore?"

"No. I still wanna fuck you."

She sighs. "You see? This is what I don't understand. I—I heard there was a difference between fucking and making love."

"There is. Although I'll admit I hadn't realized that for myself until we made love."

"You mean, until we fucked," she says.

"If you want to put it that way."

"But I thought you just said we made love." She frowns. "I'm so confused, Mason. On Thursday, you said..."

I turn on to my side, facing her and place my fingers across her lips, silencing her. "I know what I said, and I know what I meant. Just because I might say I wanna fuck your brains out, that doesn't mean I won't be making love to you while I'm doing it."

She pulls my hand away from her mouth. "This is so complicated," she says with a sigh.

"It really isn't. Trust me."

"I do," she says. "Do you, though?"

"Do I what? Trust you? Of course I do."

"No, I meant do you wanna fuck my brains out?"

"Oh God, yeah. And I will. In the morning."

Chapter Fifteen

Isabel

I'm vaguely aware of waking up.

That's to say, I'm vaguely aware of not being asleep, even though I haven't yet dared to open my eyes. My head feels fuzzy, my mouth feels dry and I'm struggling to think straight, so I'm not sure I can call myself awake… not yet.

How much did I have to drink last night?

I remember being at JC's and talking to Noah.

I remember going to the restroom and standing in line.

Oh God. I remember Mason coming in and telling me he loves me. Or was that a dream? No, it can't have been. Because I'm sure I also remember following him outside, and telling him I love him too… and didn't he drive me home? Or was that a dream, too?

I open my eyes.

Where the hell am I? This isn't my bedroom. I don't have white walls, or a huge painting of a seascape, which, even without squinting, looks like an original. I don't understand.

I turn over, taking in the white voile drapes that cover the windows at the end of the bed, and then I come up against something warm and solid, right next to me.

"Good morning."

I look up and see Mason, leaning on one elbow, staring down at me, his bare chest exposed, and although that's very distracting, I'm fixed by his smile and his deep blue eyes.

"G—Good morning," I whisper.

He leans in and kisses me, his lips brushing gently over mine, and I can't help sighing at the gentle caress.

"I don't think you're drunk anymore, are you?" he asks.

"No."

"Are you hungover?" He tilts his head slightly.

"Not really." I've certainly felt worse.

"Good," he says, and rolls me onto my back, raising himself above me as he settles between my legs, parting them with his own.

I gaze up at him, memories of last night filtering into my head… and I reach up, my hands on his chest, stopping him before he goes any further.

"What's wrong?" he asks, frowning.

"Nothing. I—It's just that I've remembered you saying something last night."

"We both said a lot of things last night. Which particular one were you thinking about?"

"The one where you kept saying you wanted to make love with me."

He smiles. "Because I do."

"I know… but I think I'd like you to make love *to* me, if that's okay. I need to feel…"

"Hey," he says, interrupting me. "I know exactly what you need, and there's nothing for you to worry about. I've got this." He bends, capturing my lips with his, and kissing me deeply. I moan into him, bringing my hands up onto his shoulders, even as he breaks the kiss, nibbling on my bottom lip, before he leans up again, staring down at me. "I love you so much," he whispers and while I need to tell him I love him too, I can't speak. The expression on his perfect face has stolen my voice… and my heart.

He reaches between us, balancing on one arm, and I feel him rub the head of his arousal against me, before he settles at my entrance, and then sinks inside. He's slow and tender and brings his hand up, resting it beside my head, pausing for a few moments before he pulls all the way out again.

This isn't what I need at all. "Give it back," I murmur.

"Why? Do you like it inside you?" he says with a smile.

"Yes."

He repeats the process, giving me his entire length this time, with that same, slow, gentle precision, before again, he withdraws, and I frown up at him.

"Why do you keep doing that?"

"Because I like how it feels when I enter you," he says.

"So do I... but I want you."

"You've got me," he growls, and thrusts deep inside me, taking my breath away. This time, he doesn't pull out – not all the way – but he takes me, moving harder and faster with every stroke.

"I told you I wanted to fuck your brains out," he says, pounding into me.

"Then why does it feel like you're making love to me?"

He slows and leans down, kissing me. "Because that's how this works, when you're in love.... evidently."

I smile up at him, and he grinds into me even harder still, and as I reach up to touch him, he captures my hands, holding them beside my head, pinning me to the mattress.

I don't know how he knew, but this is exactly what I need, and I lift my legs a little higher. He groans, swiveling his hips with every deep penetration, just as my orgasm builds out of nowhere.

"Can you come with me?" I say, looking up into his eyes. "I need this, Mason... please."

He nods his head. "I need it too, baby."

He plunges further inside me. Once. Twice. And then he stiffens and throws back his head, letting out a long howl, just as I tip over the edge into ecstasy, crying out his name, tumbling and falling.

"Are you okay?" he says, pulling us over onto our sides, facing each other. I'm still recovering, still tingling, and I smile up at him.

"That was a fabulous way to wake up," I whisper, reaching up and brushing my fingers over his stubbled chin.

"Yeah, it was." He kisses my lips, just gently. "Do you wanna do it again?"

"You want to go again? Already?"

He smiles. "Yeah. In a minute. But that's not what I meant."

"Then I don't understand."

"I meant, do you wanna wake up with me again tomorrow?"

"Oh, I see. Yes, please. I think I'd like that very much."

He nods his head. "And the next day?"

"Yes, please."

"What about the day after?"

I giggle. "Shall I save us both some time and say I'd like to wake up with you every day?"

"I like the sound of that," he says, kissing me a little harder.

I pull back, eventually, and gaze up into his eyes. "There's just one thing…"

"What?"

"You forgot the condom… again."

He tilts his head, a smile twitching at the corners of his lips. "I'm not sure 'forgot' is the best word."

"It's not?"

"No. Forgetting would imply I had any intention of using one in the first place."

"And you didn't?"

He shakes his head. "I told you, I like the idea of you being pregnant."

"I know. But the idea and the reality are two different things."

"In that case, I'll rephrase. I like the idea of the reality of you being pregnant." He leans back, studying my face. "Is that clearer?"

"I'm not sure. Are you saying, even if I'm not pregnant now, you want us to try, and to keep trying, until I am?" I ask.

"Is that what you want?" He sounds kinda nervous. But then, I know how he feels. This is a big step.

"I think so," I reply, and he shakes his head.

"Don't think, Izzy. Be sure. This isn't something we can undo, and if you're not completely certain about it, then say so, and we'll wait until you are."

"Isn't it a bit late for waiting? What if I'm already pregnant?"

He smiles and says, "Then I'll be the happiest man in the world. If you're not, though, we can…"

"We can do our best to make it happen, can't we?" I say, and he sucks in a breath, rolling onto his back. We're still connected and I kneel up, straddling him.

"Oh, God… yes. And in the meantime… no more getting drunk," he says firmly.

"No, sir."

He raises his hips, burying himself deep inside me. "You're sure about this, Izzy?"

"About having your child?" I say, just to be sure. He nods his head. "Yes, Mason. I want to have your child… or, if we're very lucky, children."

He grins now, rolling us both over, so I'm on my back again, and he starts to move. "One thing at a time, baby… one thing at a time."

"Can we shower like that every day?" I ask over breakfast in his enormous kitchen. I think it's almost as big as my whole apartment, with gray cabinets and a dark granite countertop. It might be pouring with rain outside, but I can see through the glass doors that there's a deck, and then a formal area of lawn which leads into the woodland beyond. We're sitting together at the breakfast bar and I'm watching as Mason pours us both a cup of coffee.

"Of course we can. If that's what you want."

I don't see how I could want anything else. Being taken by him, standing under the shower, the water flowing over our bodies, while he loved me so hard… it was perfect.

"Hmm… I want," I murmur and he leans over and kisses me, handing me some more toast.

"I guess we'd better go over to your apartment once we've finished this," he says, taking a sip of coffee.

"Why?" Personally, I'd rather spend the day here, with him. And that's got nothing to do with the weather being so awful.

"Because you might look absolutely gorgeous wearing my clothes, but it's not gonna be very practical for work tomorrow."

He has a point. After we showered, we worked out that I had no clothes here, other than the jeans, sweater and underwear I had on last night. The jeans are perfectly serviceable, and I pointed out that underwear is superfluous now we're together, which made him smile. But that still left the problem of a top. We went through Mason's closets and came up with a shirt, which is enormous on me, but which he says looks sexy.

"No. I guess not." I look up at him. "But what are we doing? I—I mean, are you taking me home? Or are we going back to my place so I can pack a few things for tonight?"

He shakes his head, frowning and looking doubtful. "I thought we agreed, Izzy. I thought you wanted to wake up with me every day."

"I do."

"Okay then."

I'm not sure what that means, and I'm a little nervous about asking, in case I've misinterpreted everything again, so I finish breakfast, gulping down my coffee, and once we've cleared away, we leave. While I have my coat here, it's no great protection against the rain, but Mason has an umbrella, which he holds over my head until I'm safely in his car, even though he's wet himself. Then he drives us back into town.

"Is it okay if I send a message to Noah?" I ask him, pulling my phone from my purse.

He glances over, frowning. "You don't have to ask permission, Izzy," he says. "Noah's your friend. I get that. He's probably worried about you, so of course you should send him a message."

I want to say 'thank you', but I know he'll only tell me there's no need, and instead I tap out a message to Noah…

— It's only me. Just letting you know I'm fine. I'm better than fine, actually. Thanks for last night. We'll catch up soon. Love you. Isabel xx

It only takes a few minutes for Noah to reply…

— Thanks for letting me know. I've been worried. Not that I think I need to worry about you anymore. Tell Mason from me, he's a lucky man. See you soon. Love you. N xx

I can't help smiling as I put my phone back into my purse and Mason obviously notices, being as he's now parking up behind my apartment, in the space I usually use myself.

"What's funny?" he asks.

"Nothing. It's just that Noah gave me a message for you."

"Oh?"

"Yeah. He said I had to tell you you're a lucky man."

He smiles. "I already knew that." He switches off the engine and leans over to me. "You make me so damn happy, Izzy," he says, his voice a low growl. "But I know how close I came to losing you."

I reach up and caress his cheek. "I nearly lost you too."

"Let's make sure we don't lose each other again, shall we?"

"Definitely."

He gets out first, coming around to my side, opening the umbrella as he does, and we run to the front door and up the stairs. I let us in, sighing with relief that we're actually somewhere dry at last.

"I've never seen your apartment before," he says, looking around.

"There's not very much to see," I tell him. "It's tiny."

"I'm not gonna disagree," he says with a smile as I lead him into the bedroom and grab a small suitcase from on top of the closet.

"Do you want some help?" he asks, taking it from me and putting it down on the bed.

"You could hand me some things from the closet, if that's okay?"

He passes me skirts, blouses and jackets, which I fold and put into the suitcase, filling it in no time, and moving on to a second one, into which we put jeans, dresses and tops, almost emptying the closet. I don't comment on that because, again, I'm worried I might be overthinking, and while I pack my toiletries, Mason takes the bags down to the car before returning for me.

"It's still raining then?" I say, looking at his damp shoulders.

"Not so hard, but yeah."

He takes the last of my bags and I follow him out the door, waiting while he loads up the car again, and returns to escort me out, under the protection of his umbrella.

Once we're on our way back to his place, he turns and looks at me, just briefly. "I guess we'll need to work out what to do about getting your car back as well, won't we?"

"You think I'll need it?" I say.

"You don't?" he queries.

I'm confused now, and overthinking seems to be the least of my problems. "Well, I seem to be moving in with you, so…" I'm not sure whether that was what he was suggesting earlier, when I was too scared to ask, and while I haven't exactly 'asked' him now, he's going to have to tell me what he meant, and whether that's why he's just helped me pack almost all of my clothes into his car.

"That is what you want, isn't it?" he says, slowing the car. "You don't have to, if…" His voice fades and I turn in my seat, so I'm facing him, and even though he's still driving, he glances over at me, looking worried, and I have to smile.

"You know it's what I want, Mason. I want to wake up with you. Every. Single. Day. But do you think we're taking things too fast? I mean… moving in, starting a family? It's very early in our relationship, and—"

"So?" He shrugs his shoulders. "There's no formula for falling in love, or being together. If this is how it works for us, then this is how we'll do it. Other people might do things differently, and that's up to them, but the idea of being anywhere other than where you are is all wrong to me."

I know exactly how he feels, and I place my hand on his thigh. "This is right, isn't it?"

"Yes. It's better than right, Izzy. It's perfect."

I let out a sigh. "Yes. It is."

It's dark outside now. Mason's pulled the drapes across the windows, and we're lying on his couch, in front of a roaring fire, curled up together.

When we got back here earlier, he cleared me some closet space and then left me to unpack while he came downstairs and made us some sandwiches for lunch, and then after we'd eaten, we came in here and we've been here ever since.

His living room is enormous and is decorated in neutral tones, with off-white walls and pale gray drapes. His couch is a deeper shade of gray and the alcoves on either side of the fireplace are filled with shelves, some of which contain books, although there are also photographs of his family, too. Like the one I looked at last night, of his mom.

"We never worked out what to do about your car," he says, breaking our peaceful silence.

"No." I'm tempted to make the same argument that I won't need it if I'm living here. After all, we work in the same place, so…

"I know you think you won't need a car," he says, like he's read my mind. "But our days often start at different times, and you might wanna go shopping by yourself… or drive up to see your sisters."

"Without you?" I say, sitting up slightly and looking down at him.

"Well, I wasn't sure I'd be welcome."

"Why not?" I frown at him now.

"Because when I called at your house last night, they said I'd made you cry. They were kinda angry with me."

I smile now and trace a line down his cheek with my fingertip. "They're very protective."

"I got that… all by myself."

"But I'm guessing they relented."

"How did you know that?"

"Well, you found me… which I assume means they told you where I was?"

"Yeah." He nods his head. "I'm sorry, I don't know both your sisters' names. I only know one… the one called Ash. She was the one who told me you'd gone out with an old schoolfriend. It was your other sister who gave me directions."

"That's Reagan," I explain. "Ash is short for Ashley. She's the youngest, although you'd never know it."

He looks into my eyes, holding me close to him. "When I first saw you in the bar with Noah, I wondered if your sisters had sent me there to teach me a lesson, knowing I'd find you in the company of a handsome man."

I shake my head. "No. They know the score with Noah. They're among the very few people at home who know he's gay."

"So, you don't think they'd object to meeting me?" He sounds so nervous, I have to hug him, and lower myself down, putting my arms around him.

"Of course not. We could drive up there for Thanksgiving, if you like? I said I'd go back there anyway, being as Mom and Dad have been in touch to say they're not bothering to come home – again. So I guess you could drive us both up there, and we could stay over for a couple of days, and then bring my car back again."

"We could, yeah." He tilts his head, like he's thinking about my suggestion, although he sounds kinda doubtful, and then I realize my mistake.

"Of course. You're gonna want to see your family, aren't you?"

He raises his hand, placing his fingers over my lips, and then sits up, bringing me with him, and reaches behind him to the table at the end of the couch, where he left his phone. Picking it up, he turns back around and removes his fingers from my mouth, using them to press the screen of his phone a few times, before holding it up to his ear, his eyes fixed on mine.

"Hey, Dad," he says, after a couple of seconds, and then he adds, "Yeah, sorry about that. I had someone I needed to see." He pauses and smiles, nodding his head. "Oliver explained, did he?" He rolls his eyes. "Yes, it was Isabel… and yeah, we've worked things out. She's here with me now. That's partly why I'm calling. It's about Thanksgiving." He stops talking and waits, opening his mouth a couple of times, but not uttering a sound until eventually he says, "Slow down, will you? I know Destiny and Ronan have arranged to stay until Friday, and I know you want us all there, but would you hate me if I said I'm gonna drive Isabel up to Vermont to visit with her sisters?" I grab his arm, shaking my head. He can't do this. His dad was obviously thrilled at the thought of having his whole family around him, and I can't ask him to sacrifice that. Mason ignores my silent protests and puts his arm around me, pulling me into a hug. "We'll come and see you on Sunday, if that's okay? I get that Destiny and Ronan will have gone back to Boston by then, but we can catch up with them another time." He listens again for a moment and then says, "Lunch would be great. We'll be there at twelve. Get Oliver to come too, if that's okay. I'm sure he's dying to meet Isabel." I feel awful, and can barely listen as he finishes making the arrangements for Sunday, and then ends the call, putting the phone down on the floor and turning us over, so we're facing each other.

"You didn't have to do that," I say, the shroud of guilt wearing heavily around my shoulders.

"Yeah, I did. You told your sisters you'd go, and I know how much they mean to you."

"Your family means a lot to you too."

"Yes, they do. And we'll see them on Sunday."

"We won't see your sister and her new husband," I say.

"They've just got married. I'm sure they've got better things to do." He pulls me even closer to him, so I can feel his arousal pressing into me. "Now, will you stop feeling guilty?"

"And do what?" I ask, the weight already lifting.

"I'm sure we'll think of something…"

A workday breakfast differs greatly from a Sunday breakfast. We still made love in the shower, as Mason promised, but we're now dressed much more formally, and are rushing through our toast and coffee so we can get to the office in time for my first appointment.

"What time is your first session today?" I ask Mason, licking butter from my fingers.

"Eleven," he says, watching me closely. "You need to stop doing that."

"Doing what?"

"Licking your fingers."

"Why?"

"Because it makes me wanna fuck your mouth, that's why."

I suck in a breath and shudder. "I wish you would."

"Maybe tonight," he says, with a smile.

"Don't tease."

"Who's teasing?"

I finish my coffee, feeling a little breathless at the thought of what he's got in mind, and we get ready to leave. At least it's not raining today, and we make our way out to his car, getting in and setting off for town.

"Who are you seeing this morning?" he asks.

"A couple called Lucas and Penny."

He nods his head. "So, not Ian and Vanessa then?"

"No. They're missing their session this week, because they've left the kids with her mom, and gone to the Caribbean."

"Seriously?" He shakes his head. "They've decided that sex is the answer to everything, have they?"

"It seems so, yes." I can't help feeling like I've lost my way with them. But I'm not going to worry about it... not today. I've got other things on my mind.

"What's the story with Lucas and Penny?" he asks, taking an interest.

"Lucas had a drunken one-night stand about four months ago, and Penny can't forgive him."

"Are you surprised?" he says.

"No... not at all. But it's kinda sad. Lucas clearly regrets it, and it seems like he was very drunk. He knows he made a mistake..."

"Yeah. A big one." Mason sounds very disapproving and for a moment, I'm a little piqued by that.

"As big as lying to someone you love and pretending they're your girlfriend?" I say, unable to help myself.

He slows the car and looks at me. "I thought we'd already established there was nothing pretend about what happened between us, and I think cheating on your wife is a little bigger than that... but if this is your way of saying you wanna have it out with me, go right ahead."

I shake my head at him. "That's the whole point, Mason. I don't wanna have it out with you. I just wanna forget it ever happened."

He pulls the car over to the side of the road, slowing to a stop, putting the car into 'park' and applying the handbrake, so he can turn in his seat and look right at me.

"Does this mean I'm forgiven, Izzy?"

"You were always forgiven. I love you... and love means forgiving." I lean over, cupping his face in my hand. "Of course, if you ever lie to me again..." I let my words hang between us, even though I'm smiling, and he holds up his hands.

"I told you I'd never hurt you, and I meant it. I came too close to losing you for good to risk ever doing anything that dumb again."

He closes the gap between us and kisses me, long and hard. I'm breathless in seconds and squirm in my seat, my pussy dampening already.

"I want you," I whisper as he breaks the kiss.

"Nowhere near as much as I want you," he says, his eyes on fire.

"How am I supposed to get through this session?" I run my fingers through my hair, trying to focus on something other than his body and mine. "I need to give them all my attention, and I can't even think straight."

He turns around, facing forward, and smiles. "I'm sorry," he says, although he doesn't sound it. "I'll stop distracting you."

I want to tell him not to, because I like his distractions, and I want more of them... but I have a job to do, and time's running out.

"We need to get to work, or I'll be late."

He puts the car into gear and sets off again, the smile still etched on his face. "You won't be late," he whispers, reaching over and resting his hand on my knee.

"I need to look at my notes before they arrive," I say. "Although there might be no point, I suppose."

"What does that mean?"

"It means I'm not sure Penny's heart is in it. I'm not sure she even wants to forgive Lucas. At the end of our last session, I suggested they

269

took the weekend to think things through and come back to me with a decision. I'm worried she's gonna have decided it's not worth it."

He squeezes my leg. "You get far too close to your clients, you know that, don't you?"

"Maybe… but they're nice people."

He nods his head. "Would it help if I sat in with you today?" he says. "I've got time, and I can just observe and then give you any advice you need afterwards, assuming Penny decides she wants to proceed, of course. I—I'm not interfering, and I know you can handle it, but—"

"Would you?" I jump at his offer.

"Of course. If you think it'll help."

I lean over and kiss his cheek, even though he's driving, because while I know I can handle it too, I also value his opinion.

"This is my associate, Mason Gould," I explain as I direct Lucas and Penny into my office. Mason's standing in the corner by my desk and he comes over and offers his hand to both of them.

"I'm just here to observe," he says, as they shake. "But if you'd rather I left…?" He gives them the choice, which he's duty bound to do.

"No, that's fine," Lucas says, and I wonder if that means they're going to tell me it's all over and Penny's decided their marriage isn't worth saving.

Mason backs away and goes to sit at my desk, while Lucas and Penny take the same seats they had on Friday, at opposite ends of the couch. This isn't looking good. I glance at Mason as I grab my notepad, but he doesn't respond, and I sit down in the chair opposite my clients.

"How was the weekend?" I say, breaking the silence.

"We tried what you suggested," Lucas replies. "Penny counted to ten every time she wanted to yell at me."

"And?" I look at Penny. "Did it work?"

"Yes and no," she says, shrugging her shoulders. "I still yelled at him, but maybe not so much as normal." She lowers her head. "Sometimes I'd get to ten and still want to yell. So I did."

"You didn't remove yourself from the situation, like I suggested?"

"No. I yelled." She looks kinda guilty, which she shouldn't.

"That's okay," I say. "This was never gonna be easy."

"You're not kidding," she replies.

"The problem was," Lucas says, shifting along the couch slightly as he speaks, "it all felt kinda false. I get Penny wants to yell and scream at me, and I deserve it, but having her count to ten is never gonna work in the long run. She'll just end up so damn frustrated."

"I know. This was never a long-term plan," I explain. "I just needed a way to get you both through the weekend."

They look over at me and nod their heads.

"I was kinda hoping you'd say that," Lucas says and lets out a sigh. "Because on Friday evening and Saturday, the atmosphere between us was so tense and faked, I think we'd have both gone crazy if we'd tried it for any longer. Then, on Saturday night, while I was lying in the guest room, struggling to sleep, I remembered the other thing you said, about active forgetting…"

"You did?"

"Yes, and I decided to do something about it?"

I feel wary all of a sudden. I only touched on Nietzsche's theory. It was something I intended working on with them, not something I thought Lucas might choose to develop by himself.

"What was that?" I say, sitting forward.

"I arranged for my mom to have Louise yesterday afternoon, and I drove Penny out to a lake near where we live. It reminded us both of a place we used to go when we first met." He stops talking and looks at Penny again, shifting along the couch a little more. "We're not from around here, you see, and all those early memories feel kinda distant now, but as we were walking, and neither of us was saying anything, for fear of saying the wrong thing, I think we were both remembering those happier times."

"Did it help?" I ask, feeling a little less worried now. At least he didn't try anything too drastic.

"It did. I mentioned to Penny that the place reminded me of our first kiss, and she agreed with me, and then she laughed… well, she giggled. She hasn't done anything like that in months."

"Why did you laugh?" I ask, looking at Penny now.

She moves a little closer to Lucas, although I think it's unconsciously done, and then she says, "Because I remembered how he'd kissed me that very first time, and then he'd gone skinny-dipping, to cool down." She falls silent, blushing slightly.

"It wasn't that it was a hot day," Lucas says, taking over the story. "It was just that I needed to cool down." I nod my head in understanding. "It wouldn't have been a problem, except this old guy, who used to live in the woods up near the lake, came wandering by. Penny panicked, grabbed my clothes and ran off into the bushes, and I was stuck in the lake waiting for him to leave. Believe me, I wasn't cooling off anymore. I was freezing to death."

I can't help laughing myself, and Penny giggles. As she does, I see a glimpse of the woman beneath the heartbreak and I think I understand why Lucas fell for her, and why he's so desperate to save their marriage. She's captivating.

"Reliving the story certainly broke the ice," Lucas says, and they both move closer at the same time, which almost makes me smile.

"So what happened?" I ask, because I get the feeling something did.

"We talked," he says. "For the first time since this all happened, we really talked. Penny told me how she feels, without yelling, or screaming, or hurling abuse and accusations, and I explained to her how much pressure I'd been under at work. I'd kept it from her, so she didn't worry, but the stress levels were off the scale at the time... not just for me, for everyone. It's no excuse for what I did, but I wanted Penny to understand that it had nothing to do with her. It was stress, booze and stupidity."

"You've changed jobs though, right?"

He smiles. "Yeah. It was one of the first things I did before I even moved back into the house. I just wish I'd done it sooner."

Penny sits forward slightly. "We understand that one conversation – no matter how honest and helpful – doesn't make everything right again," she says. "We know we've still got a long way to go, and I'm not gonna lie, I'm still angry with him. I still want to yell at him pretty much all the time, and I still can't forgive him. But the difference between

Friday and today, is that I think I want to try." She reaches over and puts her hand beside Lucas and he takes it in his, lifting it to his mouth and kissing her fingers. She lets him, and I'll admit, I'm astounded.

"We want you to help us get back to where we were," Lucas says, and I feel my heart sink.

"I can't do that," I reply and they both stare at me. Penny's eyes fill with tears and she shakes her head.

"B—But, I thought…"

"I can only help you move forward from where you are now," I explain, interrupting her. "Too much has happened for you to go back. And why would you want to? Going back will only make you dwell on the past, which won't help. The past is where the problem lies. Besides, relationships should always evolve and move forward, and doing that positively, together, is something I can definitely help you with."

Penny turns her gaze on Lucas, and he tilts his head, staring down at her. "Do you wanna try that?" he asks.

She doesn't answer him, but looks over at me again and says, "Are we talking about forgetting the past altogether?"

"No. Not at all." I sit a little further forward. "You proved on your walk yesterday that the past has a place in the present and the future. But you can't drag it all forward with you. It's not healthy. That's the whole point of active forgetting. It might help to think of it as selective remembering, if you prefer. You might find that more beneficial."

Penny blinks a couple of times, like she's trying to work something out, and then says, "So, it's okay for me to remember our first kiss, but I have to forget Lucas's… mistake?" She takes a moment to find the word, and I smile at her.

"I like that you're referring to what happened as a mistake now. But no, you don't have to forget it. That would be impossible. It's gonna come into your consciousness every so often, whether you like it or not. That can't be helped. But, if we get this right, with time, you'll be able to have those thoughts, deal with them, accept them for what they are, and leave them behind you, focusing more on the present and the future."

Lucas nods his head. "We could come out of this even stronger than we were before, by the sounds of things."

Penny immediately snatches her hand from his and leans back in her seat, frowning, her lips pursed in a thin line, that captivating woman hidden behind a veneer of anger.

"Say whatever it is you're thinking," I urge her. "You have to be honest with each other."

"I didn't think there was anything wrong with how we were before," she says, and Lucas closes his eyes for a second, clearly seeing the error of his words.

He moves closer, putting his arm around her, and she lets him, even though she's still tense. "I'm sorry, baby," he says. "That came out wrong. What I meant was that things could be even better, not that there was anything wrong. There wasn't."

She doesn't acknowledge his words and I notice him deflate. He's about to pull back from her when I say, "Lucas, you need to allow for Penny's pain in this. Four months might seem like a long time to you, but it's all still very raw for her. She has to work out how she feels about you, and about what happened, and you have to be patient with her."

"I know," he says, leaving his arm where it is now. "It's my fault."

I shake my head. "I want both of you to try really hard not to think of this in terms of blame and fault. It's gonna be hard, but those are very negative thoughts, and they're not gonna help. They're gonna creep in from time to time, and when they do, we can talk them through, but I want you to focus on the good times. Not just in the past, but in the present too." They both stare at me, confusion etched on their faces, and I smile at them. "You had a good time yesterday, didn't you?" They nod their heads. "And you'll have more like that. It might only be a few minutes here and a half hour there, but it will happen." I check my watch and see that we're nearly out of time. "Can I see you both again next Monday morning?" I ask, and they nod again, getting up.

"Thank you, Isabel," Lucas says as I accompany them to the door.

"You don't have to thank me. Just be kind to each other and take some time out over Thanksgiving to be together."

"We will," Penny says, surprising me.

Once I've closed the door on them, I lock it and rush back to Mason, who's still sitting behind my desk, looking thoughtful.

"Well?" I say, going and standing in front of him, looking down at his pensive face. "How did I do? Do you think it's a problem that they kind of went off on their own tangent? I didn't want them to do that. I thought we'd work on Nietzsche's theory together as we moved forward, but I think it went okay in the end, don't you? And the…"

"Can you stop talking, just for a second?" he says.

"Sure. Sorry."

He shakes his head. "Don't apologize." He sits forward, looking up at me. "Can I ask you a question?"

"Of course." I feel nervous, although I'm not sure why.

"Why do you keep asking for my help?"

"Because you're so much better at this than I am. I'm a novice, compared to you…"

He holds up his hand, and I stop talking again. "You don't need anyone's help, Izzy," he says, gazing into my eyes. "Your clients are lucky to have you. *I'm* lucky to have you… professionally as well as personally."

"Do you mean that?"

"Yes. No more lies, remember? You're exceptional at this. Never doubt it."

"Thank you."

He shakes his head. "Don't thank me. I'm just saying it how it is." I smile and he smiles back, and then he says, "It's funny, I was only talking to Oliver about Nietzsche's theory the other day."

"You two have really interesting conversations," I say with a chuckle.

"It was in the context of me telling him, in very loose terms, about a client I've been having a few troubles with, and I was explaining to Oliver that I was thinking of employing selective remembering with this guy… as a last resort. Oliver wanted to know what it was, so I told him… in layman's terms. He rubbished the idea, as only Oliver can, until I explained to him we both already use it."

"You do?"

"Hmm." He nods his head. "Neither of us remembers the bad stuff about our mom. It's still there, but we choose to forget it… at least most of the time."

"Did he understand?" I ask.

"Yeah, he did."

"That's what I'm trying to get Penny to see. She's never gonna totally forget what Lucas did, but she doesn't have to live her life around it. She can choose to park it, and focus on more positive things… at least, she can, if she wants to."

"She will," he says. "With your help."

He runs his right forefinger along the edge of my desk before he smiles up at me.

"Do you remember what you were thinking about when you were using your dildo in here the other day?" he asks, surprising me.

"Um… I was thinking about you watching me, and then coming in here and taking me over my desk."

"How would you feel about making at least a part of that fantasy into a reality?"

I blush. I can't help it. "C—Could we?"

"We could."

Then I remember something and I walk slowly around my desk, opening the top drawer. "I've got my dildo in here," I whisper. "So, if you want to, we could make both parts of it come true."

"Oh, God… yes," he groans and takes my hand, pulling me onto his lap, and while I might be giggling, I'm also fired up with anticipation.

Because that's what he does to me… and I think he always will.

Mason

The last few days have been spectacular, and while I know I agreed to us spending Thanksgiving with Izzy's sisters up in Vermont, there is a part of me that wishes we weren't driving up there now. I wish we'd stayed home and shut ourselves away… together, because there are so many things I want to do with her.

Still, there's no hurry…. not now. We've got plenty of time to do everything we want. Izzy's moved in with me, and in reality, we make love all the time… morning, noon and night.

Our mornings are slow and steady, usually ending in the shower, which Izzy seems to have taken a liking to. Our nights are a lot more passionate and intense, often by the fire in the living room, or in bed, with the lights dimmed. As for 'noon', that tends to be hard and fast, and wherever we find ourselves… her desk, my couch… to be honest, the geography doesn't matter.

Watching Izzy masturbate in her office after Lucas and Penny left was incredible. I thought it was good the first time, when I was hiding outside her door, but on Monday morning, once we'd swapped seats and I was sitting opposite her, staring openly as she played with herself and made herself come so damn hard, it was beyond words. She put on a fabulous show for me, and after she'd calmed, I walked around her desk and moved her keyboard aside, and although she'd just begged me – or rather, screamed at me – to bend her over and take her, I didn't. I wanted to see her face. So, I laid her down on her desk, and spread her legs wide… and then I took her. Neither of us had bothered to undress. Izzy's skirt was around her waist, her blouse undone and her breasts exposed, and I'd just pushed my pants down slightly, surprising her by revealing I wasn't wearing any underwear either. To be honest, I don't think it could have been any more erotic.

It's been that way ever since. Whenever we get a spare moment, we have to be together… preferably naked.

We haven't talked any more about Izzy being pregnant… and we don't need to. It's what we both want. So now it's just about waiting, and trying… and of the two, I prefer the trying. The waiting isn't so much fun. I know we'll get there. I also know many people would say we're crazy for rushing into this, but I don't care, and neither does Izzy. This is right for us, even if we can't explain it, anymore than we can explain our love for each other. It's just the way it is between us, and we're not going to question it. We're just gonna keep on trying.

I park the car alongside Izzy's Lexus, on the driveway. She's been fairly quiet on the drive up here, but then, so have I… probably for very different reasons. As I switch off the engine, she smiles and then turns in her seat, looking over at me. "You are okay about this, aren't you?"

"About coming up here?"

"Yes."

I feel like it's kinda late to be asking that question, but I nod my head. "I'm fine, although I'll admit I'm a little nervous about meeting your sisters." That's been the reason for my silence on the journey.

"You don't have to be," she says. "I called them on Tuesday and told them they had to be kind to you."

"Why?"

"Because I knew you were worried about it. I didn't want them to think of you as the man who made me cry."

"Even though I did?" I reach over and caress her cheek with my fingertips.

She leans into my touch. "That's between us, Mason, and it's in the past now. I don't think either of us needs my sisters dragging it up… and they won't now. They know we're happy, and that's all they care about."

"Thank you," I say, leaning over and kissing her.

"You don't have to thank me. I just didn't want them to think badly of you. It's negative, and we're not about negatives, are we?"

"No, we're not." She's about to get out when I pull her back. "Can I ask why you've been so quiet for the last couple of hours?"

She smiles over at me, looking embarrassed, and I know that means she's been thinking about sex. It's something I've already gotten used to with her.

"I'm just going to miss you, that's all."

"Why? Are you going somewhere?"

She giggles. "No. But we won't be able to be ourselves up here, will we?"

"What do you mean?"

I'm going to make her say it, whatever it is. She needs to stop being so shy around me. She's not like that when we're in bed, or in the shower, or on the couch, or in her office – or mine. In fact, wherever we are, if we're having sex, she's the polar opposite of shy. She's wild… and I love that about her. But when we're in a normal, everyday situation, and we're talking, like we are now, she always gets flustered and awkward, whenever the subject of sex is raised – unless, of course, she's drunk, in which case, anything goes. I'm not sure why she's so shy, but I'm working on it, because I want her to be completely comfortable with me… all the time.

She stares at me like she knows exactly what I'm doing and then narrows her eyes.

"We won't be able to make love up here," she says, surprising me, and I pull back slightly, staring down at her.

"Who says?"

"I say." She tilts her head. "If you think I'm gonna scream your name at the top of my voice, when my little sisters can hear me, you need to think again."

I smile at her. "Don't worry about it," I say, shifting toward the door and opening it. "I'll fuck you quietly."

I get out and walk around to her side, helping her out. She stares up at me, wide-eyed. "You mean, you can do that?"

"Yeah. I'll prove it to you, later on."

She leans in to me, resting her hands on my chest and looking up into my eyes. "I've spent the entire journey worrying how I was gonna survive without feeling you inside me for the next couple of days… and now you tell me we can do it all quietly?"

I laugh and hold her close to me. "Yes, we can do it all quietly, babe." I lean in and kiss her, just briefly. I don't comment on the fact that she seems to have forgotten her embarrassment... I just enjoy the fact that she has.

I hear a noise coming from behind me, and Izzy pulls away, looking over my shoulder and smiling.

"Come on," she says, taking my hand, and I turn to face her sisters.

In daylight, the similarities between the three of them are much more obvious. Ashley, who I now know to be the youngest of the three sisters, is a brunette, like Izzy, and she's maybe an inch or two shorter, with slightly lighter brown eyes. Reagan has dark blonde hair, is a little taller than Ashley, but has the same shaped face as Izzy.

"I know you've met him before," Izzy says as we approach, "but this is Mason."

I smile over at them and they smile back, and then Ashley steps forward slightly and says, "Hello. It's really nice to meet you properly."

"It's nice to meet you too."

"Do you wanna come inside out of the cold?" Reagan offers, stepping aside, and Izzy gives my hand a squeeze and a tug, pulling me into the house.

And just like that, it seems I'm accepted.

We're already full up on roast turkey, stuffing, mashed potatoes, green beans, creamed corn, cranberry sauce, and probably the best gravy I've ever tasted, although I'd never tell my dad that.

"I know it's traditional to serve pumpkin pie, but none of us like it," Ash says, bringing in some bowls from the kitchen. We're eating in their formal dining room, which they've decorated with candles, pine cones, pumpkins, and flowers.

"So, we're having apple pie instead." Reagan's following her sister into the room, carrying an enormous pie dish in her hands, which she places on the table in front of Izzy, who hasn't been allowed to lift a finger in the preparation or cooking of our meal. Neither have I, although they asked me to carve the turkey.

"I love apple pie," I say and they both smile at me, as Izzy dishes it up into the bowls.

We hand them around and once we've started eating the deliciously sweet, but slightly tart dessert, Izzy looks at her sisters and says, "When are you guys gonna see your boyfriends, then?"

"Tomorrow," they both say, in unison, before Reagan adds, "You don't mind, do you?"

"Of course not," Izzy says, although I can't help noticing she's studying Ashley. "Is everything alright, Ash?" she asks.

"Yeah. I'm just not sure how much longer I can tolerate Jax's moods, that's all."

"Moods?" A frown crosses Izzy's face and I wonder whether she's being a big sister or a psychologist. "This is the guy who was behaving like a caveman, right?"

I don't know what that means in this context, so I eat my apple pie and observe.

"He still is… and, to be honest, I've had enough."

"Maybe you should try talking to him about it," Izzy says.

Ashley shrugs her shoulders. "I did, but all he said was that he didn't see there was a problem."

"Sounds like a guy," Reagan says, rolling her eyes.

I cough, to remind them I'm still here, and they all turn to me and laugh.

"You'll have to excuse us," Reagan says. "We're used to picking Izzy's brain when she comes home. It's the age gap between us, you see. She's so much more experienced with men than…" She stops talking and blushes. "I'm sorry, I shouldn't have said that. I didn't mean—"

"It's fine," I say, holding up my hand. I feel a little confused as I gaze at Izzy, who's blushing even more fiercely than her sister. "I know all about Izzy's past, just like she knows about mine."

That's not strictly true, but I can hardly tell her sisters that. Especially as, so far as I'm aware, Izzy doesn't have a past to speak about.

Izzy's been quiet all evening, ever since Reagan made that remark over dinner. I guess that's not surprising, but now we're alone in her room, which is kinda girly, with floral wallpaper and drapes, and a fairly narrow double bed, I can't let it lie any longer.

"Why do your sisters think you have a past that you don't have?" I ask, perching on the edge of the mattress and watching her as she sits at her vanity, removing her makeup.

She gazes at me in the mirror for a moment. "Because, years ago, they assumed I was more experienced than I am, and I never disillusioned them."

"Why not?"

"I was embarrassed."

I get up and go over to her, resting my hands on her shoulders and looking at her reflection.

"Why? I still don't understand why you're so embarrassed about being a virgin. What's wrong with waiting until the right guy comes along?"

"Nothing. Unless waiting wasn't your choice."

"Was there really no-one at all before me?"

She shakes her head. "Between studying and looking after Reagan and Ashley, there was never any time left for dating."

"But you let them believe there had been?"

"Yeah. I didn't want to admit to being the oldest virgin in town."

"I seriously doubt that was ever the case, but even if it was, it's not anymore." I lean down, move her hair aside and kiss her neck, which makes her shudder. "And I, for one, am glad you waited."

"Why?" she asks.

"Because it means you're mine."

She sighs. "Yes, I am."

I move back just slightly and, holding her shoulders, I turn her around, so she's facing me, and then I crouch down in front of her.

"I know I told your sisters that you know about my past, but you don't."

"No, I don't, do I?" She frowns slightly. "Why did you say that?"

"Because it sounded better." I kneel, so I can get closer to her. "Do you wanna know, or would you rather not?"

She tilts her head. "Is there much to tell?"

"What does that mean?"

"Well… have you been in any long-term relationships before?" she asks, sounding a little wary.

"That depends on your definition of long-term. The longest I've dated anyone is six months. But we didn't live together… and we weren't in love. I've never been in love, not until I met you."

She smiles and her eyes widen slightly. "So, you've never lived with anyone?"

"No. I've spent the night with women before. I've spent weekends with a few of them. But two or three nights have always been my limit. After that, I've always wanted to get back into my own space. Which I guess was probably a sign none of them were right for me… or I wasn't right for them."

"Were there many of them?" She bites her bottom lip, and I take her hands in mine.

"I wasn't counting. Does it matter?"

She sucks in a breath. "More than fifty?" she says.

"Hell, no." I smile at her, hoping to give her some reassurance.

"More than twenty?" She's clearly not done with this.

"Yes."

"So, somewhere between twenty and fifty?"

"Are you okay with that?" I ask, feeling a little nervous myself now.

"Yes. It's not something you can change, is it?"

"No. But I want you to know, when I told you the other night that you're the best, I meant it. They weren't just words."

She leans in to me and reaches up, caressing my cheek with her fingertips. "I know," she says. "I know you wouldn't lie to me about something so important. Now, do you think we could forget about your past, and focus on more important things?"

"Of course." I stand, bringing her with me, and gaze into her eyes. "What do you wanna focus on, Izzy?"

"I want you to show me how to make love quietly," she murmurs, biting her bottom lip.

I smile down at her. "With pleasure," I whisper, and lift her into my arms. She squeals and I shake my head. "That's not a great start, babe."

"I don't think I'm gonna be very good at this," she says, as I carry her over to the bed.

"Yeah, you will. You're the best… remember?"

"Are you okay about going to JC's?" Izzy asks as we get into my car.

"I'm fine. I'll just avoid the ladies' room, if that's okay with you." She smiles up at me, and I close the door, walking around to the driver's side and getting in.

We've spent most of the day with her sisters, but Izzy arranged for us to meet up with Noah tonight, and he's evidently bringing his new boyfriend with him, which I think surprised Izzy, when he told her. I have to say, I was kinda relieved myself. I feared I might have felt like the odd one out if it had just been the three of us.

"You know the way, don't you?" she says, looking over at me with a mischievous smile.

"Yeah. Thanks."

I shake my head at her and reverse off of the driveway and onto the street, before making the short drive to JC's. I feel a lot better than I did the last time I took this journey, and I park in the same space as I did last Saturday night.

"You're sure about parking here?" Izzy says to me, looking over and frowning slightly.

"Yeah. Why not?"

"Because you parked here the other night."

"And?"

"And I don't wanna jinx our evening."

I chuckle and lean over, kissing her. "Our evening wasn't jinxed. We got back together, so it was pretty damn perfect."

"In the end… after you'd publicly humiliated yourself."

"The end justified the means, so who cares about a little public humiliation?"

She puts her arms around my neck, pulling me closer and we kiss… deeply.

"Do you think we'd better go in?" I say, breaking the kiss. We're both a little breathless and, to be honest, I can think of all kinds of things I'd rather do right now, none of which involve going to a bar. I know this is important to Izzy, though. She wants me and Noah to get along. It matters to her.

"Hmm… I guess so," she says, and I sense her reluctance too, which makes me smile.

"We can continue with this later." I kiss her briefly, so we don't get carried away.

"Even though I proved I'm not very good at silent sex?" she says, with a slight smile.

"We were never aiming for silent. We were aiming for quiet."

"Yeah. And I missed that too."

She's not wrong. I kissed her when she came last night, trying to smother the sound of her cries, but I'm fairly sure I failed. Neither Reagan nor Ashley said anything this morning at breakfast, but there's no getting away from it, Izzy was very far from quiet.

I get out of the car and go around to Izzy's side, opening the door and taking her hand, which I keep hold of as I lead her into the bar.

"They're already here," she says, waving to her right, and pulling me toward a booth on the opposite side of the bar from where she and Noah were sitting the other night.

I notice Noah standing up, and then spot another guy with him. They're both around the same height – roughly six foot two – and are dressed smartly in jeans and button-down shirts, with casual jackets. There the similarities end though, because where Noah is dark, Aaron is blond, and while Noah looks mildly amused, Aaron looks nervous. I know how he feels. The friendship between Noah and Izzy is important and I don't think either of us wants to screw up.

We walk over and Noah steps forward, just as Izzy lets go of my hand and they hug, pulling back fairly quickly for Noah to look into Izzy's eyes.

"God, you're sickeningly in love, aren't you?" he says with a grin.

"Yes." She takes my hand again, gazing up into my face. "Yes, I am."

Noah looks at me, smiling. "I'm not gonna ask how you are," he says, "because you look sickeningly in love too."

"I'm glad to hear it."

He shakes his head, and then he turns to the man beside him.

"This is Aaron," he says, and Izzy and I both greet him before we all sit down.

A waitress appears by Izzy's side and she orders an orange juice while I stick to mineral water. Noah asks for a dirty martini and Aaron a glass of red wine.

"I'm drowning my sorrows," Noah says. "So we came by cab."

"Why are you drowning your sorrows?" Izzy asks.

"Because that story I've been working on should have been published this weekend, except it's been held up by the damn lawyers."

"Oh. Poor you," Izzy says, sounding disappointed for her friend.

Noah shrugs. "It was only to be expected, I guess," he murmurs and then he looks up and turns to me. "I should probably explain that I've been working on an exposé of a local politician who's been a very naughty boy. I'd worked my ass off getting it ready to go out this weekend... right in time for the lawyers to announce they needed a few extra days to make sure I hadn't said anything that could get my newspaper sued."

"I guess they have to be sure," I say, trying to sound reasonable, and he nods his head.

"I know. It's just so infuriating."

Aaron smiles, rolling his shoulders and leans in. "Can we change the broken record now and talk about something more interesting?"

Noah narrows his eyes, although he's smiling and says, "Okay. You have listened to me whining all day. I guess you're due a break."

"Thanks," Aaron says, as the waitress comes back with our drinks, and we all settle down.

"So," Izzy says, once she's taken a sip of orange juice, "can I ask a question?"

"Of me?" Noah asks, seeing that she's looking directly at him.

"Yes."

"Go ahead."

She leans in and lowers her voice, so I have to strain to hear her. "Have you come out?"

"No." He shakes his head, frowning. "Whatever made you think that?"

"The fact that you're sitting here with Aaron, and that you told Mason you're gay the other night. I've never known you to tell anyone before."

"I only told Mason because I wanted him to know I'm not a threat," Noah says, glancing at me with a smile, which I return. "And as for sitting here with Aaron…" His voice fades and he sucks in a breath, letting it out slowly.

"We've talked it through," Aaron says, taking over where Noah left off. "And we both wanna come out fully and be a couple. At the moment only my family knows about me being gay, and I'm sick of pretending to everyone else, but we've decided it's best to wait until after Noah's article is released, to let the dust settle from that."

"Sounds sensible," I say, and Noah smiles at me.

"If we lived in a big city, I'd say to hell with it, and I'd tell my parents and just get on with living with Aaron, but in a small town…"

"It's different." I complete his sentence, so he doesn't have to.

"Yeah, it is. The only people who know are Izzy and her sisters, and you." He nods at me.

"How did Izzy find out?" Aaron asks, sipping his wine. "Did you tell her?"

Noah shakes his head, chuckling, while Izzy sits back in her seat beside me. "You're not really gonna tell them that story, are you?" She sounds worried, which is intriguing.

"Oh, I think he has to now," I say, and she glares at me, although I can see the hint of a smile on her lips.

We both look back at Noah. "We were in our early twenties, and single." He looks at Izzy rather pointedly, presumably because being single was normal for her, although he doesn't elaborate. "I think we were at a wedding, or something, weren't we?"

"Yes," she says. "It was your cousin's, wasn't it?"

"Oh, yes, it was." He shakes his head. "They're divorced now. Anyway, we were commenting on some of the couples at this wedding, and Isabel remarked on the fact that we were both single, and both looking for love and she said that, if we got to thirty and nothing had changed, we should be each other's back-ups. Before I could tell her it was never gonna happen, she gave me a lecture about how she was sure we'd both be happily married way before we got to thirty, with at least six kids between us, and a couple of dogs each, and how we could all go on vacations together. I got her to stop talking eventually, and I explained that her back-up plan was never gonna work, because I've never been into girls."

"How did you react?" I ask Izzy, looking down at her.

"It never affected our friendship, but I'll admit, I was stunned. He'd hid it very well."

"You don't need to tell me," Aaron says, rolling his eyes. "I know how good Noah is at hiding his sexuality. I couldn't work it out for ages, which is why it took me so long to ask him out."

Noah leans in to him just very slightly. "Yeah, it's taken years for me to perfect such levels of secrecy. Even when Isabel was being my fake girlfriend, no-one ever guessed we weren't together." He beams from ear to ear. "I'm that good."

"Excuse me?" Aaron says, as Noah's words ring around my head and I sit back in my seat. "What do you mean 'fake girlfriend'?"

"I mean Isabel used to come to family functions with me – you know, weddings, and barbecues and things, when my relatives would have expected me to be there with a girlfriend on my arm. It was easier to bring her with me and pretend, than to face their questions." He glances across at me. "You don't need to worry, Mason. It was purely platonic."

"I'm not worried." I'm confused.

"You're a coward," Aaron says to Noah, as I try to make sense of everything.

"Yeah, I know," Noah replies.

Aaron leans in just a little further. "But you're my coward," he says, and they both laugh.

Izzy joins in, but I can't, as much as I'd like to, because not only am I confused, I'm feeling a little hurt… not to mention angry.

I know I haven't been the greatest company for most of the evening, and we've driven home in silence, relieved that Ashley and Reagan are still out, and we have the place to ourselves. Without a word, we head up to Izzy's bedroom, and once we've closed the door and flicked on the lights, she turns on me.

"What's wrong?" she says, shrugging off her coat and throwing it onto the bed. "You've been like a bear with a sore head all evening."

"You need to ask?"

"Obviously."

I take off my jacket, hanging it over the back of the chair in the corner of the room and kicking off my shoes before I turn back to her.

"You got mad at me because I lied to you. You left me because you found out I had a 'shitty plan' to pretend you were my girlfriend at the reunion." I unbutton my shirt as I'm talking, pulling it off and hurling it into the corner of the room. "And yet, you didn't have a problem with doing exactly the same thing with Noah."

She stares at me for a moment, yanking her sweater over her head and letting it drop to the floor, her bra joining it within moments.

"Of course I didn't," she says, shaking her head before she undoes her jeans, pulling them down and stepping out of them. She's naked before me and I'll admit, I'm distracted. But only for a moment.

"Excuse me?" I say, unbuckling my belt and then unfastening my jeans, before removing them and my underwear.

Izzy gathers up her clothes and her coat, dumping them on the chest at the end of the bed, turning and glaring at me. "What do you mean 'excuse me'?"

"I mean, why is it okay to be Noah's fake girlfriend, and not mine?"

She puts her hands on her hips, tilting her head to one side. "Isn't it obvious?"

"Not to me, no."

She shakes her head. "He wasn't deceiving me," she says and I take a half step backwards.

"But I was," I say, and it's not a question.

"Yes." She moves closer to me.

"Am I really forgiven?" I ask, feeling kinda desperate.

She reaches out, her fingertips grazing over my bare chest, my breath catching in my throat at that simple touch. "Of course you are. P—Please, can we stop fighting?" There's a hitch in her voice. I notice her eyes glistening in the dimmed lights, and I grab her, pulling her close to me, holding her tight against my body.

"I'm sorry," I whisper into her hair and she pulls back, looking up at me.

"What for?"

"For lying to you in the first place. For questioning you now. I felt so hurt and so angry that you'd pretended to be Noah's girlfriend, and yet you'd left me over exactly the same thing. I guess I forgot the lies I'd told to get you there."

"It was a misunderstanding. We both know that. Can we just forget the whole damn thing?" she says, reaching up and cupping my face with her hand. "I can't fight with you, Mason. It makes me feel so... so broken."

"I'm sorry," I murmur again and I capture her face with my hands, kissing her, hard and deep.

"Make love with me?" she says, pulling back slightly and gazing up at me. It's hard not to notice that she said 'with', not 'to', and I know I can't take her... not this time.

I lift her into my arms and carry her to the bed, lowering her to the mattress and settling between her parted legs. She gazes up at me as I rub the tip of my cock against her entrance.

"Put us back together, Mason... please?"

I nod my head and she sucks in a breath, taking my length until I'm as deep inside her as I can be.

"Better?" I say, dropping to my elbows, my lips just an inch from hers.

"Better."

She circles her hips, but I reach down, resting my hand on her and holding her steady, just for a moment. "Will you do something for me, Izzy?"

"Of course."

"If I ever behave like that again; if I ever do anything to make you feel broken, or even slightly fractured, will you say two words to me?"

"What two words?"

"Just say 'puzzle piece', will you?"

She frowns. "Puzzle piece?"

"Yeah. You told me the other night that when we first made love, it was like you'd found your missing puzzle piece. And I told you I felt the same way." I move my hand around behind her and raise her ass off of the bed, grinding into her, slow and steady, my forehead resting against hers. "If I ever behave like an idiot again, just say 'puzzle piece' to me, and I'll remember. I'll remember what I'm risking and how much I have to lose."

"You're not gonna lose me," she says, reaching up and letting her fingers twist into my hair.

"I can't, Izzy." I'm struggling to speak and I cough around the lump in my throat. "I can't."

We hold each other, our bodies fused... and although I've never been this gentle in my life, I don't think I could ever love her harder.

"Why are you so nervous?" I ask, noting the way Izzy's clutching her hands in her lap as we drive to my dad's.

"Because I'm gonna meet your family," she replies, like the answer should be obvious.

I reach over and cover her hands with one of mine, leaving the other one on the steering wheel.

"They're not gonna bite you," I say, and she relaxes slightly... or she tries to.

We drove back from Vermont yesterday morning. Neither of us mentioned our fight of the previous night, and we still haven't. We don't need to. It's done now, we made up, and there's nothing more to be said… unless I behave like an idiot again, of course. In which case, Izzy knows exactly what to do.

The drive home was tedious and lonely, for both of us, and when we got back to my place, I helped her from her car, and almost dragged her inside, not bothering to bring our bags. Our lips met before the door had even closed, and while I had every intention of taking her upstairs and spending the rest of the day there, we didn't get that far, because her desperation was at least as great as my own, and we ended up tearing at each other's clothes before we'd even got to the stairs. It was a fun afternoon, and I think it was just what we both needed. I know Izzy enjoyed being able to scream my name at the top of her voice when she came, and I needed to hear her do it. Over and over… and over.

I park up alongside Oliver's Jeep and help Izzy from the car, her nerves returning as she glances at Dad's house and bites her bottom lip.

"Relax, baby." I take her hand and lead her over to the front door, just as it opens, and Dad appears, with a broad grin on his face.

"Isabel." He ignores me, which makes me smile. "It's so lovely to meet you at last."

"This is my father," I say, as we enter the house.

"Hello, Doctor Gould," Izzy replies and my father shakes his head.

"Oh, call me John. Otherwise it gets too confusing. And anyway, I can't possibly be so formal with someone as beautiful as you."

I've never seen my dad like this before and I have to stifle a laugh, just as Oliver comes out of the living room. He's holding Baxter by his collar, which is unusual, and I tilt my head at him.

"Not everyone likes dogs," he says with a shrug, even though Baxter is clearly keen to meet Izzy.

"I do," she says and Oliver releases him. He bounds forward, and Izzy crouches down, letting him lick her as she greets him.

"What's his name?" she asks.

"Baxter," Oliver replies, stepping forward. "And you must be the mysterious Isabel?"

"I'm not very mysterious," Izzy says, getting to her feet.

"Oh, I don't know. You were a huge mystery to Mason for quite a long while." He's grinning, and I punch him on the arm, hard enough to hurt.

"They're like children when they get together," my dad says, pulling Izzy away from me and taking her into the kitchen. Baxter follows, eager not to be left out. "You either have to ignore them, or go with it."

"I think I'll go with it," I hear her say as they disappear.

"You said she was beautiful," Oliver whispers, once we're alone. "You never said she was *that* beautiful. Why the hell is she wasting her time on you?"

"I ask myself the same question every morning."

"Why only in the morning?"

"Because that's when I wake up with her."

"*Every* morning?" He frowns, but then his face clears. "You mean, she's moved in with you?"

"Yeah."

"Wow. That was quick." He nudges into me.

"I'm in love with her. For some reason, she's also in love with me. Being apart doesn't seem to work very well for us."

I don't tell him we struggled with being apart for the two and a half hour journey back from Vermont yesterday. That's none of his business.

He nods his head, looking kinda sad, and I wonder if he's thinking about Jemima.

"You'll get there," I say, lowering my voice and he lets out a long breath before following Dad and Izzy into the kitchen, which is his way of telling me he doesn't want to talk about it.

Dad and Izzy are both over by the glass doors that lead out into the garden. Dad's busy explaining about the herbs he grows out there, by the sounds of things.

"Is there any chance I could have my girlfriend back?" I ask, and she turns and smiles at me.

"I'm your girlfriend now, am I?" she says, picking up on the fact that I've never called her that before.

"Yes." I'm quite unashamed, despite the presence of my little brother. "Is that okay?"

"It's perfect," Izzy replies and, giving my dad a sweet smile, she walks over to me, turning and leaning against me, her back to my front.

I put my arms around her, holding her close and glance at Oliver, who I half expect to make some kind of joke. He doesn't. He's still looking sad, and I feel sorry for him. I just wish I knew how to help. Because now I know how good this feels, I want him to feel it too.

"While I've got you here," Dad says, coming back over and checking something in the oven, which smells remarkably like lamb, "I wanted to ask what you're doing around Christmas time? We missed out on seeing you for Thanksgiving, so I wondered if we could get together over the holidays?"

"We haven't discussed our plans for Christmas Day," I say, as Izzy twists and looks up at me.

"Oh, we can't get together on Christmas Day itself," Dad replies. "Destiny and Ronan are going to see Ronan's sister, being as they spent Thanksgiving here, but…"

"Why don't we do something the weekend before?" I suggest, knowing how desperate he is to have all of us together under one roof. I kiss the top of Izzy's head to get her attention and she looks up at me again. "What are your sisters doing?"

She shakes her head. "Don't worry about my sisters. We spent Thanksgiving with them, and you didn't see your family at all. I don't feel…"

I turn her in my arms, my hands on her hips, and look down into her eyes. "Are your mom and dad coming home for the holidays?"

She shakes her head. "No."

"Okay."

I turn back to Dad, but before I can say anything, Izzy gets there first. "I'm sorry," she says. "My sisters are a lot younger than me, and I feel kinda responsible for them."

Dad tilts his head to one side, and I take over the explanation. "Isabel's parents took off when she was sixteen. Her little sisters were eight and six and she was left in charge of them."

"They just took off?" Oliver says, stepping closer.

"Yeah. They come back every so often, but only when it suits them. And that doesn't seem to include the holidays… evidently."

"So where are they now?" Dad asks.

"I don't know," Izzy replies, like she doesn't care, and I pull her back into my arms again, holding her close.

"You must spend the holidays with your sisters then," Dad says.

Izzy turns to me again, looking up into my face. "Couldn't Ashley and Reagan come stay with us?" she asks.

"Do you think they'd want to?"

She smiles. "I'm sure they would. Neither of them will be at college and, to be honest, a few days away from their boyfriends might be a good thing. It might give them a little perspective."

I chuckle, recalling their conversation over Thanksgiving dinner.

"Okay." I look back at Dad again. "If we can fix it for Reagan and Ashley to come to us the weekend before Christmas, why don't we say that everyone will come over to our place on the Sunday?"

He nods his head. "I'll call Destiny tomorrow and see how they're fixed, but I can't see why they won't be able to make it. They'll be back from their honeymoon by then, and neither of them will be working until the new year."

"I think Reagan and Ashley will really enjoy that," Izzy says, sounding enthusiastic. "They're always saying how they wish we could have a big family Christmas."

"Well, they're gonna get one," Oliver says, rolling his eyes.

"You could bring Jemima?" I suggest, and his face falls.

"Thanks for that," he says.

"Who's Jemima?" Izzy asks, looking from me to Oliver.

"She's Oliver's receptionist," I explain.

"Oh… and let me guess," she says. "He's in love with her, and she doesn't know?"

"God, am I that transparent?" Oliver slaps the palm of his hand against his forehead.

"No," Izzy replies. "But you and your brother are like two peas in a pod."

I hug her tight against me. "Not anymore, we're not," I whisper, and she looks up into my eyes. "I have absolutely no problem telling you – and the whole damn world – that I'm in love with you, and that now I've got you, I'm never giving you up… not for anyone, or anything."

Epilogue

Isabel

Mason and I haven't looked back since that argument we had up in Vermont, the day after Thanksgiving. In fact, I'm so at home here with him, in his house in the forest, I've even given up my apartment. That was a decision we took together on the way home from his father's house. I don't know whether that was because he'd called me his girlfriend for the first time, or because he'd spent the whole day being so romantic. I just know neither of us could see the point in paying rent on what was essentially a very nice storage unit for my books and other personal belongings.

So, over the next few days, I moved out properly and moved into Mason's house. Although to all intents and purposes, I'd already moved in. Since then, I've noticed that whenever he talks about the house, he calls it 'ours' and not 'his', and I like that.

It's a lovely house, and we're so happy here. We do everything together, from cooking to laundry, and deciding on the colors we're going to use to redecorate. That's our plan for the New Year. Mason says it's so I can feel like I'm putting my stamp on the house. Personally, I just think he feels like a change. He certainly seems very enthusiastic about doing it anyway, and the paint and brushes are already stored out in the garage.

Of course, doing everything together, whether that's the laundry or the cooking, often leads to doing other things too, and I have to smile as I think about all the different places where Mason and I have made love. There was the kitchen countertop when we were supposed to be making dinner together. Then there was up against the wall in the hallway, one evening after work… before we even got as far as dinner. And, of course, who could forget the stairs that Saturday after we drove back from Vermont in separate cars, the journey proving too long for us to be apart… evidently.

My favorite is still the shower, which we make use of every single morning.

I still haven't perfected the art of quiet sex, although I have tried. I had to, when Noah and Aaron came to stay, which was the first weekend in December, right after Noah's story finally broke. The publicity surrounding it was getting a bit much, so I suggested a weekend with us, and he accepted, telling us on the night of their arrival exactly what the story was all about.

"You know Senator Blackmore?" he said, looking directly at me while we sat around the dining table. We were eating the beef stew Mason had prepared that morning while I was getting ready for work, leaving it in the slow cooker, so it melted in our mouths.

"Yeah. Clean-living Joe Blackmore." I recalled the senator's campaign slogan from a few years back. "You're not gonna tell me he's your bad-boy politician?"

Noah nodded his head. "Yeah. I'm afraid so."

"How is that even possible? The guy was so… wholesome." I struggled to find the right word, and turned to Mason, who I knew wouldn't have a clue who we were talking about. "He was married…"

"He still is," Noah said, interrupting me. "At least for now."

"Oh." His tone sounded kind of final, but I ignored it for now and continued my explanation to Mason. "He had four children, or was it five?"

"Five," Noah replied. "And two grandchildren."

"So he's fairly old then?" Mason said.

"He's sixty-two." Noah shook his head. "And his career's over."

"Why? What did he do?" I asked.

He sighed, sipping his wine and then said, "Don't ask me how – because I can't tell you – but I found out that, when his wife was in the hospital last year having treatment for cancer, he was having sex parties at their home."

"Sex parties?" I struggled not to laugh.

"Yeah. I'd tell you all about them, but I think you're probably too innocent."

"No, I'm not." I glared at him, and he laughed.

"Okay. Don't say I didn't warn you, and if there's anything you don't understand, Mason's explaining it, not me."

Mason chuckled and took my hand as Noah revealed that the senator's tastes ran to being chained up and dominated by leather-clad women... several at a time, evidently.

"There were photographs," he said, shaking his head. "It wasn't pretty."

I shuddered, and Mason squeezed my hand. "Are you okay?"

"Yes. I'm just struggling with the images in my head."

Noah laughed at that point. "Be grateful you don't have the reality in there. You'd be scarred for life."

"So, you exposed him for that?" I said, tilting my head to one side.

"No," Noah replied. "To be honest, if that had been it, I'd have walked away from the story. If that's what the guy wants to get up to in the privacy of his own home, then so be it. The hypocrisy was hard to swallow, but who am I to judge?"

I frowned across the table. "In that case...?"

"My informant also told me that the senator had been procuring prostitutes for visiting dignitaries."

"Oh." That sounded significantly more damning.

"That's not it," Noah said.

"It's not?"

"No. Some of these dignitaries had particular tastes of their own, which the senator was happy to accommodate."

"What kind of tastes?" I asked, feeling a little scared.

"Everything from the mildly weird to the frankly disgusting." He held up his hands. "Before you ask, I'm not going into details about that. I couldn't put very much into the article either. They'd never have been able to publish."

"Oh, my God."

"How did he find these prostitutes?" Mason asked. "I mean, I wouldn't know where to look, and I'm fairly sure most men wouldn't."

"No," Noah said. "It transpired he'd been visiting a Dominatrix for several years – outside of the orgies – and she has a network of women working for her." He shrugged his shoulders. "There was a thread that looked like it might lead to the senator having a partial interest in her business, but I couldn't prove it, so I had to leave it out."

"You think it might be true, though?" Mason asked.

"Yeah. Unfortunately, without concrete evidence, I couldn't include it in my piece. I questioned him, though. Once I'd compiled my evidence, I went to see him, to give him a chance to defend himself. I wanted to put both sides of the story, but he called me all the names under the sun and threw me out of his office. Out of sympathy for his wife, I called him up again and offered him the opportunity to step down and resign his position in return for my silence. I probably shouldn't have done that, and if my editor knew, she'd fire me."

"What did he say?" Mason asked.

Noah looked across the table at him, rather grim faced. "He told me to go to hell."

"Then he deserves everything he gets," I said.

"I know he does," Noah replied. "I have no sympathy for the man, even though I know I'm gonna be vilified in some quarters as the gutter journalist who went looking for dirt and found it." He stopped talking and sighed. "I feel sorry for his wife and family. They didn't ask for this, and if he'd been willing to step down, I'd have buried the story, even if it had meant losing my job."

"You can't blame yourself for what's gonna happen to them," I said and although he nodded his head, I could tell he was struggling.

Our weekend together was kinda marred by Noah's mood, although it was good to see how supportive Aaron was, and how he watched him all the time. Before they left on the Sunday afternoon, Mason also spoke to Noah and offered to help him, if he needed it… professionally.

"I know Isabel can't counsel you," he said. "You and she are too close, but if you feel the need to talk to someone, just pick up the phone. I'll do whatever I can. Okay?"

I could see how touched Noah was by Mason's offer and when we kissed goodbye, he whispered in my ear, "You got lucky. Don't lose him."

I whispered back, "I won't."

Having Noah and Aaron visit with us for that weekend, especially given what Noah was going through, kinda threw us a little, so it wasn't until the Monday morning, when we got into work and I checked my appointments, that I realized the date, and went into a minor meltdown.

I rushed from my office, straight into Mason's, even though he was due to see a client in less than ten minutes.

"What's wrong?" he said, getting up from his desk and coming over to me.

"I'm think I'm late." I couldn't control my smile.

"You do?"

"Yes."

"How late?"

I could hear the excitement in his voice, and I wanted to kiss him for it. "I—I don't know exactly."

He chuckled and took my hand, leading me to his desk and sitting me down on his lap, as he called up his calendar. It took us a moment or two to count back to the first day of my last period, but between us we established I was three days late, and even though I told myself, we shouldn't get our hopes up, I could tell from the look in Mason's eyes that he already had. I had too. I could feel the excitement bubbling inside me, and I longed to let it out.

"We should get a test," he said.

"Yes." He was right. We should. We needed to be sure. "I'll go out at lunchtime."

"You can't go sooner?"

"No. I've got appointments all morning."

His shoulders dropped. "Okay. Lunchtime it is then."

He smiled down at me and then brushed his lips against mine in the softest, most gentle kiss ever.

"I love you, Mason Gould." I said in a whisper as he released me.

"I love you too."

Just then the front doorbell rang, and we pulled apart, Mason going to see who it was, while I gathered myself together.

I got through the morning, seeing Lucas and Penny first. I'd already seen them once since Thanksgiving, and while I knew they were keen to make progress, I reminded them they were on a journey. It was going to take time. That Monday, they told me they'd been spending more time together, and after a few false starts, had come up with a plan which they hoped I'd approve of. I wasn't sure they should be making plans by themselves, but Lucas outlined it to me, explaining that his mom was going to have Louise overnight for them, once a week, and that he and Penny planned on cooking a meal together, and then talking.

"I'm still not ready for anything else yet," Penny said, blushing slightly. "Lucas wanted us to go away together, to spend the night in a hotel... but it's too soon."

Lucas shook his head, staring down at his hands. "I'm sorry. I was moving too fast."

"Don't be sorry. This is fabulous progress." I kept things positive before they started beating themselves up again.

Lucas nodded and even managed a smile. "Once Penny had explained that she wasn't ready for my original plan, we toyed with the idea of going to a restaurant every week, but decided against that too."

"I didn't think we'd be able to be ourselves," Penny explained.

"So, we agreed on staying home and cooking. We thought it would be better if Louise wasn't in the house. We'll be able to talk without distractions and without having to whisper... and if Penny wants to yell at me, she can."

"Hopefully, I won't," Penny said. "I'm not sure yelling at you is getting us anywhere."

That really felt like progress, and I told them so, as well as congratulating them on their efforts, and for waiting to run the plan by me, before putting it into action. After they'd gone, I met with Ian and Vanessa, who were still basing their relationship entirely around sex, and therefore not working on the things that matter. I'm not sure what I'm going to do about them, but they've decided to take a break from therapy until after Christmas, so I'll worry about them then.

Once they'd gone, I went down to Mason's office, relieved to find his door ajar, and I pushed it open. He was sitting at his desk, concentrating on his computer screen.

"I'm just going to the bathroom," I said, and he looked up with a smile. "Then I'll head out to the pharmacy."

"Okay. Do you want me to come with you?"

"To the bathroom?" I asked, teasing him.

"No, to the pharmacy."

"No. I'll be fine. One of us should probably stay here, anyway."

"You're sure?"

"Yes. You could make us a coffee for when I get back, if you like?"

He nodded his head, and I wandered down the hall to the bathroom, feeling excited and a little nervous at the same time. My stomach was churning, like I had tiny butterflies flitting around in there, and as I closed the door, I wondered to myself whether this was what it felt like to be pregnant.

My dreams and illusions were shattered the moment I saw the blood, and although I'd told myself not to hope, I burst into tears. I couldn't help it. I finished up as best I could, washed my hands and ran from the room, straight into Mason, who was standing in the hallway.

"I heard you crying," he said, although he didn't ask what had happened. It was like he knew and he pulled me in close to him, leaning back against the wall and stroking my hair as I rested my head on his chest.

He didn't say, "There's always next month," or, "We can keep trying," or any of the other things which I knew were true, but I didn't want to hear. Instead, he whispered, "I love you so much," in my ear, and he didn't let me go.

I pulled back eventually, of course, and looked up into his eyes, seeing my disappointment reflected right back at me. I opened my mouth, wanting to make it better, but he put his fingers across my lips. "If you're thinking about saying 'sorry', then don't."

Those were the very words I'd been about to utter, but he wouldn't let me. So instead, I took his hand and kissed the palm, looking up at him.

"Can you do something for me?"

"Anything."

"Can you go to my desk and open the top drawer?" He nodded his head. "Inside, you'll find some underwear and a sanitary pad. I keep them there in case of emergencies. Can you bring them back here?"

"Of course." He bent forward and kissed my forehead, and then walked away, striding down the hall toward the front of the building.

I leaned back against the wall, sucking in a breath and stuttering it out again, telling myself it wasn't the end of the world... because it wasn't. It just felt like it.

Mason returned within moments and handed me my white cotton panties and sanitary pad. "Do you need anything else?" he asked.

I shook my head. "I won't be a minute... but then could we have another hug?"

He smiled, although his eyes were still filled with a kind of hopeless bewilderment. "Of course we can. I'll see you in my office whenever you're ready."

He turned to leave, but I grabbed his arm and pulled him back. "I'm sorry." He might not have wanted to hear it, but it had to be said.

"Don't be. This is nobody's fault."

He was right, and I knew it. "I know it's early days, but I—I wanted it so much." I fell in to him again as his arms came around me.

"I know, Izzy. I know."

"You wanted it too."

"Yeah, I did. I still do."

"What if this keeps happening every month? How will we cope?"

"By remembering we've got each other," he said, and I looked up at him, surprised to see his eyes glistening. "Nothing matters but that,

Izzy. Nothing matters but you. You're it for me. You always have been, and you always will be."

I never thought it was possible to love Mason more than I did that day, but I do.

I seem to love him more with every passing hour, and over the last few weeks, we've certainly grown closer.

We're definitely trying to get pregnant now, especially over the last couple of days, being as I'm in the middle of my cycle again. We've made love more times than I can remember, but I'm doing my best not to hope too much, and to make the most of the here and now, and let the future take care of itself.

Mason reassures me all the time that it's early days and even if it doesn't happen, we'll always have each other... and I believe him.

Tonight is the big family get-together that we planned just after Thanksgiving. Ashley and Reagan arrived yesterday afternoon, and Mason cooked us a lovely meal so I could help them unpack and catch up.

I've spent most of this afternoon arranging the Christmas tree while chatting with Ashley and Reagan. They offered to help, but I wanted to do this by myself. It's my first Christmas with Mason and it felt important to get it right. Besides, I needed the distraction of their conversations, because I'll admit I'm nervous about everyone coming over here. I know I've met them all, except for Ronan and Destiny, but I'm still a little uneasy.

I think it's just because I can't believe everything is so perfect.

I keep expecting something to go wrong... something like Mason's family telling him we're moving things too fast. I wouldn't blame them if they did, because there's no denying we haven't held back. That may be right for us, but I know other people probably think it's strange that we've moved in together already. If they knew we're trying to get pregnant as well, I dread to think what they'd say.

I put the finishing touches to the tree, and get up off of the floor.

"We're gonna go change," Reagan says, admiring my handiwork. "The tree looks fabulous."

"Thank you."

They help me clear up the boxes, offering to take them back upstairs for Mason to put up in the attic, and once they've gone, I go out into the kitchen, where Mason's busy preparing our dinner.

"How's it going?" he asks, looking up as I come into the room.

"It's all done."

I go over to him and put my arms around his waist, leaning in to him. He puts down the spoon he's holding and pulls me close.

"Where are your sisters?"

"They've gone upstairs to change."

He smiles and bends down, kissing me deeply, both of us becoming breathless within moments.

"I wish I hadn't already laid the dining table," he says, sighing.

"Why?"

"Because I'd like to lay you out on it."

My body shudders at the thought. "Then what would you do with me?"

"I'd feast on you." His voice drops a note or two, and I quiver with need… and with gratitude that, although we're trying to get pregnant, he still wants me… in all kinds of ways.

"Oh, God. That sounds…"

"Like something we need to try," he says, interrupting me. "Soon."

"Yes, it does."

"I guess we'd better get this dinner out of the way first."

"Aren't you looking forward to it?" I can't help wondering if he feels the same way I do.

"Yeah, I am. I'd just rather be feasting on you."

I nod my head, and I guess he must notice something in my eyes, or my movement, because he frowns and tilts his head.

"Is everything okay, Izzy?"

"Of course it is."

He cups my face with his hands, looking into my eyes. "No, it's not. Tell me what's wrong."

"I'm just a little nervous about tonight, that's all."

"Why are you nervous? You've met my dad and Oliver… and Destiny and Ronan are really nice."

"I know. But what if they think we're taking things too fast?" I give voice to my fears. "I mean, I've moved in with you, and we're trying to start a family, and…"

"Okay," he says, taking my hand and leading me around the island unit to sit me on one of the stools. He parts my legs, standing in the space between them, his body crushed to mine, so I can feel his arousal pressed against me. "The pace at which we choose to take our relationship is our decision, and no-one else's."

"I know, but…"

"You're worrying about nothing, baby. My dad thinks the world of you, and so does Oliver."

"They do?"

"Yeah. Because you make me happy."

"Did they tell you this?" I ask him, intrigued.

"Yes. Remember when Dad pulled me aside right before we left his place the other week?"

"Yeah."

"Well, he told me he'd never seen me so happy. He said he knew it was because of you, and he hoped I knew how lucky I was."

I can feel myself blush. "I think I'm the lucky one."

"No," he says. "Because not only did Oliver tell me how beautiful you are, within moments of meeting you, he also questioned why you're wasting your time with me. Then he called me a couple of days later and told me not to screw it up with you. He said you're too good to lose – like I don't already know that. So you've got nothing to worry about, Izzy. My family love you."

Love? Really? My eyes fill with tears. I wasn't expecting that.

"Thank you for saying that," I whisper, and Mason smiles.

"It's the truth."

I swallow down the lump in my throat and lean up to kiss him. "I guess I should go get changed," I say, and he smiles, moving back and letting me stand.

"I'd join you, but I'm kinda busy."

"If you joined me, I'd never be ready in time."

He chuckles. "No, you wouldn't."

He kisses me again, a little more deeply, and then lets me go, and I wander from the room, taking a quick peek at the living room, which is lit by the tree lights, the fire and candles. It looks romantic and although Mason hasn't seen it yet, I hope he likes it. I hurry into the dining room, just to check it out, and suck in a breath. Mason's laid the table with white china and cut glass, and decorated it with fresh pine and holly, which he must have gathered from the woodland this morning. There are candles in the center, ready to be lit, and I lean against the doorframe for a moment, taking it in, smiling to myself. Mason's made it perfect, just like everything else, and my doubts disappear as I look forward to our evening, for the first time.

It's going to be a full house, that's for sure, but I guess that's just how it should be… a house full of love.

Mason

I think I helped set Izzy's mind at rest, and I guess it's only natural to assume people might judge us for moving too fast. I can remember thinking Destiny and Ronan were doing exactly that, and they'd been together a lot longer than Izzy and I have. But what can I say? When it's right, it's right… and man, is this right.

My family knows that too. I wasn't kidding when I told her Oliver called me to tell me not to screw it all up. Dad pulled me aside, too, to tell me how happy I was looking, and that he knew it was all down to Izzy. He called her Isabel, of course, because everyone does… except me. And I like that.

I check the beef in the oven, and turn down the potatoes, making my way into the living room, to see what Izzy's been doing all afternoon.

She insisted on decorating the tree all by herself, after I'd brought it in and set it in the corner of the room, and as I enter, my breath catches in my throat. The room looks magical, with candles dotted around all over the place, and the tree itself is stunning. She's used my white lights and a few of my old decorations, and added some new ones, mainly made of wood and fabric, and the whole effect is rustic, charming, and beautiful.

She'd hoped to get this completed before her sisters arrived, but these last couple of weeks have been a little crazy. We had Noah and Aaron to stay over the first weekend in December, most of which was taken up with the fallout over Noah's article. It was obvious he was affected by it all, and I offered to help, if I could. I don't know if he'll call, but if he does, I'll do whatever I can. He's Izzy's best friend, but he's also a nice guy, and he clearly felt guilty about what had happened, even though he didn't need to. He wasn't responsible for the senator's behavior, and he gave the guy a way out, which is more than most people in his position would have done. I'm not sure he was seeing things that way, though…

It made for a kinda frantic weekend and, to be honest, I was almost relieved to get into work the following Monday, in the hope of some normality… not that I got any, because we'd only been there a few minutes when Izzy came flying into my office, scaring the hell out of me. She was a little pale, and I thought she might be unwell… until she told me she was late. I knew exactly what she meant, of course, and we sat together then, and worked out how late. It was three days, and while I think we both knew we shouldn't get our hopes up, it was impossible not to dream… so I let myself. And so did Izzy. I could tell. She was bubbling with excitement.

I suggested a test, but neither of us had time to get one until lunchtime. So we waited.

It was a really tough wait, too. How Izzy got through that morning, I'll never know. I was barely concentrating on anything. I was watching the time drag by, until she pushed my door open, just after noon, and said she needed the bathroom, and she'd go to buy the test straight afterwards.

I wanted to go with her. I didn't want to let her out of my sight at all, if I'm honest. It's been that way since the moment I met her, but my need to protect her had gone into overdrive that morning, and even the idea of her walking to the pharmacy by herself was too much for me.

It was completely irrational, of course, but that was how I felt.

She declined my offer – quite rationally – and headed for the bathroom, while I tried to keep myself busy, going over the notes from my previous client. The words were swimming before my eyes, and I couldn't concentrate at all, no matter how hard I tried to focus.

And then I heard her.

She was making a sobbing noise that tore at my heart, and I stood up and ran down the hallway, waiting outside the closed bathroom door. I think I already suspected what had happened, but the moment Izzy came out and I saw the look in her eyes, I knew. I didn't need to ask, and she didn't need to tell me.

I pulled her into a tight hug and leaned back against the wall for support... because I needed it. Then I stroked her hair while she cried against my chest. I wished I could make it better, or that I could bear all her pain, along with my own. But I couldn't. So I just told her how much I love her... and I held her until she finally pulled away from me and looked up into my eyes. I could see her sorrow and as she opened her mouth to speak, I had to stop her. I placed my fingers over her lips, so she couldn't say the word, "Sorry," to me. She had nothing to be sorry for, and I wasn't sure I could bear to hear it.

Instead, she kissed the palm of my hand, that tender action almost breaking me, and then she asked me to fetch her some things from her desk drawer, which I did.

When I came back, she was leaning against the wall, looking kinda shattered, and I wanted to kick myself for letting us both get so overwhelmed with excitement. We shouldn't have done that.

Before I left her to go back into the bathroom, she grabbed me and said, "I'm sorry," which was the last thing I wanted to hear.

"Don't be," I said. "This is nobody's fault." It wasn't. It hurt, but no-one was to blame.

She started crying again then and sobbed out the words, "I know it's early days, but I—I wanted it so much," and I pulled her into my arms.

"I know, Izzy. I know." It was a real struggle to speak.

"You wanted it too." She didn't look up at me, thank God, but she was right.

"Yeah, I did. I still do." I told her the truth.

She sighed. "What if this keeps happening every month? How will we cope?" There was a desperation in her voice that cut right through me.

"By remembering we've got each other," I said, and she looked up at me then, frowning as she noticed the tears in my eyes. "Nothing matters but that, Izzy. Nothing matters but you. You're it for me. You always have been, and you always will be."

She clung to me for a while longer and then ducked inside the bathroom, and I wandered back to my office, where I'd said I'd wait for her. As I sat down in the corner of the couch, I started making plans…

My plans haven't been that easy to bring to fruition though, because that very afternoon, not only did I have a session with Henry Bayliss, but I also had a telephone call that I wasn't expecting.

I'd reached a point of despair with Henry, and was contemplating asking Izzy to get involved, when he walked through my door, like a new man. Don't get me wrong, he still looked exactly the same. He hadn't undergone that ludicrous makeover he'd been talking about for the previous few weeks. But he had a spring in his step I hadn't witnessed before, and when he sat down, he explained that he'd 'discovered' himself. That was his way of putting it, not mine, and I'll admit, I was confused… until he handed me a large envelope.

"What's this?" I asked.

"It's the first two chapters of my novel."

"You're writing a novel?"

I was stunned. I think it showed.

"Yes. I'd like you to read it. It's still quite rough, but I'd like your opinion."

I decided against reading it there and then, in his presence, in case it was awful and I couldn't disguise that from him. So instead, we talked about how he'd started writing.

"It was something I toyed with while I was still with Madeleine," he said.

"But you never did anything about it?"

"No. I never really had the time before, but that's not something I'm short of these days, so I thought I'd give it another try. I've... I've signed up for a creative writing course, too. It's due to start in January."

I was stunned. This was all very positive. Not only was he doing something for himself, but he was going to be getting out of the house. I was impressed.

I was even more impressed that evening when I sat with Izzy on the couch in the living room at home. Neither of us wanted to talk, but I held her, and I read Henry's manuscript.

It turns out the man can write.

When I next saw him, I told him exactly that. The smile on his face was more than enough reward for months of hard work.

The telephone call, which came just after Henry had left that afternoon, was from Calvin Hart.

"Were you actually serious when you made that offer at the reunion?" he asked, rather than bothering to say 'hello'.

"Yes."

There was a pause, that was long enough for me to think about asking whether he was still there, and then he said, "Okay. In that case, we need your help."

Those weren't words I ever expected to hear from Calvin, but I ignored my surprise and we arranged that I'd see Naomi two days later, on the Wednesday.

The following morning, although I knew she probably wasn't in the mood for talking about it, I sat down with Izzy and asked if she thought she might be better placed to handle Naomi's case.

She looked up at me, sipping her coffee over breakfast. "You offered to help. Is there a reason you've changed your mind?"

"I haven't changed my mind. I'm just wondering whether you'd be a better fit for Naomi. It won't be personal for you."

"Maybe not, but I've never dealt with a case like this, other than theoretically, in college." She reached out and took my hand. "I know you and Calvin have history, and I know that's gonna make it hard for you. But it's his wife you're treating, not him. And if you need to talk, I'm here."

I leaned over and kissed her then, grateful that she's mine… and I'm hers.

I saw Naomi Hart on Wednesday afternoon. Calvin brought her to the office, looking around the place with a supercilious expression on his face, before trying to follow Naomi into my room.

"You're not sitting in," I said, getting in his way.

"But, I—"

I held up my hand, and he stopped talking, frowning at me.

"But nothing, Calvin. This first session has to be just me and Naomi. I have to assess her, without any input from you."

He stood for a moment and then nodded his head, moving back into the reception area and sitting down on the couch against the wall. That had been easier than I'd expected, and I closed my door to face Naomi.

She was reasonably lucid, considering, and although she clearly has a serious problem, at least she's aware of that, and she wants help. I came away from our session feeling like we could get somewhere, given time.

Afterwards, I went out and spoke to Calvin for a few minutes by himself.

"How is she?" His concern surprised me.

"It's gonna be a long road," I said. "But I'm confident I can help her."

He nodded his head. "I know you might find this hard to believe, but I love her very much."

I raised my eyebrows. "You remember what you said to me at the reunion, don't you? Your offer to help me keep Isabel satisfied?"

He blushed. "I only said that to rile you. I wouldn't have gone through with it."

"I wouldn't have let you." He smiled at that and shook his head. "But I'm glad to hear you love Naomi as much as you say you do, because she's gonna need your help. Now I've got this initial assessment out of the way, I think it'll be useful if you can sit in on our sessions in future…

as an observer, nothing more." He nodded his head. "These next few months are gonna be hard for her. She'll need your support."

He agreed, and I fetched Naomi from my office, where she was staring out the window. I think our session had taken it out of her. She seemed fatigued, and Calvin helped her from my office.

"What do I owe you?" he said.

"I'll send you an account for payment at the end of each month."

He smiled at that, and for once, I didn't feel smaller when he left my presence.

I make my way back into the kitchen, still smiling now, even though I know I've got a lot of work to do with Naomi, and I check on the roast just as Izzy comes down.

"Wow." I stare across the room at her. "You look beautiful."

"Thank you."

She comes a little closer, and I take the time to observe the dress she's wearing. It's dark blue and clings to her like a glove, and while it doesn't show off as much skin as the one she wore to the reunion, I don't mind in the slightest... because I know what's underneath, and I'm reminded of the other reason my plans have been hard to bring to fruition... Izzy herself.

She's diverting at the best of times, but when we're trying to get pregnant, which we are, she's beyond distracting... and while I'm doing my best not to make it about getting pregnant all the time, I want to be inside her... right now.

"Ash and Reagan will be down soon," she says, putting her arms around me.

I lean down and kiss her, letting my hands roam over her body, paying particular attention to her ass, and feeling her naked flesh through the flimsy material of her dress. She moans into my mouth and I pull back, smiling at her.

"You're so damn sexy." I flex my hips so she can feel my arousal.

"So are you," she says, looking up into my eyes, and as much as I want her, I know it's impractical. We're about to host my family to dinner... dammit.

"Talk about something else for a minute, will you?" I smile down at her. "I need a distraction before your sisters come downstairs."

She grins and pulls away, tilting her head to one side.

"Is Oliver bringing Jemima with him?" she asks.

That's a reasonable 'something else', I guess. "Not as far as I know."

"Maybe we can hook him up with one of my sisters. I don't think either of them is that impressed with their current boyfriends... especially Ashley."

"That sounds complicated.... way too complicated for Oliver, anyway. And, in case you've forgotten, he's thirty-four. Your sisters are a little young for him, don't you think?"

"How old's Jemima?" she asks.

"I've got no idea. He's never told me. I just know he's in love with her. So I'm afraid, as lovely as your sisters are, he won't give them a second glance."

Izzy steps in front of me again, resting her hands on my chest. *So much for distractions.* "You think my sisters are lovely, you do?" she says, teasing.

"Yeah. But they're not as lovely as you."

"Right answer." She leans up, kissing me, just as the doorbell rings.

We go out into the lobby together and I open the door to find my dad and Oliver on the doorstep. They must've come together, and once Baxter's bounded in, going straight into the living room, Dad follows him into the house.

"It's freezing out there," he says, clapping his hands together, and smiling, his cheeks rosy.

"Well, the fire's blazing in the living room, so go on in and get warm... assuming Baxter will let you get close enough." I take his coat and Oliver's too, hooking them up while they follow Izzy into the living room.

"This looks amazing," Oliver says, glancing around the room.

"It's all Isabel's work," I tell him, as Ashley and Reagan come in through the door behind me.

Izzy makes the introductions, and just as I expected, Oliver's polite and shakes their hands, but makes no sign of being interested in either of them, even though they're both beautiful. To be fair, Ashley and Reagan seem more interested in Oliver's dog than in Oliver, which makes me smile, and I glance over at Izzy, just before I go to fetch the drinks. She narrows her eyes, because I was right, and I wink back at her.

I'm almost into the kitchen when the doorbell rings again and I answer it. This time it's Ronan and Destiny, who comes straight in, throwing her arms around me.

"It's been ages," she says, and although she doesn't normally greet me quite like this, I hug her tight until she's ready to pull back. When she does, she looks up into my face. "You look so damn happy." She's grinning, and turns to Ronan, taking his hand and pulling him closer to her. "Don't you love being in love?" she says to me, and I smile.

"Yeah, I do."

I usher them into the living room, and quickly introduce them to Izzy and her sisters before I return to the kitchen, check on the dinner and get us all some drinks. When I get back, Destiny is telling everyone about Paris, which is where she and Ronan have been on their honeymoon for the last ten days.

"It was so romantic," she says, looking up at him.

"That's the point of honeymoons, isn't it?" Oliver says with a cheeky grin.

"Yes, but the city itself is so… so perfect." She sighs.

"It probably helped that it's Christmas," Ronan says. "Everywhere was all lit up."

"So you saw some of the sights then?" Oliver clearly can't help himself.

"Yes." Destiny turns to him, shaking her head, although she's smiling. "It's not somewhere we'll probably get to go again, so we wanted to see as much of it as possible."

"Which is why we're so tired," Ronan adds.

"Yeah," Destiny says. "You'll have to excuse us if we fall asleep halfway through dinner. Between the sightseeing and the jet lag, we're exhausted."

Oliver chuckles, sipping his beer. "You've been on your honeymoon, and you seriously expect us to believe your exhaustion is because of sightseeing and jet lag?"

"Of course I do." The corners of Destiny's mouth twist up slightly.

"Oliver," our dad says, shaking his head, "must you always lower the tone?"

"Um… yeah," he replies, like it's a foregone conclusion, and everyone laughs.

"That was delicious," Dad says, putting his serviette down beside his plate and looking over at me. Izzy made a point of explaining that I'd cooked the meal, and everyone else adds their praise.

"At least you've found a man who can cook," Destiny says to her, with a smile on her face. "Ronan's useless."

"He can't be that bad," Izzy replies.

"Yes, I can," Ronan says. "It's a wonder I didn't kill my little sister when she lived with me."

"Your little sister lived with you?" Izzy says, tilting her head.

"Yes. Our parents died when we were children, and we lived with our grandmother for a while, but then she died too, so I became Eva's guardian. She's eight years younger than me, and she was only twelve when she moved into my flat."

"That sounds kinda like us," Ash says, looking across the table at him. "Our parents walked out on us when Isabel was sixteen. I was six at the time, and Reagan was eight."

Ronan raises his eyebrows, turning back to Izzy. "You were only sixteen?" he says, with something that sounds a lot like admiration in his voice.

"Yes," she says, blushing. "But our parents came back from time to time."

"When it suited them," Reagan adds and the three of them exchange a look I think only they understand.

"That must've been hard for you," Dad says, looking at Izzy.

"It was okay." She might say that now, but I know it wasn't okay at all. I know she'll never tell Ash and Reagan how hard it really was. "We survived."

"When are you moving into the house?" I ask Destiny, sensing that Izzy would like a change of subject.

"The second week of January," she says and I explain to Izzy's sisters that Ronan and Destiny have been living in an apartment at his sister's house for the last few months, since he first came over here to live, but they've been looking for somewhere of their own ever since Ronan proposed.

"I can't wait for a slightly shorter commute," Ronan says with feeling.

"Or to have an actual bedroom." Destiny rolls her eyes.

"How many bedrooms has the new place got?" Dad asks.

"Four, but the fourth one is really a large closet," she says.

"And are you thinking about filling any of those other bedrooms anytime soon?" Dad asks with a glint in his eye. I wish he hadn't said that, but it's too late now, and I glance at Izzy, noticing that she's lowered her head.

"Not anytime soon, no," Destiny says. "We want to have kids, but I also want to go on a few digs with Ronan first, so give us a year or two, okay?"

Dad nods and even though Izzy's head is still bowed, I can't fail to spot that she's biting her bottom lip, like she's trying to hold in her emotions... and that's too much for me.

This wasn't part of my plan. I'd intended to wait until Christmas morning to do this. And I'd meant for it to be a lot more private... probably in bed, naked.

I get to my feet and walk down the table to where Izzy's sitting at the opposite end. She's unaware of my movements until I'm standing right beside her, when she looks up and stares at me, her brow furrowing.

"I'm sorry," I say in a whisper, pulling Izzy to her feet and holding her in my arms

"It's not your fault." Her voice catches and she swallows hard, trying not to cry.

"Did we miss something?" Oliver asks.

I don't take my eyes from Izzy, but I say, "Yeah. We... um... we thought Isabel might be pregnant, but it seems she's not."

"Oh, God. I'm so sorry," Dad says.

Izzy looks over toward him. "Please don't feel bad."

"But if I'd known, I'd never have said anything." I can tell he feels guilty, and I wonder now if I should've kept quiet... except I couldn't watch Izzy suffering and do nothing.

"We had no idea," Reagan says.

"I know." Izzy averts her gaze to her sister. "It's not something you shout from the rooftops, is it? It's personal. And I guess we also thought people might say we're slightly crazy for trying to start a family when we haven't been together for very long."

"Oh, I don't know," Oliver says, with a hint of welcome humor in his voice. "Mason isn't getting any younger."

"Neither are you," I reply.

"Will you to stop it?" Destiny raises her voice and we both clam up for once, as she turns to Izzy. "It's up to you guys," she says. "And it's certainly not for anyone else to judge. If you wanna have a baby, then you go ahead."

"We're trying to, thanks, Sis." Everyone chuckles and I drop to one knee, the laughter dying as they all gasp and Izzy stares down at me, wide-eyed. I pull out the box I've been carrying around with me for the last few days, and whilst keeping hold of her hand, I say, "I wanna do this right, Izzy. I've screwed up just about everything else getting together with you, but I'm gonna damn well get this right. So, Isabel Banks, will you do me the honor of agreeing to become my wife? And then the mother of my children?"

She nods her head and whispers, "Yes," just loud enough for me to hear, and I stand, opening the box I'm still holding, to reveal the emerald ring I picked out for her. "Oh," she says, smiling up at me. "My birthstone."

"Yeah."

I take it from the box and place it on her finger, and she studies it for a moment before looking back at me again.

"I think that's the most alpha thing you've ever done," she says, with a sexy smile.

"No. That's the most beta thing I've ever done. We'll do some alpha things later on." She nods her head, her eyes on fire.

"What the heck are you two talking about?" Dad says from the other side of the table.

"It's a long story, Dad," I reply, keeping hold of my fiancée while I look across at him.

"One to tell my grandkids?" he says.

"Definitely not," Izzy and I both say at the same time.

Everyone laughs and talks among themselves, while I pull her to one side and lean in closer before I whisper in her ear, "When we're old, and we're surrounded by our kids and our grandkids, I'm still gonna tell you, every single day, how much I love you."

She looks up into my eyes. "Promise?" she murmurs.

"I promise, babe."

She nods her head and then rests it against me, and as I stroke her hair and look over her shoulder at our family, I give a silent word of thanks that I found her, that she gave me a second chance, and that we're here... together. Forever.

The End

Thank you for reading *Faking the Future*. I hope you enjoyed it, and if you did I hope you'll take the time to leave a short review.

If you want to find out what happens in the last part of this series, keep reading for an excerpt from part six ...
Making Your Peace.

Making your Peace

Never Give Up: Book Six

by

Suzie Peters

Chapter One

Jemima

I park my Honda Accord at the front of the veterinary surgery, in one of the three spaces reserved for employees. I don't know why there are three, being as there are only two of us working here, but I guess that's one of life's mysteries. You know, like why the toast always lands butter side down, why there's never any ice cream in the deep freeze when I need it most… and why I had to fall for the most unattainable man in the world.

I'm talking about Doctor Oliver Gould. He takes unattainable to a whole new level. Not that he's unapproachable, or aloof. He's neither of those things. In fact, he's the opposite. He's kind, warm and helpful. Of course, there is the minor issue that he also happens to be my boss, and while I realize that falling for him is a cliché, there's not a lot I can do about it.

Because he's also gorgeous.

He's very tall, with broad shoulders, and his reddish-brown hair always looks like he just got out of bed. *If only…* As for his eyes, they're a kind of amber color, with tiny green flecks in them. If you're wondering how I know that, it's because I've looked. I do a lot of looking when it comes to Oliver… and not very much else.

It wasn't always like that. When Mom and I first moved here, at the beginning of last December, and I got the job working as Oliver's receptionist, I barely noticed him. That might sound crazy, considering I can't stop thinking about him now, but the only excuse I can give is that I was recovering from a broken heart – or at least a disappointed one. I'm not sure my heart was actually broken, because it never belonged to Donavan in the first place, so how could he break it?

Still, I'm not going to think about that now.

I need to get inside and start my working day. I know Oliver's first appointment is in twenty minutes, and sitting out here in my car won't get my computer turned on, or the coffee made.

I open the door, feeling a blast of icy wind, and pull my coat up around my chin as I get out, gazing at Oliver's Jeep, which is parked beside my car. I know he'll be inside already, preparing for the day, because he's like that. He's very diligent and good at his job… as well as being kind and helpful… and gorgeous.

But that's where the problem lies. Just about every woman in town seems to fall over herself to get to him. They're all the same… dragging their perfectly healthy pets into the surgery, just so they can spend thirty minutes with 'Doctor Gould'. He doesn't seem to object, and is universally pleasant to everyone… not just the pets, but their owners, too.

I can't really criticize them. After all, I enjoy spending time with him just as much as his clients. At least, I have since that day back in the summer, when I finally woke up from my disappointed heart, and noticed the perfect man leaning against the doorframe to his office. Somehow – and I really don't know how – he makes green scrubs look sexy, especially with his arms folded across his expansive chest. I stared at him, taking in the beauty of his face, and the way his muscles flexed when he breathed in and out, as he asked me to show in his next client. I don't know why I was staring. He didn't look any more handsome than usual, because that's not possible, and as far as I'm aware, he didn't sound any more sexy, either. He was just different.

That was when it happened.

Like a bolt of lightning.

I fell in love.

I don't suppose anyone can ever fully understand the reasons behind that. If they could, they'd bottle it, and make a fortune.

As it is, I just know from that day to this, I've been hopelessly in love with the man.

I walk to the glass door, pulling it open and take a quick glance down Main Street. Unlike Eastford, where I grew up, Sturbridge is much more of a sprawling town, its shops and facilities all spread out. Here by the veterinary surgery, we've got a sandwich shop, which I'm familiar with, because I go there every day, and a florist's, an attorney's office and a realtor. A little further down the street, there's a café and a restaurant, and Oliver's brother runs a counseling service from one of the buildings near the architect's office, I believe. The beauty salon is near there too.

Other than my hairdresser, who's called Cindy, I don't know any of the people who work in these places. I don't even know Oliver's brother. We've never met.

Why would we?

I duck inside, pulling the door closed, and shrug off my coat, hanging it up on the stand before going over to the corner of the room and turning on the Christmas tree lights. The tree is artificial, but enormous. It's so big that Oliver and I had to move the furniture around to fit it in. That's to say, Oliver moved the furniture, edging the chairs further apart and moving the coffee table so it's up against the far wall of the reception area, while I stood and admired him. Then I put up the Christmas tree, decorating it with colored baubles and white lights. He seemed pleased with my efforts and thanked me profusely afterwards. I know he was only being friendly, though. If there's one thing I've learned about Oliver since I've been working for him, it's that he's friendly... with everyone. That's why falling for him was a dangerous move. Nothing can ever come of it.

I don't have space in my life for a man like that.

Friendly is great... obviously, and so is kind. Gorgeous is a distinct advantage, too, but more than anything, after all that's happened to me, I need reliable. I need trustworthy. And unfortunately, that means there's no hope for Oliver and me. There are simply too many other women trying to get their claws into him. I couldn't handle that… not again.

Besides, like I already said, he's simply unattainable.

"Is that you, Jemima?" His voice rings out from his office.

I'm not sure who else he thinks it's going to be, but rather than being facetious, I just say, "Yes," before I walk around behind my desk, which faces the main door, and switch on my computer. As I turn to go to the kitchen at the back of the building, I almost jump out of my skin at the sight of Oliver, leaning back against the wall by his door, with a slight smile on his lips. He's already dressed for work, in his green scrubs, although I know he'll have driven here wearing jeans and a shirt, usually with a jacket over the top. He always changes first thing in the morning, in the small, curtained-off area at the back of his surgery, and then changes back before he goes home. That smile is still twitching at his lips, and for a moment, I wonder if there's something wrong with my appearance. I even take a quick glance down at myself to make sure I'm not still wearing my pink slippers. I'm not… thank God. My feet are clad in the same high-heeled black pumps that I wear to work every other day of the week, and my gray skirt and white blouse are completely decent; no hems awry, no buttons undone, although a couple of them are gaping slightly. That can't be helped, though. I'm built that way.

I gaze up at Oliver again and he pushes himself off of the wall, and steps a little closer, making a clicking sound with his tongue at the same time. The noise is answered by the patter of feet on the linoleum floor and, within a second or two, Baxter appears from the surgery behind him.

He's the most adorable chocolate brown labrador, and he follows Oliver into the reception area, going around behind my desk and flopping down into his basket. He knows that's where he spends the day, and although he occasionally gets up and wanders around, he's no trouble at all.

"Did you have a good weekend?" Oliver asks, surprising me by perching on the corner of my desk.

"Yes, thanks."

He looks at me for a moment, like he expects me to elaborate, but there isn't much to tell. I did the laundry, I tidied the house, and cleaned the bathroom. I wrapped Christmas presents, and helped my mom with some baking for the holidays. Nothing earth shattering. Just an average weekend, with the addition of Christmas preparations thrown in for good measure.

"I—I think I owe you an apology," he says, surprising me even further, not just with the apology, but with the fact that he stammered over it.

"You do?"

He nods his head, folding his arms across his chest at the same time. "Yes."

"What for?"

"Because I forgot it's Christmas."

I glance at the Christmas tree twinkling in the corner of the room, my brow furrowing. "Um… how?"

He smiles, and I melt a little inside. "I didn't exactly forget," he says. "But the party completely slipped my mind."

"Party? What party?"

"The one I have here, every year, at Christmas."

That melting feeling subsides and my stomach churns slightly. "You have a party?"

"Yes." *And I'm only hearing about this now?* "Deanna used to organize the whole thing," he says. "I guess I got used to coming into work and finding it had all been arranged, so I didn't give it a second thought. Except I went to my brother's house yesterday for a big family dinner and his girlfriend – who's now his fiancée – had decorated the house and made it look really festive, and then I realized… it's Christmas."

"I see." I'm not sure I do. "So, you didn't notice the shop windows, and the town being decked out with Christmas lights, and the freezing cold weather, or the annoying festive music that seems to play everywhere you go?"

He chuckles with a deep, sexy laugh, which makes my insides tingle and turn molten again. "I noticed all of that," he says. "I was just kinda ignoring it, until I got to Mason's house, and saw the Christmas tree they'd put up in their living room. Isabel had made it look really pretty, and it reminded me."

"That it's Christmas?" I say, shaking my head at him.

"Yes."

"I assume Isabel is your brother's fiancée, or girlfriend, or whichever it is?" I'm not really sure why I asked that question… not when I ought to be focusing the bombshell of this party he's so far failed to mention. But I'm intrigued. I'm also reeling from the fact that this is the longest conversation we've ever had. I know that's my fault, not his. Falling for him is one thing, but letting him into my life is something else, and I decided a while ago that my best defense mechanism against losing my heart completely was to keep him at arm's length, while admiring him from a distance… if that's physically possible.

"She's his fiancée now. Mason proposed to her after dinner last night. It was kinda unexpected."

"Why?"

"I guess because they haven't known each other for very long."

"Does that matter?" What's wrong with me? Why am I getting even deeper into this discussion with him? Aside from protecting my heart from him, I don't even know these people, and I doubt Oliver's interested in what I have to say.

"Of course not… if you've found the right person."

"And you don't think your brother has?"

"I'm damn sure he has. He's never been so happy." He's smiling, like this matters to him, which is kinda cute.

"Then why shouldn't they get married?"

His smile fades, and he shakes his head. "I didn't say they shouldn't get married. I just said his proposal was unexpected. Normally he tells me everything, including when he's been an idiot, but I knew nothing about this. I'm surprised… that's all."

"Sorry," I say and he frowns, standing up and coming around my desk.

"Why are you sorry?" he asks.

"Because it's nothing to do with me." I reach into my drawer for my notepad. "You were telling me about this party?"

He hesitates for a moment, like he wants to say something, and then steps back slightly. "Yeah. I was. It… It's not really a party, though."

"What is it then?"

"It's a kind of open house thing. I always hold it the day before Christmas Eve."

I frown, looking up into his whiskey-colored eyes, fighting the urge to lose myself in them. "This coming Thursday?"

"Yes. It's not a big deal." It sounds like it is, especially with so little notice. "We just make eggnog, and Deanna used to bake cookies, and people just drop in throughout the day."

'Just?' He makes it sound so simple, but I've never even drunk eggnog. I don't have a clue how to make it. And as for Christmas cookies…

"I'm sorry," he says. "I should have told you."

"It's fine," I lie. Because it feels very far from fine. It feels like a nightmare. His clients will be popping in all day, fawning over him while I hand out cookies and eggnog. I can't think of anything worse.

"Thanks, Jemima. I don't know what I'd do without you."

I'm not 'with' him, so that seems like an odd thing to say, but I don't comment, and just smile up at him. "You should probably get ready," I say. "Mrs. Williamson is due in five minutes."

"Oh, great. That's just what I need… a yapping Chihuahua."

He rolls his eyes and then steps around my chair, kneeling in front of Baxter's basket and clasping his face between his hands.

"Be a good boy for Jemima," he says.

Baxter yawns, settling his head on the soft blanket in his basket, and Oliver stands again, walking into his office and closing the door.

I let out a sigh of relief and flop back into my chair, regretting almost all of that conversation. It might have been our first, but it'll probably be our last after that performance. I should've just stuck to work, and the party, and not raised the subject of his family. He talked about them first, I suppose, but that didn't mean he wanted me to question him, did it?

I'm still shaking my head when the front door opens and Mrs. Williamson comes in on a waft of expensive perfume, clutching her

Chihuahua to her ample chest and almost smothering the poor thing.

"I know I'm early," she says as she gets to my desk, purring like a cat. "I'm sure Doctor Gould won't mind."

I smile at her as I offer her a seat, and as I make my way to Oliver's office, I wish today had never started. I wish I could still be at home, lying in bed, dreaming about Oliver, instead of facing the reality of a life spent working with him, watching other women drooling over him, and knowing he can never be mine.

∞

Oliver

"What's wrong with her?" Mrs. Williamson looks up at me from across the examination table, her eyelashes fluttering, her lips slightly parted, and I smile back, trying to look reassuring.

Mrs. Williamson – who keeps insisting I should call her Nancy – is probably in her mid- to late-forties. She dresses at least ten or fifteen years younger, and I'll admit, she's worn well. It's her hands that give away the secret of her passing years, and she has a habit of waving them around, or touching my arms, which makes them more noticeable.

I don't mind her flirting. I accept it as an occupational hazard, and my clients pay me very well for what I do; so if I have to tolerate a little flirting on the side, who am I to complain?

"I think Coco's going deaf," I say. "It's fairly common with Chihuahuas, I'm afraid, and the fact that she's ignoring you when you call her, and that her bark is getting louder, is fairly indicative."

"Oh, no." Her eyes widen, and I wonder for a moment if she might cry.

"It's not the end of the world." I soften my voice, and she manages a smile. "If I'm right, it just means you'll have to be more careful with her when you're out, and you'll have to adjust how you approach her.

You'll need to make sure she can see you, rather than coming up to her from behind. Just little things like that will make a big difference to her."

"I see," she says, nodding her head and lifting Coco into her arms.

"I've got some exercises you can try with her." I wander over to the filing cabinet in the corner of my surgery, pulling open the second drawer down and retrieving a sheet of paper, before turning back to Mrs. Williamson. "These will help us find out whether I'm correct, and how severe her deafness is," I say, handing her the sheet of instructions. "Try them out for seven days, and I'll see you again next Monday."

"My husband and I are going away for the holidays." She looks up at me with those fluttering eyelashes again, and I'm almost tempted to frown or shake my head at her. Anything to remind her that, while she's flirting with me, she's also talking about her husband. "We're leaving on Christmas Eve and won't be coming back until Monday evening."

"Okay. I can see you on Tuesday, I think. We'll check with Jemima when we get outside."

She nods her head, putting Coco down for a moment while she folds the piece of paper, putting it into her purse, before she tucks the dog under her arm again, and I head for the door, holding it open as she passes through.

"I'm so grateful, Doctor Gould," she says, resting her hand on my upper arm.

"You don't need to be." I'm just doing my job, after all. "Oh, by the way," I say, as I follow her out into the reception area, "we're having our usual Christmas gathering on Thursday. I hope you'll be able to drop by at some point?"

"Of course," she simpers, gazing up at me. "That's so kind of you."

She's acting like I've issued a royal summons, but I don't disillusion her. Instead I just smile and go around behind Jemima's desk, relishing the opportunity of being close to her.

"Can we fit Coco in for a thirty-minute appointment next Tuesday?" I ask her, trying not to get too close, despite the temptation.

"The twenty-eighth?" she says, looking up at me through her glasses, her pale blue eyes fixed on mine for a breathtaking moment.

"Yes." My voice sounds croaky and I cough.

Jemima looks away again, staring at her computer screen, and bringing up the online booking system I started using about two years ago, scrolling through to December twenty-eighth, before she turns her gaze on Mrs. Williamson.

"I can offer you ten-thirty in the morning, or two-fifteen in the afternoon."

I hope she goes for the ten-thirty. Two-fifteen is the first appointment after lunch, and I don't relish it being with Mrs. Williamson.

"I'll take the ten-thirty," Mrs. Williamson says, and I breathe out, hoping she doesn't notice that as a sigh of relief.

Jemima taps on her keyboard, her fingers moving like lightning, and then she looks up at Mrs. Williamson again.

"You'll get a confirmation email," she says. "Would you like me to write the appointment down on a card for you as well?"

"Yes, please," Mrs. Williamson replies, staring at me again, although I'm preoccupied with Jemima, watching her writing out the appointment on one of our calling cards in her neat handwriting.

I have to admit, I'm still feeling a little stunned after our conversation this morning. It wasn't that there was anything exceptional about what we were discussing; it was the fact that we had a conversation at all. I've been trying to talk to Jemima for such a long time, and this morning, it just kinda happened. I remembered Mason saying that his first proper conversation with Isabel came out of the blue, and mine with Jemima seemed to be the same.

Of course, it started off being all about work – or at least, all about the party – but she turned it around and asked about my brother and Isabel. I'd rather she'd asked about me, but we weren't talking about me. We were talking about the fact that I went over to Mason's house last night for dinner with his girlfriend, Isabel, Dad, my sister Destiny and her new husband, Ronan, and Isabel's sisters, Ashley and Reagan. We were getting together as a kind of pre-Christmas thing, because we missed out on having a family gathering at Thanksgiving. It won't be possible for us to see each other at Christmas either, because Destiny and Ronan are spending the holidays with his sister in Lexington. So, we met up at Mason's place yesterday. As I said to Jemima, that was when I noticed the beautiful Christmas tree Isabel had decorated – which reminded me about the party. It was also when Mason proposed. Jemima picked up on that and asked me about it, although she reacted weirdly when I said Mason's proposal had been unexpected. It had. That was what I was trying to explain to her. Mason hadn't mentioned it to me, and that surprised me, being as I knew just about everything that had gone on between him and Isabel when they got together; from his lame idea about getting her to be his fake girlfriend at his college reunion, to him forgetting to use a condom when they first slept together. When Isabel found out about the fake girlfriend part of that, she walked out on him and went home to her sisters in Vermont. But then, I had warned my brother it was a really dumb idea. He went after her, of course, and won her back, and it transpired that although his error of judgement with the condom didn't have any consequences, they're actually trying for a baby now, *and* they're engaged.

I didn't tell Jemima about the fact that they're trying for a baby. She seemed surprised enough by my reaction to their engagement, which she completely misunderstood. I wasn't being critical, even if she took it that way. I was just commenting on my surprise… that was all. But looking at her now, as she shows Mrs. Williamson to the door, I'll admit her response has made me wonder whether there might be something in her past that made her respond like that.

If only she'd opened up to me…

She didn't. She apologized, although God knows why. What did she have to apologize for? She said it was because it had nothing to do with her, and while I wanted to tell her it did, she seemed keen to keep the conversation professional after that.

I could hardly argue, could I?

After all, we'd just had our first real conversation, and although it hadn't gone to plan, I didn't want to spoil things completely by arguing with her.

"You've got just over ten minutes until Mrs. North is due," Jemima says, breaking into my thoughts as she closes the front door and turns around. She doesn't come back over to her desk, where I'm still standing, but remains where she is, looking across at me… or rather, straight past me. Once again, I feel dismissed.

"Oh. Okay. I guess I'd better clear up and get ready."

I move away from her desk, my heart sinking as I notice she goes back there the moment I've vacated her space.

Could she be any more subtle?

I make my way into my surgery, closing the door behind me and leaning against it for a moment.

I'm so in love with Jemima, I can almost taste it. She clearly feels absolutely nothing for me, though, and being around her so much is torture. Not that I'm thinking of letting her go. I'd rather torture myself, punish my heart, body, and mind on an hourly basis, than risk never seeing her again. I'll always be grateful she's here, no matter how much it hurts.

I can still remember the moment I first saw her, just over a year ago, when she walked in the door for her interview, answering the ad I'd placed in the local newspaper for a new receptionist.

I'd been dreading the whole process of finding a replacement for Deanna. She'd been with me for years, and with my predecessor before me. She was great at her job, but her husband had just taken early retirement, and she wanted to spend more time with him. I understood her reasons for leaving; I just didn't need the hassle of finding someone else who could do the job as well as she did.

Deanna told me her plans at the beginning of last December, giving me a month to find her replacement. I thought it would be easy.

If only I'd known…

I set up the interviews over three days, having had a lot of responses, but by lunchtime on the third day, and I was wondering whether it was a lost cause. None of them had been even remotely suitable. Then, at three o'clock on that Friday afternoon, Jemima walked in and took my breath away.

She was tiny. I estimated her to be no more than five foot four, but she wore high heels to compensate, adding probably three inches to her height. She still had to crane her neck to look up at me, though, as I stood and walked around my desk to greet her. I hadn't done that with any of the other candidates, but there was something about Jemima that made me want to be as close as possible to her. I think it was the way she was biting her lip.

It made me want to bite it too.

I shook her hand, which was small and soft, and then offered her a seat, before resuming my own and gazing across my desk at her, finding myself tongue-tied.

That's not normal for me. But I couldn't think of anything to say, and for a while, we just sat there.

She was shy; that much was obvious, just from her demeanor, from the way she wouldn't make eye contact and fiddled with the hem of her jacket, and I wondered if we were destined to remain that way forever. I wouldn't have complained. I had the most perfect view in the world. But then Baxter wandered over and nuzzled into me, wanting some attention, and while I stroked his head, Jemima studied him and said, "He's beautiful. What's his name?"

"Baxter," I replied, silently thanking him, because he'd helped break the ice between us, and then I asked Jemima what experience she had in working with animals.

She replied, "Absolutely none," which made me laugh.

"At least that's honest," I said, and she smiled.

"There's no point in lying." She shrugged her shoulders. "I didn't realize experience with animals was necessary."

"It's not." And even if it had been, I'd have waived the requirement for her. "I just wondered if you'd done any work like this before."

She tilted her head then, betraying her confusion, which wasn't that surprising. I had her resume in front of me, after all. It told me she'd had a couple of part-time jobs in her hometown of Eastford, Connecticut, one working at a bakery, and the other for a company offering hot-air balloon rides to tourists. That last job was quite seasonal, I imagined, and while I probably should have asked her what she did with the rest of her time, I didn't really care.

"I've done administrative work," she said, my silence clearly bothering her. "I had to organize the schedules for the balloon rides."

"Did you ever take one yourself?" I asked her.

"No. I'm scared of heights."

I chuckled, and she smiled as I glanced down at her resume again, noting her age, which was only twenty-one. I guessed that explained some of her shyness and her lack of experience. Being as I was coming up for my thirty-fourth birthday, it also meant she was twelve years younger than me. I wasn't sure why that thought came into my head. After all, what did it matter what the age gap was? It certainly shouldn't have done. And yet it did… because I'd fallen for her.

Love wasn't something I'd ever experienced before, but I knew, without any doubt, that I was in love. It was hard not to be, when she had the softest voice I'd ever heard, and the lightest blue eyes, which were framed by purple-rimmed glasses. Her makeup was natural, her skin smooth and flawless. Her blonde hair was tied up in ponytail, although a couple of stands had broken free and were framing her perfect face, and as I gazed at her across my desk, I knew there would never be anyone else for me.

"When can you start?" I asked her.

"Y—You're offering me the job?" We'd spent less than fifteen minutes in each other's company and I'd asked her almost nothing. Her confusion was understandable.

"Yes," I said, and while it may not have been the most sensible thing I've ever done, I've got no regrets. She's great at what she does. She's fantastic with the clients, and their pets, and their children, when they have them… and she clearly adores Baxter, who sits with her during surgery hours, and who I've noticed is often reluctant to come back to me. Her love for my dog would have been route one into my heart, if it hadn't already been hers. I just wish I knew how to tell her that. I wish I knew how to tell her anything, really. Because, even though she accepted my offer and started working for me the first week of January, I still know nothing about her, other than the meager details she included on her resume.

That means I've spent nearly a year trying to get to know her, and getting nowhere.

I've spoken to Mason about the situation, because as well as being my brother, he's also a psychologist, and even he thinks it's kinda odd that, after a year of working together – regardless of being in love with her – I know so little about her. It's just not normal to spend so much time together and have so little understanding of each other.

I guess that's why I got so excited earlier, when she asked about Mason and Isabel. I thought she was taking an interest. She wasn't… clearly. Because if she'd been interested, she wouldn't have dismissed me and changed the subject like she did. She was just querying the way I'd phrased my sentence, I think.

I push myself off of the door, realizing time's running out and I need to wipe down the examining table, which only takes a few minutes.

Of course, they're a few minutes during which I keep thinking about Jemima. Because she's all I think about these days.

I feel guilty for springing the Christmas party on her like I just did. As I explained to her, it's not a party at all. It's a lot harder work than that. It goes on for the whole day, and sometimes into the evening too, being as the surgery doesn't close until six pm… although I forgot to mention that to Jemima. We have to plaster a smile on our faces for the entire time, too… and dish out drinks and cookies to everyone who walks through the door. Of course, it's Christmas, so everyone is in good cheer, but that doesn't make it any easier, and I wonder now if I should've warned her.

I know I should've given her more notice, but I genuinely forgot. If that sounds pathetic, then there's not a lot I can do about it. I've been so wrapped up in Jemima for the last few months, trying to work out how to break down the barriers between us, I haven't been able to think straight at all. I've been trying to work out whether I should forget about conversation and getting to know her and just show my hand, and ask her to have dinner with me.

It's strange… I'm not usually a shy man. Mason is. At least, he's more shy than I am. But I'm not sure shyness is my problem with Jemima. I've contemplated asking her to dinner more times than I can think about. I've even acted out the scene in my head, and I don't think it's shyness that's getting in my way. To be honest, I think my main issue is, I'm scared. And what scares me most is that if I really showed her my hand, Jemima might leave… because dinner isn't all I want.

That's why I haven't asked her yet… because I'm scared. Not that I've got any intention of giving up. I just need to work out how to go about this without breaking my heart… or losing her.

I sit and gaze out across the lake, ignoring the icy chill and staring at the reflection of the moon on the still water. It's freezing… so cold that even Baxter has abandoned me and gone to sit indoors by the fire.

I don't care about the cold.

I just wish I could sit here with Jemima, holding her close to me, keeping her warm, feeling her soft body beside my own, and having her share this perfect piece of paradise that I call home.

I love living here in my cabin by the lake. I love the quiet and the seclusion, especially on nights like this, when I just want to think. Thinking isn't getting me anywhere, of course. It hasn't helped me work things out with Jemima. It hasn't helped me to understand why she practically ignored me for most of the day, and then ran out of the office when it was time to go home, barely acknowledging my "Goodbye."

It also hasn't helped me come to terms with the fact that, while my sister just got married, and Mason got engaged yesterday, I'm sitting here by myself. As I gaze out on the silvery shadows and dark mists lying across the lake, it all starts to blur and I let my head fall into my hands, whispering her name and letting the loneliness wash over me in waves.

… to be continued

Printed in Great Britain
by Amazon

48080935R00192